LEAVING
LYRA

Leaving Lyra

Book 2 *of the* River Oaks Series

The Taylor Sisters

LEAVING LYRA
BOOK 2 OF THE RIVER OAKS SERIES

ISBN 978-0-578-36020-1

Library of Congress Control Number 2022901597

To the late George Ramsey, our English 1A and 1B instructor at Sacramento City College in the late 1970's. You taught us to read and write between the lines, and had no idea what a mentor you were to both of us.

And to our God, the great comforter and healer of hearts, who in turn uses us to comfort others.

2 Corinthians 1:3-5
All praise to God, the Father of our Lord Jesus Christ. God is our merciful Father and the source of all comfort. He comforts us in all our troubles so that we can comfort others. When they are troubled, we will be able to give them the same comfort God has given us. For the more we suffer for Christ, the more God will shower us with his comfort through Christ.

Acknowledgments

We would like to thank our editors, Denise Blanton, Irene LaVigne, Tammy Donstad, and Rachel Lickter. Your keen eyes and sometimes difficult questions about our manuscript caused us numerous rewrites, but isn't that what editing is all about? Along with the challenges, you also gave us encouragement just when it was most needed. Thank you for the many hours you dedicated to this novel.

Thank you to Linda Kendall, EA, USTCP, for your generosity and patience with us.

We will never be able to say thank enough our real-life heroes, Father Joshua Lickter, Incarnation Anglican Church, Roseville, CA; Pastor Richard Cimino, Metro Calvary Church, Roseville, CA; and Dr. Peter Knoblich, MD. Your vast knowledge, listening ears, and caring spirits have made all the difference in these two sisters' lives.

Music inspires us and our writing. Once in a while a song comes along that changes your life—gives you new hope or courage. Such a song is a perfect backdrop for this novel, "Tell Your Heart to Beat Again," as sung by Danny Gokey (written by Bernie Herms, Randy Phillips, and Matthew West). We all have things in our past that only the Lord can heal. Sometimes He uses music.

Contents

CHAPTER 1
Little Red Toaster

Lyra Rhinehardt woke at dawn with a renewed sense of apprehension. Grateful for her car's cozy back seat, she untangled herself from the tattered beach towel that served both as a blanket and a hiding place. She sat up slowly and glanced into the rearview mirror. She saw a black Cadillac parked under some trees behind her in the parking lot. There was a flash. The early morning light caught a pair of binocular lenses, hastily lowered as the driver quickly sped away.

Lyra shook as she hurried to the front seat of her old Corolla, planted her face on the steering wheel, and forced herself to breathe. She started the engine and found the gas gauge approaching empty. Lyra reached into her pocket, fishing for imaginary dollar bills and finding only change, barely enough to take her to the next town, wherever that might be.

"What's the point?" She pounded the steering wheel, anger replacing fear for the moment. "What's the point?" she repeated, softer this time, almost ending in tears. She lifted her head as her spirit roared in reply, "I will not let this happen!" Lyra unfolded her battered map and checked out her options.

"River Oaks," she said. "I think I've got just enough gas to get there."

Living on the run had altered Lyra's personality in an unpleasant, even tragic way. Paranoia had replaced her normally open, friendly manner. Anyone who even looked at her now was a potential spy. Being in crowds was even worse. She could never tell who was watching her, and she didn't want to make herself conspicuous by constantly looking over her shoulder. Instead, she counted on her considerable weight to make herself invisible. Eyes seldom lingered on her. *No one wants to look at a fat girl,* she assured herself.

River Oaks is a friendly-looking little place, she thought as she considered the colorful welcome sign at the edge of town. *And it's so small that no one would think to look for me here. Maybe I can work for a while and save up for gas and food.* Her belly rumbled. Lyra followed the scent of doughnuts to the quaint little bakery nearby. Her heart stirred when she saw the Help Wanted sign in the bakery window. She checked herself in the rear view mirror. "Oh well," she sighed. "There's not much of a chance, but why not?" She locked the car door, donned her backpack, and entered the shop with a forced smile.

LEAVING LYRA

The smile Lyra wore when she left the bakery a few minutes later was a genuine one. She had a job. It was hard to believe that maybe her luck had finally changed.

Lyra needed a place to stay—a place not easily seen from the road, a place where few questions presented themselves. She drew her eighteen-year-old self up to her full five foot ten, squared her shoulders, sucked in as much of her ample belly as she could, and hand-combed her stringy brown hair as she readied herself at the McCreary's door. She'd squandered her last coins on a cream puff at the bakery. There hadn't been enough left to finance a trip to the laundromat. Lyra looked down at her favorite blue tee shirt depicting the classic "hang in there" cat. It seemed to sum up her life to this point.

Hiding her fear in the best smile she could muster, she knocked on the door and was surprised to see it open instantly, which could only mean that someone had been at the peephole watching her pathetic attempts at primping. *Oh well,* she thought, *the damage is done.* She would face the rejection gracefully...then find somewhere to cry. Living on the run was not the adventure it was cracked up to be, but it was a necessity.

"Mrs. McCreary?" Lyra asked. "Molly, my new boss at the bakery, said you might have a place to rent."

The retired seventy-two-year-old, Maggie McCreary, having spent most of her adult life working at Molly's Sunshine Bakery, was a student of the human heart. She saw in Lyra an honest young woman seeking peace. *Well*, Maggie decided, *peace is something we have in abundance here.* "My friends call me Maggie. Come on in." She used her well-honed smile muscles to welcome the girl into the house. "Lemonade?" she offered. "Fresh-squeezed."

"Thank you," Lyra answered.

Once they were seated at the gingham-robed table, ice clinking in their tumblers, Maggie took a sip and began. "The guest house is unfurnished. It's clean but could use a little freshening up. Now here's the deal breaker: It has heat but no air conditioning. Would that work for you?"

"It's okay. Neither does my car," she blurted. "I can take the heat."

"Well, if you're working at the bakery that's quite an asset," Maggie laughed. "Do you plan on staying here in River Oaks?"

"I sure hope so," said Lyra. "I'm planning to get my Veterinary Assistant Certificate in the future."

"So you like animals," Maggie noted, fondly recalling the many pets she had dragged home as a child.

Lyra took Maggie's smile as a hopeful sign. "Yes I do. Would it be okay—I mean, if you let me rent the cottage—if I fostered a couple of kittens?"

4

LEAVING LYRA

"Well, there's certainly not much mischief they could drum up in an empty house, now is there? As long as they're housebroken, they are welcome. Now dogs, on the other hand, well, my experience is that they'll dig and smash up my flower beds. In case you haven't noticed, I love daisies." She pointed out the French doors. A late summer display of big, bold purple coneflowers, prim white Shasta daisies, sunbursts of gloriosas, and a rainbow of gerberas beckoned. Not a weed in sight.

"Wow," Lyra exclaimed, looking through the glass. "That's really spectacular!'

"Let's go out and have a look at your new home, shall we?"

"Thank you, Maggie." Lyra followed, steadying her lip. It wouldn't do for her new landlady to see her cry, but when she heard the word, "home," Lyra heard everything that should go along with that word—safety, comfort, peace, and a sense of belonging. Her life had lacked all those things since her mother's death. Especially safety. With a sense of hope, Lyra followed the motherly woman to the cottage.

As they walked, Maggie introduced each cluster of plants as if it were a character in the play that was her yard. Lyra was eager to have a part in the colorful drama.

Lyra dragged herself back to reality. "But wait, Maggie, we haven't talked about rent. I won't be able to pay much, especially at first."

"I've got that covered, that is, if you're willing to work around the yard. I'm not as spry as I look, and it's hard for me to get on my knees—and even harder getting off them."

"Your yard's so amazing! I'd love to help. Just show me what to do."

"Then we've got a deal." Mrs. McCreary offered a warm hug, which Lyra accepted gratefully.

As they walked into the cottage, the first thing Lyra noticed was the sun pouring like honey through the enormous corner windows. "What a toasty place to sit and read," Lyra said. There was a postage stamp-sized kitchen between that room and the bedroom, which had a miniature bathroom and closet attached. "This place is perfect, Maggie. And I can't wait to start working in the garden. I'll never be able to thank you enough."

"Well, here's the key. I'll let you start settling in."

Maggie searched the want ads for a bed when she realized that her tenant would be sleeping on the floor. Then it occurred to her that if anyone could scout out a bed for Lyra, it was Molly. Her bakery was the hub of the town; very little happened without her knowledge. Not that Molly ever pried into people's lives. She was simply an excellent listener. And if anyone could hear this wounded girl's heart, it was Molly

Tauber. Maggie skipped the want ads and gave Molly's phone a jingle.

"Don't put your face on the glass, Mateo," a tall, thin Mexican American woman gently scolded her three-year-old son who had left a sticky replica of himself on Molly's display case.

"It happens all the time," Lyra responded, in Spanish. "You just happen to be one of the few parents who care. But don't worry; I have a secret weapon." In one hand she lifted a bottle of glass cleaner and in the other, a paper towel.

At the words, "secret" and "weapon," the boy's eyes widened.

"Where'd you learn to speak Spanish?" the woman queried.

"I...uh, grew up with a lady who spoke Spanish."

"Well, your accent is very good."

"Thanks. As a kid I probably spoke more Spanish than English."

"Can the secret weapon blow things up?" the boy interrupted eagerly.

"No, better than that; it makes things disappear." Lyra came around the front of the case and demonstrated. "Squirt, squirt, whoosh!"

7

"You disappeared me!" he exclaimed, lapsing into English.

"Now you get to disappear me." Lyra said, switching to English for the sake of Molly, who had just walked in from the kitchen.

Hi, Esperanza, your order's ready." Molly handed the woman two large boxes of pan dulce.

Turning her attention back to the boy, Lyra left a handprint on the glass and handed him the spray bottle. "I guess it's not a secret anymore, now is it?" Lyra paused, then said with conviction, "Secrets aren't always such a great thing, I've discovered." She straightened her shoulders. "Are you having a family get-together?" she asked Esperanza. "That's a lot of pan dulce."

"No, it's for our church. We come here every Friday to pick up a fresh batch for our service on Saturday. We rent the space from another church that has their services on Sunday. This pan dulce makes our church members and visitors feel right at home. We even have a lobby with couches and chairs where people can relax and visit after the service."

"That sounds really great. What's your church called?"

"The Church of the Broken," the woman said with a knowing smile. "Why don't you drop by sometime?" She saw a look of dismay cross Lyra's features at the word, "broken."

Lyra knew she'd been found out, but something in the woman's kind, coffee-colored eyes told her that this secret was safe.

"Oh, I'm so sorry. Where are my manners? My name is Esperanza Hernandez, and this young magician who 'disappears handprints' is my son, Mateo."

The boy beamed brightly at Lyra.

"My name is Lyra Rhinehardt. I'm new here, but I guess you already knew that." She looked down at the paper towel crumpled in her hand, placed it on the counter and looked up. "Molly's pan dulce is the best ever." Lyra directed the conversation away from church and away from herself.

"It should be," Esperanza said with a confident smile. "It's my grandmother's recipe right down to the last teaspoon. Molly knows a good thing when she tastes it."

As Lyra rang up the sweet bread, "Church of the Broken," resonated within her, and she decided she just might pay a visit…someday.

Using the hand soap Mrs. McCreary had provided, Lyra washed her clothes in the kitchen sink. With any luck her laundry would be dry by morning and ready to wear to work. If not, she'd wear them wet and hope for the best.

She stepped into the tiny shower, enjoying the warmth as it soothed her weary body and mind. Fear and uncertainty set aside, for now at least, she was home.

For the first time in quite a while she slipped into pajamas. She padded barefoot on the scuffed linoleum floor where she curled up to sleep, using her worn out sweatshirt as her pillow and her jacket as a blanket. She was asleep before the sun went down and wide awake when her alarm clock began its insistent pulse, long before the sun rose.

Lyra arrived at the bakery a half-hour early in her almost-dry clothes, so early, in fact, that Molly had yet to arrive. Lyra's rumbling belly reminded her that she hadn't had an actual meal in a long time. She looked longingly through the big plate glass window at all the enticing baked goods that were out of her reach. She could only afford to fantasize until she got paid.

Molly's lilted, "Good morning, Lyra!" startled her. "That's what I like to see, an eager employee, nice and early. You know, Lyra, I'll bet you're hungry. I know I am. How about a quick breakfast?"

Lyra breathed a sigh of relief as Molly unlocked the door.

"I've got tons of day-old bread. Pick a loaf or two to take home. I know money's tight right now, but that should get you through till payday next week."

"Thank you, Molly. I could really use this." Lyra reached for some French bread and a loaf of wholewheat and placed them next to her backpack.

"How about a couple eggs and toast?" Molly asked. "It's what I usually have. Raisin bread sound good? I'll start the eggs, and you make the toast."

"Thanks, Molly," Lyra responded gratefully.

Lyra regarded Molly's toaster with reverence. It had been a long time since she'd made toast. Little did Molly realize it was Lyra's favorite comfort food.

"There's butter in the fridge, and Maggie's famous apple butter. Help yourself."

The familiar gnawing in Lyra's stomach slowly disappeared as she mopped up the eggs with the last buttery morsel of bread.

The morning baking lessons were going well. Lyra remembered the general principles from many happy afternoons baking with her mother, but she knew she had a lot to learn.

Molly was demonstrating how to use the industrial-sized mixer to knead bread. With all the ingredients assembled in the mixing bowl, Molly flipped the switch. The bread hook made one feeble revolution then froze. Molly groaned. "No! This machine has been threatening to quit on me since yesterday. I sure could've used two-weeks' notice." Unfortunately, neither one of them could budge the dough hook. "It'll take forever for the two of us to mix and knead this all by hand. Mrs. Kramer needs a dozen braids of challah for a big shindig she's throwing tonight. I'd better call Handyman Jim."

Precisely at seven o'clock the tinkling bell announced Molly's first and best customer. "That'll be Phil," Molly said, smiling, with Lyra at her heels.

True to her prediction, Phil swaggered in.

"How you doing, Phil? Have your usual?"

"I'm doing great. Yep. A fritter and a cup o' joe. How are you girls doing?"

"Not so swift. The dough hook on my mixer just gave up the ghost. And I've got to make twelve braids of challah by this afternoon." Molly sighed.

"Stand aside, ladies. Let a professional do the job."

"But you're a computer programmer," Molly said.

"Ah, there is so much you don't know about me. Before I was a computer wizard I secretly repaired all kinds of things. I specialized in cassette decks, Tamagotchis, and nuclear submarines."

"He's such a dork," Molly laughingly whispered to Lyra.

"Let me at it. Show me the damaged goods."

Lyra whispered back to Molly, "Do you think we should?"

"What harm could it do? It's already broken," Molly replied, still hushed.

Phil rolled up his sleeves with a flourish and followed them into the workroom.

"Okay, Phil," Molly began, "this doohickey won't spin around and mix my dough."

"No problem. I know exactly what to do. It's the pinseal on the bladderwort. Happens all the time, especially with this particular model. Please step aside. Where are my tools?"

"Well, what do you need, Phil?"

"Something to fix the pinseal of course. Got a hammer?"

"Not funny, Phil." She walked over to a shelf and retrieved her dad's old tool box. "Will these do?"

"Yes, but I'm going to need a scalpel too."

"Yeah, right. Do you really have a clue how to fix this?"

"No, but sometimes I pretend like I do. Well, it can't be much harder than the SS Nucleotide. That's the first submarine I fixed." Phil surveyed the tools. "This ought to do nicely." He picked up a wrench and a screwdriver, one in each hand, and began taking the motor assembly apart, humming to himself all the while.

"We better leave Phil to work on this while we finish up the last of the pies," Molly told Lyra.

"Yes," he said. "I need to concentrate."

The pies were steaming in their racks by the time Phil announced grandly, "It is finished."

13

"Oh great!" Molly exclaimed. "Now we can get back to business."

"It was nothing," Phil said, standing tall. "All in a day's work." He cleared his throat, "Sure would like that fritter now."

"Wait, let's see how well it works," Molly said. "This fritter's on me," she beamed.

Molly flipped the switch. The motor shrieked as a fine mist of flour mushroomed from the mixing bowl like a small atomic bomb, followed by a fallout of gooey egg, milk, and poppy seeds.

"Uh, told you I could fix it." Phil's eyes shifted side to side. Finding not a hint of approval, he looked down.

The girls looked around, gaping, palms up, as a fine layer of bread flour made its new home on every available surface.

"Guess I fixed it too good?" Phil said, still seeking acclaim.

"I think you'd better stick to nuclear subs, Phil. Here's all the cleaning supplies you're going to need."

"What about that fritter you were gonna give me?"

She held his snowy-white fritter in front of him, blew the excess flour off, and looking at his flour-and-goo-covered face, she pronounced, "I'm afraid this one's on you."

LEAVING LYRA

Lyra was sitting on the floor of her little cottage about to eat some of the day-old wholewheat bread her boss had sent home with her. She was wishing for a toaster when a gentle tap sounded at her door.

"Lyra?" called a now familiar voice.

"Oh, hi, Molly," she responded as she rose to open the weathered door.

Molly stood on the doorstep, her arms piled to her chin with brand new towels and bedding.

Lyra's jaw dropped. "Oh, Molly, for me?" she said in a small voice.

"Yes, for you," Molly handed the load into Lyra's uncertain arms. "Now take this in, set it down, and come on out to my car."

Lyra took a moment to admire the towels—a plush mix of lavender and pale turquoise. She ran her fingers through the thick nap and smiled, realizing that the old threadbare towel that had served her for so long could now find a new purpose as a cleaning rag.

"Lyra," came Molly's voice, "I could use some help here." And indeed she could. Molly's car was packed with boxes and was hitched to a trailer bearing Molly's old corduroy couch. Phil stood by the car, ready to unload the couch which could easily serve as a bed. Between the three of them, they managed to get it into the cottage. With a wave and a smile, Phil drove off

15

to return the trailer to the rental company, leaving Molly and Lyra to deal with the numerous boxes. Lyra was speechless.

When the last box had been hauled into the cottage, Molly hurried home, buoyed by Lyra's gratitude, leaving Lyra to set up housekeeping.

Never had Lyra received a gift with such anticipation. She chose a box and began unpacking. On the top was a new toothbrush and a supply of toothpaste, a comb and brush, deodorant, and peach-scented shampoo, among other grooming essentials. Lyra took a moment to sniff the shampoo. It lived up to its label. Her months of scrimping and scrounging had come to an end. Even clipping a broken fingernail was no longer an unattainable luxury.

A fluffy pillow followed in the next box, along with a mirror. Lyra hazarded a glance at herself. *Yes*, she thought, *that's one happy girl right there*. She was loved and she knew it.

For the first time in ever so long she believed that God might yet have good things in store for her. "Thank You," she breathed out, fogging the mirror with her words.

Housekeeping goods filled another box, with cleaning supplies from soap and scrubbies, to a broom sticking out of the box with a red and white polka-dotted bow tied around the handle. Lyra was tempted right then and there to get to work scrubbing down the house, but her curiosity won out. Cozy blankets lined the rest of the box. Lyra lifted them to her face to experience that clean blanket smell. Finally she came to the last box. Lyra took her time with this one. She came across a collection of crochet hooks and two skeins of turquoise yarn under a pretty cloth shower curtain with a seashell pattern. *She even remembered I said I used to like to crochet,* Lyra thought. Molly had casually asked her what she liked to do in her spare time. What an amazing sneak her new boss was, plotting this surprise. Lyra was already mentally crocheting Molly a scarf when she came across a calendar which had been opened. The date she began working for Molly was circled in red ink. "Welcome to Molly's Sunshine Bakery," was written in Molly's impeccable hand. Lyra hugged the calendar to her chest. "Thank you, Molly," she said as a happy tear grazed her cheek. Under the calendar were an empty leather-bound notebook, pen, and a New Living Translation Bible with Lyra's name stamped in gold on the cover. She opened it and found a note from Molly:

Dear Lyra,

Find God's promises for you in this book. There are many. This notebook might be a great place to keep track of them. Write them down and start believing them. Here's the first one to get you started.

Jeremiah 29:11-14
"For I know the plans I have for you," says the LORD. "They are plans for good and not for disaster, to give you a future and a hope. In those days when you pray, I will listen. If you look for me wholeheartedly, you will find me. I will be found by you,"

says the LORD. "I will end your captivity and restore your fortunes. I will gather you out of the nations where I sent you and will bring you home again to your own land."

I hope you will take these words to heart.

Love,

Molly

Lyra opened the Bible and checked out the passage, afraid it might not match Molly's quotation. There it was, word for word. She let it settle into her heart, where the words were met with hopeful skepticism.

Journal Entry

What if this is true? Could it be that I have more than a past? Should I even hope that God has plans for my good? It sure hasn't seemed like it the past few years. Okay, God, it says You'll listen, and I'll find You if I look for You. I'm captive—to shame and fear. I hardly remember what it was like not to feel like this. And I haven't had a home in a long time. I hope it's here in River Oaks. I need a safe place that I can settle down in, at least for a while, and catch my breath. I'm so tired of running.

"Lyra, honey, could you help me with these boxes?" Maggie McCreary said as Lyra was heading up the pathway to her little house after work.

"Sure. Be glad to," Lyra said. "Where do you want them?"

"I was hoping we could store them in your house. They won't take up that much room."

Lyra didn't complain as she lugged the heavy boxes, though there was little space to be had in the tiny cottage.

Maggie followed her back and forth between house and cottage, chatting, until all the boxes were moved. If Lyra had given her a glance, the glee in Maggie's eyes would've spoiled the surprise. "Now, Lyra, do you think you could put all this stuff away for me?"

"I'll do my best." Lyra looked around, clearly wondering where it would all go.

Opening the first box, she found purposefully mismatched floral plates, bowls, cups, and saucers—simple enough. There was a bit of kitchen cupboard space available. Then came pots and pans which she managed to stack on the floor under the counter. There was just enough room in the drawer for the hodgepodge of silverware. So intent was she at finding places for all of Maggie's cooking gear and so exhausted from a day's work, she didn't realize these were all gifts. Housewarming, heartwarming gifts. As the realization finally dawned on her, Lyra smiled at her landlady benefactor who was trying hard not to laugh out loud.

"You really had me going there, Maggie. I didn't even realize...thank you. Thank you so very much." Lyra hastened to give her a heartfelt hug.

As Maggie walked back to the house, she sighed. It had been many years since her own mother had graced that cottage. She looked down at her hands, now creased with wrinkles, the way her mother Mary's had been back then. Those were good days. Sam McCreary, Maggie's husband, had always been such a good sport about Mary living with them. Mary had her own space in the cottage and was always as cheerful as the daisies she fostered. Most days they cooked their dinners together, mother and daughter working side by side like two knitting needles. *If only I could've had a child*, Maggie thought. *It just wasn't meant to be. Well, at least I can help Lyra on her way.* She opened the French doors leading into her dining nook and saw the soft glow of the TV spilling around the doorway to the family room. *Family. Sam is certainly that for me, and he's enough.*

LEAVING LYRA

The fruit of her first paycheck yielded four folding chairs and a card table. She draped it in a forest green tablecloth made from a folded twin bed sheet. Most monumentally, a brand new red toaster sang from the counter by the teensy sink. It was what Lyra considered a real toaster, not the hybrid toaster oven so favored these days.

Eager to test out her much-anticipated appliance, Lyra plunked in a couple slices of Molly's oatmeal walnut bread, pushed the lever down, and waited as the welcoming aroma of warm bread gave way to the flawless crisp of toast. No need to mess with the settings. *It's perfect*, Lyra congratulated herself on her extraordinary taste in toasters. Slathered butter followed— real butter. Margarine was fine for potatoes or vegetables, but toast demanded authenticity. As she sampled her simple masterpiece, Lyra was transported to happier memories of her childhood, the late-night cinnamon raisin toast she shared with her mom, toasted sourdough with her family's maid, Estrella, and the airy white bread Lyra's last foster mother used to whip up while the kids were at school. Coming home to that bread, lightly toasted, well, that truly was coming home.

And now Lyra had a home of her own. It wasn't much by most people's standards, but it was clean and it was all she needed. The next paycheck would bring curtains to hide the ugly old bamboo shades. And who knew what else she might find on her next trip to Handy's Thrift Shop?

After each day of baking, Lyra welcomed the chance to lovingly prepare her own meals. Still, it seemed a shame to eat alone. Now that she had a table and chairs, she'd have to change that.

Lyra stopped fussing with the chicken gravy and peeking at the mashed potatoes, and forced herself to sit. Her guests were due any moment, and knowing Molly, she'd be right on time. Lyra got up and checked her hair. She ran a comb through her limp locks. Scraggly as usual. She gave up and took one last peek at the potatoes.

Sure enough, there was Molly, peach apricot pie in hand at precisely six o'clock. Lyra's heart lurched. *What if my chicken's too dry?* she worried. *Did I make enough?*

"Welcome! Come on in." Lyra opened the door.

Molly put the pie down on the table and gave her hostess a hug so motherly that Lyra had to look away for a moment to compose herself. Maggie and Sam McCreary arrived on Molly's heels, bearing string bean casserole, biscuits, and those hearty family-feeling hugs.

They sat down at the small table and Lyra filled their plates from the pots and pans on the stove while her guests passed around the biscuits and butter.

"I'd like to say grace," Lyra said shyly and reached out her hands to Molly and Sam. "God, thank You for giving me this family to be part of. Thank you for my job, this house, and for this food." She paused, wondering if there was a right way to sign off from a public prayer.

"Amen," her guests sounded the chorus.

Snuggling up on her corduroy couch with her fluffy pillow and fleece blanket, Lyra took pen in hand to write down the first Bible promise she had come across in her reading that night.

Psalm 68:5-6 read, "Father to the fatherless, defender of widows—this is God, whose dwelling is holy. God places the lonely in families; he sets the prisoners free and gives them joy. But he makes the rebellious live in a sun-scorched land."

Journal Entry:

Father to the fatherless? Defender? I need that for sure. And a family? It feels like I'm getting one here in River Oaks. My life seems to be changing. Thank you, Lord. But can I ever really be free from the prison of my past? Will I ever be able to stop looking over my shoulder?

Though the questions remained unanswered, Lyra's other dreams were taking shape. Her heart was singing as she left the animal rescue center, hauling the two cat carriers to her car. The smaller kitten, a red tabby with especially broad stripes, was already yowling his protest before she even started the car. His brother, a black tuxedo cat resplendent in his neat white gloves and collar, abandoned his nonchalance and joined the chorus as Lyra pulled out of the rescue parking lot. Her attempt to calm them by singing failed miserably. She was feeling defeated by the time she opened the carriers in her living room.

The tabby, whom she'd already named Pounce de Leon, attempted to dart under the corduroy couch which, unfortunately for him, provided no crawl space. Undaunted, he squeezed between couch and wall and huddled there, hissing next to his brother, Glover.

Lyra tried all afternoon to coax them from their hiding place with food and toys. She finally gave up. Disappointed and rejected, Lyra fell asleep on the couch only to be awakened by a tickle on her nose. She opened her eyes to find Glover delicately sniffing her face, his whiskers touching her ever so softly.

She remained motionless, enjoying the little animal's growing trust until she felt the sharp pinch of small teeth on her wrist. "Ow!" she cried, shaking off the stripy offender and sending him running for cover. After a few moments, Pounce regarded her remorselessly and proceeded to stalk her hand again. "I think I liked you better behind the couch," Lyra chuckled, wriggling her fingers for his delighted fangs and claws.

Chapter 2
His White-Bread Life

Dorian had adored Brittney ever since he could remember. Maybe longer than that. It seemed like no matter where he was or what he was doing, she was foremost in his mind, and nothing could compare with the smiles she cast his way. She was a beauty even from the cradle and was easily as intelligent as she was attractive. Well liked, though charmingly shy, she was the kind of person who always had the right thing to say. Her name was as breath to him, and he loved her.

Dorian McGuire ran his hand through his windblown dark brown hair as he drove his BMW convertible through the man-made forest of windmills, feeling very much like those towers whose blades had not been touched by wind. Whatever spark of spirit he had left within him was frozen; his worries were many and his anger, impotent.

He checked his gas gauge—a new habit for him. The least of his worries was finding a car he could afford now, given his recently unemployed state. What he truly desired was a place where he could learn to trust and be trusted again.

In a matter of hours he would be reunited with his Uncle Phil, whom he hadn't seen since last Christmas. Unlike Dorian's father, Phil refused to consider Dorian an embarrassment, going so far as to open his home to his nephew while Dorian attempted to piece what remained of his life back together.

Lyra saw him as he entered the bakery—twenty-something, lean and handsome, but rumpled and lost. "Can I help you?" she asked, really meaning it. Lyra had already fostered several kittens since moving to River Oaks, each finding a good home. They had once borne the same bewildered look as this young man displayed.

He approached the counter looking right through her with his espresso-hued eyes. Lyra was used to it. Her weight held others at a distance. Sometimes it was better not to be seen. She'd learned that in high school, actually throughout her whole life. Repeatedly.

"I'm…like…I'm waiting for my Uncle Phil. I was supposed to meet him here?" His statement was delivered as a question. Even this seemed uncertain.

"Oh, Phil. He's our favorite customer. He comes in this time every morning, except of course on Sundays. We aren't open on Sundays." She caught herself babbling. He clearly didn't notice. "Can I get you something while you're waiting?"

"Uh, yeah. Some coffee. Been on the road all night. I need to stay awake. At least for a while." He seated himself facing the door—away from her. No surprise. People did that.

"Dorian! Great to see you, man!" Phil strode in and delivered a back-slapping hug. "You look awful!" he crowed with a grin. "How long you been driving?"

"Since I was sixteen." Dorian attempted a quip.

"Very funny. You know what I meant."

"About ten hours straight."

"Why didn't you pull over at some hotel?"

"I…I needed to get away. The further and faster the better."

"Yeah, I know." Phil gave his nephew's shoulder a pat. "How about we get you something to eat? Molly's is the best bakery ever." He gave Lyra a wink as he approached the counter.

Lyra's heart leapt. She had a definite crush on Phil. He treated her like she mattered. Although he was almost twice her age, she found his resemblance to Toby McGuire altogether charming. He was, after all, the best Spiderman in her opinion.

"Lyra, this is my nephew, Dorian. He'll be staying with me for a while, so get used to seeing him. I'm sure he'll be hanging around here a lot once he gets a mouthful of your maple bars. He's always loved those things. Now, as for me, maple is reserved for pancakes."

She could easily get used to seeing Dorian in spite of his haunted eyes and hair going every which way. Her life experiences had made her an astute observer, not only of appearance, but of character. It didn't require much expertise to see what Dorian was running away from. Only a failed relationship could reduce a man to this dishevled ghost in Molly's bakery. And for that loss, she actually envied him, having never had something so precious to lose.

"I still can't believe my marriage is over." Hands folded around the coffee mug, Dorian stared at the rising steam as he shook his head.

"What are you going to do, Dorian?" his uncle asked gently.

Resolute eyes snapped up to meet Phil's. "I want things to go back to the way they were."

"I guess here's as good a place to start from as any," Phil said. "Why don't you stick around for a while? You can stay with me as long as it takes; help me with the house painting and some other projects until you know what you want to do. Maybe take a couple college courses."

"Thanks, Uncle Phil."

Phil saw a hint of the open smile that characterized his nephew. *The kid's going to be alright*, he determined.

As the weeks passed, Dorian's mood had not improved. "You know, Dorian, you've been moping around by yourself for long enough now," Phil noted over his apple fritter as they shared a table at Molly's Bakery. "I want you to find yourself a pet—a dog or a cat maybe. Something to get you off your butt and out of the dumps."

"I don't know." Dorian, who was foregoing breakfast, said glumly into his coffee, "Where'd I even find an animal to put up with me, let alone like me?"

Sensing her cue, Lyra left the counter she'd been cleaning. "Could I interest you in a kitten?" she asked. "I'm fostering two new ones right now. We could see if one of them chooses you. If not, the rescue organization I work with has quite a few others to meet. Of course, none so adorable as my fosters."

"Yeah, sure," Dorian muttered, dispirited. "I can't trust my own judgment. Might as well have a cat pick for me."

Rather than accept the invitation to his pity party, Lyra rattled off directions to her home, set a time for them to meet right after work, and returned to the counter, wiping the little hand and nose prints from the display case. She smirked at the irony of it. This was the closest she'd ever come to having a date, and it was her cats he was coming to see.

At least she wouldn't have to clean up for her visitor. She was glad she had few belongings that could be left out of place. Everything she owned had fit into her backpack and the trunk of her car when she'd stumbled into River Oaks looking for a new life, and the gifts she had received from Molly and Maggie each had its place. Once more she sent up a prayer of gratitude that the first place she'd stopped in town was Molly's Sunshine Bakery, right when Molly was looking for help.

Lyra suspected her employer was fostering her the same way Lyra was fostering those kittens. Not, she was relieved to note, the same kind of fostering she'd received on the many occasions she'd been caught as a runaway. *I'm eighteen now*, she reminded herself. *I'm no longer a part of the system with its court-mandated psychiatrists and social workers and endless lies. It's MY life now,* she affirmed, *and I'm not going to waste a moment of it living in the past.* A smile brightened her broad face. She could see it reflected in the spotless glass. Though her hair hung limp, brown with no undertones, for the moment her appearance was of no concern. She was free.

Dorian followed the pathway to Lyra's house, wanting more than anything to get this pet shopping business over with.

Though he had no objections to cats, he had no particular desire for one, but Uncle Phil clearly did, so he'd go through with it for his uncle's sake.

Lyra greeted him with even more excitement than when strangers came to meet her kittens. The prospect of finding a permanent home for her felines thrilled her. Of course, there'd be good-byes; there was always a certain amount of sadness in letting go. But the joy of seeing a furry companion join just the right family outweighed all of that.

As soon as Lyra had the money set aside for vet bills, she would have a pet of her own. As it was now, the rescue group footed the bills, and she provided the love, care, and socialization that money couldn't buy.

Dorian was shocked at the starkness as he entered Lyra's house. It frankly made him uncomfortable. "Did you just move here? Where's all your stuff?" he blurted.

"You're looking at it," came her cheerful reply. "See? Makes housecleaning a cinch and gives me more time with my little friends here." She lovingly lifted each kitten from the pen and beckoned Dorian to join her on the floor.

He glanced half-heartedly at the cats as they scrutinized him. Catalina, the larger of the two, was a long-haired calico of muted peach, ivory, and gray. Satisfied with her cursory investigation, Catalina yawned and wandered off to explore Lyra's bare toes before jumping on the couch, disinterested.

LEAVING LYRA

Even to Dorian's untrained eyes, Catalina was a beautiful animal.

The other kitten, known as Catzo, was what Dorian considered a generic cat, a tabby with a dull brown cast. Her dark-rimmed green eyes, however, were anything but ordinary. He could only characterize her gaze as bright, humorous, and full of life. Already bored, Dorian tapped his fingers on the scuffed, but immaculately clean linoleum.

That was the only signal Catzo needed. She arched her back and frizzed her skinny tail like a classic Halloween cat and took a few hops sideways with all four feet off the ground before pouncing on his hand.

"Ow!" He shook off his attacker. "That one's got an attitude."

"I'm guessing you haven't spent a lot of time with cats," Lyra surmised. "There are certain rules, the first of which is to never act like a rodent."

Affronted, Dorian scowled. "So I'm a rat? Well, you're not the only one who thinks that."

Lyra could see the hurt that flickered under his anger. She chose to ignore it. "Your fingers were wiggling like a mouse. Cats can't resist that sort of thing. It's a lot safer to use toys. Here." She handed him a toy fishing pole with a cluster of feathers dangling from the end, serving as bait. He needed only to twitch it to gain Catzo's attention. She leapt at the feathers, toppling over backwards in her enthusiasm while Catalina watched, unamused, from the couch. Dorian laughed in spite of himself.

Lyra was watching with the keenest of interest. Catzo and Dorian were a perfect match. The little cat was just what he needed to cheer him up. Lyra hoped he could see that, but he continued to glance at Catalina, the prettier cat, in her glorious repose.

Unfortunately, beauty won out over personality, as it so often did. Dorian left with Catalina in a cardboard carrier along with a couple of toys, a litter box, food, and other supplies. Catzo followed her visitor to the door, as it opened and closed, and waited there for a while as if there were some mistake.

"Sorry, Catzo," Lyra said. "Your time will come."

As Lyra entered her cottage after work, Catzo chirped a greeting and purred with a vibrato that would have done an old time Wurlitzer organ proud. The little tabby jumped up on the couch, anticipating the love and attention she was about to receive.

Heeding the invitation to cuddle, Lyra threw her backpack on the floor and joined Catzo, who bumped her hand with a soft, furry head. On cue, Lyra lowered her face to receive more head butting and purrs.

Leaving Lyra

As Catzo settled into her lap, Lyra stroked the youngster's tabby-striped coat and confided, "Dorian may be handsome, but Phil is the nicest guy, Catzo. He said he likes my eyes. Said their color reminded him of a forest." She sighed. "But he's nice like that to everyone. How would I know if he really likes me? The other day he was telling Molly some far-fetched story like he always does and he winked at me. Like it was our little joke. Later on he said, 'Lyra, you make the best coffee.'" She closed her eyes and snuggled closer into her confidante.

More purrs laid the question to rest—for now, at least.

Lyra was surprised at how much she enjoyed helping Maggie with her gardening. The only part she was uncomfortable with was deadheading. It seemed a shame to cut a flower before its time was completely up, even if it made new flowers grow faster. She took these flowers on their last stem-legs and let them finish their bloom and set seed in her kitchen. Cone flowers were an immediate favorite with their spiky globes of seeds, almost as fascinating as their flowers. These hardy divas with their swept back, many-hued petals, dominated much of the garden, attracting butterflies and hummers in droves.

Lyra found weeding particularly rewarding, not that there was much in the way of weeds here. Plucking and discarding them gave immediate satisfaction though, plus Lyra could see that Maggie's down-on-all-fours days were coming to a close.

Although Maggie offered her gardening gloves, Lyra enjoyed the feel of the rich, crumbly soil. She could feel its very life between her fingers. Its scent was something she'd experienced before; it was embedded in her memory with fragile roots. Vague images of kneeling by her mother's side, helping with her roses, drifted in with the aroma. She seized the memory and held it between soil-stained hands.

"Lyra, you look like you're a million miles away," Maggie said.

"Not a million miles, just a few years. I was thinking about my mom, and how I used to help her with her roses."

"So tell me about your mother," Maggie asked gently.

"When she died, all that was good and loving in my life passed away with her. I miss her. Terribly."

"I know what you mean, Lyra. My mother lived in your little cottage. We were as close as seeds in a cone flower—but much less prickly. But tell me more about your mom."

She glanced up momentarily. "She had the sweetest voice. Mom was always singing. And she always seemed happy. Mom was so wise. She taught me about God's love and the importance of being kind. And she gave the best advice. She took time to think, undistracted by TV or radio or phone. Maybe that's why Mom was so creative. Maybe that's how she held our family together. My father was not easy to live with, but Mom never complained. She just loved."

Weeds vanquished, at least for now, Lyra stood and stretched, arching with her hands on her lower back. "So what about your family?"

"Things were real prim and proper back then. Nobody said they loved you, but you knew they did. My daddy emigrated from Ireland when he was in his teens. He was lucky to get an apprenticeship as a bricklayer. He had more energy than sense sometimes. Never saw a man work so hard. Momma was the heart of the family. She was a school teacher before she met Daddy. Left her parents and two sisters to run off with him because her daddy wanted her to marry better, him being an immigrant and all. It was scandalous. They got married by a Justice of the Peace and moved to River Oaks where I was born. Never had any children of my own—none that lived anyway. The Mister and I wanted a house full of kids, but it wasn't to be."

"I'm so sorry."

"Me too. Me too. But now we have you to watch over." Maggie regained her twinkle.

Lyra gave her a hug before she realized she was transferring a great deal of dirt onto Maggie's impeccably embroidered white blouse.

"Whoops!" They both laughed.

A real bed! Lyra sat on her sunny doorstep waiting for the delivery truck. Not that she wasn't grateful for the couch, but nothing says "home" like a comfy bed—except a toaster, of course. The question had initially been whether her narrow bedroom would accommodate a bed of any size. She had done the measurements, and it would be a tight squeeze with the small second-hand dresser she'd found at the thrift store.

The delivery men arrived with the twin mattress, box spring, and frame in their burly arms. They stared at the dresser. The older man with the skull tattoos pointed, "That's got to go. There's no way we're gonna try 'n get that bed in there with that ugly old dresser in the way!"

"Couldn't you just try?"

"Sorry. We've got other deliveries to make. Can't waste any more time on a lost cause."

"I'm sure if we..." she began.

"Like I said. A waste of our valuable time." Correctly surmising there would be no tip, they dropped the unprofitable bed in the doorway and stomped off after more important deliveries.

Leaving Lyra

Oh well, who needs their grubby hands on my bed anyway? Good thing it was wrapped in plastic. She had the frame assembled in no time and worked it in between the dresser and the wall.

"Hey, Lyra," came her friend Stephanie's voice, "you home?"

Lyra got to her feet. She'd known Stephanie for a few months at church, and they had become fast friends. "I'm here." Sensing an edge to Stephanie's greeting, she lumbered all five paces to the doorstep, her legs numb from kneeling.

Stephanie's eyes were puffy and red. Lyra engulfed her with a tight hug while Stephanie shuddered in an attempt to stifle sobs. "I can't keep doing this," Steph managed to say.

"Doing what?"

"Everything. I can't keep being a mom to my family. I'm only seventeen and I have to do *everything*. Stacey keeps little Stevie busy while I'm studying, but she doesn't do anything to help around the house. She won't even do her home school lessons. She just sits with her sketchpad and fashion magazines. She gets so mad when I ask her to do anything, I've just given up. And poor little Stevie, he knows something's wrong, and it makes him really insecure. He's been crying a lot. What can I tell him? Mom doesn't give him any attention. It's like she's been sleepwalking ever since Dad left. She never even gets dressed, just wears her worn out nightie and that horrible old bathrobe." Steph picked at a fingernail. Looking up, she asked,

"What am I supposed to do to snap her out of it? Why does it *always* have to be me that keeps our family going?"

She plopped herself down hard on Lyra's porch step and drew her knees to her chest with a deep moan. "I'm sorry. I don't mean to be a wimp. Sometimes I don't think I can keep going. I guess this is one of those times. And then there's the money...we're broker than broke. Dad hasn't sent a dime. Ever. He's off with his girlfriend, who knows where. He doesn't love us anymore and he's never coming back."

Lyra squeezed in beside her on the step. "No one person can do all you're doing without it taking a toll. You've taken on a lot of roles: mother, father, counselor, cook, maid, taxi driver, school teacher…you're doing more than I could ever do, and you're doing it well."

"Will it ever end, Lyra? When am I going to get my life back without feeling guilty, or feeling like I'm letting my family down? What can I do to get Mom back on her feet? Remember when she locked herself in her room, and we all thought she might be dead? And that police sergeant came and broke in her door and tried to get her to go to counseling? She nearly bit his head off. She did the same to me when I gave her a pamphlet on depression. I'm not going there again!"

"You're right; this is a lot bigger problem than you can handle on your own."

"Don't I know it."

"We can pray..." Lyra offered.

"Like that's gonna help." She hugged her knees even tighter and rested her head on them. Her voice drifted up from her self-imposed cave. "You have to have faith for a miracle. Isn't that in the Bible? I'm fresh out," she said.

"I have just enough for both of us right now. God cares and He has a solution. I know He does."

"So what do I do to get things to change?"

"Pray and then wait."

"Haven't I waited long enough?"

"Apparently not." Lyra closed her eyes and laid her hand on Stephanie's hunched shoulder. "Okay, Jesus, we need You. You're the only hope for Steph and her family. Please help them to become a family again soon. Heal her mom, and help Stephanie to know You love her. Give her peace, and help her to wait for Your answer. Amen."

Stephanie raised her head and gave a weak smile. "I guess we'll see."

"Hey, how about adding furniture-mover to your resume?"

"Huh?" Steph raised her perfectly-tweezed eyebrows.

"I could sure use a hand with my new box spring and mattress. They're not that heavy but it's really awkward in such a small space."

"Sure." She shrugged. "Why not?"

As predicted, the springs did not give up without a fight. The girls wrestled it into place, albeit less than gracefully, added the mattress, and dramatically fell backwards on it.

"It's weird." Lyra observed, "Your father ruined your life by leaving. Mine ruined my life by staying. I guess we don't necessarily get what we want. But I *know*," she said with conviction, "just like Pastor Vicente says, God will give us what we need."

CHAPTER 3
Well-Bread and Overworked

Work, work, work, Molly thought to herself. It was such a relief to have Lyra's help now, but she still found herself way too busy. Molly walked around the bakery's dining area on her way to the door. Stepping outside, she turned the key to lock up. *Why am I working so hard? I need a break. When was the last time I saw Jared face to face?* Her brilliant fiancé danced into her mind, then waltzed back out again as quickly as he had entered. *This is ridiculous,* she ranted inwardly. *I need to see him. We need to finally set a date for our wedding.*

She walked past Daryla's Flower Boutique on their shared boardwalk next to the bakery. Daryla Summers was busy settling in the last of a dozen yellow roses in Sergeant Morrison's weekly bouquet order for his wife. Molly caught Daryla's eye as she passed the shop. The two waved in unison. Sergeant Morrison, now there was a man who cherished his wife. Would Jared cherish her after they were married? His life had always been so busy since they'd met back in college, but had become unbearably so through the years of his med school, internship, residency, and now his fellowship in facial reconstructive surgery. *Will it ever end?* she asked herself. Still, he was everything she ever wanted in a man. She could push aside her own desires and delay her dreams for another year—or could she? Molly had a hollow spot inside her ribcage that had haunted her since the day he left for med school on the east coast. *I've got to go visit him.* She rubbed her left hand ring finger where the ever-promised engagement ring should have been residing. *Oh well, a diamond would just get all caked with flour everyday anyway,* she attempted to console herself. *A plain gold band is really all I need.*

A few blocks from her house she heard the faint notes from a piano trailing off in the distance. She had locked up a few minutes too late for the nightly nocturne.

I'll call Jared when I get home, she promised herself. *I'll close up shop for a few days and go visit him.* A sudden rush of joy filled her empty chest. *That's all we need, just to see each other again and maybe set a wedding date.* Holding onto hope and her front door knob, she turned the key and walked into her too-quiet house. Someday there would be the noise and chaos of children filling up the silent nooks and crannies. She kicked off her shoes and dug her cell phone from her favorite little red purse. The phone rang a few times before going to voicemail.

"Jared, it's me, Molly. I'm just really missing you. Going through Jared withdrawals here. I was thinking of flying out to visit you maybe next week? For a couple days? Let me know what days work for you. Call me back, Love. I've just gotta see you! I love you!" Kissie noises ensued.

As she hung up the phone, she wondered how long she'd have to wait for a call back. She wandered aimlessly into the kitchen. The leftover beef and veggie soup she made the night before stared down at her listlessly from the top refrigerator shelf. *Eat me or don't,* it seemed to mock her, knowing she would probably just settle for cheese and crackers tonight. "You may live for another day," she answered the saucy soup as she reached for the block of sharp cheddar in the fridge door. Grabbing a box of cracked wheat crackers and slicing some cheese, she headed for the family room couch and stared at her cell phone on the coffee table. The sound of her crunching crackers in the otherwise silent house was such a lonely sound that she turned on the TV to drown out the solitude. Her favorite dancing competition was on, which helped distract her, until a couple came on stage to perform a waltz. When was the last time Jared had held her that close? She couldn't remember. She flipped off the TV just as her phone rang.

"Jared!" she answered.

"Molly!" he responded. "How are you doing, sweetheart? I miss you so much!"

"I miss you more than ever, Love! When are you free next week?" she asked hopefully.

"It's not going to work for me for a while, Moll. I'm not even getting close to a full night's sleep the last few weeks."

"But you must have at least one day off in the next week or so," Molly insisted desperately.

"I'm afraid not. They've got me working harder than ever, and it's not gonna let up soon. So how are things going at the bakery? How's the new girl working out?"

Just like a man to change the subject, Molly reasoned. "She's working out great. So when are you going to have time for me, Jared?"

"Oh, Moll, you know I want to be with you! I just have this huge commitment to finish before we can be together."

"You mean getting married, right, Jared? I think we really need to set the date."

"I can't do that til I'm done here with the rest of my training. You know that. You've known that all along. We've been over this so many times."

"Yeah, I know, Jared, but I really miss you. I feel like my life has been on hold for years now while you pursue your love affair with medicine. I don't think I can wait much longer!"

"I wish I could wave a magic wand and have it all over with. I'd be back home in California, and we could set a date. I love you, Molly, I really do. Please be patient for just a little longer."

"Okay...but I don't have to like it."

"No, you don't, and neither do I. Look, sweetheart, I just got paged. I've gotta go. I love you!"

"I love you too, Jared. Talk to you soon, Love."

Leaving Lyra
"Bye." Molly heard an all too familiar silence.

To say Sadie and Kallie Waldorf's wedding was lavish was quite an understatement. These identical twins were marrying twin brothers, and to the girls' parents, money was no object. Not one to be impressed by wealth or the vices it might conceal, Lyra was nonetheless in awe of the tasteful artistry of the event. And Molly's creations were no exception. It had been terrifying delivering the two elegant cakes unscathed to their silver cake pedestals, but seeing them in place made it worth the risk.

This had been Lyra's first attempt at fondant, but she seemed to have a knack for it. So much so that Molly let her create all the eyelet ruffles for Sadie's cake. The ignorant might say it came naturally for Lyra to work with sugary creations because of her size, but she didn't have to eat a project to enjoy it. Just one of many perceptions she longed to lay to rest in this unjust world.

While Molly snapped a few shots of the cakes now safely in place, Lyra indulged in her own tour of the Waldorf's ballroom. Each expression of floral magnificence on the guests' tables represented almost a week's salary for her. Silver stands held upside-down bell jars filled with blue and lavender hydrangeas, tiny white roses, and asparagus fern, each a supreme work of art. Daryla, the florist, should be proud. She had truly outdone herself.

Lyra looked up to the ceiling where innumerable yards of sky blue fabric draped in all directions from the crown-like center of the room's ceiling to the corners of the room. They cascaded down the walls into pools of fabric on the floor. Ever the practical soul, she wondered what would become of the plethora of fabric when the wedding was over.

The orchestra was tuning up outside. A lone violin sent a sweet snippet of Pachelbel's Canon wafting its way through the French doors. Following the sound, she glanced out one of the ballroom windows that ran the length of the structure. The guests gathered outside, milling about in all their finery and clearly enjoying the ambience. It was an elegant sight to behold.

Lyra looked deeper than appearances. As a person who needed to distinguish "dangerous people" from "safe people," she let her eyes linger here and there. *Mostly safe people*, she decided, and felt herself relax a bit. And then she saw *him,* with his false smile and cunning eyes. *What is he doing here? Of course, he seeks out big events to promote himself. Why this one? Has he heard that I'm here? He has his connections, after all. I wonder if he's still having me followed?*

With no time to pity the flashy young woman on his arm, Lyra did the only thing she could do. She excused herself, feigning sickness, and ran around the opposite side of the estate, dashing through the elaborate wrought iron entrance gates, and praying with all her heart that he hadn't seen her. She ran all the way home, opened the door to her sanctuary in the McCreary's garden, stepped in, bolted the door behind her and leaned against it, panting. "God help me," she said in between gasps for air. The fairytale wedding had turned into a poisoned-apple nightmare.

CHAPTER 4
Bread Upon the Water

Dorian had not been to church since *the incident*. He had his reasons. For one thing, he feared being recognized and judged, and for another, he'd lost faith in churches in general and in the God Who was supposed to care. The church scandal had cost Dorian his wife, his home, his job—in short, his entire life. But he couldn't run any longer.

Dorian picked up the phonebook, wondering if a fresh start in a new, preferably obscure church might help. If nothing else, it would provide an excuse to sing, which he had avoided ever since *the incident*. "Church of the Broken," he read. "Sounds like me, all right. They have a service on Saturday— today." He jotted down the address and checked himself in the mirror for obvious traces of insecurity. Leaving his hair devoid of its usual gel, he headed for his car.

The church was in a strip mall, barely distinguishable from the pizza place and the liquor store bordering it. The service was already in session, and the lights were dimmed— ideal for a quick getaway.

Some of the music was surprisingly in Spanish. This was clearly not the place for him, yet he lingered. There was peace between these dark blue walls. And then he heard it, two lovely voices, disarming in their innocence and clarity. It was more than he could bear. He fled to his car and sat there, his heart pounding, until he felt steady enough to drive home.

He returned the following Saturday, this time a little too late for the music. A husky Hispanic man greeted him at the door with a genuine smile before returning his attention to the man at the pulpit, who stood on a small platform constructed of plywood and painted black. The preacher was a short man, also of Latin American descent, who bore the striking profile of his Aztec ancestors. English was not his native language, but he spoke a simple message about love that seemed to be the most profound sermon Dorian had ever heard. It had never dawned on him that Jesus had been falsely accused as he himself had been. Jesus' closest friends left Him, just as Dorian's wife and friends had all abandoned him, not wanting to be caught in the fallout. And because of what Jesus had experienced, He loved and accepted others as no one else could. He truly understood what Dorian was going through.

Dorian had lost sight of love amidst all the betrayers and betrayals—all of course in God's name. Wasn't love what he'd

51

longed for in the first place? Wasn't it what had turned his heart Godward? What he wanted even now? And yet, an act of kindness was behind the very disaster that had destroyed him. As the service concluded, his head bowed, he shook the hand of the man at the door and hurried to his car.

He wanted to talk with someone. But it would have to wait. Uncle Phil would be gone until Tuesday, attending some kind of computer programming convention. Reluctant to return home in such a state, he drove around aimlessly for a while and eventually ended up at Molly's Sunshine Bakery.

Lyra gave him a smile as the bell jingled his arrival. She looked as if he were the very person she wanted to see—the way she smiled at everyone entering her domain.

Dorian plopped himself down at a wrought iron table by the counter.

"Coffee?" she asked. "No, you look wound up already. How about some chamomile tea? That should mellow you out."

"Sure. Whatever." He waved her away dismissively.

She placed the china teapot, cup, and saucer in front of him and then went to get herself a glass of water. Returning to his table, she said, "Now you can't expect me to let you leave here carrying—whatever it is—that's eating you up inside." Her eyes told Dorian that she was prepared to take whatever measures needed to get him to spill his guts, but instead she spilled her own.

LEAVING LYRA

"I had that same look as you have when I first came into town. No one to believe in, and no one to believe in me." She took note of the slow wince that came over his face. "Yeah, it hurts, doesn't it? Like when your foot goes to sleep. It's numb, but it hurts all the more for it. I was lucky—I guess 'blessed' is a better word—that I stumbled in here. I'm learning to trust again. Without trust you can't love anyone, even yourself or God." She took a deep breath. "I'm working on it, but I've got a long way to go." She took the seat across from him and waited, unhurried, like a cat lounging by a fireplace.

He opened the lid of the teapot and sniffed at its contents. It smelled like old-fashioned postage stamp glue from his grandfather's stamp collection. Harmless enough. Absently, he poured a cup and began to gulp it down. His mouth singed, he spluttered hot tea all over Lyra's red apron.

"This is boiling water!" he accused. Lyra gave him her glass of water to cool his mouth down.

"Duh. Boiling water *is* how you make tea." She smirked. "I thought you knew that."

"Sorry, Lyra. I didn't mean to spew on you."

"Yeah, that's what it's like," she observed, "trying to hold scalding water in your mouth. Sooner or later, you gotta let it out before it causes more damage."

He crunched an ice cube. "You wouldn't understand."

"Try me."

"It's like…It's a guy thing," he muttered.

"Well, I guess that leaves me out then." She gave a nervous chuckle as she rose, heading over to tend the already spotless counter. "I've spent long enough being 'one of the guys.'" She looked up. "Phil will be back on Tuesday. He's a really good listener. You're lucky to have him as an uncle."

In fact, Lyra could not imagine a nicer uncle—or a better friend. In his blue eyes she saw the smile they displayed and the sadness they hid. Cerulean, that was the color. It reminded her of her favorite crayon color from her childhood. Most of all she enjoyed the spark of mischief in his eyes during their morning banter.

At the rate she was going, Lyra was at least two years from her goal of being a veterinary assistant. Every spare moment and every extra dollar she made was devoted to this one end. Evenings found her on the couch with Catzo, who stalked her pen and tried to catch textbook pages with her teeth. Rather than a hindrance, Lyra appreciated the cheer the little tabby brought. She dreaded the day she would have to part with her and send her away to someone who could afford the care Catzo deserved. In the meantime, Catzo would continue to share Lyra's bed every night and would wake Lyra each morning with chirps and head-butting.

LEAVING LYRA

After a night of studying Lyra curled up on the couch with her journal and Bible. Catzo was at her feet, kneading the squishy throw blanket. She read Proverbs 16:3 out loud. "Commit your actions to the LORD, and your plans will succeed." Lyra wrote this quote down in her notebook and added a journal entry after it.

Journal Entry:

My only plans were just to survive after Mom died. I feel like something new is awakening in me now. Can I call it hope? If I give Him my plans, He promises to make them work. I guess that means they will succeed. But how do I believe that? My life has been such a disaster. How do I change my way of thinking and believe that God really cares about my future when my past is so full of garbage? God, help me. I want to believe in Your promises, but I look at my past and I think You don't care about me.

Dorian started seeking solitary places. He found a park nearby where the summer river had narrowed. Cottonwoods lined the banks flanked with rounded river rocks worn smooth with years of winter flooding. The rocks clattered as he made his way slowly over them. He picked up a stone and tossed it into the clear water, watching the concentric circles fan out toward the shore.

The movement of the water reminded him of the first time he told Brittney that he loved her. Alone together on his father's ski boat, he had cut the motor in the middle of the bay. They drifted with the waves slapping contentedly at the sides of the boat. He remembered the nervousness in the pit of his stomach as he summoned up the courage to tell her how he felt. It was quiet, very quiet. *She's so perfect. How do I tell her I love her?* he'd wondered. He was just about to speak when she dove overboard. As she resurfaced, he saw her sun-kissed golden hair sinuously caressing her bronzed shoulders.

"Come on in, Dorian. Cool off."

Had she seen the sweat trickling down his forehead? Did she realize how nervous he was? Did she know what he was about to say? *Aw, forget it*, he told himself. Throwing caution to the wind, he dove in and surfaced face to face with Brittney. He heard himself saying out loud, "I love you, Brittney. I always have." The water encircled them. There was a moment's pause. She grabbed his shoulders and said, "You have no idea how long I've waited to hear that." She kissed him, then dove down playfully, leaving a single set of ripples in her wake. He never would have dreamt that she'd eventually disappear. Forever.

I've got to let go. I can't keep living like this. She's never coming back. Even though I did nothing wrong, she's never

going to believe it. I have to give this all up to You, God. Your
will be done.

He stepped into the water and knelt down. In a baptism
of sorts, he lay on his back, arms spread. He let the gentle
current wash over him. Even though it was late summer, the
river ran cold. At first, the water took his breath away. Ignoring
the discomfort, he settled in. *Will I ever be whole again? Will I*
ever be home again? Will I ever find love again? As he lay
there, the chill shocked the truth into him. What he really
needed was to believe. *I've lost touch with Jesus. My faith needs*
to become real. Like this water.

His spirit lifted, he rose, throwing his head back. The
water formed an arch from his hair back down to the river
behind him, dancing over the stones. He was feeling more at
ease than he'd felt in quite a while.

He wandered the riverbank until he heard the sound of a
classical guitar, expertly finger-picked. Not wanting to disrupt
the music, he stood a respectful distance away, venturing
forward only when the last notes had ceased.

He discovered that the guitarist was a large-framed girl.
A loose rock clanked under his foot.

Startled, the girl turned. "Oh, hi, Dorian. You scared me.
How come you're all wet? You're not exactly dressed to go
swimming."

"Got hot and just decided to jump in. I didn't know you
played guitar."

Smiling, Lyra held up the battered instrument. "One of the ushers at church gave me this. His son had given up on learning to play."

"You've obviously had some experience playing," Dorian observed.

"It's been awhile. I had to hock my six-string for gas money." She shrugged. "Playing really helps keep me sane." Lyra pushed her hair behind her ear.

"I've played a song or two. Nothing like you, though. I'm more of a strummer."

She handed him the guitar.

For the first time in ages, he felt music stirring inside. Surmounting his fear, he began to sing.

"You've got a really nice voice," she noted as he finished his song. "You're a Christian, right? Have you ever thought of singing solo at church?"

"I've got to go." He shoved the guitar at her, almost dropping it. Clattering across the rocks, he disappeared.

"That's the worst case of stage fright I've ever seen," Lyra commented to a passing duck.

CHAPTER 5
Five Loaves

"I was wondering how long it'd take for you to tell me the details." Phil's blue eyes beckoned, promising compassion.

"Nothing much to tell." Dorian studied the reemerging calluses on his left fingertips. "The same old story. You do something nice and you get punished for it." He shrugged.

Phil was silent, his head cocked expectantly, obviously dissatisfied with the explanation. The clock on the wall behind him was the only discernible sound in the breakfast nook. He watched quietly as Dorian flicked a bread crumb from the table top, thought the better of it, and bent over in his chair to retrieve it.

Dorian looked up, grateful for his uncle's patience, so unlike the accusations and demands of his church's Board of Directors and the rejection of his father and his wife who should've known him better. "There was this girl at church. She was maybe sixteen years old and mentally unstable. At first I felt sorry for her. She became a nuisance, then she became a noose."

Phil's brows came together. He waited.

"I met Kari after church one day. She was in a wheelchair. I could tell she was troubled, so I lent an ear a few times. It didn't take long to see that her issues were more than I was qualified to deal with, so I gave her the name of a good Christian counselor—a woman at church. I thought nothing more about it until I got called into the senior pastor's office. There was Kari, looking totally freaked out. The whole staff was there and worst of all, Brittney. They were all staring at me as if I were a monster. Kari told them that I had taken advantage of her—you know, sexually—and she told it convincingly. She said that I had told her that we were meant to be together, and that God had told me to leave my wife for her. The scary thing was that she really seemed to believe it. And so did Brittney."

He leveled his gaze. "Brittney never let me explain. Her mind was made up from the beginning. In exchange for my resignation and leaving the church, Kari and the church agreed to keep things quiet, but you know how churches are. Word gets out and there's no stopping it. I heard through the grapevine that Ashton, the backup singer, had immediately taken my place on stage, just like he always wanted to do. I got tired of feeling ashamed over something I'd never done. I was too embarrassed to show my face in town and sick of wondering who knew about it." His shoulders rose and fell. "So here I am."

"And Brittney?" Phil asked.

"Has already filed for divorce."

"I'm sorry, man. I'm really sorry. It's so unfair. I can't believe Brittney would fall for that." Phil said, adding with conviction, "We'll get you through this."

Phil had always been a good listener. No problem was too great or too small to merit his attention, and his kind eyes never held a hint of judgment. Though he sometimes asked intimidating questions, Lyra never felt threatened. And so it was on this particular afternoon.

"Are you still getting by with Molly's old worn-out couch?"

"I don't need much to get by," she countered. "But now I have a bed, dresser, and a table and folding chairs too. But most importantly I have my very own little red toaster."

"Molly says you came here with all your belongings in a backpack."

"Oh, I'm not that into things—except toasters." Her smile betrayed an unaccustomed wariness.

"Look, you don't have to tell me anything you don't want to," Phil said, as he gently patted her arm.

Lyra thrilled to the touch of his hand. She had never come so close to confiding in anyone about her past. "Thanks," she said. "Maybe someday I'll tell my story. Just not now."

"I'll be here." He smiled.

As she lay in bed that night Lyra relived the sensation of his hand upon her arm. Was it concern or love in his eyes? She got up and opened her Bible to distract herself.

Journal Entry:

I wish I could tell Phil about my past. I'm weary, Lord, from carrying this heavy load. It drags me down, but I'm afraid to let it go. It's all I know. I'm used to it. I was reading tonight in John chapter 6, about how Jesus had just finished preaching. He must've been tired from dealing with all those people.

He decided to leave for the other side of the lake, but a large crowd followed Him. He gave of Himself and gave up His own need for solitude, and ministered to the needs of others. He had compassion even though He and His disciples needed rest. Jesus knew their greatest need was for the Word of God. He looked ahead to their physical needs as well. He gave them bread and fish to eat. They were in an impossible situation. Phillip told Jesus that even eight months' wages couldn't feed the crowd. But Andrew, who was always bringing people to Jesus, found a boy with five loaves and two fish and brought him to Jesus. Andrew was totally dependent upon Jesus' power. He didn't worry about the outcome. He just gave what he had

available to his Christ. He didn't try to manipulate the outcome;
it wasn't Andrew's problem to worry about. It was Jesus'. Jesus
called food into existence that wasn't already there.

Lord, I bring You my five loaves and two fish. Everything
I've got. Make a miracle of my life. Bring into existence Your
healing from my humble five loaves and two fish.

"Isn't Catalina supposed to…like…do something? I'm afraid she might be sick. She just lays on the couch with her eyes looking far away. It's like she's looking for something." Dorian pushed his plate aside for Lyra to pick up.

"You've got that right," Lyra said. "Catalina belonged to a little girl who died in a car crash. Her folks couldn't bear the sight of the poor cat after the accident so they took her to the shelter. I was hoping that your broken heart would bond with hers."

Dorian bolted to his feet. "My heart? What do you know about that? Did my uncle say something? That's none of your business!"

Lyra's brow furrowed. "He didn't say a word. He didn't have to. A broken heart's easy to spot. And hard to heal." She rose to attend to another smudge on the counter left by an overenthusiastic young doughnut connoisseur.

Dorian sat back down, drained the last of his coffee, and went home to his broken-hearted cat. He sat down beside her on the couch and sunk his hand into her silken coat. "I know how you feel," he said. He poured his heart out to the cat who had ceased her aimless staring and trained her amber eyes on Dorian. Eyes blinking slowly, she continued to regard him as he spoke.

"Lyra told me about your little girl. I'm sorry. I lost someone too. Maybe we can…like…be there for each other."

Catalina nudged his head with her forehead in response.

Lyra sat down on her corduroy couch, a toasted slice of delicate lemon poppyseed bread in hand. "I guess I do have a crush on Phil," Lyra confided to Catzo, who had tumbled into her lap and was grappling with her own tail. The spunky tabby squeaked when she bit it too hard. "But who wouldn't? He's the nicest guy I've ever met. He may be older than me, but he's funny and smart and cute too." A dreamy sigh escaped. "Of course, I can't think of a single reason why he'd be interested in me. I'm just someone he kids around with, just one of the guys." Another sigh followed as crumbs drifted down to her kitten. "I've spent most of my life trying to be invisible to men. So what do I do now?"

Catzo looked up from her own attempts at tail-destruction and gave her a knowing wink.

"I'm glad you've got it all worked out, Catzo."

Why can't I be more like her? Dorian asked himself as he watched Lyra at the counter catching up on the details of an elderly couple's lives. As always, she was quick to smile and equally quick to commiserate. Lyra seemed to sense her customers' needs before they could even voice them, and she had an incredible knack for remembering names, faces, and coffee and pastry preferences.

As for himself, Dorian had little to offer in social situations. Unlike his loquacious uncle, Dorian was tongue-tied in crowds and could barely look anyone in the eye, so great was his shyness. When forced to speak, he peppered his speech with the word, "like," as he groped for the right words. Back at his former church he had been asked to lead a Bible study for his fellow worship band members. After one agonizing session, he decided to give the leadership roll over to Ashton, the outgoing backup singer and keyboard player who now, in Dorian's absence, directed everything.

How ironic that despite his taciturn nature Dorian had once been the worship leader of one of the biggest megachurches on the West Coast. With a guitar in hand and hair spiked, he was transformed. Fully alive. He couldn't expect that kind of exhilaration to ever happen again.

As she did for everyone, Lyra put Dorian at ease. In fact, lately he looked forward to talking with her every morning at the bakery. He thought it odd though that other than her love of cats, her sparse furnishings, her skillful playing of guitar, and her outgoing nature, he knew nothing about her personally. On this particular morning he resolved to turn their conversation Lyraward.

"What's your favorite thing here...like...to eat?" he asked lamely, immediately regretting his reference to eating habits. "I mean, what do you recommend?" He smiled, satisfied with his attempt to uninsult her.

"I was going to say the people, but not being a cannibal, I'd say the cream puffs. Not so much fun to make, but I love the way the plainness on the outside hides the perfect sweetness on the inside. Life can be like that. People too. Even cats. Of course, even the finest of cream puffs cannot rival a good slice of toasted whole wheat."

Only Lyra could turn a discussion of baked goods into a cheery philosophical observation. "What's your favorite? As if I didn't know," she asked over the counter.

"I think I'll try a cream puff this time," he said.

"What, no maple bar?" She raised her eyebrows in amazement then smiled. "Coming right up."

LEAVING LYRA

As Lyra turned and headed toward the display case, Dorian studied her. *She sure wears that shirt a lot. It's not part of her uniform.* It was clear to him that Lyra needed some new clothes. *That kind of thing doesn't seem to matter to her,* he concluded. *And why on earth should that matter to me?* His visit to her cottage confirmed the fact that she was not into external appearances. What a contrast between her and Brittney. Back in the day, he could barely afford his wife's constant shopping excursions. But it was worth it. Brittney looked good. Really good.

Lyra returned with an extra large cream puff and a matching smile.

"So what's your story, Lyra? What brought you here to River Oaks?"

"I don't think you want to know."

"Yeah, I do. I really do."

"I can't talk about it."

"What are you, some kind of spy?"

"Well, if you must know, it's all about toast," she said in a conspirator's whisper.

"What? What's that supposed to mean? I didn't think spies ate toast. It leaves too many crumbs behind."

"That's what they'd like you to believe. But I never said I was a spy. I knew you wouldn't understand," she said, rolling her eyes playfully.

"So...what then? Are you here spying out the perfect toast recipes?"

"What if I am? Toasting is an exact science, you know."

"I always just thought you just stuffed bread into a toaster and pushed the lever down."

"Ha! Shows how much you know."

"So, what makes it the perfect piece of toast then?"

"Not only does it have to be toasted for exactly the right time and temperature, which I can't divulge or I would have to find a way to silence you, permanently, but the essential toppings are of the utmost importance."

"Such as?"

"Depends on what kind of mood I'm in."

"So if you're feeling miserable?"

"Oh, that's easy. Blueberry preserves capture the essence of the blues."

"How about when you're feeling up?"

"That's a cinnamon and sugar day." She proceeded to do her best James Brown impersonation.

"I feel good. Na na na na na na na
Like I knew that I would now.
I feel nice like sugar and spice now.
So good, so good. I got toast,
Da da da da. Ow!"

Dorian's mouth dropped open as he tried not to choke on his half-chewed bite of cream puff. He put up questioning hands and said, "Where'd that come from?"

"I'll admit it. I have a thing for toast. Why do you think I work here? What do you think I'm doing in that back room?"

"Okay, so what does toast have to do with being a spy?"

Lyra crossed her arms in front of her. "I guess you'll just have to figure that out." Unable to restrain herself, Lyra began to laugh. It'd been a long time since she'd had the chance to goof off, and it was extraordinarily freeing.

Wondering what had just transpired between the two of them, Dorian joined in her laughter, feeling lighter than he'd felt in quite some time. *So this girl has a sense of humor. Nice.*

There it was again, the giddy little tickle in Lyra's tummy every time Phil looked her way. The thing about Phil was that he didn't just look; he really saw. Normally that would disturb a girl who'd spent so much of her time and effort on not being noticed, but his gaze was caring. Safe. *Of course, he looks at everyone the same way*, Lyra reminded herself.

"What's up, Lyra?" He seemed to *mean* her name when he said it. Soft, yet deliberate.

Lyra put down the toasted slice of raisin bread she'd been nibbling on during her break. "I, uh..."

"I absolutely agree." Phil's blue eyes sparkled. "Hey, Molly, wasn't I just saying that the other day?"

"As a matter of fact, you were." Molly approached the table where Lyra was taking her break. Molly tried to wipe off the flour from her own nose with an equally floury finger, smudging it irreparably.

Lyra stood. "I guess I should be getting back to work."

Molly gestured to the table where Phil was finishing his apple fritter. "We need to talk, and this is as good a place as any. Sit."

Lyra's heart sank to her knees. She took her seat, expecting the worst. After all, hadn't she dropped that sheet of almond macaroon cookies last week, ruining the whole batch? Lyra resolved not to cry. If only her hands would stop shaking. In the short time she'd been working here, she'd come to love the people and the job. She took a deep breath and let it out slowly. *Why did this have to happen in front of Phil?* Molly looked serious. This was going to hurt. Bad.

"Lyra," she began, "you've been working here for a while now. How would you say it's been going for you?"

"I love it. I know I've made some mistakes, and I understand if..."

"Well, I think you're doing fabulous, but there's one thing I have to ask of you."

Lyra's eyebrows lifted. *What is happening here?*

"Can you work more hours? I really need your help. Of course, there'll be a little raise in it for you."

"I, uh..."

"My sentiments exactly," Phil smirked.

"Yes," Lyra said, receiving a big hug from a grateful Molly followed by a brotherly pat on the back from Phil.

"Glad you'll be sticking around," he said as he discreetly licked a bit of glaze off the tip of his thumb. "Who else would I have to tease without you here?"

Lyra's pounding heart unleashed a fiery blush. She looked down at her hands, at the flour stuck under her nails. Looking up, she said, "Thank you, Phil. That means a lot." How generous his name felt on her tongue. She found herself seeking occasions to speak it, but finding all too few, she said it again and again in her heart.

CHAPTER 6

Cinnamon Twist of Fate

The elderly couple thanked Lyra for the patient, detailed directions she gave to lead them to the freeway.

"You haven't lived here that long," Dorian observed. "Yet you seem to know your way around better than my uncle does. Why is that? Are you, like, some kind of...like...directional genius?"

Lyra's eyes were far off, watching the old man open the car door for his wife and carefully shut it once she was seated. Dorian was beginning to think she hadn't heard him when she replied, eyes still trained on the departing couple, "Over the years I've found it helpful to always have a way out to some other town or city I could reach in a matter of hours."

"So you've traveled a lot?"

"You could say that. How about you?" As usual, she seamlessly deflected the conversation from herself. As usual, he failed to notice.

"Nah. I lived in the same house in the same town until I got married, and we lived real close to Mom and Dad's. Even went to the same church all those years. That's where I met her. That's where I lost her."

"She died in church?" Lyra ceased polishing the counter. "How awful! I'm so sorry, Dorian." Lyra walked over to his table.

"She's okay," he said drearily. "It's our relationship that died...at the church."

She waited, kitchen towel poised.

"I'd rather not go into it."

"I don't blame you." Her towel resumed its work.

Dorian wasn't sure in which context she spoke the words, whether she didn't blame him for the breakup or whether she didn't blame him for not wishing to discuss it with her. He chose the first possibility.

Lyra looked up. "Did you see that?" She was pointing at an antique truck as it passed the window of Molly's Sunshine Bakery.

"That old thing?"

"Old thing? It's a classic and a rare one at that. A Dodge truck from the 30's, I'm guessing."

"How do you know about old cars?" Dorian asked.

"I knew a family, the Barker's. Mr. Barker loved 'old cars,' as you call them. Not that he had the money to buy any, except for a '27 Ford Roadster he was able to salvage for next to nothing. I helped sand and paint it. It was a rust bucket when he got it, but it really shined when he was done restoring it. He'd always dreamed of having a Dodge from the 30's, just like his dad had. I saw the pictures. I could tell that his dad was really proud of his ride. I guess that got passed on to Mr. Barker, and on to me in the short time I knew him."

"You're full of surprises, Lyra," Dorian said.

"No, just full of toast."

"Lyra?" Molly called from the back room, "Can you watch the bakery on Friday and Saturday while Phil and I fly to Seattle? I'm his 'pretend date.' His ex-girlfriend, Ronnie is getting married. Should be a lot of fun, helping her realize what she's missing." Her brown eyes gleamed with mischief.

"Sure. I'd be glad to," Lyra said, faking it. "You two kids have fun." She plastered on a smile, picked up a cleaning rag, and commenced scrubbing the table tops with the sense that things would never be the same at Molly's Sunshine Bakery.

That night, Lyra wrote in her notebook:

Well, that's the end of that! Phil has asked Molly to go with him to his ex-girlfriend's wedding in Seattle. I know what that means; means he's gone on her and wants to make his ex

jealous and wish she'd never broken up with him. They'll come
back here all starry-eyed, I just know it. I'm not even going to
look for a promise from God tonight. I'm too upset. Why bother?

The following Monday rolled around with quite a
surprising twist of fate. Lyra wasn't sure quite what to think.

Journal Entry:

Well, looks like Molly's finally taken. Her fiancé Jared
showed up with a honking diamond and proposed right there in
the bakery. The look on Phil's face let me know how he really
feels about Molly. He slunk off quietly and I wanted so badly to
follow him, but I had to run the shop because she took off with
Jared to celebrate. There was a time not long ago that it would
have made me happy to see Molly out of the picture with Phil,
but seeing how crushed Phil was made me see how totally into
her he really is. I care too much about him to see him hurting
like this.

The following day brought yet another strange twist of
fate.

Journal Entry:

Major drama at the bakery. Molly broke up with Jared last night! Phil and Jared duked it out on her porch when Jared wouldn't back off after Molly said she was breaking up with him. I always knew Phil was a hero. Well, I guess that's it. I'm glad Phil's happy.

Lyra put her journal down and flopped on the couch.

"Well, Catzo, Ever since they came back from Ronnie's wedding Molly and Phil have been, well, together all the time." She sighed as the little cat bounced into her lap and attempted to lick her nose. Lyra guarded her nostrils, narrowly escaping the raspy tongue. "I knew I could count on you for sympathy. I guess I was just being silly, thinking that..."

She tickled the kitten's tummy and barely missed the outstretched claws. "Molly looks happier than I've ever seen her, and that makes it easier to take." Lyra smiled. "And they're so cute together. And it's great to see that kind of love exists anymore. Love..." She scooped up the little tabby and kissed her head. "You know all about that, don't you, Catzo?"

CHAPTER 7
Hello From the Burned Side

"Dorian's not a very common name," Lyra observed, sitting with him at his customary table in the bakery.

"Tell me about it," he grumbled. He was not about to let on that he was known in his student days as *Dorkian*. "Lyra's not a very ordinary name either."

"My mother said I've been singing since the day I was born. I must've had a set of lungs and some pretty cool baby lyrics back then." She returned her toasted challah bread to her plate and studied him.

"What do you like to sing, opera?"

"Just because I'm overweight doesn't make me an opera fan," she scolded with surprising gentleness. "Actually, I can't stand the stuff. Too stilted and theatrical to be real, at least a lot of the time. And real is what matters most to me in music…in everything, I guess. If you're not sharing what's in your heart, what does any of it matter? It'd just be sounds."

Dorian looked out the bakery window. There used to be so much inside him, irrepressible joy and a passionate love for God and humankind. Now he was feeling empty, save for the bitterness that still from time to time bathed his heart like fouled blood with each pulse.

"You sing, right?" Lyra asked eagerly. "I've been looking for someone to jam with."

"Used to." He fingered faint scratches on the table's shiny surface with his left hand. "Haven't had much to sing about in awhile."

"You do realize that Dorian is the name of a musical scale?"

"Huh? What's a scale?"

Lyra grinned. "Never mind."

"Hey, Dorian, I just wrote a new song last night. Well, I didn't write the song; Adele did. It's called, 'Hello.' I just 'toasted' it."

"Toasted it? What do you mean, 'toasted' it?" Dorian wondered.

"You know, kinda like Weird Al does with songs, only I make them about what's really important to me—toast. Do you want to hear this or don't you?"

"Now I'm intrigued. Hit it." Dorian's eyes turned up at the outer edges.

Lyra took a deep breath and began quietly, in her lowest possible Adele-like voice, instead of her normal soprano:

"Hello. It's me.

I was wondering after all these months if you might feel deplete,

LEAVING LYRA

And come over, just to eat.

I know toast, it is your favorite,

And I ain't done much cooking.

Hello. Are you hungry?

I just bought a brand new toaster

And I'm practicing my toasting.

I hope you like rye, but if sourdough's your pleasure

Then that is what I'm making.

It's no secret that both of us are running out of bread.

Hello from the dark side.

At least I can say that I tried

To tell you I'm sorry for ever burning your toast,

But when I call you always seem deaf as a post.

Hello from the pushed aside,

You thought your jam was misapplied,

But I tell you I'm sorry for ever burning your toast,

Next time I'll cook you a perfect pot roast.

There's such a difference between breads and a million toasting
times.

Hello from the self-despised,

You said my toast's formaldehyde.

I tell you I'm sorry for being such a bad host.

If you come back, I'll make you light sepia toast.

Hello from the pushed aside.

You thought your jam was misapplied,

But I tell you I'm sorry for ever burning your toast,

Next time I'll make you the toast you love most.

There's such a difference between breads and a million toasting times.

Hello from the burned side.

You hate my toast; it's been implied,

But I tell you I'm sorry for ever burning your toast.

Now my heart's been tied to your old whipping post."

Laughing hysterically, Dorian began slowly clapping, increasing in tempo.

Molly came out of the back room. "What the what? Lyra, you have some crazy talent!"

Lyra took a deep bow.

Journal Entry:

I heard at church this week that long ago a German school teacher would take off his hat and bow to his students each day. When asked why he did that he replied that you never know what these boys will become one day. One of those boys was Martin Luther.

I have a humble gift of music. I give it to You, God. It's all I have. It may not be much, but in Your hands even insignificant dust became man. Fame, wealth, and talent mean nothing unless it's surrendered to you. Please use my insignificance not just to entertain but to get Your work done.

After a few weeks' attendance, Dorian found himself eager to go to church. The sermons were bringing healing to his soul, and the music lifted his spirit higher than he thought possible, considering his state of disgrace. The two lovely voices continued to intrigue him, but because the singers were situated up in the dark balcony, he had never been able to figure out to whom the voices belonged. It was the pastor's belief that his congregation should be focused on the rough wooden cross behind him at the front of the church. Attention bestowed on gifted individuals in the gathering could pose a threat to their humility, a threat which Dorian had to admit was very real. At least it had been in his past.

On this Sunday, while an usher was engaged in helping a mother and crying baby to the nursery, Dorian stood at the foot of the wooden spiral stairs. Unable to stand it any longer, he crept up to the loft where the two voices intertwined in an intricate harmonic dance. No one noticed his presence; he was free to observe, though he saw very little in the dark. Then came the high, sweet solo, calling goosebumps to his skin, a lump to his throat, and weakness to his knees—so much so that he found himself kneeling.

Hoping to escape unnoticed, Dorian rose on uncertain legs and staggered down the stairway. He found a seat at the back of the church as the pastor began his message.

In his simple way, Pastor Vicente spoke of forgiveness. His broken English conveyed his simple point. "Jesucristo's forgiveness was a sacrifice," he said. "He gave up His place in Heaven for a while and even gave up His life for us. When we forgive, we give up something too. Maybe it's revenge, maybe self-pity or shame, or wanting to say or think bad things about someone who hurts us. Jesus said we are supposed to forgive people the way He forgave us: free, as a gift, a sacrifice." The message was short but profound.

As the congregation filed out, Dorian sat there, staring.

"Dorian?" he heard a familiar voice say softly as a hand gently touched his shoulder.

"Lyra? What are you doing here?" he said.

"I go to church here," she replied as she sat down next to him.

"That was some sermon. I can't take it all in yet," he said.

"I know, I have some major forgiving to do," she said, glancing up at him from the corner of her eye.

Dorian sighed and leaned forward, elbows on knees, hands clasped. "Looks like we both have our work cut out for us."

"Grace," she responded. "No amount of effort on my part can bring about that change in me. The hurt is too deep."

"Grace," he repeated as if hearing the word for the first time.

The following Saturday it happened, the singing began. He felt himself coming apart. Dorian wondered why he subjected himself to this, but something very hungry in his soul begged for sustenance, and something very tired in him longed for rest. God's Spirit living within him told him that what he longed for was to be found here.

The pastor spoke of worship in terms of emptying of self and allowing God to fill the empty spaces with love, adoring Him freely in a place where nothing else matters. This struck Dorian deeply. *Worship is not a performance?*

His heart beat a crazy rhythm as the service came to its end. Dorian hurried to the stairway, hoping to catch a glimpse of the two singers as they descended. He was about to meet the wielder of that soprano voice which had cut him so deeply, so beautifully. When no one came down, he decided to investigate. Halfway up, he nearly collided with a teenage girl in baggy clothes. Feeling like a groupie, he gushed, "Your high notes were amazing. Where'd you learn to sing like that?"

"Oh, I'm not the soprano. She is." She pointed up the stairway.

He took the steps two at a time.

The other singer sat in her folding chair, leaning forward, her head bowed and hands clasped.

As the lights in the church were being turned off, Dorian resisted the temptation to interrupt. After all, she might be praying.

The pastor, however, did not hesitate. "Lyra, mija, are you still up there?"

Lyra? Dorian asked himself. *What are the odds that two women with such an unusual name attended the same church?*

The odds tipped when the young woman rose, stretched, and called out, "I'm just leaving."

She was greeted with Dorian's gaping mouth and wide eyes. "Dorian, what are you doing up here?" she asked, amused at his dumbfounded expression.

When he failed to answer, she said, "Come on, Dorian, Pastor Vicente needs to lock up."

As they walked out the door, Dorian asked, "Hey, you wanna...like...go get some lunch or, you know, something? To eat. Not that you eat that much…" There. He'd stepped in it again and hurt her feelings.

"Sure. Are you okay, Dorian?" She chuckled, no offense taken. "Is there something you need to tell me?" Concern merged with amusement as they walked to the parking lot. She stopped at her car. "You do have a weird look on your face."

"Your voice. I love your voice," he blurted stupidly. "I've been hearing you and that girl do your duets week after week. I didn't know it was you up there. You're killing me, girl."

"Sometimes it kills me too," she confessed. "It can take awhile to put myself back together."

"I thought worship was supposed to be happy."

"It can also be a cry for help," she said knowingly. "And that might just be what you heard."

"Wanna go in my car?" Dorian asked.

"Sure. Where are we going?"

"I hear they serve a mean French toast at Mr. Pancake Head."

"French toast? Did you say 'toast?' I'm all in."

It was a short wait for a table at Mr. Pancake Head. Sliding into the booth Dorian said, "I was working on something last night."

"Oh yeah, what was that?" Lyra asked, opening her menu.

"I was, like, practicing some 'toasting' myself."

Lyra looked up from her menu quizzically. "Literally or song-wise?"

"Song-wise, of course. I already *know* how to make perfectly toasted bread. I don't *need* to work on that."

"You're saying that you make perfect toast every time, no exceptions," she sputtered.

"Well, yeah. Toast is not *hard*."

"It is if you burn it." She glared.

They both laughed.

The waitress arrived to take both of their French toast orders.

"Now what were you saying about toasting last night?" Lyra scooted forward in her seat, elbows on the table, head resting on her hands.

"You're not the only one who can toast a song, girl."

He noticed I'm a girl, she squeaked inwardly. *Well, at least that's a start.* "Well then, let's hear it."

"It's to the tune of 'Ramblin' Man;' the Allman Brothers band made it famous way back in the seventies, I think. I heard it on the radio yesterday at Swiss Sisters Coffee, you know, where I'm a barista. My manager likes country and old 70's and 80's songs. Whenever he comes in, first thing he does is change the station from what we all like to country or oldies. It's usually that twangy old stuff, but yesterday this song came on. I hadn't heard it in years, but it got...like...stuck in my brain the rest of the day. Last night I found myself singing it for the two thousandth time, so I figured, why not toast it?"

"You're stalling now, aren't you?" Lyra smirked.

"Yeah, well, I'm not used to singing at Mr. Pancake Head's."

"Just sing it softly then." Lyra enjoyed his squirming immensely.

"Okay, here goes. It's called 'Light Toast Man.'" He pulled a paper with lyrics out of his jeans' pocket.

"Lord, I was born a light toast man,
Gotta a really old toaster and doing the best I can.
At breakfast times it burns it,
So I make it in a pan,
'Cos I was born a light toast man.

My toaster once was new and really shiny.
It made the perfect toast on number one.
Nowadays it turns my bread into pure charcoal.
I'm thinking target practice might be fun.

Lord, I was born a light toast man,
Really gotta watch it or turn on the exhaust fan,
But then I get distracted by my short attention span.
Guess I should switch to raisin bran.

On my way through Amazon this morning,
My smoke alarm bugs my neighbor, Mr. Chan.
Guess I'll buy me a new one,
Throw the old one in the can.
Put it on the old installment plan.

Lord, I was born a light toast man,
Don't want nothing that's darker than slight tan.
You might like it crisper, but I'm just not a fan
'Cos I was born a light toast man.

Lord, I was born a light toast man.
New toaster just arrived in the delivery van.
You can't make toast better from Spokane to San Fran.
I was born a light toast man."

Lyra was gasping for air by the time the song ended.
Wiping her tears away with her napkin, she was at a loss for
words.
"Did you like it?" Dorian asked.
"Did I like it? Did I like it! Man, you got me beat by a
mile, Dorian. You know what this means, don't you?"
"What?" He beamed.
"This means 'Toast Wars', Suckah!"

"Bring it on!" Dorian narrowed his eyes. "I can take it! You ready for this?"

"I was born ready for this! I am, in fact, the Toast Queen."

"Here's your bill, Toast Queen." Their waitress slapped the bill on the table and walked off.

"I've got this one," Dorian said, snatching up the bill before Lyra could grab it. "I got a lotta big tips this week."

Lyra protested, but Dorian won out. It was the first time a guy had ever paid for anything, almost like a date. She pushed the idea from her mind.

"Hey, mistah big spendah," the waitress dropped by with her Bronx accent for the check payment, "you gotta pretty good voice there. I overheard your song to the lady. Me and Charlie, the cook, think you oughta be singing professional-like. I know a guy."

"Ah, thanks…" he read her name tag, "Midge, this is just for fun. I don't take music seriously anymore."

"Anymore? So you tried to make it big time before? What stopped ya?" Midge snooped.

"Life. Keep the change." Dorian put his wallet back in his pocket and stood up.

"Thanks for the French toast," Lyra said as they walked out the door and strolled to his car. "I'm seriously impressed with your toasting skills and your voice."

"Yeah?" Dorian looked down at his beat up Nikes.

"Yeah! What's to stop you from being a professional musician? You've got the talent, that's for sure."

"Life," he repeated, "Life."

Later that evening Lyra picked up her journal and curled up on the couch.

Journal Entry:

Now I've got that song, "Lord, I Was Born a Ramblin' Man," stuck in my brain. Dorian drove me to lunch at Mr. Pancake Head. It was almost as if we were on a date. I know we weren't, but inside my head I pretended that we were.

He didn't know all this time that it was me singing up in the balcony every Saturday at church. He said that he "loves my voice." Can you believe it? He heard me sing that toasted Adele song the other day in my lowest voice, but he didn't realize I could sing soprano. He LOVES my voice! Now if I could just get him to sing WITH ME...I wonder why he quit singing? What's in his past that's holding him back? Why is he getting a divorce? I wish he'd open up and tell me about it, but who am I to talk? Talking about the past is like reliving it, and it's something I just can't do.

She picked up her Bible and opened it to the book of Philippians where she'd left off yesterday.

Philippians 3:8-14

Yes, everything else is worthless when compared with the infinite value of knowing Christ Jesus my Lord. For his sake I have discarded everything else, counting it all as garbage, so that I can gain Christ and become one with him. I no longer count on my own righteousness through obeying the law; rather, I become righteous through faith in Christ. For God's way of making us right with himself depends on faith. I want to know Christ and experience the mighty power that raised Him from the dead. I want to suffer with him, sharing in his death, so that one way or another I will experience the resurrection from the dead!

I don't mean to say that I have already achieved these things or that I have already reached perfection. But I press on to possess that perfection for which Christ Jesus first possessed me.

No, dear brothers and sisters, I have not achieved it, but I focus on this one thing: Forgetting the past and looking forward to what lies ahead, I press on to reach the end of the race and receive the heavenly prize for which God, through Christ Jesus, is calling us.

CHAPTER 8
Horizontal Stripes on Toast

On her break, Lyra swung a chair around and straddled it next to Dorian. She crossed her arms over the back. It had been a slow day, and she was eager to talk even if it entailed distracting Dorian from his scholarly duties for a while. Writing an essay?" she asked.

"Huh?" He hit "send" and quickly closed the screen on his laptop. "Oh, no, I'm just writing an email to my mom." He stopped, realizing too late how nerdy he sounded.

"Cool." She sat, smiling, obviously waiting for him to elaborate.

When the silence became too loud, he said, "She's the only one back home who believes in me. Sometimes I can't believe I have a future. Anywhere."

"I believe in you," she said softly.

"You wouldn't if you knew what's been said about me." He refused to meet her gaze.

"Look, Dorian, I grew up surrounded by lies and I've gotten pretty good at detecting them. You're hiding something, all right, but it's not about anything you've actually done. Am I right?"

He looked her square in the eye. "How can you know that?"

"I've had my share of accusers." She shrugged. "But there was always another town, another identity. Until now. I've found my home and I hope to stay here."

"I'm glad," he said.

The bell over the door jangled as a mom with four children entered.

"Gotta get back to work." Lyra smiled as she walked back to the counter, calling the kids by name.

Dorian sat with his maple bar and java. He opened up the mailbox on his computer. Although he would never admit it, he enjoyed his mother's emails. She was his sole connection to his former life, and he loved her dearly.

"Son," it read, "Your father and I could use some time away from each other—you know how underfootly he can get—so I thought this would be a good time to come and see my boy. I've already arranged it with your Uncle Phillip. Sandra Lee will be accompanying me, of course. I'm certain she'll get on fine with your Catalina. I should be driving in at around three on Saturday afternoon. Can't wait to see you. Love, Mom."

He stared at the letter and, not knowing what to do with it, he hit the "delete" button. His mother would arrive in three days, and he didn't know how to prepare for it. Maybe he should just let her *happen* as she so often did.

Three days later, the bakery welcomed a new visitor. "Now you must be Lyra," A smartly-dressed woman of generous proportions with an oversized handbag marched into the bakery and reached out a brightly manicured hand to Lyra. "I've heard all about you. Oh, I'm sorry. I didn't introduce myself proper-like. I'm Bette Anne," she said in her very Southern drawl.

Lyra's brows curved upward as she tried to put an identity to the effervescent face before her.

"I'm sorry, Sugar. You still don't know who I am."

"Can't say that I do," Lyra replied, shaking the stranger's hand. "A lot of people come through here, and I normally have a good eye for faces." Accepting the challenge, she planted her hands on the counter and leaned forward, unabashedly studying Bette Anne, much to the older woman's delight. "Your eyes— I've seen them before," Lyra said. Very little of the whites showed in Bette Anne's eyes as if they were meant for merriment. Little smile wrinkles confirmed Lyra's observation. She stood up straight and adjusted her apron. "I've seen that sparkle before, though rarely. You must be Dorian's mom. So nice to meet you."

The scent of honeysuckle reached Lyra's nose as her visitor leaned forward. "I'm surprised my boy didn't tell you to expect me. You're in all his emails, but I guess ya know that."

"I—uh—I didn't know that." Lyra began folding a napkin on the counter into progressively smaller pieces.

Bette Anne reached out a hand and touched Lyra's arm. "Don't you fret none. It's all good stuff. Real good stuff. I'd say you're about the best thing in his life right now, exceptin', of course, our Lord and Savior. Dorian's so aloneful lately."

"Are we talking about the same Dorian? He's never treated me special...And what is 'aloneful?'"

"Just like it sounds. He's so full of alone, there isn't much room for anything else. He was a little shy back home, but everyone loved him. I think he feels lost."

"I think he's losing some of that 'alonefulness.'" Though she longed to know more, Lyra restrained herself. If Dorian didn't feel safe telling her about his troubles, it would only be right to wait until he did. "So what can I get you? Dorian should be here in about twenty minutes."

"All I want is a glass of sweet tea and your sweet company."

Lyra brought Bette Anne a tall glass of tea. Rattling with ice and damp with condensation, it looked so good that Lyra brought along another for herself.

"You and me, we're going shoppin'."

Lyra's eyebrows were getting an inordinate amount of exercise today. "Shopping? Well, I'd be happy to show you where the stores are after I finish my shift. What are you shopping for?" She took a long sip. "Something for Dorian?"

"No, Sugar, somethin' for you. You've been a good friend to my boy, so humor this crazy ol' southern lady and let her take you shoppin'."

"That's not why I'm his friend. Repaying me for my friendship doesn't feel right to me, but I appreciate the thought behind it. I'm sorry, Bette Anne, but that makes me uncomfortable." Lyra wondered what other wild suggestions the "crazy ol' southern lady" might make and willed another customer to take her away from this well-meaning woman before she concocted even stranger ideas.

"Mom?" Dorian walked in on cue. "What are you doing at the bakery? I thought we were meeting at Uncle Phil's this afternoon."

Lyra couldn't help but notice how Dorian's eyes crinkled just like his mother's as he received Bette Anne's welcoming hug and a kiss on the cheek.

"You didn't shave today, boy, now did ya? And ya know how important appearances can be." She brushed a stray hair from his forehead. "No shower either, judging by the hair. Dorian, don't let yourself go like this."

"I was late to class even without a shower, Mom. Sometimes it's just so hard to get out of bed," he said drearily. "And I don't think you should be discussing my personal hygiene in front of my friend."

Lyra drew in a deep breath. It was the first time Dorian had referred to her as a friend. In fact, she missed out on much of the mother/son exchange, so taken was she with having a male friend.

A small whimper arose from Bette Anne's stylish handbag. Was there no end to the surprises this woman had in store?

Bette Anne brought forth a Yorkshire terrier with a pink bow on the dog's perky little head. "This here is Sandra Lee." She held the dog to her face, unconcerned that the dog's frenzied licking would ruin her perfect makeup. "She's Mama's good little girl."

Lyra chuckled.

"You're not serious about taking me shopping." Lyra stared, incredulous, as Bette Anne popped into Molly's bakery at the end of Lyra's shift.

"Bette Anne doesn't make any offers Bette Anne doesn't intend on keepin', Sugar. Now hurry up and get out of that apron, and I'm gonna teach you how to shop."

"Mrs. McGuire, I don't have any money for clothes. Really, I'm fine with what I have." Lyra forced a smile.

"And that's why I'm taking ya on this little shoppin' spree. Before I met Dorian's father, I was on my own, and money was scarcer than hens' teeth. I didn't let that hinder me one bit from lookin' my very best."

"What's that got to do with me?" Lyra said over her shoulder as she hung up her apron.

"You'll see, Sugar," Bette Anne answered with a playful twinkle in her eye.

Lyra was surprised at how easy Dorian's mom was to talk to in spite of the woman's overzealous manner. The drive in Bette Anne's red Mercedes convertible passed swiftly with Lyra fielding questions, freed from her usual reserve.

"What do you see as your next great accomplishment?" Bette Anne asked.

Lyra's face lit with excitement. "I'm studying to become a veterinary assistant."

"A dream. That's good. Now my boy—he's not so dreamful these days." Bette Anne sighed. "That girl, she tore all the dreamin' right outta him."

"Girl?" Lyra asked, too caught up in the conversation to consider the line she was about to cross.

"Oh yes, she said all manner of terrible lies about him. Sad to say, people believed her. Even his wife. Can you imagine that? My sweet boy ever takin' liberties with a poor disabled girl?"

"Dorian would never do anything like that!" Lyra blurted loudly.

"Well, you know that, and I know that, but the church board sided with the girl, leavin' my boy without so much as a hope for the future. The good Lord says people perish without a vision. I don't want that happenin' to him."

"He's going to college…"

"With no idea of what he's really good at 'ceptin' music. The church board agreed to keep things quiet as long as he left the ministry. You know how it is when word gets out among churches. I guess everyone loves a scandal—'cept for the scandalated. It was such a big congregation, and he had such a high profile position, with all the recordings and being on TV and all…"

"Dorian was on TV? He seems so shy."

"You never seen him leadin' worship?"

"I don't have a TV. Studying takes too much time for that."

"Well, believe you me, he was good. Goosebumple good. The light and love of Jesus was on him, and it moved people. Really moved them—to tears even. You know, like your singin' does to him."

Lyra was unable to express her surprise or ask for clarification before they reached their destination, a used clothing store on the edge of town.

"Even with GPS it took me forever to find this place, seein' as how I'm not familiarated with these parts. Now that we're here, we won't waste a minute." She rubbed her hands together. "Let's get to work."

Lyra followed her mutely into the shop, wondering what Bette Anne was up to.

"We full-figured ladies need to accentuate our curves without callin' attention to the space in between. Take this tee, for example." She held up a seemingly harmless orange and white-striped tee shirt. "Now this innocent-lookin' shirt has three strikes against it. You may have figured out the first one since you're wearin' a lot of black. Orange is a looky-here color. It's too conspicuating. Orange is fatterin', black is flatterin'. Got that?"

"How do you know what colors I wear?"

"My boy texts me photos of all the Sunshine Bakery clan. You are in a lot of 'em." She paused to let her words sink in then resumed her lecture. "Do you know the second rule for us curvaceous gals? Judgin' from the horizontal stripes on your shirt, I suspect you don't. The only place horizontal stripes belong are on toast. With clothes, they make you look wider than you really are. Vertical stripes do just the opposite. The same holds true for short shirts. Tunics and longer shirts are so much better. We need to lengthify, not shortify."

Lyra found herself instinctively crossing her arms across her chest as Bette Anne carried on, plucking a tank top off the rack. "Now looky here, sleeveless attire will make your arms look big, and fabrics with large, bold patterns...Sugar? Are you listenatin' to this crazy ol' lady?"

"Why are you doing this?" Lyra asked softly.

"Because no one ever did it for me. They just told me I was fat, I ate like a pig, and needed to go on a diet. They never taught me to love myself and make the best of what the good Lord gave me."

"Thank you." Lyra's response came at a whisper.

In the course of the afternoon Lyra tried on innumerable tops and jeans. Bette Anne waited outside the dressing room and critiqued each piece of clothing Lyra modeled. It wasn't long before Lyra was able to predict what would work to her advantage in the mirror.

"Now, if you had the money for three tops and three pairs of pants, which ones would you pick?"

Lyra held several articles of clothing up to herself in the mirror and narrowed it down to three of each.

"Nice pick, Sugar." Bette Anne swept up Lyra's choices to the cash register and paid for them before her protege could voice a protest.

"Why are you doing this for me?" Lyra asked again with humble gratitude.

"Like I said, no one did it for me. It took a lot of years and unflatterin' clothes for me to come up with my own rules."

"It'll be a long time before I can repay you."

"One of your beautiful smiles is all the payment I need, Sugar."

Lyra opened her Bible to Psalms 69:29-34

I am suffering and in pain.
    Rescue me, O God, by your saving power.
    Then I will praise God's name with singing,
    And I will honor him with thanksgiving.
For this will please the LORD more than sacrificing cattle,
    More than presenting a bull with its horns and hooves.
The humble will see their God at work and be glad.
    Let all who seek God's help be encouraged.
For the LORD hears the cries of the needy;
    he does not despise his imprisoned people.

    Praise Him, O heaven and earth,
    The seas and all that move in them.

Journal Entry:

"This scripture fits me. I am afflicted by my past, and I am poor, but I do praise You, God, and give You thanks for all You are doing in my life. You really do hear me and care about my needs. You promise that You will, and You proved that today with Bette Anne. What a blessing she is! She makes me feel like I matter to her, and to Dorian too. But I don't want to get my hopes up about Dorian. He's just a friend, and I should just be grateful for that."

Lyra took a moment to study herself in the mirror on the bathroom door as she got ready for work the next day. Part of her recoiled against the loss of anonymity her new wardrobe represented. Starting today she would have to face the challenge of being somebody—someone with dreams, and more importantly, a future.

By the time she reached the bakery, Lyra had become so self-conscious she practically sprinted to the restroom to put on her apron. Her new clothes made her feel conspicuous.

The bell above the door jingled. "Stephanie!" Lyra greeted her friend. "I see you brought little Stevie for a snack. What'll it be, cowboy?" Smiling, she noted the four-year-old's soon-to-be outgrown hat and cowboy boots with a silver plastic revolver tucked into his belt.

"Cookies!" he shouted as he did an excited little dance, lifting his cowboy boots high.

"And what kind of cookies does this cowboy want today?" Lyra asked.

"Peedy Putter!" Stevie proclaimed at the top of his lungs. The dancing intensified. If she hadn't known better, Lyra might've feared this was a potty dance.

"Peanut butter cookies coming right up!" she said, reaching behind the curved glass display case and pulling out two. "And guess what? There's a peanut butter cookie sale today. Two for the price of one and a glass of milk to go with it." Lyra would reimburse Molly later. Given Steph's financial situation, a cookie could just about break the bank.

Stevie danced off, a cookie in each hand. Molly came out of the workroom to watch his show. He started singing, "I'm an old cowpan from the Rio Grande..."

Lyra turned to Stephanie, "So how are things going at home?"

"Same as usual. Mom is still dazed and depressed. I've gotta do something fast. She's not snapping out of it. Forget going to college, I've gotta find a job. I don't know what to do about Mom." Stephanie took a deep breath and tried to act perky for Stevie's sake. "Yee haw! Rope them cattle, Stevie."

"Have you tried looking for a job at your gym? You love that place."

"I'm not eighteen yet. Will be soon though. They don't hire people under eighteen. I checked. I'm gonna have to quit going to the gym soon. I can't afford the ten bucks a month, not with my family in the state they're in."

"I'll keep my ears peeled for any possible jobs. Something will turn up."

"Thanks, Lyra. You're the best." She hugged her. "Hey, is that a new shirt and jeans you have on?"

"Sure is! Courtesy of Dorian's mom!"

"What? Dorian's mom? Girl, you've got some stories to tell. Wanna get together after work?"

"My place, about six?" Lyra suggested.

"See you then." Steph took Stevie's hand. "Come on, little cowpoke, we've gotta mosey on over to the library." Stephanie attempted to pay for the cookies, but Lyra refused it.

"I've got this," she said emphatically, happy to give to someone else for a change.

CHAPTER 9
French Bread Toasting on an Open Fire

As she sat on her corduroy couch two days before Thanksgiving, Lyra decided any holiday was a terrible time to be alone. Still, being alone sure beat the old alternative, suffering in silence at her father's political holiday gatherings, dreading what would happen when everyone left and he was all liquored up.

Her first foster home wasn't much better. It seemed once you were in the system, you had no voice, no defense except to run. Still, the holiday did conjure up some fond memories, when her dad was a struggling nobody lawyer and her mother was still alive.

Her mom was such a warm, loving woman. She had managed in her all-too-short life to keep the monster in him at bay.

It must've been the music, Lyra thought. *Mom could turn any situation around with her count-your-blessings voice, the kind that made you happy just to be in her presence.*

She and Lyra would make up silly songs while cooking. It became such a part of her life that Lyra was shocked that other families did not share in this gift, that what she shared with her mother was, in fact, an oddity. She continued to write silly songs even now. Most were her mom's favorite tunes borrowed from the 1970's and 1980's. Embellished over time, they could still make her smile. Even Catzo appeared to be smiling when Lyra sang them to her. She'd never shared them with anyone at the bakery. They might think she was weirder than weird, but Dorian appreciated her musical sense of humor.

"I miss you, Mom," Lyra said, a tear rounding her cheek. She picked up her old, beat up Bible, instead of the new one Molly had given to her. She pulled out of it her most prized possession: an equally weathered photo of her mother smiling that about-to-sing smile, the only image that had survived Lyra's many hurried exits.

Estrella had come to live with the Rhinehardts as a maid, a few years before Lyra's mother's death. Estrella stepped into Lyra's world with a furious devotion as they watched Mr. Rhinehardt fill the loss of his wife with career and cognac, his drug of choice. By the time he had ascended to his judiciary throne, he acquired another addiction, taking an unhealthy interest in his daughter and his maid.

Lyra and Estrella created their own celebrations, singing Spanish songs over hot chocolate with cinnamon and toasted sourdough—an odd combination, but it worked its magic nonetheless.

Estrella never spoke of her prior existence in Mexico. Lyra could only imagine what kept her in the States, although it was hard to fathom anything much worse than the nightmare they shared.

Now here was Lyra in a new town with no plans for the holiday. Molly had gone to meet Phil's family. She knew that Dorian would be there too. Lyra was grateful for her little house in the McCrearys' garden, but she sure wished there was someone to share it with. Unwilling to invite herself to anyone else's celebration she had stocked up on frozen turkey dinners and a couple cans of turkey-flavored cat food for Catzo.

A knock sounded at the door, exactly three knocks, evenly spaced. Lyra recognized the nonverbal greeting. Grinning, she opened the door.

As usual, Mr. McCreary was smiling. "We were wondering if you'd be off with your friends for the holiday. The Missus wanted to give you these." He presented her with a platter of cinnamon rolls. "You do have plans for Thanksgiving, don't you?"

"Everyone's off doing family things. It's just me and Catzo this year." She manufactured a smile while stifling a sigh. "Well, thank you for the rolls. You know how much I love them."

"Now that simply won't do," he said. "You and Catzo are sharing Thanksgiving with us this year."

"Oh, I couldn't. Besides, I have all those frozen turkey dinners..."

"Well, keep them in the freezer and come on over on Thursday. Even though it's just the two of us, Maggie always cooks a full turkey. We wind up eating turkey for days and freezing some besides. So, you see, you'll be doing us a favor." He patted her shoulder and turned to leave. "Dinner's at five, but you can come whenever you're ready. I imagine the Missus could use a hand in the kitchen," he said over his shoulder. "And by the way, Catzo's welcome too."

"Thank you," was all she could say.

Thursday afternoon Lyra stood at the McCrearys' doorway dressed in her best tee shirt and jeans, Catzo in her arms. She brought along a dozen fresh croissants from the bakery along with a can of cat food. Lyra was welcomed into the scent of sage crouton stuffing and turkey. Catzo wriggled free and set about exploring behind the floor-length curtains.

"Good," Maggie said. "You're just in time to help whip the potatoes." She handed Lyra the mixer. "And use plenty of milk and butter. That's how the Mister likes his potatoes, nice and smooth."

"Nice and smooth, coming right up," Lyra beamed and proceeded to whip up some glorious, swirly potatoes that could well have sat atop one of Molly's cakes.

The turkey beckoned, browned, rested, and ready in its aluminum foil nest. Mr. McCreary heeded its call as he transferred it to Maggie's favorite harvest-themed platter for carving.

So this is what a real family feels like. I'd almost forgotten. Lyra thought, e*ven if it's just a family of two.* For tonight, though, they'd be a family of three. Four with Catzo.

Journal Entry:

I am grateful for my new family. It was almost like being with Mom again.

Psalm 68:5-6

Father to the fatherless, defender of widows—this is God, whose dwelling place is holy. God places the lonely in families; he sets the prisoners free and gives them joy. But he makes the rebellious live in a sun-scorched land.

The bakery was bustling on Molly's return from Thanksgiving. But even the hectic pace did not dim Molly's heart of gold. She'd heard from Lyra that Stephanie and family were struggling financially and emotionally after Steph's father had given them all up to follow his lust for a younger woman that worked at his construction company. Knowing that, Molly had offered Stephanie Harrison a job at the bakery. Holiday season was especially harrowing this year, since the wealthy clientele on the other side of the lake had recently discovered Molly's Sunshine Bakery. Molly and Lyra could barely keep up on all the extra orders coming in. It was a win/win situation hiring Stephanie. Molly didn't bother posting a help wanted sign but immediately offered Stephanie the job. Her young recruit just as quickly accepted the offer on the spot and started work the following morning at 4:00 am.

Yawning, Stephanie began working on her first batch of sugar cookie dough.

"You'll get used to these hours soon," Lyra encouraged her.

"I hope so," Steph yawned again.

"Coffee will help." Lyra walked over to the ever-busy coffee brewer and poured Stephanie a cup and added cream and sugar. "Here you go." She handed it to her friend.

"Thanks, Lyra."

Molly was busy rolling out pie crusts for the forty-plus apple and pumpkin pies ordered by the Waldorfs for their annual employee appreciation dinner. "I'm not going to want to see another pie crust for a while," Molly grumbled.

"I'll help you with those as soon as I get these gingerbread cookies in the oven," Lyra offered cheerfully.

"Great. And Steph, when you're done with your cookies, I'll teach you to roll the perfect pie crust," Molly promised.

"I've made lots of sugar cookies for Stevie in the past, but I've never rolled a pie crust. Mom used to make pies, but it's been a long time since..." Her voice trailed off. She paused, "Thanks again for the job, Molly. I'll do my best to learn fast."

"I know you will, Steph." Molly swept back a stray curl from her heated forehead.

At break time, Lyra and Stephanie sat together nibbling a few of Steph's broken sugar cookies. The vast majority had turned out splendidly, but there were always a few that managed to break, usually the star-shaped ones for some reason unknown to mankind. Molly encouraged them to eat their "flops."

Lyra couldn't help but notice how slim Stephanie was. Everyone else seemed to notice too. Steph was regarded with favor everywhere she went, but seemed oblivious to it all.

"How do you stay so thin?" Lyra asked with a hint of envy she wished wasn't there.

"It's the gym. My dad got me a year's membership just before he left us. I guess that's one thing to be grateful for. My membership is just about to run out. Now that I have this job, I can just pay monthly. Working out has really helped me deal with all the stress my family is under."

"I could never be thin like you," Lyra said, truly believing it.

"You'd be surprised what exercise can do," Steph encouraged.

"I've been fat for so long; I can't change it, and I hate it. I see how you turn every guy's head when you walk by. No one ever notices me, unless it's to make some rude crack about my weight. I hate looking in the mirror."

"I don't turn guys' heads, Lyra. I'm just your average seventeen-year-old kid. But if you really want to make a change, put up the ten bucks a month and come to the gym with me. This month the membership fee is free. Quit feeling down on yourself and let's do something about it."

"I can't change. Fat is who I am."

"Maybe that's who you were, but your father is out of your life now. You told me about your past, and that's just what it is, the past. You don't have to be trapped there for the rest of your life. You are the only one who can do something to change it, with God's help, that is. You've used that weight to try and protect yourself. It was how you made yourself unattractive. You've been hiding behind your weight. You don't have to hide anymore. Come on. Come with me to the gym tonight."

"I don't know," Lyra hemmed and hawed.

"What do you have to lose?"

"Sixty pounds or so, I'd say." She smiled weakly.

Reluctantly, Lyra dragged herself to the gym with Stephanie after work. She plunked down ten whole dollars on the counter and said to the paper-thin woman behind it, "Where do I sign?"

After a flurry of paperwork, Lyra found herself in the locker room standing on a scale, afraid to look at the truth it revealed. "It's worse than I thought, Steph. I've gained more weight since I moved here."

"Well, we gotta start somewhere," Steph said, scratching her head. "So what's your goal? How much do you want to lose?"

"Maybe sixty pounds? I don't really know. You tell me. I don't know anything about this stuff."

"Let's look at a chart for your age, height, and bone structure and see what it suggests."

The girls set about it, and Lyra's guestimate was accurate. They set her goal at sixty pounds.

"Okay, let's work on this ten pounds at a time," Steph suggested. "I've got a great workout plan just for you, my friend. Cardio and weights, we'll alternate day to day, and work on a different target area each time. You'll lose a pound or two a week. It's safer that way. We gotta talk about what you eat too. Here we go..."

"Ugh," agonized Lyra. "This better be worth it."

Lyra dragged herself into work the next morning with aching muscles in her legs and arms.

"So how'd the gym go last night?" Molly inquired, already guessing the answer.

Lyra just looked at her. "Ugh," was all she said.

Stephanie bounced in the door as the guttural comment was leaving Lyra's lips.

"That's becoming a favorite phrase of yours, huh, Lyra? Don't let her kid you, Molly, she was a real trooper last night."

"And you were the drill sergeant," Lyra moaned.

"Well, no weights today, we'll give those muscles some time to heal. Just some cardio tonight," Steph said innocently.

"If I'm still alive tonight," Lyra whimpered.

Journal Entry:

Well, I did it. I survived two evenings at the gym. And I hate it! The worst thing about it is how great everyone looks there, and how huge I am in comparison. All I can say is this better work.

Lyra had been working on a Toast Wars song for Dorian in secret. She could hardly wait for a chance to unleash it. Her opportunity was just about to arrive.

After church on Saturday Dorian asked, "How about hitting Mr. Pancake Head for lunch?"

"Sounds like a plan," Lyra eagerly agreed. *Date trumps weight*, she justified.

Off they went in Dorian's ancient Corolla. His luxury BMW sports car had long since been traded in for an old economy car.

Once they were seated at the restaurant, Midge brought them menus and a quick smile. "Oh, it's you two again. Hey look, Charlie, Mr. Big Spendah and his girl are here again. You gonna make with the voice this time? Huh? Think our customers would enjoy it." She grinned, revealing a mouth full of bridgework.

LEAVING LYRA

Lyra got shivers when she heard Midge say, "his girl." She tried not to show any reaction on the outside when Dorian didn't correct the waitress.

"Nah," Dorian said, "haven't written any more toast songs lately. It's actually Lyra's turn. Toast is her favorite food so we have this friendly competition to outdo each other with *toasted* songs."

"Kinda like that Weird Al fella. Hey Charlie," she yelled, "they're warping songs like Weird Al here!"

"Ya don't have to yell, Midge baby, I can hear for myself, ya know," Charlie replied.

"Well, ya got one for us there, Lyra?" Midge inquired. "Maybe a nice Christmas tune or somethin'?"

"As a matter of fact, I do have some Christmas toast up my sleeve." Lyra cleared her throat. "It's sung to the tune of, 'Chestnuts Roasting on an Open Fire.'"

"Did ya hear that, Charlie? Leeera's gonna sing us all a *toasted* Christmas sowng."

All other talk in Mr. Pancake Head ceased. "I heard, I heard already, Midge. Let the girl sing, will ya?" Charlie reprimanded.

A bit nervous, but used to singing in front of people at church, Lyra stood and began:

"French bread toasting on an open fire,
Toaster's up in flames again.
Need a quick snack 'fore it's time to retire.

117

Don't want no rice by Uncle Ben,
Only toast will do.

Got my butter and some marmalade.

Needing more than just a bite,

Heading out on this grand escapade,

I'll have to buy a toaster tonight.

You know that stores are all a'craze

With all those last-minute shoppers in a daze

And all those toasters sold and wrapped up tight

If only one is left, it just might mean a fight.

And so I'm wandering down the appliance aisle

For a toaster to boost

None on the shelves, then a clerk with a smile

Says for sixty bucks she'll cut the last one loose.

Yes, there it is, it's in her hand.

If I grab it from her, I'm sure I'll be banned

So I pay the ransom she requires.

If I complain maybe next week she'll get fired.

And now I'm toasting up a loaf or two,

Butter oozing down my chin,

Although I'm so full, I'm about to spew,

I'll be sleeping with a Christmas grin."

LEAVING LYRA

The entire restaurant erupted after her last note. Lyra bowed. Dorian's smile was blazing. He stood and clapped.

Lyra's heart thudded as if she'd just stepped off of the elliptical.

"Now that's what I'm talkin' about," said Charlie, slapping down his spatula.

"And to think it all started here at Mr. Pancake Head." Midge pushed her rhinestone glasses up on her nose. "Breakfast's on me today, kids. You two should be doin' music togethah. Ya know it?"

CHAPTER 10
Hey You with the Pie Crust

"What ya doing for Christmas, Lyra?" Dorian asked over his maple bar.

"Handyman Jim said they're looking for volunteers at the homeless shelter. I thought I'd lend a hand. And I'm planning to go to the McCrearys', to listen to old classic carols of Bing Crosby and watch a couple of his movies. They're big fans of his, and it's their tradition. Anyway, it sounds like fun. What are your plans?"

"We'll all be meeting at my grandparents'—you know, Phil's parents' house. We'll probably be fighting over Mom's egg rolls, as usual. Phil and his brother Matt stash them and fight over them. Her egg rolls really are that good."

"Never met an egg roll I didn't like," Lyra said, sweeping a straw wrapper from the table.

"I'd bring you one, but it'd never make it back from the Bay Area," he said.

"Well, it's the thought that counts."

"Hey, Steph, it's Lyra. Molly's got the flu. I just sent her home, can you come help me out at the bakery tonight?" Lyra clutched the phone with a desperate hand.

"Sure thing. I could really use the hours. Poor Molly. Tomorrow's Christmas Eve too. There go her plans with Phil and his family. I'll be right there. Just gotta tuck Stevie into bed."

"Thanks, Steph." Lyra hung up the phone and closed up for the night. She did a quick assessment of priorities and shook her head, "How many pumpkin pies can this town eat?" Her list was complete by the time Stephanie unlocked the door and breezed in, announcing her arrival with an extra jingley-sounding bell.

"Put me to work, boss," Steph joked.

"Boss? I'm not your boss."

"You are now; Molly's not here." She tied on her red apron. "I'm ready to roll."

"Roll? You better be. We have a bajillion pumpkin pie crusts to *roll* out tonight. Let's get 'er done."

Pie crusts had gotten easier for Stephanie, but she still couldn't match the speed of Lyra's rolling pin. "Can't wait til I'm faster at this, Lyra. I can't keep up with you."

"Just takes practice." Lyra looked up. "What was that?"

Both girls heard the bell over the front door.

"Didn't you lock the door when you came in, Steph?"

"Oops! I guess not."

The girls stuck their heads out of the workroom doorway. "Sorry, we're closed," Lyra informed the handsome fireman who had just entered the bakery.

"Sorry, the door was unlocked, so I thought..." his voice trailed off as Stephanie stepped through the door. "...I can come back...tomorrow."

"No, it's okay. What can I get you?" Stephanie asked eagerly, stepping up to the counter.

Oh brother, thought Lyra as she stepped back into the work room. *She stopped this one dead in his tracks just by walking into the room. She's definitely got the "It Factor," whatever "It" is. And she looks like she's in her twenties instead of just seventeen.* Lyra could hear them talking in the other room.

"Just got off duty," the fireman explained, "and I could sure use a cup of coffee and something sweet."

"Like what?" Stephanie asked with a lilt in her voice.

"Like you," he chuckled. "Are you free after work for a late dinner?"

"Actually, I'm just starting my shift tonight." She placed her hands on her hips. "Besides, I don't even know you," she said playfully.

"I'm sorry, my name is Spencer Haus. I work at the fire station a couple blocks down. Are you new here?"

"Yes, uh, no. I'm new here at the bakery, but I've lived in River Oaks for a long time."

"Funny, I've never seen you around. Did you go to high school here?"

"Kind of."

"Kind of? What do you mean?"

"Homeschooled." Steph apologized.

"Oh, gotcha."

"So," Steph changed the subject, "what would you like to go with your coffee, pie? Cake?"

"Pie's good. What do you recommend?"

"It's after hours; we've only got apple and banana cream left." She handed him a steamy cup of coffee.

"Banana cream it is then."

"Cream?" she asked.

"Yes, banana cream."

"No, I mean cream for your coffee?" she giggled.

He laughed. "No, I take it black."

Overhearing their banter, Lyra rolled her eyes.

Steph cut an extra large slice of pie and served it with a smile.

"What did you say your name was?" Spencer probed.

"I didn't," Steph cocked her head to the side, her long ponytail sweeping her shoulder.

"So what is it?" He scooted forward in his seat at the counter.

"Why do you want to know?"

"Just curious."

"Well, you're just going to have to figure that out. If you'll excuse me, I've got to get back to work. Just shout out if you need something else, okay?" She put his check down next to his pie slice.

"What should I shout out? I don't know your name."

"'Hey you,' works." She tossed her ponytail in the air as she headed into the workroom.

Steph high-fived Lyra and resumed rolling out pie crusts.

A few minutes later they heard Spencer leave. Steph went out front to lock the door for the night. On her walk back she noticed a huge tip along with his payment. Clearing his plate and coffee cup, she saw a note written on his napkin. "Great pie, even better smile. I'll be back, and next time I'll find out your name. Until then I'll call you Shanaenae."

Stephanie beamed, folded up the napkin, and tucked it in her skinny jeans' pocket. With a spring in her step she launched herself at the rolling pin.

When Lyra served at the Homeless Shelter, she felt a kinship with the residents, especially women escaping violent boyfriends, husbands, and, yes, fathers. Were it not for the McCrearys and Molly, she could easily have landed there herself.

On this occasion, one woman in particular embraced the sentiment that things would never get any better, that luck was always meant for someone else. Her name was Roberta, but everyone called her Bobbie. It was hard to tell how old she was; sun, disappointment, shame, and years of heavy smoking had carved deep lines into her face. She wasn't about to let anyone in, or so said her harsh reaction to even the smallest kindness.

After Lyra finished serving dinner on Christmas Eve, she joined Bobbie, who sat alone at a nearby table, chewing her filthy fingernails.

"Hey," said Lyra.

"Hey," Bobbie replied, still nibbling away.

Thus began a silence that lasted well beyond the limits of comfort.

"My name's Lyra," she finally broke the silence.

"Bobbie. So what do you want?" Bobbie demanded. "What are you doing here? Who are you trying to impress? God?"

"I just thought I'd drop by here and lend a hand. It wasn't that long ago that I was on the street myself."

"You're fat," Bobbie accused.

"I know." Lyra walked away. "I know," she whispered.

Lyra was about to skip dinner and go to bed without opening her journal when she nearly slipped on an envelope lying on her floor. It shot off from under her foot only to fly into the clutches of Catzo. Lyra pried it away from her kitten's meddling claws and carried it to the desk lamp. Switching it on, she recognized Dorian's characteristic scrawl. It was a song sung to the tune of "Every Breath You Take" by The Police. "This better be good," she said gloomily. "I could sure use a laugh."

Don't give me corn flakes
Or some rare flank steaks.
No more chiffon cake;
I cannot partake.
Only toast will do.

Whatever else you make,
Pie crust with a flake,
It just can't be fake,
Don't care what you bake.
Only toast will do.

Oh, can't you see? Give that toast to me!
My poor head aches with everything you bake.

LEAVING LYRA

Don't give me a hot cake
The size of Great Salt Lake,
How I start to shake
Like I've seen a snake.
Only toast will do.

Without toast I'm lost in a rat race,
Like I'm stuck inside my guitar case.
There's just no words inside my knowledge base,
Like I can't breathe in a tightly enclosed space.
I keep begging, baby, no more cheeeeese!

For a small fee
Bring some toast to me
No more ten-layer cake,
Got a stomach ache.

Do I seem opaque?
Burn me at the stake,
Hit me with a rake,
Drain my hydraulic brake,
Only toast will do,
Only toast will do,
Only toast will do…

"Dorian—that little scamp. He must've slipped this
under my door before he left for the holiday. I'm sure glad he

did," she confided to Catzo who was still trying to grab the envelope. "Mine. Get your own envelope, you rascal."

Journal Entry:

Bobbie's little comment about my weight really punched me in the gut. I almost ran away crying. I know God wants to use me at the shelter. Bobbie's right. I am fat.

I was really feeling down after all that when I found that Dorian had slipped a toast song under my door. I guess he figured with the holidays and no real family to spend it with, I would be having a rough day. That was so thoughtful of him, but now I suddenly crave toast.

I've got to change my attitude. I don't have to be a model-thin like Steph, but I don't have to be overweight either.

CHAPTER 11
You're Chewin' on Something and it's Not Toast

New Year's is about hope, Lyra told herself. She'd just about run out of it when she'd happened upon Molly and the McCrearys. Now here she was, with a job she loved, going to school, living in a cozy cottage with her spunky little kitty, and going to a caring church she actually belonged to. She even had *real* friends.

After convincing Dorian that she needed his help, Lyra and Dorian would be singing together at their church's candlelight vigil, bringing in the new year. Lyra loved singing with Dorian. In fact, she liked everything about the young man. He was smart, funny, kind, talented, not to mention good-looking. But more than all that, he treated Lyra with respect, and when warranted, concern. He was a far cry from the self-absorbed young man he had been when he had first come to River Oaks.

Lyra and Dorian decided to walk together to church for music practice. They had taken to walking together around the lake—a brisk hour's journey when they hadn't much to say. More often though they'd stop to admire the trees in their various states of leaf. Even in their bare-limbed condition the trees were of lovely shape and texture. They'd often pause to pick up a fallen leaf of rare hue or to feed day-old bread to the mallards and the gaudy Mandarin ducks. A wealthy citizen of the other side of the lake had donated the colorful birds to the community, and not surprisingly, the birds had stayed. The lake had everything they needed, and the shores were full of admirers with an excess of bread crumbs.

Like the ducks, Lyra was happy to have found a safe place to land. The foster homes she'd lived in had been in sketchy neighborhoods at best, with some foster parents milking the system with each kid they brought in. The one exception was the last family she stayed with. The Barkers' home was alive with music, especially old songs from the '70's and '80's. Lyra learned to enjoy many kinds of music from the Barkers, ranging from swing to rhythm and blues. Mrs. Barker could always be counted on for a listening ear and a legendary hug. Mr. Barker could always tell when Lyra was sad and went to great lengths to make her laugh. She remembered her eighteenth birthday, the presents, cake, and the offer to let her stay on with them even though she had just aged out of the foster system. She'd been so happy, but then it happened. Lyra saw her father's Lexus pull up to the Barker's modest home and she slipped out the back before he could poison their lives too. Running—that's how she found herself in River Oaks. Fortunately, she had evaded the man her father hired to find her. A wave of gratitude swelled in her chest. For a second time she found herself among people who loved her.

"You're sure quiet today," Dorian observed. "Whatcha thinking about?"

"Toast."

"Come on, Lyra. You're chewing on something, and it's not toast."

"Just thinking about places I used to live. Sure thankful to be here. What about you, Dorian? You're quiet too. What are you thinking about?"

"Ah, just wallowing."

"Wallowing? In what?"

"Just the way things used to be," he said.

"When are you going to open up and tell me what happened? Why did you move here, Dorian? What happened between you and your wife?" Lyra knew the gist of his story from Bette Anne spilling the beans, but Dorian had never told Lyra himself. She pretended to know nothing about his past.

"Why are you always running, Lyra? What are you afraid of?"

"Did your wife find somebody else?"

"Who's the guy that hurt you so bad, Lyra?"

"I don't want to talk about it."

"Well, neither do I."

They walked on in silence.

The next day as Lyra sat on her couch studying, a knock sounded, a tapped version of the first line of, "Jesus Loves the Little Children." She answered from her side of the door with the second line, then they pounded out the rest of the verse together, laughing. *He must be over his hot mess from yesterday,* she thought.

"Are you going to let me in or what?" Dorian asked through the closed door.

"I guess so," Lyra tried to sound begrudging, "even if you *are* early."

He walked in, guitar case in hand, and slouched onto Lyra's sofa. "I thought we might do something to celebrate the end of this year."

Lyra quickly banished the ridiculous thoughts of romance that had floated into her mind uninvited. "And that would be?"

"Well, since this has been such a wild *ride* for both of us, I asked Uncle Phil if we could take his old Bentley to church. That should get people talking."

"Phil's got a Bentley?!"

Dorian knew Lyra loved old cars—at least vintage ones. Was that why he was doing this, just for her? Regardless, she would check the ride off her bucket list.

They went out to the car and stowed their guitars in the trunk. To her amazement, Dorian stood at attention and opened the door for her. "Your carriage awaits, Milady," he Britishized his voice for her benefit.

She responded in kind. "Thank you, Jeeves. To the cathedral, if you please," the reference to their little storefront church was quite a stretch, though it revealed God's glory and love to rival the world's finest churches, past or present.

Lyra stifled a giggle as she watched Dorian struggle with the gears. After grinding and lurching his way around the lake, he got the hang of it. Much to Dorian's disappointment, no one was at church yet to observe his triumphal entry into the parking lot. They unloaded their guitars, settled on the curb, and began rehearsing the song which would welcome the new year, a song Lyra had written for the occasion.

His tenor and her soprano attracted the attention of a woman walking by. Lyra recognized her as the woman she had met at the homeless shelter. Lyra stopped singing and patted the curb. "Hey, Bobbie, are you joining us tonight at church?"

"There'll be lots of food," Dorian contributed, trying to be helpful.

"I don't believe in no churches," Bobbie said, her face both sullen and sad.

"You don't have to," Lyra explained. "You're welcome anyway."

"Yeah, well, we'll see," Bobbie grumbled. "Got any money?" she asked without preamble. She raked her stained fingernails through her greasy, sandy blond hair. "I could sure use a smoke."

Lyra elbowed Dorian as he reached for his Corinthian leather wallet, a holdover from more prosperous days, while Lyra created a diversion.

"So you had some bad experiences in church," Lyra said. "So have I. You know why that is?"

Mildly curious, Bobbie shook her head.

"Cause there's people in them."

Bobbie threw her head back and cackled a cynical smoker's laugh, ending in a sputtering cough. "Yeah, get rid of all the people, and the only thing left would be God. If there is one," Bobbie added.

At just that moment, Stephanie arrived with her mother, Sylvia, her sister, Stacey, and little brother, Stevie.

Sylvia instinctively put her youngest behind her as Steph stepped forward to greet the homeless woman.

"Hi, I'm Stephanie." Smiling, she reached out her hand, choosing to ignore Bobbie's unwashed state.

"Bobbie," the homeless woman said warily, reluctantly extending her hand. Nice people had agendas, she had learned, even if it were just to look holy by associating with "the poor."

"Hi, Bobbie. My name's Stevie!" The boy had bounded up from behind his mother in the cowboy attire he insisted on wearing.

A genuine smile creased Bobbie's weathered face. Leave it to a kid to see her humanity.

Stacey stood back, arms crossed in teenage angst, hoping no one would see her with this dirty, disgusting woman. She made no attempt to greet the pariah.

A*t least that one's honest,* Bobbie thought, looking at Stacey, *not trying to show off. Not like Mr. Fancy Car, offering food to lure me into this god-trap.*

"Where are my manners?" Sylvia stepped forward and gingerly shook Bobbie's hand, trying not to recoil. Bobbie embodied Sylvia's deepest fear—to be a homeless mother of three. The kids had no idea how close they had come to that reality. Before Stephanie got her job at the bakery, they had been facing eviction. Now, with that small income added to their welfare check after the divorce, they'd have a roof over their heads and enough day-old baked goods to keep their bellies full.

Stephanie had convinced her family to attend the New Year's Eve service at Church to hear her sing a solo. Sylvia's deep depression had prevented her from leaving the house much. It was the first time Sylvia had set foot in church since her wedding, and she felt terribly awkward. *I've always tried to do the right thing, to be a good person,* she thought. *Isn't that what it's all about? So why have all these things happened to*

me? Why did Kirk leave us? Where was God in all that? If it
weren't for Stephanie's solo, Sylvia would never have cast her
shadow across the threshold of this or any other church.

A car door creaked from across the parking lot. Pastor
Vicente gathered up an armload of Molly's pink boxes and held
them close, balancing them under his chin. The church keys
dangled from his little finger. "Lyra, would you open the door
for me? And Dorian, there is a flat of tamarind and an ice chest
full of horchata and bottled water in the back seat. Would you
bring them in for me?"

"Hello," he attempted to greet Bobbie, but the boxes
shifted and spilled down on her. Good thing Molly had the
foresight to seal her boxes with those shiny labels bearing her
logo. Ignoring the boxes, he reached out his hand. "Sorry, let me
try that again. Hi, I'm Pastor Vicente. And you are?"

"Bobbie," she said with a half smile.

"Would you like to join us for New Year's Eve?"

The church service dragged on for Sylvia, with people
standing up and giving thanks for various events of the soon-to-
be passed year, any of which she could have attributed to blind
luck. *Poor people,* she thought, *what will they do when this god
of theirs lets them down, and there's nowhere to go* but *down?*
She hoped that Stephanie's song would come soon; she didn't

know how much more of this god-stuff she could take. It was depressing, thinking about all these people who would be as disappointed as she herself had been.

Then it happened; a sweet voice came drifting down from behind her in the unadorned, darkened, candlelit room. She turned around. No one was even trying to see Stephanie. Instead, many just sat with hands raised and eyes closed. *Whoever heard of hiding performers up in a dark balcony and not letting them be seen?* she wondered, more than a bit angry that her beautiful daughter would be made invisible. The song was over all too soon, and replaced by a reverent silence—with no applause or acknowledgement of any kind. Sylvia was infuriated.

Steph was joined by a soprano and a tenor for several more songs before Pastor Vicente invited the congregation to help themselves to food and drink laid out simply on two long tables.

Homemade tamales, enchiladas, street tacos, refried beans, salad, and rice were all prepared by the ladies of the church.

In the row behind Sylvia, Bobbie was starving. She decided to stay and find out just how ridiculous things might get. Besides, there *was* food.

The food was beyond amazing. The women at the church had outdone themselves. Everyone was overstuffed. Bobbie couldn't remember being quite so full in years.

Pastor Vicente stood up and got everyone's attention. *Ah, here it comes,* Bobbie told herself, *he's gonna start preaching and ruin everything.* She picked up her backpack and stood up to leave.

"It's time for our annual Church of the Broken Talent Show," he announced. People began to clap. Chairs were shuffled around to face the podium. "Dessert will be served afterwards, so stick around."

Bobbie put her backpack down and sat in the last row so she could make a quick getaway if needed. *I guess I can stay for a little while. Ain't got nothin' better to do, and it's nice and warm in here.*

The children were up first, yawning and wiggling around as they often do, oblivious to the fact that everyone was watching them, all except one little boy. He seemed to be basking in the light of his newfound fame. He grabbed the microphone stand and began his best Elvis impression while the other kids sang, "Yes, Jesus Loves Me." The crowd's laughter seemed to feed the boy's frenzy. When the song ended they nearly had to use a shepherd's crook to get him off the stage. His mortified parents had to come up to remove him from the limelight. Stevie clapped extra hard.

LEAVING LYRA

Kids! thought Bobbie. *I wonder whatever happened to mine. Ain't seen 'em in years. I wonder what they've been up to? Prob'ly no good. They never did amount to nothin,' just like their father. Maybe if he'd 'a stayed, things might'a turned out different. Okay, Bobbie, buck up, don't be gettin' all soft now. The past is the past. You ain't got nothin' to depend on but yourself, old girl. Stay strong.*

Her thoughts were interrupted by the announcement of the next act, Cincinnati Pig and the Dancing Figs. A man stunningly dressed in a tuxedoed pig costume, complete with snout and curlicue tail, danced his way in front of the audience followed by three reluctant dancing men in green fig costumes. A song by the same name as the act played over the PA system. Bobbie was beside herself. She couldn't help but laugh out loud. Maybe this place wasn't so bad after all. The laughter didn't die out until long after the music ended, and the Barnyard Mr. Big himself oinked his way out of the room.

Numerous acts followed. Lyra, Steph, and Marta—the alto who sang with Lyra on Saturday mornings—finally got their turn to perform in old-fashioned wool suits and matching pill box hats, gleaned from a thrift store. They did their rendition of an old Andrews Sisters' song, "Elmer's Tune," in three-part harmony.

Next was a family of teenage kids performing mariachi music. They were doing pretty well until one of the kids lost control of his gigantic guitar and smacked his brother in the head. They never quite regained their rhythm, but they finished strong.

They were followed by a better-than-average standup comedy act, traditional Mexican folk dancing, a man sitting on a stick horse singing, "Mule Train," and cracking his fly swatter whip while making outrageous faces, and a kazoo band of elderly men playing their own version of Aretha Franklin's, "Natural Woman." Pastor Vicente's contribution of juggling stuffed kittens provided a lively pre-finale.

The evening finished with Lyra's song, "Down From the Wall," that she had written for the occasion:

How long did I watch You, imprisoned on Your throne,
Suspended animation behind these walls of stone?
How was I to realize that You're the One I'd known
On the wall?

I saw You in some paintings that hung along the way,
In stained glass presentations when the clouds had rolled away.
How was I to recognize the symbol from the Truth—
The Jesus that I'm living for from images of You?
And You've come down.
Down.
Down from the wall and into my heart.
I see that You are Life and I want to be a part of You.

I nailed You high upon the wall.

I couldn't see Your face as I prayed to You and cried to You
To fill my life with grace.
But looking back upon the wall, an empty cross I see.
The world had tried to keep You dead,
But You chose to live in me,
And You've come down.
Down.
Down from the wall and into my heart.
I see that You are life, and I want to be a part of You."

Sylvia was rooted to her chair, so stunned she couldn't even clap. She'd gone to church as a kid, but she never heard mention of God actually living in a person's heart. *Is this something new or was I just not listening back then? An empty cross? 'The world had tried to keep You dead, but You chose to live in me?' What does that even mean? Is this what Stephanie believes? I just don't understand this.*

Stacey shook her mother's shoulders. "Mom. You're not listening to me. I said I wanna go home. Stevie's been sleeping on my lap for at least a half an hour. My legs are totally numb."

Without a word, Sylvia reached for Stevie and they walked out, Stacey staggering on prickly legs, and her mother pondering gently piercing lyrics.

Dessert was served after the music with pan dulce, ice cream and chocolate cake. Bobbie had some of each.

The pastor stood up and said, "No sermon tonight; I think my cat juggling said it all." Everyone laughed. "Just love one another, okay? Happy New Year, Feliz Ano Nuevo, everybody."

That's it? Bobbie was puzzled. *No hell fire and damnation? What kind of church is this anyway?* She decided, *Maybe not such a bad one.*

Lyra's visit to the homeless shelter had haunted her. Perhaps that is what drove her to pick up her guitar and jump in her old Toyota with its dented passenger side door that all too often got stuck shut. She drove through the winter storm to the shelter.

Handyman Jim welcomed her with a smile, discolored from years of tobacco and alcohol, yet brightened with years of recovery. "Well, if it isn't Miss Lyra come to bless us with her singing."

"That remains to be seen." She gave him a wink and set herself up in a folding chair on the sidewalk under the tattered green canvas awning. Beside her were three men and two women puffing on their cigarettes and staring as if life's answers might be found in the smoke they exhaled.

Though the smoke stung her eyes and rasped her throat, Lyra started singing and strumming, her fingers stiff with the cold. She wished someone would grasp the meaning of the songs she sang, but her listeners vacantly watched the smoke rise. She packed up her guitar after a short set.

"A lot of these folks have to keep their walls up to survive being on the street, Lyra," Handyman Jim explained softly. "The street gets a lot tougher in the city than it is here in River Oaks, and a lot of them have been all over the place. You can't gain their trust overnight. Give 'em your time and give 'em your ear and see what happens." He patted her shoulder by way of farewell and left to join a couple fellow casualties of the Vietnam War in a heated discussion of the inadequacies of the Veteran's Administration.

Lyra left with a lightened heart and Handyman Jim's assurance that she had been heard.

The following week found Lyra at Dorian's door. "Your mission, should you decide to accept it, is to join me for an impromptu concert at the shelter."

"I don't know, Lyra. You saw how I was with Bobbie. I didn't have anything to say. I felt like an idiot."

"It's not about you, Dorian. It's not how you talk, it's how you listen," she said.

"Has Bobbie opened up to you yet?" he challenged.

"Handyman Jim says it takes time. I think he's right. When I found myself living in my car, I hid my fear by making myself super outgoing. Some other homeless people just plain hide."

"You mean you were faking being friendly at first? Sure fooled me."

"No one knew how scared I was. The only one I've told was Catzo." She paused awkwardly. "And now you."

"Miss Lyra, I see you brought a friend," Handyman Jim said with his bright olive green eyes. "How about we set you up inside this time? Too dang cold out." He sat them down at the hub of a dozen circular tables.

Dorian's hands grew clammy as the residents entered the dining hall, some chatting comfortably in loose groups, others fiercely alone. Bobbie was among the latter. With a curt nod at Lyra, she joined the line filing past the food serving station. As they took their seats with their food, the homeless guests clustered the tables around Lyra and Dorian whose harmonies were quite serviceable given the lack of amplification, the overall noise, and the echoes that inhabit uncarpeted spaces. For once, it didn't matter to Dorian how they sounded or even the lack of response from some of their audience. He sensed God's pleasure.

As they packed up their instruments, Lyra said, "Now comes the fun part; we get to meet the guests."

Over the course of the evening, Dorian met war veterans, an art teacher, a librarian, a single father, several homeless mothers with kids in tow, a couple of entire families, and a few people exhibiting signs of mental illness and addictions—not at all the homogeneous group he would've anticipated. Instead, they comprised a microcosm of individuals brought together by poor fortune and, in some cases, poor choices.

It was then he realized that, were it not for Uncle Phil, he himself could have wound up somewhere like this. Humbled, he stared down at the Rolex that no longer belonged on his wrist. Bobbie came alongside Dorian and nudged him, looking straight into his eyes. "You get it now, rich boy, don't you?" She gave him a wry smile and marched off to join the smokers on the sidewalk.

CHAPTER 12
Rising Decibels and All Sugared Up

The gift card for Robin's Nest Yarn Shoppe that Phil had bestowed upon Molly at Christmas, was burning a chasm through Molly's jeans' pocket. Today was the day to put the fire out. She had done her research on Ravelry.com, the worldwide website for yarn addicts of all ages, and had narrowed the sweater of her dreams down to a handful of patterns. Today after work she would be off to Robin's to choose the yarn that would bring one of those patterns she had purchased online to life. It was interesting how looking at the right fiber and color would help her choose which pattern. Funny how life sometimes works that way; looking at many choices can help determine the right path to take, narrowing down your options finally to just one. *If only people would take the time to examine all their options and the possible consequences before making their final choices in life,* Molly philosophized.

Her dad had taught her well. "Think, Molly, think," he had advised her in her teens. "Every choice you make leads to different consequences. You need to look down the road, ten, twenty years, and see where that choice will take you." His advice had clearly irritated her in her teens, wanting to make the easiest and funnest decisions, but as she grew up, she began to see the wisdom in her father's instructions. She wished she could thank him, now that he had gone the way of all flesh, and seek his wisdom on how to balance life with business.

Molly was overwhelmed with her workload. Even with Lyra and Stephanie's capable help, she was having a hard time keeping up with demand. But it was just these thoughts that were driving her to the haven of the yarn shop and as Phil had put it, her need to *unwind. Dear Phil,* she mused; *he only gets the crumbs of my time.*

Molly had just about cleaned a hole right through the portion of the counter she had been polishing as she considered this.

Lyra derailed Molly's train of thought. "Do you think that counter is clean enough now?" she asked with a knowing smile.

"Nope. Several more hours should do the trick," Molly replied.

They both laughed.

"You look like you've lost some weight, Lyra. That exercising with Steph must be working. You look great."

"I've lost fifteen pounds so far. Thanks for noticing."

"Hey Lyra, want to come with me to Robin's Nest after work? We can celebrate your weight loss with yarn," Molly suggested. "I hear that Robin has just gotten a new shipment of Madelinetosh yarn this week."

"I've been wanting to check that place out. Sure, let's go."

It was fifteen minutes from closing time, and the two looked at each other.

"That's it," Molly said wildly, "Let's just close early. It's been unusually slow this afternoon anyway."

They readied themselves and were just about to put up the "Sorry, We're Closed" sign when the bell jingled over the front door. "Ah, nuts," exclaimed Molly none too softly. She put down her purse and wiped the frown off her face. Stepping out into the service area, she saw an extremely well-dressed woman, a stranger to Molly. This mistimed customer had two rambunctious children with her who had already made their way over to the display cases and were pawing the bent glass windows separating them from their observably unneeded sugar high. Lyra came out of the back room, hearing the decibels rise. They would not be closing early. More probably, quitting late. *Ah, well, such is life,* Molly reminded herself.

"Give them whatever they want," the woman stated flatly. "And whip me up an iced coconut milk mocha macchiato."

Molly wanted so badly to roll her eyes at that particular moment, but instead queried, "Is that with or without whipped cream, ma'am?"

At the word, "ma'am," the woman recoiled and gave a little humph. "Surprise me," she said, disinterested, and turned on her heel. She walked away to the furthest table from her kids.

Molly had seen her kind before but determined to stay pleasant no matter what.

The children were now licking the display windows, laughing and pushing each other around. The older of the two, a seven year old boy, pushed his sister a bit too hard, and she landed on the floor, bursting into tears. Lyra was there in a flash, helping the little girl to her feet. Way too occupied with her cell phone, the woman ignored the tussle.

"Hey mister," Lyra admonished, "be nice to your sister."

"She's not my sister, she's a toad. She's an ugly old toad!" the boy yelled.

"I'm not a toad!" Tears again.

"Okay, that's enough, you two," Molly interjected. "What would you like to order? Doughnuts? Cookies? Cake?"

"Yeah!" the kids said in unison, jumping up and down and temporarily forgetting the boy's claim to his sister's amphibian ancestry.

Molly walked over to their mother's table. The woman looked up slowly. "Yes?" she said, laying her cell phone down, clearly annoyed at the interruption.

"What would you like your children to have, ma'am? They clearly can't make up their minds."

"I said whatever they want. Can't you understand English?"

"But they want everything," Molly replied.

"Do you have a problem with that?"

"No, ma'am!" Molly said with emphasis on the *ma'am*.

The next thirty-five minutes felt like hours. Well after closing time, Lyra and Molly were wiping the last of the lick marks off the display case and getting ready to lock up for the day. The unpleasant woman had provided them with the largest single sale they'd had in days, but at what cost? The floor was littered with crumbs, frosting, and various states of partially-eaten cupcakes. Pink boxes full of the rest of their purchases would be consumed around their house for days. The only consolation was that the woman had to take them home all sugared up.

"Okay, Lyra, we're out of here. It's a good thing Robin is open late tonight for her knit along."

The two walked at a good clip, anxious to fondle yarn between their fingers. It wasn't long before they reached Robin's Nest. Robin had cleverly designed the nest on her sign out of many different colors of yarn woven together. Three little blue balls of yarn served as eggs inside of it with a felted robin perched on the edge with a snippet of yarn that served as a worm in its beak.

"Ah, here we are at last," Molly sighed as she pushed the door open. "Yarn heaven!"

Lyra was overwhelmed by the huge inventory and sheer volume of color and texture. Molly was about to give her the grand tour until Robin noticed the new face and came to greet Lyra.

Robin Banks was a boho beauty, thirty-seven years old, always smiling, and often humming a tune to herself. She moved about the shop like it was her home, and usually had some knitting in her hands, walking and talking as she knit, rarely looking at her projects.

How does she do that? Molly wondered. As Robin swept Lyra off into fiber-land, Molly was now free to explore on her own. *Now where's that new shipment of Madelinetosh?* She wondered. *Alpaca or merino wool? She tossed the ideas around. Well, if I do the intarsia sweater, it should be wool. If I do the lattice-textured cardigan, it could be alpaca, but it's gotta be Tosh for sure. Hmm...but what colors?*

Yarns were organized by fiber content and weight. She wouldn't be looking at the cobweb-like lace weight yarns today. Sweaters needed a heavier, thicker yarn. She referred to the patterns she had brought with her. *Let's see how much yarn these sweaters call for. The "Birdie Fair Isle Cardigan," by Hannah Fettig, with its flying swallows circling its yoke requires a lot of yarn, but I do have that gift certificate from Phil. The intarsia colorwork is new to me, but I'm up for the challenge. Or will it be "Peanut Butter," by Linda Permann, the lattice-textured cardigan? That would be great in an autumn shade with cute wooden buttons.* Molly adored buttons. She leafed through her patterns in their clear, protective sleeves, and continued to muse. "Ah," she said out loud. "How will I ever make up my mind?"

Robin had just left Lyra in the colorful, affordable world of acrylic yarn and had heard Molly's sigh. *"Can I help you choose something, Molly? What are you making?"*

"Well, Phil gave me this giant gift certificate and I'm having a hard time deciding on which pattern to use. I haven't even started browsing for colors yet." Molly handed her the patterns. "What do you think?"

Robin flipped through the patterns. "They're all lovely, but have you seen the <u>Knit, Swirl</u> book, by Sandra McIver? I've got it right over here. It's the last copy too." She led Molly to the white book shelves near a sunny window where two overstuffed couches and some upholstered chairs beckoned. "I think one of these would look stunning on you. Maybe the "Sheer Beauty" jacket. Here, take a look." She handed Molly the book.

Molly was enchanted. "This is it, Robin! How did you know?"

"Knitter's intuition." She smiled, turning up one side of her mouth more than the other. "I've got some new

Madelinetosh and Malabrigo skeins in this week. Wanna see? Just took them out of their boxes this morning."

Molly followed along like a junkie to a meth lab. *No wonder knitters call their abundance of fiber their "stash,"* Molly thought.

Countless skeins later, Molly finally decided on Madelinetosh's "Tart," a ruby red jewel of a yarn. She walked up to the counter hardly able to contain herself. "I can't wait to get home and get started," Molly told Robin.

Lyra had finished her yarn expedition and was right behind her.

"What did you find?" Molly asked her.

"This aqua blue variegated acrylic yarn. It was on sale too." Lyra beamed. "I'm going to start crocheting scarves for the homeless shelter. Handyman Jim said their supply is getting low. Can't let them run out."

"So you're crocheting for charity, Lyra?" Robin asked. "Well, let's just take another 15% off. Let it be my little contribution."

"Thanks so much, Robin. It'll get put to good use," Lyra said. "So what did you find, Molly?" she asked.

"Look at this sweater pattern. It's a wool hoarder's dream. And check out this red yarn."

"Amazing," Lyra replied. "It'll look gorgeous on you."

Molly whipped the gift certificate out of her wallet and plopped it on the counter. "Bam! And it's paid for by my sweet Phil."

Lyra wished she had a sweet man of her own, but she'd have to content herself curling up with a ball of yarn and a warm kitten.

"I remember Phil coming in to buy this gift certificate before Christmas," Robin reminisced. "He wandered in like a little lost lamb. Nearly had to shear him on the spot," she said with a chuckle. "He didn't know what the heck he was doing and walked around aimlessly for a while until I thought he had suffered enough. I asked him if he was here for knitting lessons, just to rattle his cage a bit more. He turned rather white and stuttered that he needed to buy enough yarn to *build* a sweater. I said, 'So you already know how to knit and you're making a sweater?' He didn't seem to take to that idea any more than the lessons. I finally decided to play nice and asked if it was a gift for someone. Boy, was he relieved when I suggested this gift card. Sure was fun toying with him though. You've got yourself a heck of a man there, Molly."

Molly beamed, "Don't I know it!"

CHAPTER 13
Dough's on the Table

The next morning Molly and Lyra were hard at work. It was a half hour before the bakery was to open—their "crunch time," as they called it. "What about these mini carrot cakes, Molly?" Lyra asked. "Want me to put the cream cheese frosting on now? They seem cool enough."

"Perfect timing, Lyra. These things will sell like hotcakes. They'll be gone in an hour, once word gets out that we made them today." Molly's carrot cakes were always a best seller. Her mom had perfected the recipe over the years. They were Molly's personal favorite. "Can you put a couple aside for Phil and me?" She knew Phil would be delighted.

Lyra was frosting the last of the mini cakes and Molly was glazing the fresh raised doughnuts when there was a loud pounding on the glass door of the bakery.

"Phil must *really* want his morning apple fritter," Lyra quipped.

The pounding came again. Molly set her wooden-handled spatula down and wiped her hands on her red apron. "Guess I better answer before he breaks down the door." Molly was irritated, wondering why Phil was so impatient to get his fritter so early in the morning. She heard the knocking again. "I'm coming. I'm coming," she shouted.

There at the door was an irritated man in a business suit, and someone was with him. Could that be the well-dressed lady that had the two 'most-likely-to-lick-the-showcase' kids with her yesterday? It sure was, but the children weren't with her today. *Aww, how sad,* Molly thought, finding her sarcasm ready even at this hour of the morning.

Molly unlocked the door and opened it a hand's breadth. "We aren't open yet, but if you'd like to come back in twenty minutes, we would be happy to serve you."

The brash man pushed the door open and barged in, followed by the aggravating woman with her bejeweled cell phone in hand. Molly stumbled backward, aghast.

"I said we aren't open yet, sir." She rose to her full height and squared her shoulders.

"I'm not here to ingest carbohydrates. I'm here on business," the stranger spoke.

"Business? Look mister, you can come back in twenty minutes like everybody else."

Lyra stepped out of the work room, holding an industrial-sized rolling pin and trying not to look flustered. "Molly, do you need some help out here?"

LEAVING LYRA

"No, Lyra, this man is just leaving. You too, ma'am." She looked at the well-dressed woman and couldn't resist admiring her Jimmy Cho shoes.

The man handed Molly his business card. Molly read, "Haskill and Haskill Investment Group. Neil Haskill, CEO."

"Well, Mr. Haskill," Molly said, narrowing her eyes, "what is this all about?"

"I'm not going to beat around the bush, Ms Tauber. My firm is prepared to offer you a handsome sum for the purchase of this bakery."

"My bakery is not for sale."

He sat himself down at a table near the register.

"I'll have an iced. Coconut milk. Mocha. Macchiato," the woman demanded, slowly emphasizing each word as if Molly were simple-minded.

"I said we're not open yet, ma'am."

"Get my wife her order," Mr. Haskill insisted.

"How many times do I have to say it? We. Are. *Not.* Open. Yet!" Molly said, enunciating every word.

Lyra stepped up beside her, slapping the rolling pin firmly into her left hand several times to present a united front.

"You wouldn't be saying that, Ms Tauber, if you knew what I am prepared to offer," he said with a sardonic smile.

"And just what would that be, Mr. Haskill? You could promise me the world. This bakery is *not* for sale! It has been in my family for generations. *You* are wasting *your* time."

"Am I?" He removed a leather-bound notebook from his inner breast pocket and scribbled an outrageous offer on a sheet of paper. He tore it out, folded it in quarters, and pushed it across the marble-topped table toward Molly. "We've had our eyes on this bakery for some time now. Canterbury Heights doesn't have much of a bakery, and we have found the majority of your wedding customers have come from *our* side of the lake. We would like to buy you out. Haskill and Haskill Investments is planning on building an all-inclusive wedding event enterprise which we will call 'Indulgence Weddings' for your customers on the *right* side of the lake. My wife Delilah here will be spearheading the project with her impeccable taste and expert event-planning skills."

Delilah stepped forward in her black suede stilettos. "Now where is my iced coconut milk mocha macchiato?"

"As I've been saying, we're not open yet, and I'm afraid you'll have to leave so that we can prepare for our *real* customers. You've put us behind this morning. Good day, Mr. and Mrs. Haskill." Molly strode to the door and held it open.

The duo did not move an inch. Molly stood firm as a customer walked by the plate glass window.

"Phil!" Lyra exclaimed.

Molly turned to see Phil headed toward the open door with a puzzled look on his face.

"Opening a little early today, Molly? What's up? Customers already?" Phil stepped inside.

LEAVING LYRA

"These people were just leaving, Phil." She made an unmistakable gesture toward the open door.

"We'll be back," Neil Haskill said smugly as he and his wife departed.

"Oh, yes we will," Delilah looked back with disdain. "And, by the way, your customer service, as *your* people would say, sucks!"

Molly wanted to boot the unwelcome guests out, but settled for locking it in their wake with a resounding click.

"What the heck was that all about?" Phil wrapped his supportive arms around her.

"I'm so mad I could spit! The nerve of those two, coming in here so high and mighty!" Molly fumed.

"What did they want? How did they even get in here? It isn't opening time yet."

Lyra interjected, "We were in the work room, and that jerk started pounding on the door. He wouldn't stop until Molly unlocked it to say we weren't open yet. Once it was open, he just pushed his way in like he owned the place. As a matter of fact, that's what he's planning to do, own the place. Like Molly would ever sell her business, especially to someone like him! He came in here so full of himself with his snippy little Barbie Doll wife, and he slid an offer across the table to Molly, just like they do in the movies," Lyra continued.

"What did it say?" the ever-curious Phil questioned.

"I don't know and I don't care," Molly said, walking over to the now-tainted table and grabbing the neatly-folded paper. She gave it a toss into the trash. "Good riddance!"

"You aren't even going to look at it? Oh, come on now, Muffin. Aren't you curious?" Phil walked over to the trash and fished it out.

"I've got doughnuts to finish glazing." Molly planted her hands on her hips and stomped off to the work room.

Phil unfolded the paper with Lyra looking over his shoulder. "Whoa! Molly, I think you should look at this. Seriously!" Phil exclaimed.

"Nothing is gonna make me sell this bakery. It doesn't matter what that paper says," she shouted.

"You really should see who you're dealing with here," Lyra coaxed. "He's not joking around."

"Oh, all right." Molly gave in, walked back over, and snatched the offer from Phil's hand. Speechless, Molly dropped the paper to the floor.

Molly prepared to leave early with a dreadful headache as Stephanie came in for work. "You don't look like you're feeling so good," she observed.

"I'm not. I'm going to lie down. Lyra, you can explain to Stephanie what happened this morning?"

"Sure. I hope you feel better," Lyra said. "See you in the morning?"

"In the morning." Molly drooped out the door.

"Spill it, Lyra! What's going on?" Steph demanded.

Lyra spilled. "Well, these two 'Canterburians' forced their way in here this morning before we opened..."

"What? Two people from Canterbury Heights? What did they want?"

"This bakery," Lyra delivered the shocking news.

"Huh?" Step's perfectly-tweezed brows furrowed. "They want to buy the bakery? Molly would never sell this place."

"Yeah? Well, look at this." Lyra displayed the notorious paper which Molly had left behind.

"You've got to be joking. She can't turn this down." Steph's lip started to quiver.

"I know. Looks like you and I will be looking for jobs soon." Lyra looked down at the many digits on the paper, willing them away.

Stephanie's tears were rising. She grabbed a napkin. "Don't tell her I'm upset. I'm happy for her, really I am. It's just that my family depends on the money I'm bringing in."

"I know what you mean, Steph. I'm not sure what I'll do either. It was good while it lasted. Well, let's get back to work while we still have a job."

Stephanie blew her nose and tried to look cheerful. "Let's hit the gym after work. I need to work off some of this stress."

It wasn't clear to Molly what she should do. Phil dropped by her house to bring dinner and talk things over. Molly greeted him with an ice bag on her head.

"Still have that headache? Come here, my love." Phil wrapped his arms around her. "Want to talk about it?"

They sat down on Molly's new microfiber couch. "I've never dreamed of having so much money before, Phil. I've been thinking about what this would mean for us."

"Don't let money cloud your thinking, Molly. Do what you think is the right thing for *you*."

"For us! After all, the subject of marriage has come up. This could make our lives so much easier. I could stay home and be a full-time mom someday."

"And what makes you think you wouldn't be a full-time mom either way? Your mom took you to work with her every day, and you turned out great, didn't you?"

"Yeah, but I know how hard it was for her. This money would make our lives so much easier. We would have financial stability."

"Nothing is really stable in this world, Molly."

"You don't want me to sell, do you?"

"I never said that. I just don't want you to make this decision based on money alone. We would be just fine without it. I will always take care of you. You wouldn't have to work either way. I make a good enough salary for both of us—and any future kids too. So what it comes down to is what do you really want? Only you can answer that question. I'm okay either way."

"Doesn't it bug you that I keep such ungodly hours?" Molly's mind churned out questions.

Phil smiled. "Never has, never will. And who are we to call any hour ungodly?"

Molly picked up her ice bag and twisted it as she considered the consequences. "And what about Lyra and Stephanie? If I sell, they'll be out of work."

"Maybe the new owners will hire them. They're already trained. They'd be crazy not to." Phil kissed her on her beleaguered forehead. "Now let's get some food in you and get rid of that headache."

CHAPTER 14
Glutenous Maximus, But Some Call Him Ronald

At the gym Lyra and Stephanie commiserated over the possible sale of Molly's Sunshine Bakery. Lyra's legs were about to fall off while Steph increased the speed of her own treadmill without so much as a whimper.

"Hey, aren't you that hot girl that works at the bakery?" A tall, muscular jock strutted up to the girls. He flashed his best Tom Cruise-inspired smile.

"We both are," Steph replied.

"I was talking to you." He pointed at Steph.

Oh no, Lyra thought, *another guy hitting on Steph. It happens every time we come here. It wouldn't be so bad if they weren't so stuck on themselves. Aren't there any nice guys at the gym? Steph can handle it though, she'll see right through him.*

The man in question flexed his biceps in a failed attempt at nonchalance. His ridiculously-oversized headphones seemed out of place at a gym where everyone else used earbuds.

Kind of matches his ego, Lyra reasoned.

"I noticed you on the weight machine before. You're really in good shape, if you know what I mean."

Stephanie smiled a reward for his compliment.

Oh oh, thought Lyra, *she's cracking. Come on, Steph, don't fall for this loser. You're too smart for his musclebound ego.*

"Lyra, I'll be back," Steph said. She turned to Mr. Muscle. "Are you challenging me on the weight machine? She brushed the hair from her sweaty face and swept it up into a messy bun. "What did you say your name was?"

"Ron, but some people call me Ronald," he doddered, puffing out his pecs like an overgrown rooster.

Lyra watched them walk away, his legs so muscled that he walked bowlegged. Morbidly fascinated, she watched the neckless wonder approach the bar, adding additional weight. He took his turn first, managing to lift it above his head. Steph then added an additional forty pounds to the bar.

"What? You gotta lift my weights first before you go adding more," he protested.

"Are you afraid, Ronald? Some people call you that, don't they? I'll make you a little wager. If I win, you leave me alone..."

Ronald broke in, "and if I win, you go to dinner with me tonight."

"You're on, Ron...ald." Steph lifted the additional forty pounds with relative ease. "You're up."

He added twenty more pounds. The competition continued until Steph could lift no more and she returned to Lyra, crestfallen, yet excited. "Well, looks like I'm going to dinner with Ron tonight."

"Steph, are you sure? With that stupid head?"

"Well, some people do call him Ronald," she said defensively before bursting into laughter.

"Look at him preen. You sure you want to go out with *him*?"

"It's just for fun. Besides, it's a free meal, isn't it? But you're right, he never even asked my name." She brightened. "I'm meeting him at Tortugas at seven. He'll be surprised how much this girl can eat."

"I want all the details tomorrow," Lyra said as they headed out the door.

Lyra walked on past Stephanie's and took the long way home through the park. Two young people were seated on a bench, holding hands, talking. Their eyes never left each other. Would she have to move and leave Dorian behind to find another job if Molly sold the bakery? She plodded on home, missing Dorian already.

.

LEAVING LYRA

The gate squeaked as she entered the McCrearys' yard. There was a lone figure sitting on a bench near the daffodils. "Dorian?" she asked hopefully.

He stood and walked toward her, arms open. "Uncle Phil told me about what happened this morning at the bakery. I thought you could use some company."

She walked into his embrace. "Oh, Dorian, I don't want to leave here! I can't stay if I don't have a job."

"Who said anything about you leaving?"

"If Molly sells, I'm out of a job. And why wouldn't she sell? It's a huge chunk of money. She could stay home and live her dream of raising a family with Phil." Lyra could no longer hold her tears in, soaking Dorian's tee shirt.

Dorian held her close. "It's gonna be alright, wait and see," he comforted. "Besides, even if you lose your job at Molly's, it doesn't mean you have to move away. We could find you another job here. As a matter of fact, one of the baristas at my work is getting ready to head off to college soon. I can put in a good word for you." He smoothed the hair from her cheek. "You can't leave vet assistant school, and you can't leave...me."

Lyra could hardly catch her breath. "You're my best friend, Dorian," she managed to choke out.

"And you're mine." Dorian held her tighter.

167

The three women worked side by side in the workroom of Molly's bakery. The air was charged with tension. None of them spoke until the smell of burning cookies filled the air.

"Oh no, I forgot to set the timer on the snickerdoodles!" Molly flew to the oven. "Burnt to a crisp." She tossed the cookie trays into the sink.

"Molly," Lyra began, "we want you to know that whatever you decide is fine with us. You just do what is best for you."

"I've decided. I can't sell this bakery." Molly walked over to the sink and started vigorously scrubbing the burnt cookie sheets. "Why don't you girls go up front and start loading the display cases while I finish up here."

"She doesn't sound very happy about her decision," Stephanie whispered to Lyra as they wheeled the racks of eclairs and pies to the front.

"She sounds downright depressed," Lyra said in a low tone. "Maybe we should just leave her alone for a while. In the meantime, how did your date go with aka Ronald last night?"

"You know, he's not so bad. He even asked what my name was. Ha!" She grinned. "He said he was embarrassed for not asking before. He was really polite. He pulled out my chair for me, told me to order whatever I wanted, and he even picked up the check, thank God, or I'd still be washing dishes. He told me that he thinks I'm gorgeous. No guy has ever said that to me before—not since dad left."

Lyra inwardly rolled her eyes, thinking, *When was the last time anyone ever said that to me? Oh yeah, never. Steph has it so good, and she doesn't even know it. She has the looks of a supermodel, but not the ego to go with it. Better keep my mouth shut and let her figure this out for herself. Never trust a flatterer, especially if some people call him Ronald.* "So you think you're going to see him again?"

"Tomorrow night. He's taking me to meet some of his friends that work with him at Takashimi's Taco Grotto. We're going to some fancy-schmancy restaurant on the other side of the lake. Can you believe it? He wants me to meet his friends!"

Lyra could stand it no longer. "You don't even know this guy. How do you know you can trust him?"

"I'm just having fun, Lyra. It's just a date, for goodness sake. And how do I get to know him unless I give him a chance? You're starting to sound like my mother."

"Just be careful. I don't want this guy taking advantage of you."

"I'm seventeen years old now. I know what I'm doing."

Famous last words, thought Lyra.

Stephanie had just finished primping in the bathroom at work. Hair, dress, shoes—everything was perfect. Meeting Ron's friends was sure to be amusing, and the promise of a fine meal sealed the deal.

"Steph, your Ron—I mean, 'some people call him Ronald' is here."

The red Trans Am flexed its motor noisily from the parking lot, followed by an impatient honk of its horn.

Real classy, thought Lyra.

"See ya, Lyra," Stephanie said, model-walking to the door.

"Wow, you're awfully dressed up for Ron—I mean Ronald."

"He is taking me somewhere fancy tonight, and I have to look good for his friends."

"Well, they'll be impressed," Lyra replied.

As Steph headed out the door, Lyra thought to herself, *I hope she knows what she's doing. Lord, keep her safe. I don't trust that guy.* Lyra picked up a broom and swept furiously.

"We're meeting my friends at the Fillmore on the other side of the lake. I like it cause they *fill* you up *more*. Get it? They got really big plates."

"Ha, ha," she courtesy-laughed. Steph had never been to the other side of the lake. Canterbury Heights was the epitome of upper crust living. *I hope I know what fork to use,* she thought.

As they drove by the palatial mansions, Ronald saw his old high school. "Hey Stephanie, that's where I actually graduated from. I was quarterback for the Canterbury Carnivores..." He launched into a lengthy discourse on yards, touchdowns, and so many head and neck injuries.

Hmm, that explains a lot. Stephanie studied her cuticles as he droned on.

Half an hour later she was jolted back to his incessant monologue by the question, "So, uh, where did you say you went to high school?

"Oh, I'm home-schooled."

"You're, like, joking me, huh? You're too hot not to go to a real high school."

"Uh, thanks, I think."

"No, seriously, where *did* you go to high school?"

"I study at home. I haven't graduated yet."

"Oh, so you stayed back too? I spent two years in seventh grade. Don't feel bad." His Trans Am's tires squealed in agony as he peeled out from the stoplight. "Look! There's the Fillmore. Remember what I said about the Fillmore? You laughed. Remember?"

Stephanie did not wait for him to open the door as they pulled in. *Forget the chivalry. I'm hungry, and I just want to get this date over with. I didn't realize just how into himself he is, and how much he talks.* She walked on ahead of Ronald, no easy feat in stilettos.

"Hey, wait up! You must be looking forward to one of those big plates I was talking about. You sure can put that food away, Stephanie. Remember on our last date?" He beat her to the hefty restaurant door and wrestled it from her grasp. "Remember?" he repeated.

"Oh yeah." *How could I forget?* she thought.

They met the other two couples in the bar.

"Stephanie, this is Brandi and Brayden, and Madison and Jackson."

"Nice to meet you," Stephanie responded, as they nodded a greeting to her.

"What'll ya have, Stephanie?" Ronald asked.

"Seven up."

"No, I mean, what are you *drinking*? How about a nice cold beer?"

"I can't drink. I'm not twenty-one yet."

"It's okay. I'll order one for you...Hey, barkeep. Couple cold ones down here."

The drinks arrived. Steph took a sip and tried not to spew. *Oh my gosh! This tastes like dog pee left out on a hot window sill...for a month...in the middle of summer. How can they drink this stuff?* Her glass remained stationary on the table for the rest of the evening.

Brandi was already sloppy drunk. Boyfriend Brayden displayed too much PDA and was quite handsy with his date.

LEAVING LYRA

Madison spoke incessantly of the rowing team in college. As far as Steph could tell she was a total gym flea, overly conscious of her own good looks and mildly threatened by Stephanie.

Jackson, Madison's date, was paying Stephanie an unwelcome amount of eye-attention.

"So where are you going to college?" Madison asked Steph.

"Um, I haven't decided yet?" Steph replied.

"You mean you're not going to college? What? Are you just working or something?" Madison condescended.

"Uh, I'm still in high school."

"Yeah, but isn't she hot?" Ronald interjected. "Don't make fun of her 'cause she stayed back like I did. She can dead weight as much as she weighs."

"Thanks, Ronald." Steph took his left-handed compliment in stride.

"So where do you go to high school? Are you a Canterbury Carnivore like the rest of us *were*?" Madison taunted.

By this time Stephanie was feeling smaller and smaller and wishing she were home. "Well, actually, I'm home-schooled."

Everyone threw back their heads and roared with laughter.

Jackson said, "Yeah, right. You're too hot to be..."

"That's what I said, dude!" Ronald smacked him on the back.

A few rounds later they were finally called to their dining table.

"So what looks good to you, Ronald?" Steph inquired, not wanting to take undue advantage of his finances.

"You do!" He congratulated himself on his quick comeback.

"I mean, on the menu," Steph corrected him.

"Well, if you're talkin' food, did I mention they have really big plates here? Well, I really like prime rib. Lots of meat. Big plates," he slurred.

Funny. He's stinking drunk and he doesn't sound any dumber than he did before, Stephanie observed. "Uh, yeah, I guess I'll have the same."

Dinner conversation consisted of raunchy jokes, bragging, wild party remembrances, big plates, and sports stuff, most of which Stephanie didn't get. But at least the food was good, and there was lots of it, as Ronald had promised.

Near the end of dinner, Madison said, "So what do you do for fun, Steph? Why so quiet?"

"Um, I work at a bakery, take care of my younger siblings, and hang out with my friends mostly."

"Oh, simple things for a simple girl. So what do you like to bake? Whole wheat bread? You're just so *wholesome*."

"Yeah, I like punching dough."

"Hey, she works out at work. Ha, ha, ha! You're funny, Steph," Jackson beat Ronald to the punch. He gave Steph a slow, meaningful wink.

"Thas wud I wuss gonna sssay." Ronald was clearly slowing down.

Madison saw the wink, and fueled by it, continued her hostile take-down of Stephanie.

"What's a good little girl like you doing hanging out with bad-boy Ronald? Huh? Bet your mommy doesn't know you're out with a grown man tonight. Jackson, get your eyes off her!"

"I need to use the restroom," Stephanie excused herself. She stood up and walked to the back of the restaurant. A number of men's heads turned as she passed their tables. When she got there, she was alarmed that the other two girls had followed her.

Once inside the restroom, Madison's tirade continued. "Where do you get off trying to steal my man? I see the way Jackson is looking at you. You think you're so hot, little girl. But that's all you are. A little girl," Madison condescended. "Don't come dancing in here like you're one of us and then flirt with our guys and every man in the place. Still in high school! All you are is jail bait!"

"Yeah," Brandi added. "Brayden can't take his eyes off you either. Go home to your mommy while you still can."

"Look, I'm not interested in either of your guys. I'm not flirting!" Stephanie defended herself.

"What? Our men aren't good enough for you? Is that what you're saying?" Brandi taunted.

Madison spat, "I didn't come here tonight to babysit! It's past your bedtime! Get out of here and let your mommy tuck you in!"

If they only knew what my home was like, Stephanie thought. *But even as bad as it at home, I'd trade this for home any day.* She quickly stepped out of the restroom and headed back to the table.

While the three girls were having their discussion in the "little girls' room," the men had plans of their own.

"Let me help you out here, Ronald," offered Jackson. "I don't think you're going to get anywhere with this girl tonight, unless..." He slipped a club drug into Stephanie's drink. "There ya go man, that should take care of it."

They all laughed appreciatively.

"Shhh. Here come the girls," Braydon warned.

"Ronald, can you take me home? I've got a blistering headache," Stephanie begged.

"Sure Steph. Finish your beer first. That will reeeally help your head," Ronald coaxed.

"Yeah," Jackson encouraged, "It's a well known fact that beer takes away headaches. You should drink it all down."

"He's right," Braydon joined in. "Works every time and only takes a couple minutes. I drink beer whenever I have a headache. It'll fix you right up, girl."

"No, I really want to just go home. Now!" Steph repeated.

"Come on, just a couple sips. Do it for me," Ronald begged. "You'll feel much better soon."

"Oh for the love of...gimme that," Madison grabbed the beer and drank it down in one gulp. "And that's the way we do things around here, little girl!" She smacked the empty beer glass down on the table.

Stephanie headed toward the door. Ronald reluctantly followed her.

The guys at the table laughed hysterically at the slight change of plans.

"What are you guys laughing at?" Madison yelled.

"Guess you took care of her," Jackson laughed knowingly. "Say, baby, let's get outta here."

Once outside Stephanie raised her voice, "Are you gonna take me home, or do I need to call for a ride?"

"What's wrong, Steph? I thought we were having fun."

"You thought? Now there's an interesting concept. Your friends' girlfriends were so mean. Didn't you hear how they talked down to me?"

"Aw, don't pay any attention to them. They make fun of everyone they like. They do it to me all the time. That's how they always act. That's how you know they like you. You'll get used to them."

"No I won't, because I'm never going to see them again!" Stephanie fumed. "They were the rudest, most insulting people I've ever met!" Steph got in the car and slammed the door.

He clambered into his seat, started the engine and peeled out of the parking lot. "Listen, babe, they didn't mean anything they said. It's just their way. You gotta learn to get along with them. They're my best friends' girls. They didn't mean nothing by it."

Stephanie was fuming, but decided to say nothing more, until Ronald's drunk driving nearly drove them into an oncoming car. Stephanie screamed and grabbed the wheel just in time to swerve out of the way and onto the side of the road.

"Calm down, girl. I've got everything under control," he slurred.

"Are you trying to kill us both?" she yelled. Steph opened the car door and started walking away as fast as she could in stilettos.

"Wait! Where you going, beautiful? Get back in the car."

"The only way *I'm* getting back in the car is if *I'm* driving!" Steph made herself clear.

"Ok, you win, Princess. I'm not drunk, but I know you wanna drive my car. Every woman does!"

LEAVING LYRA

Steph put the car in gear and sped off towards home. "Hey babe, you're a pretty good driver. I'll bet you're good at a lot of other things too." Ronald put his hand on her knee.

"Get your hand off me. And don't call me babe."

"Ok...baby," he crooned.

"I am *not* a baby!"

As they pulled up in front of Stephanie's house, she left the car running and made her way to the front door, leaving him behind in the car. He eventually followed her up to the door where she was fumbling through her purse looking for her key. Realizing she had forgotten it when she changed purses, she knocked on her front door. No answer. She continued knocking, harder each time. After a few minutes, her knuckles were sore.

"Well, you can always come over and sleep in my bed. You just gotta be gone before my parents get up."

"Are you out of your mind?" Steph answered. "What makes you think I'd *ever* want to sleep in your bed?"

"Well, I did buy you dinner. Twice!"

Steph continued pounding on the door. "You idiot! Your ego outweighs you! Get off my porch and take your swag with you."

Ron, better known as Ronald, swore at her, jumped in his Trans Am, and burned rubber, just as her sister Stacey opened the front door. Moments later, as he screeched his tires around a nearby corner, the two girls heard the wail of a police car's siren.

"Who was that?" Stacey said sleepily.

"Ronald, but let's just call him Ron.

The next morning at work Stephanie recounted the whole ordeal to Lyra and Molly. "You were right, Lyra. I should never have gone out with someone like Ronald. What should I say in the future when creepers like him ask me out?"

"What we need here is a list of anti-pickup lines to have ready for those on-the-spot occasions when you really want to make a guy disappear fast," Molly suggested. "Legally."

"Like what? Give me an example." Steph was intrigued.

"Well, like when a guy says, 'Are you sure you're not a parking ticket because you have *fine* written all over you; wanna go out?' you can say, 'Can't! I've got the cholera,'" Molly suggested.

"What's the collar ah?" Steph wanted to know.

"I guess that one won't work for you then, but there's more where that came from. So how about, 'Who's that guy over there? Oh, never mind; it's just my dead Uncle Joe.'"

Lyra shouted, "I've got it! How about, 'Johnny's in the basement mixin' up the medicine,' can he come too?"

"Now you got it. Come on, Stephanie, give it a try," Molly encouraged.

"How about, 'I'm allergic to pushy?'" Stephanie ventured.

"Or maybe, 'Better start your obituary now. The autopsy will show nothing—if they ever find your body.'" Lyra contributed. "Or, 'So...you're back. Looks like the taser wasn't enough. I'll have to step it up a notch this time.'"

Steph was definitely getting with the program by this time. "You've got a booger hanging out of your nose," she said. "Or what about, 'My nickname is Jail Bait.'"

Not to be outdone, Molly contributed, "Just a minute; I'm receiving a message from the Mothership." She took off her shoe and mumbled gibberish into it.

The bakery resounded with laughter.

"What skills do you have? I'll expect your resume on my desk in the morning, but I'm telling you right now, it doesn't look promising," Lyra said.

"Do you do windows?" Molly interjected. "If you do, I've got a great first date idea."

Stephanie said, "I've got diarrhea, and you're making me *really* nervous...ooops!"

Lyra chimed in, "Maybe...when I get this darn house arrest ankle bracelet off."

"Well, it's tempting," Molly said, "my viral meningitis *seems* better today. I don't think I'm *that* contagious right now."

"You don't bathe often, do you?" Steph chuckled. "Smells like you got that latrine-digging job back again. Congrats!"

"They let me play with crayons now. Do you hear the voices too? They let me play with crayons now. Crayons now!" Lyra nodded.

Molly began clicking her heels together, harder and harder. "There's no place like home, there's no place like home, there's no place like home," she said through clenched teeth.

"I can't think of why I would. You must crave rejection," Steph said.

"Ding! Whoops! This is my floor. See ya," Molly said. "Then if you're sitting at a table you can slither down in your chair and hide."

"Ha!" said Steph, "If Ronald ever asks me out again, I can say, "Remember what happened the last time I went out with you? You had that potty accident. *Very* embarrassing."

"Whatever happened to a simple, 'Hi, my name's Fred?'" Molly asked. "Guys used to just introduce themselves."

"Well, not anymore." Stephanie was definitely getting into this. "I could always say, 'Didn't I meet you while you were working in that tampon factory?' That would freak them out. Guys are so squeamish about that stuff."

"Oh, wait! I got one," said Lyra. "You need neutering. I know a guy..."

Molly said innocently, clasping her hands at her waist and leaning forward, "I collect stamps. Do you?"

"I have tapeworms," Steph confided. "Do you want to go out for sushi?"

"That's a tough one to beat. But how about, 'Just wait til I switch to my other head,'" said Lyra. "Then you pretend to unscrew your head from your neck."

Molly grinned. "Gosh, this impetigo's *so* itchy. I just got over poison oak, then it was ringworm, and now it's impetigo. Always something..."

"Why don't you go somewhere where you can be alone?" Lyra offered.

"How about this?" Stephanie said, "Aww, nice try. Keep practicing, but next time try it *without* the drooling."

"Mom's been wondering where you've been. You better run home now." Molly made a shooing motion with her hand. "Off you go!"

"You've got a nice butt—oh wait, that's your face!" Steph said. She thought for a moment. With unmasked bitterness, she asked the imaginary guy, "Who do you think you are to come crawling back here after all you've done to me and the kids?"

After a respectful moment of silence, Lyra pretended to dodge something. "Where are all these bats coming from? Did it hurt when you crawled out of hell?"

The three of them burst out laughing then returned to work, enlightened and refreshed.

CHAPTER 15
When Yeast Expected or No More Ms Macchiato

Mr. Haskill was standing outside the door of the bakery, quietly this time, waiting for Molly to appear and open for business.

"Oh no," said Molly to Lyra. "He's back. Call Phil for me and make sure he's on his way over, will you?"

"You got it, Molly." With growing trepidation, she called Phil, then reported to Molly that he was already on his way.

"Good morning, Mr. Haskill," Molly said, unlocking the door.

"Good morning, Molly. Please call me Neil," he said stepping inside.

"Listen, Mr. Haskill, I've given your offer a lot of thought and talked it over with my boyfriend—oh, here he comes now."

Phil jingled the bell over the door extra loudly.

"Phil, I was just telling Mr. Haskill here that we've thought about his offer, but the answer is still no." With hands on hips, she faced the Canterbury Heights businessman. "Thank you for your generous offer, but I won't be selling."

"You drive a hard bargain, Ms. Tauber. What will it take for you to walk away from this place a wealthy woman? Is it having a position in the wedding conglomerate? Is it more money? Whatever it is, I can make it happen. You see, my wife has always wanted a business of her own, but planning weddings is not enough. She wants the whole, all-inclusive package under her control. We need this bakery. It's the missing jewel in her crown, and she *will* have it. And you, sir." He turned to Phil. "If you were her husband, you would understand how important your wife's dreams are. What is your dream, Ms. Tauber?"

"For you to leave now. I'm *not* selling."

"Everyone has their price. New home? Security? College education for your future children? Name your price."

"I think we're done here." Phil stepped forward. "The lady said no."

"Before I go, let me give you my last offer." Again he wrote down a sum, folded it in quarters, and placed it gently on the table with his business card, and walked to the door. "You have my card. I'll give you two days to think it over." And he was gone without a backward glance.

"Good riddance," Molly muttered. "Thanks for stepping in, Phil. That man scares me."

"You gonna look at his offer?" Phil asked.

"No. As far as I'm concerned it's a closed matter."

"Okay if I look?" Phil's curiosity was piqued.

"Go ahead." She crossed her arms tightly and looked away.

Phil unfolded the paper. "Molly, you'd better sit down. He just doubled his offer."

"Phil, my bakery isn't worth a tenth of what he's offered. Why does he want it so badly?" Molly ignored the menu sitting on top of their table at Clyde's Fine Dining that evening.

"Desperation, I think. My guess is that his shrew of a wife wants what she wants, and he wouldn't dare deny her. She's quite a bit younger than him and a whole lot better looking. She might just be in the market for another sugar daddy if he doesn't come through."

"The question remains. What am I supposed to do?" She found herself wringing her linen napkin. She was oblivious to their observers, the Petersons and the McCrearys, at their usual Friday night table for four.

The Misters cast pleading gazes to heaven and shook their heads as their Misuses settled in for an evening of people-watching and eavesdropping.

"Look at the way she's handling that napkin. Death in the family?" Betsy surmised.

"No, River Oaks is the only family she has," Maggie responded knowingly.

"He lost his job?" Betsy tried again.

"I don't think so. He's not the one who's flustered."

"Cheating's out of the question," Betsy stated fiercely.

"Absolutely," Maggie concurred.

"A break up, maybe?" Betsy wondered.

"Shhh...did she say, 'smell the brisket?'" asked Maggie.

"I thought it was something like, 'smell the bee's wax.' No, I think it's, 'smell the picnic.' I don't recall seeing either one of them with a picnic basket in ages. Not that I would notice, of course," Betsy said.

"Of course not," their husbands chorused. At this rate they'd never finish planning their deep sea fishing cruise away from their wives, a much-needed escape about now.

"If you piped down, you might just find out that she's selling the business. At least that's what I overheard Lyra talking to Dorian about the other day." Sam sat up tall, proud of his newfound sleuthing skills and relishing Maggie's envy.

"Selling the business?" the women hissed in harmony, looking over at Molly who hadn't reacted to their whispered outburst.

"She can't be going broke," Maggie said. "The shop's as busy as it's ever been—busier, in fact, since the folks from Canterbury Heights discovered it. Maybe it's too much for her. I guess I could pitch in a couple days a week. Then we'd really know what's going on around here. And since I worked for her parents for so many years before I retired I could step right in and help. Poor dear, it must be just too much for her, even with Lyra and Stephanie's help."

"Good idea," Betsy said. "I could offer to help too."

"Wait, they're ordering; we don't want to miss something," Maggie said.

The husbands, completely fed up with their gossiping wives, decided to play their hand. "Look Sam, he's picked up a piece of bread!" Bob gasped.

"And it's sourdough! What do you think that's all about? Look, now he's chewing with the left side of his mouth. Three, four, five times," Bob exclaimed softly. "What could this mean?"

"Well, I heard from Dr. Pullemout's cousin's niece that he just had a temporary crown put on his right lower bicuspid," Sam divulged.

"No!" Bob put his hands over his mouth in mock horror.

"Now you boys stop this. You're ruining our dinner, and we haven't been able to hear a word of their conversation," Betsy whined.

"But wait, there's more," Bob hushed his wife. "Did you hear her say she needs...a diamond?"

"Why yes, Bob. I think she did," Sam said. "And he told her he'd have to buy a box of Cracker Jacks and hope for the best."

189

"What's that? He says he wants to honeymoon in the Kalahari Desert?" Bob went on.

"She says that's fine as long as he brings his Tinker Toys and rock collection," Sam's eyes gleamed.

Both men could contain themselves no longer and burst out guffawing.

"Next week we girls are getting our own table." Betsy slapped Bob on the arm.

Molly didn't eat much of her chicken marsala. She slid the food around on her plate listlessly. "What should I do, Phil? I need your help. This is our future we're talking about here."

"Have you prayed about it?"

"Yes," she replied.

"Have you gotten alone, cleared your mind, and really listened? That's my advice."

"Phil, you're not helping. I need you to tell me what *you* think I should do here."

Phil put his hands up. "I can't tell you what to do. This is your decision, and I will support you either way."

"I'm thinking about taking the money. Is that so wrong?"

"No," Phil said softly, taking her hand across the table. "You do what you think is right. Why don't you take tomorrow off and spend some alone time thinking it over. Maybe go talk to Pastor Joe."

She abandoned her half-hearted pursuit of the cold chicken on her plate and looked up. "And there's just one of the many reasons I love you, Phil. You're right. I need to talk to Joe."

Phil saw the first smile he'd seen all week on Molly's sweet face as she squeezed his hand.

Pastor Joe leaned back in his chair, the back of his head resting in his hands. "So let me get this straight. This man from the other side of the lake wants to give you a ridiculous sum of money in exchange for your bakery, and you're asking my advice? My question to you is why do you want to keep the bakery?"

"I...uh..."

Pastor Joe waited, focusing on the watercolor print of a German brown trout which was studying a fishing fly with interest. As usual, the fisherman's patience worked its magic. Joe knew that most people can't stand the tension that silence brings in a conversation. He could easily wait her out.

Eventually she spoke, "Molly's Sunshine Bakery has been at the heart of this town for generations. We've been part of all the weddings, parties, funerals, holidays, and everyday celebrations in River Oaks. I guess I like being part of that, carrying on the tradition. I love the work—the art and science of making that perfect eclair..."

"And coconut cream pie," Joe interjected.

Molly smiled. "Yeah, especially those."

"So what's the downside of your most noble profession?" Joe asked, still thinking about pie.

"The hours," she said without hesitation. "I'm on a different schedule than most people. It's not so important with Phil. Being self-employed he works his own hours. But if we get married and have kids, well, it'll get complicated."

"How did your mom manage?"

"I've been wondering that myself. Even with Maggie McCreary's help, Mom was in the bakery a lot. I'd walk to the bakery every day after school with my friends. Mom'd always have milk and cookies for us. My friends thought I was the luckiest kid in school." She studied her fingernails, looked up and smiled. "Even at work, no matter how tired she was, she always had time for me. I guess that's why I felt pretty lucky. And proud too."

"Is there anything you'd change about your childhood? How you were raised?"

"It would've been nice if Mom had been awake to tuck me in at night, to read me stories and say good night prayers with me, but she barely had time to kiss me goodnight before she conked out. And we didn't do much as a family except at the

LEAVING LYRA

bakery. We rarely went anywhere, and if we did, it was only for a couple days, and the folks were stressed out the whole time, worrying about the business. I didn't mind helping her at work, though. In fact, we had a lot of fun together in the kitchen. That's one thing I do look forward to with my kids someday."

"How do you feel about your children taking over the bakery eventually? Would you wish it on them?"

"I...I don't know. I guess it would depend on their personalities. It'd be hard for the kids if they love sports and the outdoors. Phil would be there for them, but I..." Tears glistened in her eyes. "I'd miss out on a lot."

Joe leaned forward, sunlight glinting off his rimless glasses. "If you hadn't had the offer to sell, would it have even occurred to you?"

Molly pondered for a moment. "No, I don't think so."

"So what has you considering it now? Besides your baker's schedule, is money an issue?"

"Phil makes plenty of money. We wouldn't need a second income," she said defensively.

Joe rested his chin on steepled fingers. "So what is it you don't like about affluence?"

More than a bit shocked at his question, Molly answered deliberately, "Nothing—but I mean, I wouldn't want a change in lifestyle, surrounded and owned by things, caring about stuff instead of people, or thinking I'm better than anyone else. Money often changes people," she completed her rant.

"Phil comes from a wealthy family. Does that bother you?"

Molly looked down at the coffee stains on Joe's desk. "It did. At first. Until I got to know them."

"And where's Phil in this picture anyway?"

"He's not giving advice one way or another."

"Good man, but how do you think your decision will affect him?"

"I think he'll be fine either way. He just wants to see me happy."

"And what makes you happy, Molly?"

"People. People make me happy."

"And how would you feel seeing the place gutted and remodeled and owned by the Haskills, catering to people like themselves?"

Molly's eyes misted. "You really want that pie, don't you?"

"We've covered a lot of ground here." Smiling, Joe rose and stretched his back. "I only have one more question for you."

"What? All questions and no advice?" Molly stood, miffed at his elusiveness.

"My advice: listen to your life, Molly." He grinned. "You already have the answer."

Molly gave a grumbly sigh. "So what question have you been saving for last? It'd better be good."

"If you decide to sell...can I have your recipe for coconut cream pie?"

"Men!" Molly growled as she stomped out of the office.

Molly left Joe's office and headed for the dock on the lake where she had taken life's questions over the years. She brought out her cell phone and did what her parents had taught her to do. She composed two lists, one for and one against selling. Unfortunately, both were equally compelling. She shrugged. "A lot of good that did me!" she said aloud, stuffing her phone into her pocket. "I'll get an answer out of Phil even if I have to withhold his apple fritters for a week and put truth serum in his coffee. Somebody's gotta help me, and it should be him, doggone it!"

As she got to her feet, she caught her shoe's heel between two loose boards. She shook her foot loose. "You're not a bit of help either," she scolded the weathered wood.

Just then her cell phone proved its usefulness. "Denisie?" Molly practically shouted. "Where have you been? I've been trying to reach you!"

"Something happened with the phone service. I was without a phone for a couple days. What happened? You sound frantic."

"Well, I am!" Molly proceeded to explain the situation, grumbling that no one seemed disposed to give her any answers.

"Remember going to the bakery after school?" Denise recalled. "How warm and welcoming it was? How your mom always took the time to ask about our days and really listen?"

"Do you remember her looking tired?" Molly asked pointedly.

"I can't say I do," Denise responded after a brief sweep of her memory banks. "Do you?"

"If she was, she never showed it. But when she got home she was pretty much done. I want to be that milk-and-cookies mom and work too."

"If you'll pardon the pun, it sounds like you want to sell your cake and eat it too."

Molly groaned. "Not only is it a terrible pun, but it's no help at all! I expected better from you," she said, more than half serious.

"Look, there's no one who's going to be more impacted by your decision than Phil. Talk it over with him."

"I tried that. No one's willing to help me." Molly tried to drive the drama from her voice, but Denise had known her for too long.

"Talk to him again, Molly. He's a smart guy. You'll figure this out together."

"Tried that."

"Try again," Denise insisted. "Recess is over. I've got to go get my class now. Keep me posted." Denise signed off before Molly could resume her whining.

Molly pushed her shoulders back. "Okay, Phil. No more Missy Nice Gal. I'll get the truth out of you, so look out." Avoiding the treacherous loose boards, she stepped from the dock and up the bank, then marched down the sidewalk around the lake. Her tortured mind devised strategies for overcoming Phil's reticence and just as quickly discarding them as manipulative, counterproductive, or illegal. It was in this tormented state that she pounded on Phil's door, ready to hash it out.

Phil opened the door. "Molly, are you okay?"

She strode past him into the living room. "How can I possibly be okay when I have this huge decision to face *on my own?*"

"You're not alone, Molly." He laid his hand on her shoulder.

"Well, you all have a funny way of showing it—you and Pastor Joe and Denise. You just throw it back in my face. You call that helping?"

"You're not alone," he repeated. "There's Someone Who holds the future in His hands, Who knows the outcome of your every decision. Have you *really* picked His brain yet?"

Molly studied her dusty shoes. "No, I guess I haven't listened. Not really."

"Go after Him. He has the answers you need." He hugged her then held her at arm's length, smiling. "Go get Him, Muffin, and tell me what He says."

Stunned, Molly shuffled from Phil's living room to his porch. She turned to see him nerdily waving at her. How she loved that man! He gave her the best advice she'd had all day. How could she have missed it? Without Phil she probably would have.

Back at home, Molly finally followed Phil's advice and collapsed to her knees at her bedside. "Okay Lord, I'm listening." She knelt in silence.

Her fate decided, Molly hurried to the bakery.

Her resolute steps drew Stephanie's and Lyra's attention. Dreading the news, yet wanting the waiting to be over with, they silently followed her to the work room.

"What is it, Molly? Have you decided?" Lyra dared to break the silence.

"Do you two want to be bakers?" Molly asked.

"I love working here." Lyra's voice caught a little.

"Me too," Steph said in a small voice.

"Then bakers you shall be," Molly said with a flourish.

"Does that mean you're keeping the bakery?" Lyra's eyes sparkled with hope.

LEAVING LYRA

"I'm keeping it all right, and when the time comes for having kids, I'll turn more of the work over to you two with a sizable raise for each of you. If this works, and I have it on good Authority it will, you can count on careers with good pay, the town will still have Molly's Sunshine Bakery done right, and I'll have time for a family. Everybody wins!

A flurry of hugs and high-fives sealed the deal along with more than a few tears of relief.

CHAPTER 16
Getting Carawayed

"Well, I guess that's it." Dorian folded an official-looking paper and tucked it back in its envelope with a sigh.

Lyra had been sitting with him at his favorite table at Molly's Sunshine Bakery where he was going through his mail. She guessed it hadn't been attended to in quite some time based on the volume of ads and credit card applications that towered off to one side. "What is it?" she asked gently, having noted the address of a law firm on the envelope.

"My marriage—it's done. Officially." He stared at the envelope in his hand.

"Do you want to talk about it?" she asked.

"Not much to tell, actually. Married my beautiful Brittney who later believed an awful lie about me, and she just walked away. I'm left with my reputation at risk if I so much as make myself visible in the Christian music scene. That was a stipulation of them dropping the false charges against me."

"Does that seem a bit suspicious to you?" Lyra asked.

"Doesn't matter much, does it? Everything about my life is over. I don't have any skills except for playing music. I'm back in college now, but I don't know what for, other than to make my parents happy."

"Then what about rebuilding your life? Every time I left a foster home I had to start over. Sooner or later, it'll land you someplace good. At least it did for me. Eventually."

Eager to turn the conversation elsewhere, Dorian asked something that had been on his mind for quite awhile. "Lyra, where'd you come from? I mean, how come you showed up here in River Oaks with nothing but a car and a backpack? And why all the foster homes? Are you running from somewhere—or someone?"

Lyra looked to one side and then the other. Finding the bakery empty, she began hesitantly, "My father is a horrible, violent, abusive man. Unfortunately, he's also a highly respected judge. I was about to try getting help through Child Protective Services, but before I could, he had me sent to a mental hospital in his attempt to discredit me and shut me up. No one believed me. The foster homes weren't much better after that, but they were a whole lot easier to escape from. Now that I'm eighteen, I'm my own woman. I just pray I don't ever see my father again. Even though he made me look like a liar, I'm still a threat to him, and there's no telling what he'd do to shut me up."

Dorian felt a chill course through his body. He took her hand and squeezed it. "So you know what it's like to be lied about. I'm sorry, Lyra, I really am."

"Well, I finally took the big leap and adopted Catzo," Lyra announced to Molly while Phil listened in.

"That's wonderful news, Lyra!" Molly said. "You've worked hard and you deserve it, and so does Catzo," she added with a smile.

Lyra beamed. Working at the bakery had given her enough of an income to provide for a pet on her own, to be Catzo's caregiver for life. She smiled, thinking of the frisky kitten and the special tuna casserole they would share in celebration tonight.

"Oh, Lyra, I almost forgot," Phil said as Lyra donned her apron. "If you want my old desk and chair, they're all yours. I'm sure Dorian wouldn't mind delivering it after work."

Dorian looked up from his studying. "I don't mind at all."

"It would be really useful for my studies," Lyra said. "Oh thanks, Phil. I'll take you up on that. See you after work then?" She awaited Dorian's nod before ducking into the kitchen where Molly had started working her culinary magic.

Lyra was looking forward to having a desk, especially with all the books and assignments she'd have to keep track of as she continued her studies in the veterinary field, the culmination of a lifetime love of animals. Not that she wasn't also grateful for her couch and card table. It would just be nice to have an area set aside for her studies.

Dorian was waiting with the desk at Lyra's front door at the end of her shift, his face in an inexplicable grin. It felt good helping her pursue her dream. Studying would be so much easier from a desk than from the couch or overused card table. He admired her drive and her intelligence. Lyra would make one heck of a vet assistant.

She met his smile with one of her own.

It hadn't occurred to either of them that Catzo would see the intruding furniture as an excuse to escape her confines and play amongst the butterflies in Mrs. McCreary's black-eyed Susans; neither had they considered that the kitten might have followed them to the street. By the time Lyra realized it, she was too late to prevent the rambunctious kitten from darting in front of an oncoming Chrysler. As such things happen, the realization dawned in slow motion, and Lyra could only watch in horror as her little friend was struck and flung to the sidewalk as the car sped away.

Dorian could see that Catzo was in dire need. "Quick Lyra, get in my car. I'll drive you to the vet's."

She tenderly scooped up Catzo and sat in Dorian's car. Catzo cried out with every bump in the road, breaking Lyra's heart a bit more each time. "I'm sorry, Catzo," she sobbed. "I should never have let you out of my sight." Lyra longed to hold her close, but there were too many broken parts, so she just cried. Thinking of Catalina, Dorian glanced over at his passengers, his own eyes filling with tears. He sped up, only to see the telltale red and blue lights of a police car in pursuit. He pulled over reluctantly.

Officer Morrison assessed the scene instantly. "You, follow me. I'll get you to the vet's office. We'll talk about speeding and seat belts later."

Dorian shooed away curious dogs as he led Lyra to the front desk. One look at the vet assistant drained whatever hope remained in his heart. Lyra was about to lose her dear friend. Again his thoughts turned to Catalina, how he'd poured his heart out to her, how she always listened, never judged. Lyra would be needing a friend like that, real soon. He glanced over at her. Lyra was clearly in shock, barely registering her surroundings as Catzo was rushed off to Xray.

"I'm not sure we can save her," the vet said. "Treatment would cost a small fortune." He handed her an estimate. "And she'd need a great deal of aftercare. I hate to say that I recommend we put her down."

"I can't afford it," Lyra said in a shallow voice. "I can't even give her a chance."

The vet's words and Lyra's response raced like rapids over the stone of Dorian's heart, wearing it down once and for all. Dorian was holding it together, knowing he would have to get Lyra safely home before falling apart himself. "I've got this, Lyra," Dorian said. "See what you can do to save her," Dorian said.

"I can't make any promises," the vet replied, turning quickly and exiting to attempt the seemingly impossible.

Dorian paid with his credit card at the counter. He led Lyra and her thin thread of hope out to the car, unaware of how the waiting room hushed in respect as they passed through. On the windshield was a note from Officer Morrison that read:

1. Wear your seat belts.

2. Mind the speed limit.

3. I hope you got there in time.

Lyra, the capable, upbeat epitome of a strong young woman, sat beside Dorian in the car in tears, utterly broken, desolate.

Dorian knew it was time for him to take charge. "We're not giving up, Lyra. She's not giving up either." He pulled out of the parking lot.

"It's all my fault," she cried into her bloodied hands.

"It was an accident." His words fell on dulled ears. He pulled the car over, leaned across the front seat, and enveloped her in a lengthy hug. "It's okay, Lyra. Don't hold back. We'll get through this," Dorian soothed, "no matter what."

After she regained some composure, he drove her home and let the McCrearys know about the accident. He told them to expect a call from the vet. Next, he stopped at the bakery, letting Molly know why Lyra might not be at work for the next couple days. Finally he drove to church, spoke to Pastor Vicente, then hid himself away in the loft, and prayed fervently for his best friend and her Catzo.

Dorian spent the rest of the day with Lyra, just being there. It was late when he arrived home. The lights were out; Uncle Phil was no doubt sleeping off a night of video games.

Alerted by the sound of his car, Catalina was at the door, mewing a soft greeting. With a grateful heart, he scooped her up and felt her forehead press into his. He wondered if the contact enabled her to read his mind. He hurried to the kitchen to give her a midnight snack, which she ignored, preferring a place on his lap in Uncle Phil's recliner.

Dorian sat there for a long time in the dark, trying to make sense of a senseless accident that had left a sweet and caring young woman so terribly alone and a joyous little kitten so pitifully injured. He relived leaving Lyra at the cottage. It was so stark. She had so little. It wasn't fair. He left her there all cried out, completely empty. *How could I have left her there all alone?*

He had spent a lot of time trying to convince her that accidents happen to the innocent as well as the guilty. At least that's what he'd learned in Sunday school. When she failed to respond, he gave up and concentrated on holding his own emotions in check as he held her hand, being strong for her. Now, at home alone and under the cover of darkness, he felt tears rising to the surface.

Phil heard the unfamiliar sound. Molly had told him about Catzo. He took heart. For the first time since Dorian's arrival, Phil saw his nephew, once so absorbed in his own pain, caring deeply for another.

Early the following morning, Maggie McCreary sat at her white wrought iron table on the patio, watching Lyra's cottage for signs of life.

Her husband came and sat down next to her. He reached for a steaming hot cinnamon roll poised on the ornate platter in the middle of the table. He took a bite. Just the right snap of cinnamon. His Maggie could have opened her own bakery shop. But her devotion to the Taubers was even more admirable. He followed her gaze. "Took it pretty hard, did she? You'd think she'd lost family."

Maggie stirred her tea slowly, watching the milk swirl. "Well, she hasn't lost her yet. From the look of things, though, that kitten is the only family she has. I pray that the poor little thing makes it." Maggie rose, resolute. "Let's see if I can convince Lyra to eat." Gathering her as-yet-unused plate and a couple pastries, Maggie followed the big daisy beds to the cluster of recently replanted moonbeam coreopsis that covered the bare patch by the cottage door. The ferny leaves were a bit limp, but coreopsis are a hardy lot and they would surely perk up. As she paused to inspect the transplant, she remembered her own barrenness. She'd lost a child, barely larger than Lyra's kitten when she'd miscarried. Her home had always seemed too large after Clara. No one seemed to understand the terrible loss she felt, not even her husband. Well wishers would mutter assurances. "There must have been something wrong with it," "It's probably for the best," and "You're still young. God'll give you another baby." Well, He never did, and even if He had, it would not have been her little Clara.

LEAVING LYRA

It was with a sense of her own personal grief that she approached the cottage and knocked. Hearing muffled crying, she tried the door and found it unlocked. "Lyra," she called, "Can I come in?" Hearing no objections, she opened the door to the mournful scene. Lyra was seated on the floor, balled up against a wall in the dim room which was scattered with an assortment of cat toys.

Maggie set down the plate and rushed to Lyra's side and knelt beside her. "I'm so sorry," she said. Maggie did not try to explain Lyra's pain away, offer false hope, or accuse or excuse God. She didn't tell the girl not to feel bad, and never used the words, "just a cat." She simply knelt there, gently rubbing Lyra's back until her arthritic knees informed her that if she didn't arise soon, there would be no walking today. "Lyra—my knees. I can't get up."

Lyra stood and helped Maggie to her feet. "Are you okay?" she asked haltingly.

"I'm going to need some help walking, Dear, if you don't mind getting me back to the Mister at the patio table." She whispered. "Thank you for helping me up, Lyra. I'm not sure he can get me off the ground anymore with his bad back. Don't tell him I said so. You know how men are."

Lyra saw the warm exchange as Maggie's eyes met Sam's, and her heart lurched. Lyra knew true love when she saw it. She longed for it, grieved and hungered for it. She guided

Maggie to her seat where the old woman's legs promptly gave out. Lyra steadied her as Sam looked on with concern.

"Are you all right, Mags?" he asked.

"Just overdid it a bit, I'm afraid."

Lyra could see Maggie's smile was strained. So could Sam.

"Lyra, Dear, could you sit with us a while? It might take the two of you to get me back in the house." She patted Lyra's hand. "And please do me the honor of sampling a couple of my cinnamon rolls. I've got milk in the fridge if you'd like."

Lyra sat with the McCrearys, keeping careful watch over her landlady. Lyra had never met anyone with bad arthritis, but she had met an elderly dog, Hero, who'd suffered untreated for longer than he should have been allowed to, at one of her old foster homes. That was when she had decided she'd be a veterinary assistant, to make a difference. Now she wasn't so sure she could handle it.

"See that Shasta daisy over there?" In an attempt to divert Lyra's attention, Maggie pointed to an enormous clump of classic white flowers with bright yellow centers. "You and I will be dividing it up this winter and putting it behind the coneflowers. And wait 'til you see what I have planned for around the sundial."

Lyra blinked. Maggie was assuming that Lyra would stay. But, of course, her landlady needed Lyra's strong, young knees. Still, it sounded as if Lyra was…wanted.

Catzo's recovery was just as expensive and arduous as the vet had warned. Her jaw had been broken in front and was wired back together at the chin. She was enjoying her diet of soft canned foods, though even they proved challenging to eat. Dorian offered to take care of the little tabby in between his classes while Lyra was at work. He was impressed with the kitten's determination to return to her playful ways, even with the loss of her right front leg. She had beaten the odds.

Dorian had just received the credit card bill for the veterinary care. He knew he had to pay it off before the interest ate him alive. It was then he decided he would sell his Rolex and his priceless custom guitar.

CHAPTER 17
Loafing on the Dock

"Gabriela's birthday is next month," Lyra informed Dorian. She waved good-bye as the forever-child lumbered, peppered with sprinkles, from the bakery with her parents, Pastor Vicente and Esperanza Hernandez.

"How old will she be?"

"Fifteen..." Lyra brought a finger to her lips. "Hmm..." She left Dorian wondering what she was up to as she headed for the room where Molly was coaxing some clingy raspberry jam-filled cookies from their sheets.

Lyra explained her idea.

Molly grinned. "It's short notice, but, with a little help, I think we can pull this off. She'll love it—especially if there are sprinkles involved." The last of the cookies gave up with reluctance. "Too much jam," Molly confessed. "I guess I've been a little distracted lately."

"Don't worry, I'll do all the planning," Lyra said with a wink. She headed back to Dorian for the grand announcement.

"Okay, so you got Molly to make a cake for Gabriela. That's cool," he said as he finished his maple bar and slurped down his coffee.

"Oh, but that's just the start. Have you ever heard of a quinceañera?"

You mean that big party for Hispanic girls? Yeah, our last maid, Maria Elena's daughter had one of those. Set her folks back a few paychecks, that's for sure. There's no way Pastor Vicente and Esperanza can afford something like that."

"No, they can't. But if we all work together and pool our resources, we can get it done and make it a surprise for Gabi."

"What about her dress? They cost a fortune."

"Your mom showed me the coolest thrift store. I was there just last week. They were practically giving away a prom dress that would really look beautiful on Gabi. I'd just have to hem it."

Dorian did not question, as he once might have, whether it would be worth it to go to the trouble for someone with Down Syndrome, who would never embrace the entry into adulthood that the celebration symbolized. Dorian volunteered, "Maybe you and I could work out some music. As I recall, music was a big deal for Emilia's event. We may not be mariachis, but you know plenty of songs in Spanish, and maybe we could even write one for the occasion."

Lyra gave him a smile so sweet, he had to blink a couple times before he could manage to smile back.

"I write best when I'm outside," Lyra said. "When I'm done with work, maybe we could grab your impressive guitar and go for a walk?"

"Uh, I decided an economy model would work just as well."

"What does that mean?" Lyra questioned.

"Like, I, uh, didn't need that fancy guitar anymore."

"Dorian, is there something you're not telling me?"

"I don't need it. I figured I'd put the money to better use."

"Like?"

"I...uh..."

"Dorian, did you sell your guitar to pay Catzo's vet bill?" Her eyes opened wide, incredulous.

He turned his head away.

"Dorian, look at me. Look at me!"

"I did it 'cause I care. I care about you, okay? I care about Catzo. That guitar's just a part of my old life. It's not who I am anymore. You're more important than that old guitar."

"I can't believe you did that! We've got to get it back. I'll repay you every penny. It may take a while, but I..." She brought her hand to her mouth, trying to hold back imminent tears.

He wrapped his arms around her and let her cry. "You're worth it, Lyra. You really are."

LEAVING LYRA

Whether it was the light in her eyes or the prospect of writing again, Dorian's heart beat in double time as he accompanied Lyra to her house to get her guitar.

"I know this great little dock not far from here that no one uses," she said. "It has a great view and it's really quiet there except for the red-winged blackbirds when they're nesting in the cattails. They can get pretty rowdy." She gave Catzo a quick nose rub, picked up her guitar and notepad from the couch, and headed out the door.

As they walked toward the lake, Dorian noticed the way Lyra held her instrument. She carried it with a reverence that comes from having next to nothing. He thought about his one-of-a-kind guitar with its elaborate mother-of-pearl inlays. It had been his companion on stage and off. He'd kept it as a symbol of hope, hope that things could go back to the way they were, when he was somebody with something to offer. In relinquishing it, he had given hope to his friend—his best friend.

The spot was every bit as pleasant as Lyra had described, though its boards creaked threats beneath her weight. Before long, the two had come up with a simple melody. While Lyra pondered over the words, he strummed the guitar softly and hummed the tune to himself. The nylon strings were easy on his fingertips. As he began fingerpicking, music flowed from his hands in ways he had almost forgotten. He closed his eyes and continued to play, like the little drummer boy of old, an offering to his one and only King, the God Who had seen him through the toughest months of his life. When he opened his eyes, it was getting dark.

"I guess we'd better go. I can barely see what I've written," Lyra said.

"Come over to my place," he offered, "I'll bring out my new econo guitar and we can, like, jam for a while."

The protesting boards on the dock made good on their threat, buckling under Lyra's foot, trapping her shoe and irretrievably devouring it along with her pen.

"Lyra, are you okay?"

"Sure," she said, pulling her foot out of the hole. 'It's just a bruise. Happens all the time." She forced a laugh. "I've gotten used to it."

"It's a long walk to my house in just one shoe. I'll go get my car and pick you up."

Recognizing that she'd be on her feet all day tomorrow, she accepted his offer. It seemed her feet were always sore, and a barefoot stroll could prove disastrous.

Dorian sat at Phil's kitchen table, watching Lyra as she put the finishing touches on Gabriela's birthday song. Here she was, just Lyra. And here he was, just watching. Lyra was a big girl, that fact was undeniable, although she was losing weight from her frequent trips to the gym. Her face was wide and her eyebrows unplucked. Her brown hair was straight, parted on the left. Definitely in need of a trim.

But her eyes were remarkable—deep shades of brown with a generous dash of green. She turned them on Dorian, startling him. "I think I've just about got the final verse." She paused. "You okay?"

Dorian nodded and took a swig of Dr. Pepper. "Let's hear it." He cleared his throat.

She lifted her sweet voice:

"Little star, how bright you shine,
Your smile will light our way,
Remind us of what is pure and good.
When you laugh, the angels play.

"Angel from birth,
God's message of love
Where imperfect words always fail.
You live love, you teach love,
And in you we reach love.
We're humbled by the words that you pray."

"It's beautiful, Lyra." It was hard to believe that he had ever been weirded out by Gabriela. She was everything they would be singing about her—an angel, a message, a teacher. He had come to see Gabi through Lyra's eyes, those incredible eyes that always seemed to see the best in people. For a moment he wondered how Lyra viewed him. The term, "small-minded," arose from his conscience. Small-minded and selfish. Surely she'd see him more charitably than that.

"Seriously, Dorian, are you all right?"

He smiled sheepishly. "Just tired, I guess. That was one heck of a midterm this morning."

Catalina waltzed into the kitchen, her plumed tail swaying back and forth at the tip as if touched by the faintest breeze, her banner of welcome. She greeted Dorian's fingers with the air of a dignitary shaking hands as she sat down, facing him.

He buried his hand in her luxurious coat while she purred up at him with contented, half-closed eyes.

Unlike Catzo, who instantly befriended everyone, Catalina reserved her affection for Dorian alone.

Lyra was grateful to have played a role in Dorian and Catalina's coming together. She already saw changes in both. Neither of them were brooding anymore. In fact, Dorian was proving to be almost as goofy as his Uncle Phil, and Catalina had even begun playing in the cat tunnel Dorian had bought her. Lyra was also grateful for where God had taken her these past few months. Yes, life was good.

LEAVING LYRA

It was Lyra's lunch break at the bakery. With a slice of oatmeal walnut toast in hand, she settled into a chair to wait for Dorian. She couldn't help but notice Phil and Molly sitting at a back table. They had been dating for some time now and were like lovestruck teenagers.

Phil slid his hand across the table and covered Molly's hand with his.

Molly said something only Phil could hear. They both chuckled.

Lyra was very happy for them, but seeing Molly and Phil together left her feeling lonely. After all, who would ever look at her like Phil looked at Molly?

Dorian heaved his backpack onto Lyra's table, startling her. "You didn't forget about our Spanish tutoring lesson, did you?"

"Uh, no, I didn't. Well, maybe just a little." She grinned at him. "I guess I got distracted. Look at those two." Lyra sighed. "I guess I'm a romantic at heart."

"Being around the two of them would make a cyborg feel romantic," he said with a grin.

"Yeah, well, I've got a half hour, so let's get to it."

In their discussion of imperfect, subjunctive, and preterite tenses, they both found it hard to concentrate. "Maybe we should finish this tonight at my place," suggested Dorian. "I have a package of all-beef hotdogs that are still good. I think Uncle Phil left some hot dog buns. I could even toast them."

Lyra couldn't resist his boyishness. "But do you have relish?"

"I wouldn't have invited you if I didn't. I know better than that. I don't know what you see in that slimy green stuff."

"I'll have you know it's comprised of small, crisp pickle bits. No slime whatsoever."

"Yeah, whatever." He elbowed her. "So ya coming or not? Por favor?" There went those eyes of his, crinkling again.

"How could I turn down such a compelling offer?" She added her smile to the mix. "What with the relish and all." *Not to mention*, she told herself, *those dark eyes that my heart relishes.*

"I guess I should let you get back to work." He lingered nonetheless, looking uncertain, backpack slung over his shoulder.

She stood, equally awkward, uncertain of what would happen next.

Dorian gave her a one-armed hug while a smile dawned on Lyra's face.

"Yeah, well, see ya tonight," she said.

"I'll be there." *Stupid*, he admonished himself. *Of course I'll be there. I live there, remember?* He sure seemed to be saying an awful lot of dumb things lately, especially around Lyra. Dorian headed out the door and turned to wave just in case she might be watching.

She was.

He waved like a dork.

Molly leaned into Phil. "Aren't they cute?" she whispered. "I wonder how long it will take them to figure it out." They shared a knowing smile.

With a flourish, Dorian lifted the lid to the pot on the stove in which four hotdogs simmered. "Las perras calientes!" he announced, jabbing each unceremoniously with a fork and slapping them down, two on each plate.

"I hope you have no idea what you just said," Lyra chuckled. "You just called them hot ladies of the night. Ever thought of being a famous chef as well as a linguist?" she inquired.

"Nope," was as nonchalant reply.

"Good!" she said. "The holes you left in those poor doggies are nothing short of barbaric."

"And I suppose you could do better?" he challenged.

Lyra picked up a set of tongs near the sink and snapped them at his nose. "Tongs," she said simply.

How can she make tongs sound witty? he wondered.

She started a demonstration of the proper way to apply relish and mustard to the toasted bun, complete with a stilted, nasally English accent that had him in stitches before she'd even finished her presentation.

Man, this is fun, he thought. A far cry from his life when he'd first come to River Oaks. And a far cry from the fame that had kept him continually concerned with appearances back home. He was free and he loved it.

"There was a mockingbird singing in Mrs. McCreary's loquat tree last night," Lyra told Dorian. "Out of season, but it sounded so silvery, I just had to write a song about it."

"Silvery?"

"Something shining in the dark like the moon, so sweet and pure. I love the way mockingbirds make up their songs with bits and pieces of other birds' tunes."

"But they make it their own. Like you do, Lyra, when you're up in the worship loft at church. Sure, the songs have been sung before, but not like you sing them. You're pretty silvery yourself. So are you going to play it for me or not?" Dorian asked.

"Okay, it's called 'Mockingbird' and it goes like this:

Midnight singer, rooftop song,
Pale gray voice on a darkened summer sky,
Moonlight could not contain your praises as you fly away
Into morning.
The trees and the sky awaken.

Bare-veined leaf, life-lace exposed in my hand,
No one told you the Hand that wove you
Was pierced in the heart of man.
He died and arose, winter into spring.

Rain-fed winter, polished stone,
Holy river, Jesus will take you home.
He will fill you, cleanse your shores.
Keep on flowing, you know His love is yours.
And you will overflow."

Dorian sat, silent, stricken by the beauty of her melody and each carefully painted word. It was the most beautiful thing he'd ever heard

"You okay, Dorian? It wasn't that bad, was it?" Her smile was the perfect finale.

"How? I mean, like, how did you write that, Lyra? I know you're great at toasting songs, but that was really amazing!"

"Remember the first time you ran into me at the park? The time you went swimming in your shorts and T-shirt? I was working on it back then. The rounded river rock, the worn-out leaves made their way into the song. It was just waiting for that mockingbird to come along to complete the picture."

"And the melody with all the fingerpicking, how did it all come together?" asked Dorian.

It's what God does when we give Him the little we have to offer. I'm just glad to be part of the process." She shrugged.

Several days later, Dorian found himself standing alone in the rain, aching for Lyra. *What just happened?* he asked himself. His thoughts were so full of her, and yet he felt so very alone, so terribly empty.

Just a moment ago they had been laughing, carefree, in the unexpected rain. They were slogging through the puddles together in the twilight as they returned from a walk to the lake for no reason in particular. Then it happened. She got a few steps ahead. He caught her arm impulsively and turned her around to face him. Their eyes met—unwavering. He reached up his hand to brush the rain-drenched hair from her face. "Lyra," he said softly, "I've been wanting to tell you..."

She took three steps back, turned, and ran.

He called for her to come back, but she was gone. Dorian puzzled over her disappearance. It had seemed so natural up until then, walking side by side. Something had changed in her eyes. Had she been for that moment not a friend but a woman?

Am I losing my mind? This is Lyra I'm thinking about for goodness' sake. Friendly, funny...fat...Lyra. He winced at that last thought as it made its appearance in his brain. *That's how everyone views her, isn't it? Good old fat Lyra.*

He lifted his head to the rain and felt the water as it ran down his body, leaving him inwardly changed. *I will no longer allow outward appearances to define someone,* he resolved.

Mrs. McCreary had been dozing in front of the television set when she was awakened by the sound of someone pounding on Lyra's door.

Mr. McCreary put down his paper and removed his reading glasses. "Sounds like someone's desperate to talk to our Lyra," he said. He cinched up his bathrobe, picked up a flashlight, and marched, slipper-clad, into the rain.

His flashlight illuminated a very wet and disheveled Dorian. "I don't know what I did," he explained. "Lyra..."

"We menfolk seldom do know what we're doing—at least that's how it looks through the eyes of a woman." He smiled. "Why don't you come in and dry off? Give Lyra time to compose herself. Maybe Maggie can offer a bit of her wisdom. In case you haven't noticed, my wife knows what makes people tick. She's got me all figured out anyway, along with most of the town."

"Uh, okay. Sure. Thanks." Dorian followed the flashlight's beam to the house where he was welcomed with hot chocolate, a dry towel, and listening ears.

Lyra peeked out the window. "Good. He's gone," she sniffled to Catzo. "Something happened when he touched me. I can't let him know. I'm scared, Catzo. I'm so scared." She buried her face in the warm, stripey coat and let the throaty purr soothe her. "He's my best friend. I don't want to lose him. If he knew how I feel, he wouldn't want to hang out with me anymore. I just can't let him know that I—I love him. There. I said it, Catzo. I love him."

The little tabby gave an encouraging nudge and set about drying Lyra's tears with her little pink tongue.

Journal Entry:

What just happened? Dorian and I were walking along just like always, it started raining, and then Dorian grabbed my arm and turned me around to face him. That look in his eyes. I was terrified. It's like he saw who I really am. I know it's not possible, but it felt like he wanted to kiss me. I don't understand. We're just friends, right? I feel like I misunderstood, and now I'm so embarrassed. He came pounding on my door, but I just couldn't answer. I can't face him right now. I'm so confused.

LEAVING LYRA

I'm seeking healing, Lord. I'm a lost lamb, crying out to You. My past is my future without Your help.

Reading Your Word tonight, I came across this scripture:

John 14:1 and 27.

"Don't let your hearts be troubled. Trust in God, and trust also in Me...

"I am leaving you with a gift—peace of mind and heart. And the peace I give is a gift the world cannot give. So don't be troubled or afraid."

"What would make her run?" Dorian asked the attentive Maggie. "One moment we're sogging along in the rain, and the next minute she gets this scared look on her face and runs away."

"So you say she looked afraid," Maggie prodded, warming to the mystery, enjoying herself immensely. "What happened just before that?"

"I caught her arm and was just going to brush the wet hair out of her face..."

"Well, I think that explains it. She must've thought you were making a romantic gesture, and that scared her off. I'd say if you want to stay friends then stay friends and forget about any boyfriend/girlfriend stuff."

Dorian found her advice disappointing. But after all, they were *just friends,* right

Neither made mention of the incident the following day at Molly's Sunshine Bakery. In fact, Lyra avoided his gaze. He'd been trying to catch her eye all morning and was determined to hang around until he did. He still had to know what it had meant to her when their eyes had met. He finally caught her attention before she quickly looked down to polish the display case for the fifth time.

"Hey, Lyra, I guess we had some kind of misunderstanding last night. I had no intention of scaring you off. We're still friends, aren't we?"

"I don't know what you're talking about," she said, scrubbing harder.

"Well, you just ran off and left me behind."

"But...but it was raining."

"I followed you and knocked on your door, and you never answered. Aren't we friends anymore?"

"Oh yeah, we're friends," she said flatly. "I gotta get back in the kitchen." She tightened up her apron and hurried off.

Stephanie came through the front door and hurried into her red apron. She was so sparkly these days with her job at the bakery and the stability it brought to her family, that she found herself singing happily away in the workroom.

Molly was delighted to have found such cheerful and reliable help, as her frequent outings with Phil had made it hard to keep up with her work even with Lyra and Steph's help. Molly considered herself blessed indeed.

"What's up with you and Dorian?" Stephanie asked. "Spill it, girlfriend."

"What do you mean?"

"Dorian's sitting out there looking all upset. Did you just have an argument or something?"

"What do you mean, upset?"

Stephanie crept to the curtained doorway and peeked out at Dorian. "Now he's got his head in his hands. "Either he has a really bad headache or you two have a problem. Which is it?"

"Maybe he just needs a caffeine fix," Lyra suggested lamely. "You know how a lack of coffee can do that to you."

"When are you going to admit it to yourself, Lyra?"

Lyra busied herself arranging a chocolate kiss on the exact center of each snickerdoodle on the waiting cookie sheet. "I don't know what you're talking about, Steph."

"I think you do," Molly barged in. "It's pretty obvious to just about everybody. He likes you. A lot."

"So what are you going to do about it?" Stephanie asked.

"Well, I thought I might start by finishing these cookies." She turned around, a chocolate kiss melting in her hand. "What makes you say that anyway?" Lyra said with forced casualness.

Molly crossed her arms and leaned against the wall. "Do you want a list in alphabetical order?"

"Well," Stephanie began, "you spend all your free time together. You're always laughing. You're both always talking about each other. He sold his prized possession to pay for your cat's vet bill, and you go on all those long walks by the lake. Seriously, can you picture your life without him?"

"And that wasn't even in alphabetical order," Molly said, uncrossing her arms.

CHAPTER 18
Toast of the Town

The Church of the Broken's plain interior had taken on a dazzling, festive ambience. Pink rosebud bouquets with flowing white ribbons, courtesy of Daryla's Floral Boutique, lined the central aisle of folding chairs. A table with a cake inundated with garish sprinkles surrounded by fifteen electric candles of varying heights, waited behind the humble podium.

As principal members of Gabriela's Court of Honor, Dorian and Lyra were dressed to the nines, Dorian in his only suit and Lyra in a flowered dress from the thrift store. Dorian looked over at her. Her unadorned hair framed her face in rich brown, and her eyes shone bright even without makeup. Her pink and green dress with gauzy, flowing sleeves made her look as if she might take flight. Lyra's frequent trips to the gym with Stephanie were showing outstanding results.

Lyra looked at him and smiled.

His heart had taken to racing whenever she did that. He smiled back, wiping his sweaty hands unceremoniously on his pants.

As they took their place in Gabriela's entourage, Dorian was aching to take Lyra's hand in spite of his clamminess, but heeding Mrs. McCreary's advice, he played it cool.

A young Mexican American couple and their two developmentally disabled girls from Gabi's school, resplendent in hot pink dresses, made up the rest of Gabriela's Court.

A church deacon announced Gabriela, her parents, and godparents, along with her attendants.

Gabriela's godparents placed a heart-shaped locket around her sturdy neck and a tiara on her head as she clapped joyfully. Pastor Vicente led his daughter to a seat at the table where brightly-wrapped gifts awaited her clumsy but eager hands.

When it came time for sparkling cider toasts, it seemed as if everyone in the congregation had a word to say about the birthday girl. She was obviously well-loved by all.

Dorian watched Gabriela enjoying her first dance with her father—more a rocking back and forth motion—but no one, including himself, saw it as less than beautiful, especially when he realized that Gabriela might never wear a wedding gown. This pink ruffled dress would be the closest she would come. But oh, how she shone in her father's arms.

Dorian and Lyra came forward to sing the song they'd composed for Gabriela, leaving more than a few of their listeners teary-eyed.

Gabriela's godmother then gave her a doll dressed just like Gabriela—the Last Doll, they called it—and her godfather gave her a pair of sparkly flat healed shoes to wear.

Dorian marveled at Lyra. This event was her doing; she had organized the whole thing. He felt proud, so proud to call her his friend. Recklessly, he put his hand on her shoulder, secure in the unlikelihood that she might bolt again in front of everyone. He was relieved to feel her leaning into him. As the next song began, a rolicsome gift of the local mariachi band, he took the plunge and asked her to dance and was quite surprised by her ability to polka. The ballroom dancing class he'd taken in preparation for his wedding didn't help much with folkloric dancing, but he found Lyra's steps pretty easy to follow. "How'd you...?" he began.

"Our maid, Estrella," Lyra replied. "She didn't just teach me Spanish. She made me a part of her culture. We were...family," she said wistfully.

"Well, now you have family here too."

The music abruptly changed to Spanish hymns. "I don't suppose she taught you to waltz," Dorian said, hopeful.

"Matter of fact, she didn't."

"Well, it just so happens that I can. You want to give it a try?"

"Sure. Why not?" came her response.

Lyra's heart fluttered as they danced. *So this is what it feels like to dance with someone you...love.* She didn't let the fact that she wasn't loved back get in the way. She'd learned to live in this make believe place she'd created for herself. *It may not be real, but it sure is fun...until he decides to dance with someone else.*

Sure enough, after their waltz ended, Dorian excused himself and left to seek another partner...the birthday girl.

It did Lyra's heart good to see them laughing together, to see Dorian whole. She could scarcely believe it when she saw Dorian turn down a dance offer from Gabriela's very attractive older cousin. His words, "No, thank you. I already have a dance partner," would be replayed in Lyra's fantasy realm for years to come.

He looked across the room. Their eyes met, and Lyra sent him a radiant smile. Their reverie was broken by Gabriela, who, determined to dance with each of her friends, asked Lyra to dance.

"Dorian's nice," Gabi said as she danced with Lyra. "He likes you. I can tell. Do you like him back?"

"Of course I like him. He's our good friend, Gabi." Lyra dodged the proverbial bullet.

Dorian watched, chuckling, as Lyra taught her a bouncy step that looked more like a basketball throw than a dance move. *Has life ever been this good?* The dance ended, and Gabi went off to dance with one of her attendants.

Lyra and Dorian took a quick break, hurriedly eating their hot dogs—Gabriela's favorite main course—and her mother's renowned tamales, then played for the guests as they dined. Doing music together felt so natural. It was as if each could anticipate the other's improvisations. They had never sounded so good.

At last it was time to sample Gabriela's birthday cake. Molly and Lyra had set new standards for sprinkles. The gooey chocolate cake was a hit with everyone, especially Gabriela, who continued to lick the buttercream frosting and sprinkles from her fingers long after all traces were gone.

The evening ended with a Tree of Life ceremony in which Gabriela took the fifteen candles and handed them out in honor of special memories she shared with family and friends. She asked Dorian and Lyra to share a candle for making her laugh. "You're always together, so you should share," Gabriela said.

Journal Entry:

The quinceañera was a complete success. I'm surprised Gabi didn't get sick from eating so many sprinkles. She's such a lovable kid. She totally deserved this party. When I was dancing with Gabi she said, "He likes you." Could that really be true? He did ask me to dance. A waltz. And he turned down some pretty girl so he could keep dancing with me. I feel free for the first time in years.

What do you want to do for your birthday?" Stephanie asked, delicately blotting her face with a towel as she stepped off the elliptical.

"I dunno. Gotta study for that test on Monday. Could take all night. It seems to take longer with Catzo helping."

"How about you take a break for dinner, and we meet up at Mr. Pancake Head? They've been advertising that cream cheese-stuffed French toast..."

"I'm so there." Lyra mopped her beaming face.

Mr. Pancake Head lived up to expectations. Lyra ate slowly, letting the blend of creaminess and toastiness overwhelm her senses, barely listening to Stephanie complain about being used as a trophy. *That's something I'll never have to worry about,* Lyra told herself, resigned to her lack in the looks department. *No one will ever make an object of me.* Her thoughts drifted to Dorian.

Interrupting her own lamentation, Stephanie arched her eyebrows. "You're thinking about him again."

"Who?" She longed to hear his name.

"Dorian," Stephanie said, congratulating herself on her rudimentary psychic skills.

Lyra's smile broadened. "I guess I was. How'd you know?"

"You were smiling. Why don't you invite him out to dinner for your birthday?"

"I'm already having dinner with you, and that's my last dime. How's that supposed to work?" She took an uncharacteristically large bite of toast and chewed slowly. "Besides, it'd be really awkward, making a big deal about myself."

"Just saying if you want him to make a big deal about you, you should start by..."

"Thanks, but no thanks. I'm not begging for attention from him or anyone else. Besides, what if he doesn't want to go?" She reminded herself of the risk.

"Whatever." Stephanie shrugged.

"He *really* likes you, you know." Stephanie looked up from the thin, elastic dough she was now rolling with expert hands.

Lyra's heart quickened. "What?"

"Dorian. And don't you deny that you like him too." She rested her rolling pin even as she rested her case.

"Of course, I like him. He's a great guy." Her voice betrayed her, and Lyra knew it.

"Quit playing games! You know what I'm talking about."

"Assuming you were right about this, and you were me, what would you do?"

"I'd find out how he feels about me."

"This isn't high school, Steph. What am I supposed to do? Ask my girlfriends to ask his guy friends as they pass notes in the cafeteria?"

"You can just leave that to me." Stephanie's green eyes had a dangerous glint that Lyra had never before observed.

"No thanks. I don't want any interference."

"Then how are you gonna find out?" Stephanie wanted answers.

"Steph, don't bother. I'm not sure I'm ready to find out how he feels," Lyra said. She groaned and went back to rolling peanut butter cookie dough in her hands, forming perfect balls to be placed on the huge cookie sheets. *But what if she's right?* Lyra wondered. *What then?*

"Suit yourself," Stephanie said, flipping her ponytail as she walked from the workroom to start a new pot of coffee.

Lyra had never had a boyfriend, and up until now it hadn't mattered much. Now it did. Terribly. Fear, hope, and desire warred within her as she dedicated herself to filling the next cookie sheet with precise globular blobs of dough. She startled at a hand on her shoulder.

LEAVING LYRA

"What's on your mind, Lyra?" Molly asked genially.

"Nothing," came the standard answer.

"Those cookies tell me otherwise," Molly observed. "When I've got something troubling me, my cookies get perfectly round just like those." She pointed at Lyra's orderly rows of oven-ready cookies-to-be.

"Steph said something that got me thinking is all." Lyra wasn't exactly lying.

"This wouldn't have to do with a young man who seems to know when you take your breaks and shows up with a convenient sweet tooth at exactly those moments?" Molly said, enjoying each word.

"Uh, yeah, it might." Lyra tried not to look too hopeful.

After a dramatic pause, Molly reassured her, "It's just a matter of time before he realizes he's totally gone on you. Hang in there and be patient." Molly turned to leave, then stopped. "Just don't wait too long. I know all about waiting, and sometimes you can wait too long."

Great, Lyra thought. *Be patient but don't wait too long. What's that supposed to mean? What does waiting too long look like? Days? Weeks? Years? Seconds?* With renewed internal conflict, she continued forming rows of perfect little cookie balls, putting them on the sheet, and wishing her life could be so easily aligned.

CHAPTER 19
Cornbread with Little Sister in Fields of Topaz

Dorian burst into the bakery. "Hey, Lyra, check it out." His eyes gleamed as he held out a black satin jewelry box.

Not quite knowing what to expect, yet hazarding a hope that the mysterious container might be for her, she took it from him and opened it. "Oh, Dorian, what a beautiful pendant. That's a topaz, isn't it?" Snug in its intricately filigreed, yellow gold setting, hemmed in with a bevy of small diamonds, the sunshiny stone seemed to be smiling up at Lyra. It reminded her of a sunrise, bright with promise.

"Yep. My mother's favorite gemstone. Do you think she'll like it?"

Lyra released the breath she'd been holding and handed the box back to him. "She'll absolutely love it!" She smiled in spite of herself.

"It's really hard to find anything for Mom. She's already got everything she wants, says the 'gatheration' of family is all she wants for her birthday, but I wanted to get her something special this year. She's been such a blessing to me."

"She was a big help to me too," Lyra agreed. "Your mom is just like that topaz—bright and sunny, warm and welcoming. You made a terrific choice, Dorian. It totally fits her."

There was that little boy grin she loved. Bette Anne had raised herself a thoughtful son. For that and so many other reasons, Lyra loved her.

"Well, that's weird." Dorian looked up from his laptop that rested on his favorite table at Molly's Sunshine Bakery and caught Lyra's gaze. "Not really weird, but Mom wants to invite you down for her birthday."

"Doesn't she live in Southern California? That's one heck of a drive. Tell her I said thank you. I just wouldn't feel comfortable..."

Dorian grinned. "Try convincing her of that. You've met my mom. She'll make sure you're comfortable whether you like it or not. Southern hospitality at its finest. You may as well pack your backpack and get ready."

"I can't. There's all the baking—I can't leave Molly with that. And what about Catzo? And church, and..."

"Can't leave Molly with what?" Molly entered with a tray of buttermilk spice muffins—with just the right amount of nutmeg—and commenced restocking the display case.

"Dorian's mom wants me to come down for her birthday, but I can't leave you with all the baking."

Molly turned to Dorian. "How long would you be gone?"

"Four days tops," he said, hoping for Lyra's sake, and his own, that she could get away from the bakery for a few days. Aside from church, and the gym, she had very little social life. Like him. It'd do them both good, he decided.

Molly responded with a knowing smile. "It just so happens that Maggie McCreary offered to help out in a pinch, and with Stephanie here, we've got you covered. You could really use some time off." Before Lyra could protest, Molly picked up her tray and headed back to the kitchen. "You two go and have fun. Tell Bette Anne hi for me."

"I'll tell her yes then," Dorian said, thinking, *this will be fun.*

Images of sunrises and wheat fields danced in Lyra's head as she picked up her guitar that evening. She hoped to paint such a picture with words and capture the rippling of heads of grain with her guitar. More than that, she wanted to portray the beauty of people like Bette Anne. No, Bette Anne in particular.

LEAVING LYRA

After a few hours with her guitar, the song was complete. "Yes," Lyra concluded, as she put down her guitar and finished scribbling the last of her new lyrics.

God has sown His love in your heart, Bette Anne. And I'm so grateful to have received some of that love, she thought.

Dorian's vast music library was put to use the next day during the long journey. The two of them sang, laughed, and even enjoyed the occasional comfortable silence between them. As they neared Dorian's parents' house, he seemed to drift from Lyra.

"What's up, Dorian?" Lyra asked, hoarse from all the singing.

"This will be, like, my first time back since...you know. Some people don't know about it, others do. A lot of them think I'm guilty. My father—I put his position on the church board in jeopardy. He's still mad at me. We never really...talked about it. He's kind of...like...quiet that way."

"But your mom did invite you. They obviously want you there."

"I'm not sure if Dad knows I'm going to be there. Mom has this way of...surprising people. Like putting them in positions where they have to, like, squirm, but with the best of intentions. I remember this one time when my sister Hannah and

I were fighting about some dumb thing, like using the car. We were really going at it, and what does Mom do? She signs us up for rock climbing classes together. Considering possible equipment failures and the prospect of falling to your death, it made our arguments seem pretty stupid. Instead of fighting, we wound up helping each other and cheering each other on."

"So your dad might not know about me being there either." Lyra shrugged and sighed. "Great. I wish you could've told me before I got in the car this morning."

He patted her hand. "I really wanted to have you along. I am sorry for putting you on the spot though."

"Yeah, sure. I see a bit of your mother in you. Hadn't noticed it before." She gave a wink along with a half smile. "It's a good thing I like your mom."

Dorian's humble Corolla was a far cry from the luxury car he'd last driven onto the palm tree-lined driveway of his parents' home. His used economy vehicle seemed completely out of place there.

Sandra Lee's yapping announced their arrival, and Bette Anne emerged from the heavy mission-style door. Tucked under one arm was the wiggling little Yorkie whose tongue was licking the air in anticipation of greeting her guests.

LEAVING LYRA

"Welcome home, Sugar," Bette Anne said, hugging her son. "And Lyra, how nice to see you." She motioned with her free hand. "y'all must be hungry and tired after that long drive. Come on in."

"Here we go," Dorian muttered.

Lyra hadn't noticed how nervous he was until then. She socked him in the arm and smiled even though she was equally anxious. Suddenly it didn't matter if she was expected or even welcome here. She would be there for Dorian. Nothing—not even her own apprehension—mattered.

He looked up, eyes merry in spite of his circumstances.

"I've got your back," she whispered.

"I'm counting on it." It felt good having a friend.

"We have company, Timothy," Bette Anne lilted as he walked out of his study. She beckoned Dorian and Lyra forward.

"Lyra, this is my dad, Timothy. Dad, this is Lyra."

"Isn't it a bit soon to be dating? Is your divorce even final yet?" his father asked, more concerned than angry.

Lyra stepped forward and offered Dorian's father a sweaty hand. "We're just friends. We play music together at church," she said breezily.

Timothy looked down at her hand and up at her flushed face. After a firm handshake, he nodded and retired to his study.

"Nice to see you too, Dad," Dorian mumbled.

"Don't let him bother y'all none. It's his way. He's not talkful. I guess y'all could say he and I are opposations, and ya

245

know what they say about that." She smiled. "Come along now. I have sandwiches all made up."

The sandwiches were constructed of freshly-cut ham and cheddar cheese with unexpected alfalfa sprouts on sourdough bread, so thick in ingredients that they were difficult to eat. Their plates were soon littered with stray sprouts and escaped chunks of ham.

"She's always trying to get me to eat like this," Dorian confided when his mother had left the room in pursuit of a jar of her homemade garlic dill pickles for them to sample.

"I'll be lucky to finish half of it," Lyra groaned in dismay.

"That's okay. All that matters is that we enjoy it." He grinned. "At least that's what she always told me and my sister, Hannah."

"Oh, your sister? You've hardly mentioned her."

"Yep. I've known her ever since I was born. Ha!" He smiled. "She's older than me, and she lives in Colorado. We're not that close. She and Dad never really got along, so she doesn't come to visit all that often."

Bette Anne returned, reverently carrying a large mason jar of sliced pickles with chunks of garlic hovering at the bottom of the container. "This is all that's left of last summer's batch. Let me know what you think."

Not knowing what she'd do if the offering was inedible, Lyra gave the pickles a cautious bite and was relieved to honestly praise Bette Anne's handiwork.

"Mom makes the best pickles," Dorian said with his mouth full of food, sending sprouts flying again. He reached for a slice of pickle and gave it a contented crunch.

He and his mother chatted while Lyra continued to tackle the insurmountable sandwich. She had to give up halfway, as Dorian had.

"Well now, I guess I'll be showing Lyra up to her room," Bette Anne said.

"And I'll be in my room taking a nap." Belly beyond full, Dorian yawned and stretched then followed them, barefoot, up the stairs and off to his room.

"Here's your room, Miss Lyra," Bette Anne crooned as she opened the door to a lovely room done in dusty pink and sage. A bouquet of English roses matching the decor, perfumed the air. Like the sandwich, it hinted at overkill but was welcoming nonetheless.

"Wow, Bette Anne, what a beautiful room. Thanks for inviting me."

"Now I have a little present for you in the bathroom."

Wondering what kind of gift might lurk in a bathroom, Lyra followed.

The room was dominated by a long mirror with what Lyra's mother used to call "makeup lights." And there, by the sink, was enough makeup to paint a thousand circus clowns.

"In case I never told you, I'm an Executive Director and distributor of Moi Toujours Moi Cosmetics." She studied Lyra, appraising and approving. "I can see Stage One was a success." She faced Lyra and put her hands on Lyra's shoulders. "Lookin' good, Sugar. Now let's see what a little highlightifying of those lovely features of yours will do." Bette Anne stepped back and said, "Well, I do believe that someone has lost more than a few pounds since I saw her last."

"Yeah, my friend Stephanie and I have been going to the gym."

"Well, it shows, Sugar. You just keep that up, and you'll be all slimified in no time. I'm proud of ya."

It had been a long time since anyone had said they were proud of her. "Thank you," she said.

Bette Anne went on to elaborate on her theories of color and proportion for the larger woman. With brushes and palette, she applied subtle color to Lyra's face with the hand of an artist. To her amazement, Lyra liked what she saw in the mirror for the first time. It reminded her of her childhood when she had stood beside her own mother, watching her put on her make up. Lyra's mother was beautiful. "I...I look like my mother!" Lyra was dumbfounded, admiring Bette Anne's artistry.

LEAVING LYRA

A little blush, colors to highlight her smoky brownish green eyes, a touch of mascara to thicken her eyelashes, lip color, and she looked, well...like a different person. A person people might just want to know.

"Now, sit yourself down here in front of the mirror. Let Bette Anne work her magic with that dark chocolate-colored hair of yours." She brushed out Lyra's lifeless hair. "Girl, you need you some bangs. Mind if I do a little stylifying?" She raised her scissors and snipped twice in the air.

"I've never had bangs in my life."

"Well, girl, it's about time you had you some. Ready?"

"I guess so." Lyra closed her eyes in faith, believing Bette Anne knew what she was doing. Was she ready for this change? Lyra hesitated, then opened her eyes just long enough to catch Bette Anne's smile in the mirror. Resolute, she said, "Okay, let's do it." With each falling lock, she asked herself how this daring move could change her life. Was she ready to be an attractive young woman? Would this really still be her? How would this affect her relationship with Dorian? Having used her plain looks as a hiding place for so many years, she was feeling terribly exposed. She kept her eyes tightly closed until the snipping ceased.

Bette Anne announced, "You can open your eyes now, Sugar."

There, facing her in the mirror, was a woman she did not recognize. *Could that really be me?* The bangs were feathered, continuing down each side of the length of her hair. The contour of feathering made her face look thinner than she had seen it since she was a child. She blinked several times. Her mouth was open but wordless.

"Well, what do ya think, Sugar?"

Lyra touched her hair. "That's really me?"

"Sure enough. You look prettier than a North Carolina sunset." Bette Anne stood back, admiring. "Ya know that it's not what's in the mirror that makes a woman. It's what's on the inside. And I'd say you're beautiful inside and out. Ya just need time to recognize yourself in the right mirror."

Lyra wasn't quite sure what she was feeling as she gazed at her reflection. She had never felt pretty before. Was that what she was feeling—pretty? She turned her head side to side, marveling at the feathered locks. Could she face the attention she would get from everyone who knew her? From the time her father had begun abusing her, she had wanted to vanish not only from *his* sight, but from all men. She knew in her heart that she had let herself overeat in order to make herself unattractive. She wanted to merely blend in with the scenery. Now, looking at a new Lyra, she knew she could no longer disappear.

"So whatcha thinking, Sugar?" Bette Anne asked.

"I'm not sure what to think," Lyra said honestly. "You did such a beautiful job, but frankly, I'm kinda scared to look like someone I'm really not."

LEAVING LYRA

"Ah, but this *is* you, Lyra. Maybe it's time to heal from your past and move forward. You are beautiful, ya know! If you'll let yourself be. A haircut doesn't change who ya are inside, and girl, you've always been beautiful. Don't let your daddy rob ya of the rest of your life. Don't let him control you for one more minute."

"How do you know about my father?" Lyra's eyes opened wide.

"When you've been there yourself, ya recognize all the signs. It went on in my family for generations. And it stops with me." Bette Anne put her hands on Lyra's shoulders and prayed, "Lord God Almighty, please don't let your daughter Lyra hold onto her past hurts anymore. Set her free from the hold her earthly father has had on her. She has suffered terrible bad at the hands of her daddy. Release her now from the sins he perpetrated on her. And if there are generations of this sin in her family, stop it now. Help her to feel clean and pure in Your sight. Only You have the power to transform her life and bring healing. Help her grow into the woman she was meant to be. Give her a new start now, in Jesus' name. Amen."

Lyra was reaching for the tissue box as Bette Anne ended her prayer. Wiping her eyes, she smudged her eye makeup.

"Now don't you go a worrifying about that makeup. These here are healing tears, just let 'em flow, girl. We can freshen ya up later." Bette Anne wrapped her arms around Lyra.

As she heaved sobs onto Bette Anne's shoulder, Lyra felt years of her stored-up pain melt away. She felt a safeness that she hadn't known since her mother died.

"There now, my girl, he can't hurt ya anymore. You are free of his hold, and now God Himself is gonna heal ya, as only He can."

Tears subsiding, Lyra released a jagged breath. "So how did you get free, Bette Anne?"

"'Bout the same way you just did, Sugar. Someone recognized my hurt like I recognized yours. She led me to my path of healin' in Jesus. I was much weaker than you back then and very timid."

Lyra couldn't imagine Bette Anne ever being timid. In fact, that was the polar opposite of what she was today.

"God has some mighty plans for ya, darlin'. You wait and see. You betcha. Now, take some time to freshen up and I'll meet ya downstairs in an hour. We can work on supper together. Just wait'll everybody gets a look at ya!"

After Bette Anne left the room, Lyra went right to her journal.

Journal Entry:

I feel a shift in my emotions. Ever since Bette Anne prayed for me I'm beginning to pity my father now. The hate is growing smaller. Bette Anne mentioned sin being carried from one generation to the next. I'd never thought about that before. Was this part of my father's childhood?

Wondering about her dad, Lyra picked up her Bible and searched for the word "generation" in the concordance.

Exodus 34:7

"I lavish unfailing love to a thousand generations. I forgive inequity, rebellion, and sin. But I do not excuse the guilty. I lay the sins of the parents upon their children and grandchildren; the entire family is affected—even children in the third and fourth generation."

Psalm 79:8

Do not hold us guilty for the sins of our ancestors! Let your compassion quickly meet our needs, for we are on the brink of despair.

Does this mean I'm not guilty for what my father did to me? I've carried this weight of guilt around for much too long. Could it be that I don't need to feel guilty anymore? Her heart renewed at the hope of such healing, Lyra set aside her journal.

Lyra found herself excited but nervous as she prepared herself for Dorian's reaction to her new look. *This is it*, she thought.

Bette Anne and Lyra were in the kitchen, cooking up a tornado of southern dishes when Dorian entered the room. He grabbed the counter, almost falling over when he first caught sight of Lyra.

"What the...Lyra, is that you?" he asked in disbelief.

"It's me," she mumbled, dropping her gaze. There was nowhere to hide.

"So Dorian, what do you think?" his mom prodded.

"You look beautiful! Uh, I'm not saying you looked bad before, but...uh, you know, you look good. You look good, I mean, like, really good!"

Lyra appreciated him stumbling over his words. She always loved it when he did.

Unaccustomed to any kind of compliments, Lyra quickly changed the subject. "We've just about got dinner ready. I hope you're hungry."

"Can ya go get your daddy and tell him supper's 'bout to hit the table? Thanks, honey," his mom said.

Dorian turned his head to get one more glance at Lyra, missing the doorway entirely and running into the counter.

Lyra wasn't sure she was truly ready for this new self she'd discovered today, but she couldn't help but giggle.

Over dinner, Lyra noticed Dorian continually glancing at her. She swept back the feathered hair behind her ear, unaccustomed to having hair hanging loosely at the sides of her face.

"Well, Lyra," Timothy started a new strand of conversation, "looks like Bette Anne is at it again. I hope she hasn't pushed you into a whole new look, but I must say, she's done a stunning job. She has such a knack for that kind of thing."

Lyra wasn't sure what to say. "Thank you," she mumbled.

As dinner ended, Dorian and Lyra insisted on doing the clean up. They both reached for a red and white polka dotted serving bowl at the same moment. Their hands touched. They looked at each other before setting the bowl down. They'd never had so much fun doing dishes before.

Dorian and Lyra walked with Bette Anne out to the garden and invited her to sit on the bench by the fountain of succulents spiraling down a dry fountain. Dorian handed her the box, then standing with hands in his pockets, he leaned forward eagerly.

"Now I tellified ya I don't need a thing!" Her attempt at a stern look failed utterly. "But I do appreciate a remembrification now and again!" She pried open the box, and her face glowed with delight. "Oh, Dorian! It's...it's stunnin'!" She picked up the pendant to examine it more closely, her smile grew wider by the moment. She held it out to her son.

With equal joy he took it and walked behind her to clasp it around her neck, then returned to revel in the happiness he had brought her. "I love you, Mom."

"I love ya too, Son." Tears glistened in her eyes. "And I'm so proud of ya."

Lyra was feeling every bit the intruder on this mother and son moment, but she couldn't walk away either. She waited, growing increasingly unsure of herself.

Dorian cleared his throat, "Uh, Mom, Lyra has something for you too."

Lyra stepped forward shyly, toting her guitar. She sat next to Bette Anne and said simply, "I wrote this song for you. I hope you like it."

The first few notes were a bit sloppy, but her guitar began to soar, bringing her voice up with it.

Dorian had not yet heard the song. With pride he watched Lyra as she sang, her eyes brimming with her offering.

Bette Anne listened, smiling, beholding with wonder her own field of topaz.

"There is beauty in living more precious than gold,
More beauty than our eyes can behold.

LEAVING LYRA

From autumn's haze to where Jesus stays,
Our treasure is knowing Him.

He has sown the fields of topaz,
Bending low as the harvest draws nigh,
Rip'ning in His loving sunshine,
Nurtured in His light.

He has worn the robes of a shepherd
And He's walked the paths that know our feet,
Feasted at the rich man's home
And thirsted in the desert heat.

He's known the gold in the song of the meadow bird,
In the sweet-smelling autumn land,
In fresh bread warm from the kitchen,
In the touch of an old friend's hand.

But He did trade each image of gold,
Wrought by time or hand of man
To be an earthen vessel,
Resting in His Father's hand.

He has sown the fields of topaz,
He has sown the fields of your heart.
He has sown the fields of topaz,
He has sown the fields of your heart."

That night as Lyra lay in bed, she relived all the highlights of the day. Bette Anne's delight had given her spirit wings. The touch of Dorian's hand had thrilled her. Was it *possible? Nah, just friends…* she told herself and closed her eyes to dream of a future with new possibilities in it.

Dorian's sister, Hannah, surprised everyone the next day, arriving with her seven-year-old twin girls, Freedom and Liberty. Hannah and Timothy exchanged obligatory greetings to each other without ever making eye contact, then each retreated to their respective rooms.

The twins unreservedly converged on their grandmother.

"How are Granny's little princesses?" She enveloped them both in a single hug.

"Who's she?" Liberty paused to acknowledge Lyra with a pointed finger.

"This is my friend, Lyra," Dorian said.

"Who is she really?" Liberty insisted.

"Uncle Dorian just told you, this is his friend, Lyra," Bette Anne explained.

LEAVING LYRA

The little girl narrowed her brown eyes. "Is she why Uncle Dorian and Aunt Brittney aren't together? I miss Aunt Brittney. She used to do our nails and let us play with her makeup and stuff."

Lyra crouched down to meet the girls at eye level. "Dorian wasn't with Brittney when I met him. So I didn't steal him from her—or anyone. That would be mean. Besides, we're just friends."

Liberty rolled her eyes. "I guess you're okay then."

"Granny, where are the cookies?" the twins chimed in unison.

"Y'all will have to find them, just like always."

"Aww, Granny," Freedom whined, "can't you give us a hint?"

Bette Anne put her finger to her lips as if considering it for the first time. "When it's snowy, what do you look for?"

The girls scampered off to make their usual random guesses.

"That should keep them out from underfoot for a while." Bette Anne grinned affectionately at the twins as they disappeared upstairs, squealing.

"Your cookies must be pretty good to create that kind of excitement," Lyra observed.

"They are. Believe me," Dorian said.

Not to be left out of the conversation, Sandra Lee insisted noisily that Lyra was to pick her up without delay. Lyra

259

lifted the diminutive Yorkie who waggled and air-licked with delight.

Hannah emerged from her room and glanced around. Seeing that the coast was clear, she came up to Lyra with outstretched hand.

Lyra juggled Sandra Lee to receive a hearty handshake.

"I'm sorry I couldn't give you a proper greeting. Things were...uh, tense, as you could see. I'm Hannah, the prodigal daughter. I wouldn't be here except it's Mom's sixtieth birthday, and I wouldn't miss that for the world." She gave her mom a sideways squeeze.

"I'm Dorian's friend, Lyra." She gave a sympathetic smile.

The twins came thundering down the stairs.

"Come and say hi to Dorian's friend, Lyra," Hannah said as Liberty and Freedom disappeared down the hallway.

"Already did," came a shout from the pantry followed by another from the laundry room.

"Well, in case they didn't do a proper job of it, the blond one is Liberty—Libby for short. She's my most outspoken one. I admire that in a woman, though in men it can be so bothersome." She grinned. "Now Freedom—Frieda for short— she's more of the artistic type. She doesn't say much but when she does, look out; she's spot on and doesn't care who's listening. I'm afraid Dad doesn't see the value in openness and honesty."

LEAVING LYRA

Lyra was thinking "Openness" and "Honesty" would no doubt be the names of Hannah's next batch of twins, should she be thus favored again.

Hannah turned her attention to her brother. "Dorian, you're looking good. I'm glad to see you survived the scandal."

Dorian's face dropped and he looked away.

"Hey, don't be sad, little brother. The church board is just a bunch of proud, stuffy, judgmental old men. Who cares what they think?"

"It mattered to Brittney, didn't it?" he said.

Bette Anne retrieved her dog from Lyra and redirected the conversation. "So Hannah, Sugar, how are things back in Colorado?"

Hannah's face was rapt as she described the knife-sharp air, the silence of snow, and the soft whispers of autumn aspens leafed like gold coins on a dancer's skirt under the guardian Rockies, the fields of July dandelions, and streams so cold they seemed to tear the skin. She took it all in, both beauty and brutality, and breathed it out in her words.

"Are you a writer?" Lyra ventured.

"As a matter of fact, I am. Started writing articles for nature magazines and now I have a couple books under my belt. How did you know?"

"You use words...like a paintbrush.

"And what do you do that gives you such insight?"

"Oh, I'm just an assistant at a bakery."

"She listens a lot too," Dorian ventured. "Really well. And she writes songs. Beautiful songs, like the one she wrote for Mom's birthday." He smiled at Lyra, who was embarrassed at all this attention.

Lyra excused herself and returned to her room for a much needed dose of solitude.

Seizing the opportunity for some sisterly advice, Hannah forged ahead. "There's a lot to that girl, Dorian, and I don't mean size. Depth, honesty. I see it in her eyes. You see it, don't you? And I'll bet she's one of your churchy friends too..." Dorian did see it but didn't know what to do about it.

He had been up half the night, joking around with Lyra as he showed her around the place in the light of the full moon —the tree fort where he'd broken his collarbone and the path— still visible—he had carved across the lawn on his bicycle, the swing set kept in good repair for grandkids or bigger kids who needed, for the moment, a bit of kiddishness to lighten their souls. "This is where I broke my arm attempting a backflip off the swing. It's also where I learned once and for all not to take any more dares." He grabbed the chains of the first swing and nodded toward the second one. "Come on, Lyra."

LEAVING LYRA

Lyra's hands came up, fending off the offer. "No way! You saw what happened at the dock. I'm not about to fall on my butt."

"That dock was made of rotten wood. It was ready to break at any moment, no matter who stepped on it. This is made of metal. Besides, my mom loves riding on the swing. She says it helps her to 'thinkinate.'"

Lyra looked up to the top of the swing, a dull and distant glow in the moonlight. With its exceptional height, it should reach unparalleled altitudes. She looked at Dorian and smiled. "Okay. I guess I'll give it a try." After a couple tentative pumps she was swinging with her head back, laughing, carefree as a child.

It occurred to Dorian that her laughter was every bit as beautiful as her singing voice. It made his heart feel full. He wanted to tell her so, but didn't want to sound dumb. Instead, he commented, "I've never heard you laugh like that."

"I guess I needed to," she said, catching her breath. "It's been such a long time since I've felt like a kid."

"Well, you should do it more often."

"I'd look pretty stupid on the kiddy swings at Lakeside Park."

"So? Looking stupid never stopped Dorkian."

"Is this a dare?" She studied his never-quite-tan face with its ever-so-dark eyes and wanted to laugh again—a joyous kind of laugh meant to be shared.

He beat her to it. "I guess it is," he chuckled.

All the upstairs lights were off by the time they made it back into the house. They parted with whispered good nights and each retired to their own room.

Lyra found sleep slow in coming as she relived the last days' events. The hours on the road—the company of silence and the intimacy of words. But she would have to be careful from here on out. She had ventured further than she should with her feelings for Dorian. But for now, she would allow herself the joy she felt.

Journal Entry:

Dorian can't be serious about me, but he's been so nice. Is it possible he has more than friendship feelings for me? I have a ray of hope, but then I keep remembering how dirty I feel. No man could actually be interested in a used, fat, filthy piece of trash like me. That's what my father always told me.

The old lies came rushing back.

Maybe it's not true. Bette Anne went through the same sort of things I went through, and she's so respectable. No one would ever guess about her past. I see changes in myself happening. I am losing weight. Bette Anne has helped me dress better and look better. But I feel like I'm playing dress up. When

LEAVING LYRA

I look in the mirror I wonder if it's really me or just someone I want to be. Can God really change me and make me lovable?

She thumbed through her Bible and came on a scripture she had highlighted weeks ago.

Psalm 51:10-12, 15-17
Create in me a clean heart, O God.
    Renew a loyal spirit within me.
Do not banish me from your presence,
    and don't take your Holy Spirit from me.
Restore to me the joy of your salvation,
    and make me willing to obey you…
Unseal my lips, O Lord,
    that my mouth may praise you.
You do not desire a sacrifice, or I would offer one.
    You do not want a burnt offering.
The sacrifice you desire is a broken spirit.
    You will not reject a broken and repentant heart, O God.

Accustomed to bakers' hours, Lyra woke early—too early. She pulled her Bible from her backpack and read her favorite passage from the book of Jeremiah, Chapter 29:11.

"For I know the plans I have for you," says the Lord. "They are plans for good and not for disaster, to give you a future and a hope."

She stared out the window at the first light dawning through the palm trees. *Could that hope and future be for me?* For once, she dared to believe it might be true.

Dorian was awakened by the sound of Lyra screaming and shouting in a frenzy of Spanish. Her voice was joined by a woman's tearful voice, and even more Spanish. Pajama-clad, he joined his sister and nieces on the landing, watching the strange spectacle.

Lyra was downstairs in the arms of his parents' maid, sobbing. The maid's little daughter looked on, twisting her nightgown in uncertainty.

"It's barely dawn. What's going on down there?" Timothy demanded from the top of the stairs. "Is anyone hurt?" His tone softened ever so slightly as Bette Anne hurried from their bedroom to join them.

Lyra had been oblivious to her audience until that moment. "No one's hurt. It's just that I never thought I'd see Estrella again—and here she is!" Lyra blinked back another surge of joyous tears eager to join the ones that had already flooded her reddened face. Stubbornly resisting them, she swiped her face dry with her arm. "Estrella took care of me when I was just..." Lyra glanced down at the little girl who looked disturbingly familiar. Eyebrows raised, she locked eyes with Estrella.

"Yes," Estrella replied to the unspoken question as she beckoned her daughter to her side. "Sonrisa is your half-sister."

Lyra dropped to her knees and reached out her arms to the little girl. "Hello, little sister," she murmured.

"What kind of man takes advantage of his maid like that? Who knows what else he might have done?" Timothy asked Bette Anne as they closed the door to their room.

She arched her eyebrows.

"I'd hoped Dorian would choose friends from more respectable families. That's all I'm saying," Timothy complained.

Bette Anne's eyebrows froze.

"What?" Timothy asked.

"There you go, judgifying again. Lyra can't help who—and what—her father is. Neither could I. Remember? She's a nice girl, and I don't want to be hearin' another hurtinizing word about it. Do you hear me, Timothy?" She bristled.

Timothy knew better than to argue. She was right all too often, and he hated being a sore "loserator."

Estrella was given the day off. She whisked Lyra away to the little cottage in the backyard by Bette Anne's cascading bowls of succulent plants, each bowl replete with its own miniature fairy garden.

Dorian was left to wonder what this revelation might mean to Lyra. Would she want to leave River Oaks—and him—to be near Estrella? The thought distressed him. He could never move back here. Besides, he much preferred singing in the dark loft at Church of the Broken to the blazing lights of his father's church.

Lyra asked her long-held questions at Estrella's kitchen table. "My father told me that you'd been deported. How'd you wind up here?" Lyra paused long enough to take a bite of the honey cornbread that comprised their breakfast.

Estrella replied, "I tried to stay for you as long as I could, mija, but I couldn't expose my child to him. When I found out that I was pregnant, I had to leave before he found out. I didn't want to leave you. I'm so sorry." Estrella began to cry. Little Sonrisa padded over to her mommy and begged to be picked up. "He lied to you and told you I was deported. I really just ran away."

"I ran away too and hit the foster care system after you left, and I just kept running," Lyra said. "In fact, since you were gone, there was no reason to stay. Your leaving actually helped me get out. Eventually I found a nice place to live in River Oaks. It looks like you found a home too. Things worked out. No need to feel bad. You did what you had to do."

"God has been good to us," Estrella said, giving her daughter a hug and kissing her glossy black hair.

They spent the rest of the day discussing the paths their lives had taken over the last few years. Estrella's brother had found work for her in a local hotel, then got her a job with Bette Anne and Timothy when their much-loved maid, Maria Elena, had retired.

"Bette Anne," Estrella asserted, "should be named a patron saint of domestic workers."

"And assistant bakers as well," Lyra seconded. "She's been helping me with...I guess you'd call it my 'look.'" She went on to describe how much her life had changed since finding her place in River Oaks. Apparently, she spoke of Dorian more than she'd realized.

"He's a very nice young man, Lyra. He's always treated me kindly, not like some of the people who visit here. I think he likes you or he wouldn't have invited you. Bette Anne talks about you all the time whenever she gets a text or email from Dorian. So he must be talking about you to his mom."

Lyra insisted, "We're just friends," even though her mutinous heart argued to the contrary.

Journal Entry:

Did I hear You right, Lord? Did You just tell me to forgive my father? After all he's done to me? After all he did to Estrella? He's a monster. It's going to take a miracle, Lord. I'm willing to be willing to forgive, but by myself it's impossible. This has got to be You, because I just can't do it alone. You're telling me to forgive and let go, so You do it. Here are my five loaves and two fish. Let's make some toast!

CHAPTER 20
Long Ago and Farro Wheat in Search of the One True Ring

Lyra wore her makeup on the drive home with Dorian. If she was going to make a change, she decided to go cold turkey. The mascara bugged her the most. She always felt like there was something stuck to her eyelashes, and without thinking she'd rub her eye and wonder if she had smeared her mascara. Not wishing to appear overly vain, she was reluctant to use a mirror. This would take some getting used to—and perhaps some expert tips.

As they pulled into River Oaks, Dorian suggested they stop by Molly's bakery for a treat.

Lyra started rambling off excuses, fearful of too much attention or forced compliments on her new look.

"They're all going to see the new you sooner or later. Believe me, you have nothing to be nervous about."

"I guess it's now or never," Lyra surrendered.

Maggie McCreary was just taking off her red apron and preparing to go home to the Mister, when Lyra and Dorian walked in the bakery door. "Good golly, Miss Molly," she gasped, "look who just came in the door looking like a million bucks!"

Molly and Stephanie looked through the workroom doorway. Molly's eyes opened wide in wonder and Steph let out a squeal and ran to Lyra with outstretched arms. Stephanie threw her arms around Lyra and started jumping up and down.

Walking up to get a closer look, Molly said, "Lyra, you look incredible."

Having never dealt with such compliments before, Lyra didn't know what to do. She looked down at her shoes. Lifting her head she asked, "You don't think it's too much?"

"Ooooooh noooo!" Stephanie assured her. "It's just right. Now how did this happen?"

Dorian smiled proudly. "My mom decided it was time for a makeover. I agree with Stephanie. It's just right." He gave Lyra a smile that could have melted the soles right off her shoes. "I just thought I'd bring her by and show her off a bit."

"I'm not here to show off."

"Well, maybe you should," he said.

LEAVING LYRA

Molly and Steph gave each other secret glances while Maggie just smiled and nodded her head.

Though Mrs. McCreary was kind enough to care for Catzo while Lyra was out of town, Catzo was over the moon to see Lyra when she got back. Lyra was in the garden playing with the rambunctious kitten when Dorian opened the gate cautiously, a desperate look on his face. As he closed the gate, he said, "Lyra, you've gotta help me!"

Lyra didn't know what she was about to get into; all she knew was that Dorian was in a state of panic.

Dorian explained, "Phil's lifelong crush, Ronnie, came to his house last night, claiming her husband beat her up. Phil let her sleep upstairs while he stayed downstairs on the couch. In the morning he was fixing breakfast, and she came down the stairs, wearing one of Phil's shirts and not much else, just as Molly came to the front door. You can imagine what she thought. Molly ran off crying. She won't speak to Phil. And somehow in the middle of all this, Ronnie switched her own wedding ring with the ring Phil had just bought as an engagement ring for Molly. Ronnie must've found it in his room."

"What? Phil's going to propose to Molly? It's about time!"

"Yeah, but don't say anything. It's a secret. We've got to get the ring back!"

Lyra had heard enough about Ronnie to know that she was not the sharpest bread knife in the bakery—after all, she had passed Phil over.

In spite of Molly's accounts of Ronnie's vindictive nature, Lyra thought it might be fun to match wits with her. Besides, Dorian was so cute when he squirmed, and she rightly assumed he'd be doing a lot of that on this mission.

They tucked Catzo indoors and jumped into Dorian's car. As he drove, Lyra and Dorian plotted on their way to the Lavender Luxury Hotel & Spa where the ring was being held prisoner.

Once there, Dorian begged her to accompany him into Ronnie's lair but Lyra decided to give him an opportunity to "man up" while she waited in the hallway, ready to come to his rescue if need be.

Ronnie opened the door, clearly disappointed that it wasn't Phil. She dragged Dorian in. After a short while, Lyra could hear the talk on the other side of the door become heated. It sounded as if Ronnie's musclebound husband was about to clobber Dorian. Lyra burst in. Dorian thought quickly and said Lyra was his fiancée, and that the ring was hers. Lyra felt a happy little thrill pass through her, a what-if sort of state that she indulged in. *Why not?* she told herself. If they happened to be acting, she might as well enjoy her part. And she did, probably more than she should have.

The act paid off. Dorian and Lyra left Ronnie's hotel room triumphant, bearing Molly's pilfered engagement ring, and leaving Ronnie to explain herself to her angry, confused husband. They hadn't escaped unscathed though; Ronnie had made cutting remarks about Lyra's weight, which had visibly wounded her, and she was brooding in the car as they headed home. When she could take it no longer, Lyra reminded Dorian that she was fat.

"Lyra, you're a wonderful person," he assured. "Any guy would be lucky to have you." The conviction in his voice sent a shiver of hope down her spine.

"Yeah, right," she said, half believing him even as she tried to dismiss the hope. This make-believe stuff needed to come to an end before it felt any more real.

"I mean it, Lyra." No hint of condescension emerged from his words. Instead, she felt Dorian's anger—anger at the Ronnies of the world. He was mad on her behalf.

She looked into his dark eyes as he glanced away from the road and toward her. His indignation quickly gave way to fondness, a genuine fondness she longed to bask in. "Really?" she dared to whisper.

"Really," he replied.

They drove on in silence for a while, with Lyra clinging to that last word. *Really.*

Dorian finally spoke up. "You're much too hard on yourself, Lyra. If I've learned nothing else from my divorce it's not to focus on how things look on the outside. I was hung up on everything looking so good to everyone. I thought I had it all, the seemingly perfect Barbie doll wife, perfect marriage, my music, fame, and my circle of perfect-looking friends. Where did it all get me? My wife left me when things didn't look good, when I was accused of molesting that poor girl, and I was kicked out of my church and my ministry. All of my friends left me in the dust. My own wife didn't want to believe me because it messed up her perfect-looking world. My dad believed me but put pressure on me to leave town and live with Uncle Phil. I guess I made Dad look bad too."

"I believe you, Dorian. You would never do anything like that. Your family and friends should've supported you."

"Thanks, Lyra. That means a lot to me. For a long time, I wished Brittney had believed me, and then I realized that maybe she did, but she just couldn't stand the stigma of being my wife when things looked so bad to other people. She cared more about what other people thought than she cared about me. I guess what I'm trying to get at is that my life no longer has to look perfect, and neither do I or the people I choose to spend my time with. I'm looking deeper than skin level now. You, my friend, are funny, intelligent, hard-working, independent, kind-hearted, and you toast a mean brioche. You are crazy musically talented. That song you wrote for my mother was incredible!

Leaving Lyra

You love animals, really listen to people, you're super perceptive, you put yourself out for your friends, you love God, and you have the most amazing eyes, with or without makeup."

Lyra digested the things that Dorian had just said. She was still unsure of what to do with compliments.

"You're all that, you know. And you're fun to be with," he added.

"You wouldn't think so highly of me if you knew more about my past."

"Try me."

"I don't think so."

"Trust me. I've told you all about *my* past."

Lyra was silent.

Eventually Dorian pulled over at a deli. "Let's get something to eat. I don't know about you, but I never had breakfast this morning."

"Okay."

They walked inside. "What'll you have?" Dorian asked.

She discreetly pulled her wallet out of her pocket. Lyra shrugged and said, "Uh, I'm really not all that hungry."

"Well, I'm buying, and you have to get something. Might as well be something you like."

"Okay," she resigned herself. "You win. Thank you. I'll have whatever you're having."

"Hope you like sardines and anchovies."

"Eew! You are joking, I hope?"

277

"Of course. Never touch the stuff." He spoke to the man behind the deli counter. "We'll have two meatball sandwiches with extra mozzarella on them, please."

"Coming right up, sir."

As they walked away with their sandwiches, Dorian muttered to Lyra, "I hate when they call me 'sir.'"

"Yeah, me too." She smiled in spite of herself.

"And this 'sir thing,' does it happen to you often? They gotta be blind," Dorian inquired.

"Not so much lately. Not since your mom took me on as a fashion disciple."

"You really do look great, you know. Hey, let's go sit in the shade at that park across the street."

Clutching her sandwich, Lyra followed him, her heart beating out of control. As they sat down on the grass under a willow tree, Lyra asked, "Did your mom put you up to this?"

"Put me up to what?"

"Why are you being so nice to me?" Her question came out feeling like an accusation.

"Nice to you? What are you talking about?"

"All these compliments. What's wrong with you? Did your mom say, 'Dorian, you just have to help this poor, lonely, ugly, fat girl?'"

"Get over yourself. You've been using your weight to protect you and keep people away. Sooner or later you're going to have to let somebody in. Why shouldn't it be me? And don't keep calling yourself fat after you've lost so much weight. What are you so afraid of?"

"You have no idea what I've been through."

"Then why don't you tell me?"

Lyra's eyes pooled. She lifted up the paper napkin she had been meticulously folding and wiped her eyes.

"Come on, Lyra, let me in. I'm your friend. You know all my dark secrets."

"It's my father, okay?" she blurted before she could stop herself. The silence that followed was punctuated by a trio of children playing tag at the nearby jungle gym.

"It all started when my mom died. I was twelve. My dad started drinking—a lot. He wanted me to play this 'game' with him. I didn't want to play, so he forced me. I think you can guess what kind of 'game' he had in mind. He'd come into my room at night. Oh, Dorian, it was so awful! He forced me to do things I can't even talk about. He said I was a dirty girl, and maybe he was right. I felt so dirty. I still do." She began to sob.

Dorian put his arms around her and let her cry it out. "Don't hold those tears back, Lyra. You get them out, girl. I'm here for you." He rocked her gently in his arms.

Lyra looked up. "As I got older, it got more frequent and more brutal. As you know, we had a live-in maid, Estrella, who now works for your parents. She was my only friend. That's where I learned to speak Spanish. I thought she was here illegally. My father threatened to have her deported if I told on him. Towards the end I found out he had been abusing her too. I just couldn't stand the thought of him hurting her the way he did me. But no one believed me. My father is a judge with lots of connections. He had the power to deport her. When Estrella left, he told me that he had sent her back to Mexico and that it was all my fault. He obviously lied since she's been living with your family. When I threatened to get help from CPS, he knew all the right people and had me declared mentally ill—delusional, so no one would ever believe me. I started running away. Then I was passed off into the foster care system, but kept on running until I landed with this great family, the Barkers. My father found me at their place the day I turned eighteen. I had to slip out the back door. Then he had me followed by a private detective. I gave him the slip and found my way to River Oaks. So yes, Dorian, I did use my weight to keep him away, to keep everyone away."

"I'm so sorry, Lyra. I had no idea." He smoothed back her hair and handed her a fistful of napkins allowing her tears to continue to flow. "You're safe now. He's gone."

"I'm not safe! I saw him at the Waldorf wedding when Molly and I dropped off the wedding cakes. I don't know if he saw me, but I saw him. I don't want to have to run anymore. I like it here. I have a home, a job, friends...you."

"If he shows his face in this town again, I'll beat the living snot out of him. I don't care who he is. He's not touching you again."

LEAVING LYRA

Lyra heaved out years of pent up anguish, hopelessness, and fear. She wondered why Dorian would want to defend her. She had long since run out of napkins when she began calming down. "I can't believe I told you. Thank you for listening, Dorian."

"I'm sorry you ever had to go through any of that. Your father had better hope we never meet. My justice will be swift."

"We got it! We got it!" Dorian announced as he and Lyra erupted, triumphant, through Phil's front door only to find Molly and Phil in the middle of a serious conversation on the couch. Dorian quickly concealed the engagement ring in his pocket.

"What'd you get?" Molly asked, turning around.

Lyra, quick on her feet, came up with a story about finding missing lyrics to a song they'd been working on. Molly thwarted their attempt to disappear upstairs. She insisted on a private conversation with Dorian about what had transpired between Phil and Ronnie.

Lyra and Phil stepped outside, leaving Dorian to face the furious Molly.

Dorian, bolstered by his brush with death at the hotel, responded confidently while Phil and Lyra prayed in silence on the porch.

Journal Entry:

Man, talk about a close call! Ronnie's muscle-brained husband almost clobbered poor Dorian when he went to retrieve Molly's ring from Ronnie. When Dorian lied and called me his fiancée in order to get the ring back, I couldn't help but feel, just for a moment, what that might feel like, to have someone make that kind of promise to me, to really belong with someone. It felt amazing. I never thought I'd ever feel that. Ever. Even if it was only for a moment.

I finally told Dorian my secret. I guess it isn't a secret anymore, and that makes me feel stronger somehow. He was so kind and understanding. He didn't make me feel dirty or ashamed. I don't think I've cried that hard since Estrella disappeared. But it felt good to get it all out in the open. I know I can trust him. That feels even better.

I sure hope Molly can forgive Phil. Dorian said he was able to explain things pretty well, and that she was listening, but she was really hurt and jealous. I get it. I'm only just now beginning to trust, but I get how important it is. It has to do with knowing who someone really is and counting on it. Like when

we trust God; we know He's good even when the situation's
sketchy.

She looked up "trust" in the back of her Bible.

Proverbs 3:5-6
Trust in the Lord with all your heart;
do not depend on your own understanding.

Seek his will in all you do,
and he will show you which path to take.

Romans 15:13
I pray that God, the source of hope, will fill you completely with
joy and peace because you trust in him. Then you will overflow
with confident hope through the power of the Holy Spirit.

Joy, hope, and peace. I could use some of that.

A few weeks after Phil had managed to patch things up
with Molly, she had taken a day off to go on an outing with him.
Little did she know that he would propose to her.

The following day at work, Lyra and Steph listened as
Molly described Phil's perfectly planned and executed proposal
in minute detail. Both girls were spellbound. Stephanie was
surprised, unlike Lyra who had helped rescue Molly's

engagement ring from Ronnie's clutches. She would never let on about the ring's dramatic return.

At the end of the story, Molly asked both girls to be bridesmaids at the wedding, letting them know that she and Phil would be paying for their dresses and shoes. Lyra and Steph were thrilled and honored to be a part of such a momentous event.

Immediately the three of them went into wedding planning mode.

CHAPTER 21
Relationship Burnt to a Crisp

"So here's my list, Phil. Not entirely complete yet, but off to a good start." Molly plopped the notebook on the marble-topped table that Phil frequented daily.

"Wow," Phil gasped, looking down on the multi-paged list screaming for immediate attention before him. "You've been busy, Muffin."

"Well, yes I have. Planning a wedding is no small task, and unless we want a long engagement, I figured we'd better get started right away. I want to know what you think of all of these ideas, like what colors, what food to serve, where the ceremony should be, not to mention the reception, and how many guests to invite, what flavor of cake, flowers..." Molly droned on, satisfied to see Phil's eyes glazing over. "So many details to decide on, especially the date."

"As soon as possible," Phil interjected. "I'm good with whatever you want. I don't care about any of the details, as long as you'll marry me. Really. Just surprise me, and I'll show up, the happiest man on earth."

"You're saying you want me to decide on everything?"

"Yes! I want this to be your dream wedding with everything the way you want it. Just give me the bills."

"No way, Phil. I have a nice-sized nest egg from my parents that will pay for everything."

"That's *your* nest egg. You keep it for the future. I've got this all handled financially. You just plan the wedding and I'll plan the honeymoon. Deal?"

"But I want to contribute money to both."

"Not happening, Muffin. Look, I've been putting away money for years. I'm single, I own the house, and I don't spend much, except at your bakery." Phil gave a serene smile. "I'm rollin' in the green."

"You drive a hard bargain, but I guess I'll let you plan the honeymoon. I'll take care of the wedding plans if that's what you r*eally* want."

"I really do want."

"Okay, but not Brazil!" She winked at him, reminding him of her former fiancé's less than desirable honeymoon plans in a remote village in Brazil. She stood up to head into the back room as her timer for the bread was going off impatiently, demanding her prompt response.

"I've gotta go get some work done, Molly. I'll see you tonight." Phil bestowed a quick kiss before she hurried to tend to the bread.

Molly heard the bell over the door jingle, and Phil's footsteps on the boardwalk outside as she launched herself into the workroom. "Yahoo, Lyra!" she cried. "He started going all comatose when I read the list, just as I'd expected. He doesn't care about any of the details for the wedding." Molly rubbed her hands together. "Now let's do this!"

They high-fived each other and started discussing flowers and wedding colors in glorious detail.

"Can't wait to see you, Denise," Molly chirped to her best friend on the phone. "When's your plane getting in on Friday night?"

"Five, so let's make an evening of it and go to dinner, my treat. I can't wait to feast my eyes on all those wedding gowns with you. It's like we always dreamed about as kids!"

"I know! Can you believe this is really happening?" Molly asked.

"Couldn't happen to a nicer person," Denise said emphatically.

"So what's going on with you and Sean? Is he getting on board with the idea of marriage yet?"

Denise sighed. "No, he's got the lack of commitment gene. Our relationship is going nowhere. I'm seriously thinking of breaking up."

"Oh, Denise, I'm so sorry! And here I am all jazzed about the wedding while you and Sean might be breaking up," Molly apologized.

"No, Molly, don't feel that way. My miserable relationship can't dampen my excitement for you and Phil. To be honest, I was inspired when you broke up with Jared and found the right man. It gives me hope. I've wasted enough of my life on Sean. It's time for me to move on."

"Speaking of moving on, have you ever noticed the way Clyde looks at you?" Molly raised an eyebrow.

"What? Clyde Vanderlande? No way. We are talking about Clyde from the restaurant, right?"

"Yep. I can tell he's interested...very interested. Remember when he had that tropical mango iced tea the last time you were in town?"

"Yeah," Denise said. "It was really delish, but what's that got to do with the price of papayas in Polynesia?"

"Well, the next time I went into Clyde's, I tried to order it, and he said he didn't have it. It was for a 'limited time only.' Everyone knows you adore mangos. Later when Phil and I were eating, Clyde made a point of coming by our table and asking about you and how you were doing."

"That's ridiculous, Molly. He's not interested in me, and how would he know I adore mangos?"

"Don't you remember back in high school when we had Apprentice Day and the seniors had to set up fake restaurants in the multipurpose room as a project for economics?"

"Yes, but I don't get it. What's the point here?" Denise wondered.

"Remember you and I were juniors and we went up to Clyde's booth because we knew his dad owned a restaurant in town and we figured the food would be really good?"

"Uh huh." Denise was still puzzled.

"We ordered the tacos, and he asked if you wanted fresh mangos on yours. You said you were crazy for mangos, and he loaded up your Chinet with chunks of mangos, so much, in fact, that there were none left for me. Don't you remember?"

"Oh, yeah. I guess I'd forgotten about that. You have a memory like fly paper, Molly. No, it's more like spilled honey— sweet and super sticky."

"So trust me, he's interested. Hey, let's go to Clyde's for dinner. You just watch how he treats you," Molly suggested.

"Hmmm... I think you're wrong, but let's go. I always thought Clyde was really smart, not to mention cute. My relationship with Sean is as good as over anyway. Maybe I should just end it sooner rather than later and move on like you did with Jared."

"Don't do anything rash. Do you still love Sean or are you just sick of waiting?"

"Actually, I'm not sure how I feel anymore. It's comfortable having someone to go out with on the weekends, but it's getting really stagnant. I feel taken for granted. He never makes an effort anymore and I think we're both bored but too complacent to do anything to change it. There's not much life left in our relationship. Whenever the subject of marriage has come up in the past, he gets all antsy and finds a way to change the subject. I don't want this kind of relationship to become permanent, so I guess I should just break it off." She paused. "Do you really think Clyde could be interested in me?"

"I really think he is, Denise. Let's see if we can find out," Molly giggled.

"That's it! I'm going shopping tomorrow after school for something new and gorgeous to wear on Friday. I'm gonna pray about breaking up with Sean. I think it's time for a change."

"I'll be praying for you. See ya Friday at five."

"Can't wait! Love you, Molly," Denise said with enthusiasm.

"Love you more," Molly replied, hanging up the phone.

Clyde, thought Denise, *he always seemed like such a nice guy back in school. He didn't have much of a social life, though, poor kid. Seems like he spent most of his time behind a book or helping out at the restaurant. He had that charming quirk where he'd reverse the first letters of words in a sentence. Spoonerism, I think it's called. It'll be nice getting to know him —that is, if I get the chance.*

She started planning her break-up speech in her head as she reached under her beaded lampshade to turn off her bedside lamp. The dangling beads danced in the darkened room, unaware of their invisibility.

"Sorry, Phil." Molly looked sheepishly at him as she replaced the coffee pot on the coffee-maker. "It's the weekend that Denise is coming to help me find my wedding gown. I'm afraid I'll be busy Friday night through Sunday." She handed him his cup of coffee and customary fritter.

"Wow, all weekend?" Phil puzzled. "How long can it take to find a dress?"

"Gown, Phil. It can take a lot longer than a weekend to find the right one. It has to be completely perfect. Plus, we've got to find bridesmaids' dresses too. That's not easy. The girls have to agree on styles they all like and look good in. It all takes time. And then there's the shoes..."

"All right, all right. I get the picture. It sure is easier being a guy. We just go in, pick out a tux, get measured, and, bam, we're done. The shoes come with the tux, so it's one-stop shopping. Done in an hour or less."

"You're not joking; it *is* much easier being a guy, but you miss all the fun of trying stuff on, going to more stores, trying more stuff on, not being able to decide, worrying about prices, finding exactly the right shoes to go with the dress you can't afford, et cetera."

"Well, I know you'll have fun, Muffin. So how are you all gonna go together on Saturday? Someone's gotta run the bakery with that Girl Scout troop coming by like they do every third Saturday."

"Denise and I will go dress hunting Saturday morning, and Lyra and Steph will just have to join us when the bakery closes late Saturday afternoon. I wish we could all go together, but that's just how it goes."

"Hey, why don't I run the bakery for you on Saturday? I'm not scared of no Girl Scouts, and as long as the baking is already done, all I'd have to do is run the register and serve up pastries and coffee."

"What? You'd do that for me, Phil? Really?"

"Really," Phil replied, receiving a big bear hug from his petite fiancée.

"I can't wait to tell the girls! This will make things go so much easier, having everybody together. Oh, thank you, thank you, thank you, Phil!" Molly repeated rapidly between kisses. "Are you sure you can handle this? You'll be severely outnumbered when the Girl Scouts arrive."

"Piece of cake," he punned, looking proud of himself.

Molly kissed him one last time, then ran to the back room to tell Lyra and Stephanie the good news.

Friday evening, Molly was waiting downstairs at the Sacramento International Airport, anticipating Denise's arrival. Molly had arrived a little early and had brought her knitting to keep her occupied while she waited. She was working on a forest green cowl in alpaca yarn for Denise and was almost ready to cast off. As she watched the yarn pass from one needle to the other, she marveled at her good fortune of having the same best friend for all these years. Denise and she always picked right back up where they left off whenever they got to see each other. Molly wondered if Denise had actually broken up with Sean this week. At least Denise had seemed pretty determined to.

Molly had dropped by Clyde's during the week and made sure she mentioned Denise was coming to town for the weekend to help find a wedding gown. Clyde had misunderstood and thought Denise was coming to shop for her own wedding dress. His face had instantly fallen. "I didn't know Denise was metting garried," Clyde said. He had long since given up on explaining or apologizing for his inadvertent letter reversals. If anything, they actually seemed quite normal to all who knew him.

As Molly set him straight, she was delighted to see his smile resurface. *Yep*, she congratulated herself on her keen observation, *he's definitely interested. I can hardly wait to tell Denisie!*

Molly had just finished casting off her project when she looked up and saw Denise at the top of the escalator. She jumped up and ran to meet her at the bottom of the moving stairs. They both giggled like schoolgirls as Denise stepped onto solid ground. Hugging, they started in on their nonstop weekend-long conversation. After rescuing Denise's luggage from its wild carousel ride, they made their way to Molly's car, chattering all the while. On the drive back to River Oaks, Molly told Denise about her conversation with Clyde that week.

"You're kidding," Denise asserted, then daringly asked, "Really? I can't believe he reacted like that. Maybe you're right, Molly. I sure hope you are," she added shyly.

"I'd bet my knitting needles on it," Molly asserted. "So what happened with you and Sean this week? Did you break up with him?"

"Well, I had a talk with him Tuesday night after work. We went to dinner at our usual Mexican restaurant, The Matador, and had the *same old orders* we always have, sat at the *same table*, and had the *same waiter* with the deep voice who *always* makes such a production of seating me. When the food came, I looked at Sean and asked, 'Are you getting bored with us?' He asked me what I meant. So I said, 'We go to the *same*

294

place every week, do the *same* things, and pretty much say the *same* things to each other. Isn't it time for a change?'"

"He told me he was happy with the way things were. I informed him that I wasn't, that I needed some variety, some excitement, something to look forward to when I'm grading papers and doing lesson plans all week."

"He asked, 'What do you want from me?'"

"I said, 'Something more than this.' I asked why he always changed the subject when I brought up marriage. He told me not to 'rock the boat,' that he wasn't ready to commit. I told him that our relationship was going nowhere."

"He said, 'Can't we just enjoy our enchiladas and talk about this some other time?'"

"I told him, 'No, Sean, we need to make some changes.'"

"He didn't want to talk about it and said that he hated change. I said, 'Then you're going to be one lonely man.' I got up and walked out, called my friend Melinda from work, and asked her to come pick me up. He didn't even follow me outside; he just let me leave."

"Later that night, he called me to try and patch things up. I told him it was over, that he would be forced to make a change anyway since I didn't want to see him anymore. He kept trying to smooth things over, saying everything would be okay between us, but I told him it wouldn't. He said I'd be back in a week when I'd calmed down. I told him to keep dreaming. It's over between us. Honestly, I feel so relieved. I was trapped in that stalemate relationship for so long, and now I get the chance to breathe. It's so good to get away this weekend. I'm not even sad about the breakup, just angry that he was so blasé about it."

"I'm proud of you," Molly said. "You finally took a step forward, and that one step left him in the dust."

"I realized after I talked with you on the phone on Monday night that I was wasting precious time waiting for him to commit himself when I wasn't even sure I loved him anymore."

"What if he comes back and says he'll change things up? What if he pursues you and tries to win you back?" Molly probed.

Denise shifted in her seat, readjusting her safety belt. "I don't think I'm interested in him anymore. My mom always said that men are on their best behavior before you marry them. If this was his best...well, I'm not sticking around to see his worst." She drew in a deep breath. "I'm feeling like I've been let out of a cage. I'm not going to settle for a sloth anymore. The next guy is going to have to work pretty darn hard to catch me and even harder to keep me."

They pulled up in front of Clyde's Restaurant as their conversation about the aforementioned sloth ended. "Let's go have some fun tonight and forget all about What's His Name for the weekend," Denise proclaimed.

"Now you're talkin'!" Molly agreed.

LEAVING LYRA

Clyde had been waiting all week for Denise to come to town. He had been hoping against hope that she would stop in for dinner with Molly, and now here was Molly's car pulling up outside, and there Denise was, ready to walk into his restaurant and hopefully into his life.

Before they got out of the car, Molly had an idea. "Let's be sure we're talking about your break-up when Clyde approaches our table. We want him to overhear that you are a free agent now."

"Great idea, Molly. Let's do it." Denise was checking out her hair and makeup in the tiny visor mirror. "Guess I'm as ready as I'll ever be," she said, opening up the car door and stepping out. She had chosen wisely while shopping that week. Her new dress was an enthralling shade of emerald green, setting off her long auburn tresses that trailed the V neckline. Her slim waist was accentuated by the full skirt that swished as her forest-colored suede heels stepped confidently up the curb, following Molly into the restaurant.

Clyde heard the door open and turned to see Denise entering, looking even more gorgeous than he'd ever seen her before. He nearly dropped the tray he was carrying to the table the Petersons shared with the McCrearys. The two couples were out on their usual Friday night double date, and by the looks of things, Maggie and Betsy considered it a very lucky thing they had chosen to go to Clyde's that evening.

Clyde recovered the tray and served the two couples their meals. He hastily made his way to the front of the restaurant to greet his *most valued customer*, Denise.

"Goodness gracious, he almost dropped his tray. Did you see that, Maggie?" asked Betsy.

"Looks like he's distracted by who just came in the door," observed Betsy. "Is that Denise Kaughman with Molly?"

"It sure does look like her, all right. She has grown up to be quite the beauty, hasn't she?" Maggie noted. "That long curly auburn hair. She's the image of her mother."

"My, yes. I wonder what she's doing in town. Didn't she move down south to be a school teacher years ago? Glad to see her back in River Oaks. Let's see if we can hear why she's back and why Clyde is acting so fidgety," Maggie suggested.

"All right, you two," Bob Peterson broke into their speculations. "No gossiping now."

"Yes, right," Sam McCreary concurred. "This is supposed to be a double date, not a gossip fest."

"Fellas, please shush. We can't hear what the girls are talking about. I think Denise said something about breaking up with her boyfriend," Betsy recounted.

"Yes, I think she said she needs a change. Maybe that means she's interested in Clyde. You know how we girls drop hints loud enough for the right ears to hear," Maggie contributed.

"Ladies, please. If you're not going to quit eavesdropping, at least let the two of us men sit together so we can talk man-talk," Bob pleaded.

"Oh, all right." Betsy gave in and switched seats so the men folk could get a reprieve.

Meanwhile at a nearby table, a different man-talk conversation proceeded uninterrupted as Spencer spoke to his fire chief mentor. "So, Chief," Spencer got his boss' attention away from the friendly bickering couples in the next booth. "I met someone. She's the prettiest woman I've ever seen. She's got this long, long hair, and legs to match. She's sassy but sweet. And she seems really dedicated to her younger brother and sister. I don't know what it is, but I just can't stop thinking about her," Spencer confided.

"Sounds like you finally met your match. That last girlfriend of yours was a hot mess, so cold and into material things. So how old is she, and how did you meet her?" The Chief picked up his coffee cup.

"I met her at Molly's bakery. She works there. I'm not sure exactly how old she is. I'd guess twenty-three, twenty-four, somewhere in there."

"So what's her name?" He raised his cup up to their passing waitress in a silent plea for a refill.

"That's the problem. She won't tell me."

"Well, how are you gonna ask her out if you don't even know her name?"

Denise could stand it no longer. "Now tell me what kind of dress you're looking for. Full length, tea length, with or without a train, straps or strapless, sleeveless, low-cut back?" Denise asked

"Not strapless, for sure. I've seen too many brides wrestling with their dresses at weddings to want to fuss with having to hike it up throughout the day. I definitely want straps of some sort. No train to have to mess with either. Brides always have trouble getting them bustled up for the reception. I don't want to have to fuss. Something I can dance in, for sure. And I really love low backs on bridal gowns. They're so gorgeous. I think women's backs are very underrated."

"I totally agree," Denise said

"You men are talking too loud," Maggie nagged.

"We can't hear what the girls are saying," Betsy scolded.

Maggie craned her neck. "I think Molly is talking about wedding dress styles."

"Ah, maybe that's why Denise is in town. She's probably maid of honor," Betsy surmised.

"Those two were inseparable as kids. I remember they were always popping in and out of the bakery," Maggie reminisced. "It's good to see them back together again."

Now who's too loud?" Sam chided.

"Oh, shush. We're trying to listen." Maggie was indignant.

The men just chose to ignore their wives and went on with their conversation about catfish and lawn mowers.

"So, ladies," Clyde smiled the words as he came up to Molly and Denise's table, "What can I dret you to gink as you look at the menu? I mean, what can I get you to drink?" He ran his hand through his freshly-cut sandy-blond hair, checking to make sure his brain were still there.

"I would love to have that delicious tropical mango iced tea—the one I had the last time I was here. Molly said you don't have it anymore, though." Denise looked up at him, batting her ultra long eyelashes and pushing back the waves of her cherrywood-colored hair from her face.

Clyde bent down to retrieve the pen he had dropped. Righting himself, he said, pronouncing carefully, "Well, I think I could bring it back on the menu for tonight."

"Make that two," Molly chimed in, barely suppressing a giggle.

As Clyde hurried away to *det their grinks*, Molly whispered, "See, what did I tell you?"

CHAPTER 22
I'm Afraid We Lost the Fritter

Having exhausted all local bridal shops, Molly, Denise, Lyra, and Stephanie decided to drive into Sacramento.

"Those dresses were all starting to look the same," Molly lamented.

"But they all look lovely on you," Denise insisted, "You could pick any one of them and be the most gorgeous bride ever."

"Now you're just being silly," Molly said. "I want something different, not like every other bridal gown. I think we need to go to Miosa Bride on J Street. Many of the brides I make wedding cakes for have raved about the exceptional selection and service."

Michael was the owner and well-known gown designer at Miosa Bride. If she couldn't find the right gown there, it didn't exist.

Soon the girls found themselves talking to Michael. He made recommendations for the perfect style of dress for Molly according to her figure type.

"I know you said you don't want a strapless gown, but I'd like you to try a couple that I have in mind along with the gowns you've already chosen to try on," Michael suggested.

"Oh, just try them, Molly," Denise coaxed.

"Yeah, you haven't tried on a single strapless gown today," Stephanie added.

"I just don't want to worry all day about falling out of my dress. I've seen too many brides constantly pulling up their dresses," Molly reiterated.

"If the dress has the correct fit and the back isn't too low it will stay put," Michael assured her.

After an hour, the gowns were starting to pile up in Molly's upstairs dressing room. Many gowns came close to being "the dress." One had the right lace but not the right back. Another had beautiful Swarovski crystals and a sweetheart neckline, but too much train for an outdoor wedding. She finally agreed to try a strapless gown and thought she had at last found her dress with clean lines and plenty of sparkle delivered by narrow beadwork cascading into bouquets of lace flower appliqués. "I think this could be it!" Molly declared.

"This strapless gown works for you, Molly," Lyra said.

Denise and Stephanie agreed wholeheartedly.

Molly turned and saw the yards of English net pooling on the ground behind her.

Michael bustled the sweeping train up.

"I love this dress, but I'm kind of concerned about the train. This is going to be an outdoor wedding, and even bustled, this train is pretty long."

"I have one more dress I'd like you to try," Michael said. "It's one of my own designs." He brought out a stunning ivory gown. It had a lightly ruched bodice with lace appliquéd flowers blooming below the bust line and flowing down the very full skirt of fine English net. No sweetheart neckline here. It was strapless but straight across the top and very form fitting.

"Oh my." Molly's mouth dropped open. "I've got to try this on."

Denise hurried into the dressing room to assist Molly. Moments later the curtains parted, and out stepped the bride-to-be.

A chorus of ooh's and ahh's followed.

"It fits you like a glove. This dress was made for you," Michael said.

Molly was breathless. "It's...it's perfect. This is it!"

"I didn't think you could do better than the last dress, but this one is the most exquisite gown I've ever seen." Denise grinned. "Can I borrow it for my wedding—if it ever happens?"

"Sure thing. I'm only gonna wear it once."

They both laughed.

"Now let's find those bridesmaids' dresses," Molly enthused.

Lyra groaned. "Do we *have* to? Things were going so well."

"We're going to find something that looks good on all of us," Stephanie assured.

Michael suggested, "You might think about using the same fabric and color with different-styled dresses for each bridesmaid so that everyone feels beautiful."

"Pink," Molly spoke with authority. "They could be different shades and styles, as long as they're all pink."

Lyra sighed with relief, knowing that she wouldn't have to try to fit into something that Stephanie and Denise would look good in. Having recently lost a few more pounds at the gym, the prospect of finding a dress was not as daunting as it would have been, but she was still insecure.

Molly, Denise, and Stephanie were already busy checking out the selection of sleek dresses, leaving Lyra stranded, uncertain.

Sensing her hesitation, Michael stepped in to assist in her search for flattering dresses. He led her to a peony pink chiffon dress that seemed to float on its hanger. The bodice was a high V-neck with pleated strips appearing to wrap diagonally twice around the bust line. They tapered and crossed at the top and flowed over the shoulders to settle onto the horizontally pleated back of the bodice. The floor-length skirt was softly pleated as well.

Leaving Lyra

"Try this on, Lyra," Michael encouraged. "I think it will be amazing on you."

Lyra stepped into a dressing room. *I'm going to look like a beached whale, but this isn't about me.* She shrugged out of her comfortable jeans and tee shirt and slipped into the airy chiffon dress. Not wanting to look, she turned her back to the full-length mirror and fumbled with the zipper. She hesitantly turned to the mirror and drew in a deep breath. *Oh wow! This isn't half bad.* She turned sideways to admire her results from the gym. *All the working out was worth it.* With her new hair style and make up she felt almost glamorous in this dress.

Steph spoke through the dressing room curtain, "How's it going in there, Lyra?"

Lyra slowly slid open the curtain.

"Lyra, you rock that dress! Look, you guys!" Stephanie announced.

The girls all crowded around Lyra. They were all in total agreement that she looked stunning.

"It's perfect on you, Lyra," Molly spoke for them all.

"Great style," Denise said. "Maybe we should all try on the same design."

Michael beamed.

In less than an hour the girls were headed out the door, dresses ordered, and ready to try on shoes. After several stores and a quick coffee break, they were about to give up on shoes.

"No!" Molly insisted, "Never give up on shoes! Ever!"

Heading back to the car, they stumbled upon a small shoe store called The Glass Slipper. "Come on, girls, one more store," Molly coaxed. Multiple sighs followed.

Stepping in the door, Molly immediately beheld "the shoes." Ivory satin, medium-heeled pumps covered with appliquéd flowers with faux pearl centers across the toe and a smattering at the heel area. "That's it, girls! These are the shoes."

The sales lady approached. "We have them in a variety of colors as well."

"Oh," said the bridesmaids in unison, suddenly forgetting how tired they were.

"Pink?" Molly asked.

"Three different shades," the lady answered with a smile.

"Sold," Molly pronounced.

High on estrogen, the girls were returning back to River Oaks from their successful shopping excursion.

"Hey, what's with the flashing lights?" Denise pointed at the fire engine parked in front of Molly's bakery.

Through the smoke pouring from the front door they could just make out Phil wringing his hands. Fire fighters were hustling their hoses through the doorway.

Molly jumped out of the car and ran up to Phil.

He grabbed her shoulders and held her back. "It's not that bad—really. We can get the place up and running in no time. At least the grease fire didn't spread to Daryla's flower shop."

Molly gaped, wordless.

"I'm sure your insurance will cover the damages," Phil consoled.

Molly muttered, "How?" her hand on her forehead.

The girls stood frozen near the car, afraid to approach.

"You know that fryer, I think there might be something...wrong with it."

"Phil, I told you not to touch the fryer," Molly spoke through clenched teeth.

"Well, I know, but I really needed a fritter, and how hard could it be? But the stupid fryer, it just seduced me, lulling me into a false sense of security, making me feel...invincible. What was I supposed to do?"

"Not touch it!"

Spencer walked out the door, hose in hand. "We've got it under control now. At least no one was hurt."

"But what about my fritter?" Phil pleaded.

"I'm afraid we lost the fritter, Phil." Spencer patted him on the shoulder, comforting him on his loss.

Stephanie hurried over to get a better look at the handsome firefighter. "Spencer, what happened?"

"You all left this party animal in charge of a highly flammable substance. You should have known better, Shanaenae."

"What'd he just call you, Stephanie?" Lyra was puzzled.

"Ah, thanks! I've been trying to find out her name for weeks. Stephanie."

"Thanks a lot, Lyra," Steph muttered, glaring at her.

A young firefighter came out, dragging a hose. "Ma'am, it's safe to go in now." The smoke was dissipating as they entered the dining area...no damage.

"You guys must've gotten here fast. The dining area looks untouched," Molly marveled.

"But wait til you see the work room, that's where the real damage was done." Phil stared guiltily down at his shoes.

Molly and the girls followed and found the rest of the firefighters sitting around the work tables stuffing their laughing faces with an assortment of brownies, pies, cookies, doughnuts, and cake. A large smoke machine was in the corner, chugging out scentless smoke. Molly looked at the fryer. Not a sign of fire anywhere.

"Where's the fire?" Molly seethed.

"Fire? Who said anything about a fire?" Phil said. "The firefighters are the ones who've done the damage, I'm afraid. Look at all those crumbs! They've wiped you out, Molly. Who would've known they'd be such messy eaters?"

LEAVING LYRA

"Thanks for the pastries, Phil," one firefighter yelled. A round of applause ensued from the rest of them. "Sparky! Sparky! Sparky!..."

"You...little..." Molly pointed her finger at Phil. "You will pay!"

"I already did. It was expensive but well worth it. And you thought you couldn't leave me in charge here," Phil whined. "I took out your entire inventory, sold every last crumb. I think I have a new calling."

"I don't think so, Phil." Her forced calm held a deadly edge.

"Didn't you ever throw a party when your parents were gone?" Phil offered in his defense.

Arms tightly crossed, Molly pierced his soul with gimlet eyes.

"You know, smoke machine, large and manly hoses, coffee instead of beer—black with no foo foo sugar or creamer? No fryer fire. Honest. Just good manly fun. The smoke machine was just to lend that 'I'm at a deadly blaze' mood. The guys and me, we're simpatico. What red-blooded guy hasn't dreamed of putting out a gigantic grease fire in their fiancée's bakery? How was I supposed to resist this kind of temptation? It's in the blood. These guys understand, don't you, Captain Spencer?" He grabbed the firefighter and dragged him back into the fray. *Spencer will protect me,* he hoped.

"We most certainly do, Sparky." Spencer stood up extra tall. They fist-bumped a secret code of honor from one pyromaniac to another.

"Sparky?" Molly asked icily. "Did you just call him Sparky?"

"My secret firefighter code name; Spence here gave it to me after I fixed the smoke machine the second time. They don't make those things like they used to. Very inferior quality these days. The important thing is no one got hurt," Phil placated unsuccessfully.

"Well, not exactly," Spencer corrected, "Parker did choke on that pecan pie, laughing at you and that gig you did of Molly and the rolling pin. Almost had to do the Heimlich on him." He turned to Molly. "This man is a danger to the well being of the firefighting community."

Molly stood, glaring at the both of them, her crossed arms tightened further.

"Well...okay then," Spencer said, "the party's over, gentlemen; time to wrap up the hoses. Stevens, Hemitt, grab the brooms; I want this place spotless."

"Oh, no you don't," Molly ordered. "Sparky here is doing *all* the cleanup by himself." She turned her lasers on Phil, blistering his retinas. "Do I make myself clear? And I want it so clean that I could eat off this floor. Got it, Sparky?"

In spite of his extensive experience in emergency situations, Captain Spencer gave an involuntary shudder, as if someone had just walked over his future grave. "That's it, guys, let's *move!*" As his men loaded the hoses, Spencer turned to see Stephanie walking away. He strolled over and tapped her on the shoulder, setting her ponytail swinging. "So, Stephanie, looks like you're off work for the rest of the night. How about we go get a cup of coffee at Swiss Sisters?"

"Aren't you on duty? Besides, I have to get home and take care of my little sister and brother."

"Well, how about Monday after work, say five o' clock?"

"I don't know. I don't really know you."

"Well, how are you gonna get to know me then? It's just coffee, Shanaenae."

"Aren't I a bit young for you?"

"I don't know. How old are you?"

She hesitated. "How old do you think I am?"

"Maybe twenty-three, twenty-four?"

"Wow, you're a good guesser."

"So, what do you say? Monday?" He gave her an impish smile.

"Let me think. Nah." She tossed her ponytail and turned to head home.

"Walk you home?"

"No thanks. I know my way."

Sunday after church Molly and Phil were discussing the wedding. They had decided beforehand that they didn't want to do the traditional bouquet and garter toss at the reception.

"Let's make what we throw something that our guests will really want," Molly said to Phil. "Something they'll really compete for."

"Like chubs of salami?" Phil suggested, shaking his head yes.

Molly rolled her eyes. "Only if you have an EMT standing by. Those chubs are more like clubs."

"Okay, okay, I've got it. I'll throw a *big* roll of duct tape. It's round, easy to catch, and a guy can never have too many rolls of duct tape!"

"Do you think guys would really compete for a roll of duct tape, Phil?"

"Just you watch."

"All right, this is your thing. Do whatever you want, just have it ready to go at the reception."

Phil rubbed his hands together. "Easy! The guys are going to love this!"

"Whatever." Molly couldn't care less what he threw at this point.

"Who's your best man going to be?" Molly looked up from the invitations she was stamping at her kitchen table.

"Well, Mitch of course," Phil responded, absently placing another stamp on his pile of invites.

She stopped mid-stamp. "Phil, are you sure? He owes you a prank. What would be a more glorious revenge than ruining our wedding?"

"He wouldn't do it. He'd have to be lower than a sublunar scumdog to do that. I've known him all my life. He knows the wedding is off limits. But if it makes you feel better, I'll talk with him. I promise he will not cast a tricorder into the solemn proceedings."

"Tricorder? What's a tricorder?" Molly was puzzled.

"Didn't you ever watch Star Trek?" Phil was aghast.

She shrugged.

"Well, in the episode where…"

"I hope you're right." She cut off his soon-to-be lengthy monologue and continued stamping, this time with furious energy.

CHAPTER 23
Don't Take it Out on the Dough

"Here comes your firefighter again," Lyra teased Stephanie. "He's heading across the street towards the bakery."

"He's not my firefighter! Oh oh, you're right; he's heading towards the door."

"I'm outta here!" Lyra disappeared into the workroom, leaving Steph all alone. She pretended to wipe down the counter as he entered.

"Does that bell over the door ever drive you crazy?" Spencer asked.

"What bell? You must have ringing in the ears," Stephanie taunted. "What can I get for you, Captain?"

"A date with you," he replied.

"I told you I don't date perfect strangers."

"Oh, so you think I'm perfect then."

"I stand corrected! You are just a stranger." She tossed her ponytail over her shoulder, being coy.

"I wouldn't be a stranger if you would just go to coffee with me after work tonight."

"How do I know you're not some crazy axe murderer, hmmm?" She smiled.

"Well, I do carry an axe frequently at work."

"See what I mean? Besides, you're way too old for me, Captain."

"Don't call me 'Captain.' I'm just Spencer to you. And what do you mean too old? You've gotta be around twenty-four. I'm only twenty-eight."

Stephanie didn't answer him at first. She reasoned, *Oh man, he's eleven years older than me! He wouldn't even be talking with me if he knew I was seventeen.*

"Twenty—I'm twenty," Steph blurted. She couldn't believe that she had actually just lied to this guy. *What? No, not some guy. He's a man.* She reminded herself. *He thought I was twenty-four. I only wish I was. What'll I do now?"*

"I'm so sorry! I didn't mean you look old or anything. You're just so darn gorgeous; I don't know. Would you at least agree to coffee and give me a chance to get to know you?"

"I don't know. You did insult my age and all..."

"Come on, it's just coffee."

"Well, okay. But *just* coffee. I get off at five tonight. Come by, and we'll walk to Swiss Sisters."

"I can't pick you up?"

"Nope. You might carry an axe in your car. How am I supposed to know?"

"All right, all right. I'll walk over at five." He left, self-satisfied, with confident step.

"I'll be here," she said. *Gee, Steph, what a snappy comeback,* she thought. *You sounded like the seventeen-year-old that you really are. What'll I do if he finds out?* She walked into the workroom.

"So now you're twenty?" Lyra challenged. "Why did you lie to him?"

"I don't really know, Lyra. He's so handsome. If he knew my age, he'd never speak to me again. What harm can it do just to go to coffee one time? I'll never go out with him again," she lied to herself and Lyra.

At five on the dot the bell jangled.

"At least he's punctual," Lyra whispered to Steph before disappearing again into the workroom.

"Ready to go?" Spencer asked.

"I'll get my purse. Be right back."

As she ducked into the back room, Lyra cautioned her, "Be careful, Steph. You really should tell him the truth. He's gonna find out eventually."

Steph took down her ponytail and loosed her silken locks, running her hands through her hair. It fell dramatically around her shoulders and down her back. "I will, but just not tonight. It's just coffee after all." She stepped out of the room, purse slung over her shoulder.

"Your—your hair is amazing," he stammered. "I had no idea it was so long."

She ran her hand through her hair again. It flowed like a cascading waterfall.

"So how did it go last night?" Lyra's inquiring mind wanted to know.

"Oh, you know..." Steph trailed off.

"No, I don't know! What happened?"

"Well, we walked to Swiss Sisters, had coffee, and talked a lot. He likes hiking, dogs, and bacon. Just your regular guy."

"Come on! What happened already?"

"Nothing *happened*. We just got to know more about each other. He's so amazing!" she said dreamily. "He's taking me out to dinner someplace fancy on Saturday."

"So he's okay with your age? I'm surprised."

"No, Lyra. I haven't told him yet. I want to see if he really likes me first before I risk telling him the truth."

"You better tell him soon, or he'll be really mad that you lied."

"I don't know how to tell him. If I do, he'll never ask me out again. He's just everything I'm looking for—strong, hunky, sweet, funny, and I found out he goes to church where Molly and Phil go. I want a strong Christian husband someday."

"Wait a minute, Steph. You're getting way ahead of yourself here. What did your mom say about you dating a guy eleven years older than you?"

"I didn't tell her his age. I knew she'd be upset. I just told her he was a nice guy I met here at work. That's true enough. She probably thinks he's in high school, like I would be if I weren't home schooled. Besides, she never asked. She's still so depressed that she doesn't seem to care what I do anymore. She's in her own self-centered world. I need to get away from the house this Saturday. Her wallowing is driving me nuts. What better way to do it?"

"I don't know about this. What if he's just trying to..."

"You're not my mother, Lyra! He's not that kind of guy! I know what I'm doing. I'm almost eighteen now; I can handle myself."

Stephanie spent a sizable chunk of her paycheck on just the right dress and high heels to wear on her date. She took them, along with her makeup and curling iron, to work with her. She stepped out of the bathroom in a dark burgundy-colored, body-hugging dress and black suede four-inch heels. The curling iron had made her tresses even more irresistible.

Leaving Lyra

Lyra was amazed as she watched her friend glide gracefully across the floor in those heels as if she were born wearing stilettos. "How do you walk in those things? You look like a model!"

Steph practiced her runway walk as Lyra continued to be amazed. "You think he'll like this outfit?" Steph pivoted and walked the opposite direction.

"Wow! He'd have to be blind not to. Speaking of...he's headed this way. I'll duck out." Lyra once again disappeared through the curtained doorway, listening protectively.

Spencer strode in and nearly tripped over his jaw. "Wow! You look..."

"You like?"

"I like!" His eyes feasted from head to toe.

She turned around.

"I really like!"

"You don't look so bad yourself," Stephanie said. "Shall we get going?"

"I just want to look at you a little while longer," he gawked.

"You silly! Let's go!"

Lyra said a lengthy prayer as her friend headed out the door.

321

Their dinner on the other side of the lake was a fantasy for Stephanie. He had opened all the doors for her, pushed in her chair, and hardly taken his eyes off her all evening. She'd never eaten at such an expensive restaurant as Chez Brigitte. Her former date with Ronald at the Fillmore couldn't begin to compare to this swanky place with its low lighting and candles everywhere. The prices weren't even on the menu.

He asked all about her likes and dislikes, and they found they had many things in common. Their mutual love of the outdoors left an opening for many possible future adventures together. Stephanie, being both feminine and athletic, impressed Spencer; he could definitely see this relationship going somewhere. Fast.

After the filet mignon, he brought up a sore subject.

"So tell me about your family, Stephanie."

"What can I say? They're just a family," she attempted to skirt the issue.

"What? You don't get along with them?"

"It's complicated."

"That's all right. I'm a good listener. Tell me about them."

"Well, Mom married her high school sweetheart. They had three kids. You know, the stuff dreams are made of."

"Something tells me there's a lot more to this story."

"Yeah, well, there's a villain in every fairytale."

"So what happened?" Spencer leaned his elbows on the table and clasped his hands together.

Steph shifted uncomfortably in the brocade-covered seat. "It just gets ugly from there. You don't want to hear about it."

"Yes, I do." Spencer leaned forward, taking her hand.

Stephanie held on to his hand, feeling the warm current flow from his touch. She caught her breath. "Maybe sometime I'll tell you."

The waiter came by with dessert menus and they reluctantly let go of each other's hands.

Stephanie began to feel guilty that she hadn't been honest about her age. How could she ever tell him now? She had already waited too long. She'd have to find a way tonight, she promised herself.

"What looks good to you?" Stephanie asked Spencer casually.

"You do!" he replied.

She had heard that line before from Ronald, but this time, she felt a shiver run down her spine. *Who needs dessert with this delicious feeling running through me?* "I'm talking about dessert."

"So am I."

The waiter returned. "What may I get you for dessert?"

Spencer rallied. "I'll have your dark chocolate cheesecake. What would you like, Shanaenae?"

She smiled. "I'll have the mango key lime cheesecake, please." She handed back the menu.

"Any coffees for you, sir?" the waiter addressed Spencer.

"Two coffees, please." He gave Stephanie a slow stare.

Rather stuffed, they drove to the lake and parked nearby. *Now's the time to tell him the truth,* Stephanie told herself, *before this goes any further.*

He reached for her hand. The full moonlight shone on the two of them silhouetted in the car. The lake shimmered like a mirage, its reflection illuminating each of their faces.

"So tell me about your family," he spoke softly.

"Well, my dad was my hero, you know. He just about walked on water. He always made me feel safe and loved. Then one day he was just...gone."

"He passed away?" Spencer asked sympathetically.

"That would've been easier to take. He ran off with the typical young secretary from his construction company. Gone— into thin air." Stephanie looked down.

"I'm so sorry." Spencer wasn't sure what else to say.

"Mom still hasn't come out of the shock and depression, so I'm pretty much 'Mom' to both of my younger siblings." She wiped a tear away. "It's been pretty rough. What about your family?" Stephanie tried desperately to change the subject. She needn't have tried.

A blinding light shone in her eyes. "Stephanie Harrison? Is that you?" Sergeant Morrison asked in an uncharacteristically harsh voice.

Startled, Spencer and Stephanie dropped each others' hands.

"Captain Haus. What are you doing out with Stephanie after eleven o' clock?"

"We're on a date, sir," Spencer replied.

"It's after curfew, you know. You are aware it is eleven fifteen?"

"What does that matter?" Spencer asked innocently.

"Stephanie, let's see your ID," Sergeant Morrison commanded.

She shrank down in her seat. "There's something I've been meaning to tell you, Spencer...I'm...seventeen."

"What?" Spencer blurted. "You're what?"

"I'm almost eighteen, in a few months."

"Get in the police car, Stephanie." Sergeant Morrison opened the back door. "I'll take you home to your mom. I hope this doesn't send her over the edge again." He leaned his arm on the open door and addressed Spencer. "And you, Captain, you should know better than this."

"Sergeant Morrison, I had no idea, really! She told me she was twenty. Look at her! Does she look seventeen?"

"I must admit she doesn't, but this is the end of it. Head on home now and wise up."

Spencer shot his date an angry look.

"I'm so sorry, Spencer," was all she could say as Sergeant Morrison closed the back door of the squad car on her last word.

In the police car the sergeant lectured her, "What were you thinking, Stephanie? Does your mother know you were out with a grown man who's almost thirty? Did you think Spencer wouldn't find out? Why did you lie to him? Well...what do you have to say for yourself?"

Stephanie cried softly in the back seat, feeling ashamed. Why hadn't she told him the truth from the start? Now he would never want to set eyes on her. She wasn't the type to lie. *Why?* She asked herself again. *And now here I am sitting in the backseat of a police car like a criminal.* The thought of the kind of person who typically sat in this seat turned her stomach. *How can I face my mom? What'll I say? What if she really does go over the edge? I better come clean and hope she doesn't.* "I'm sorry, Sergeant Morrison. This was all my fault."

"Don't go too hard on her, Mrs. Harrison," Sergeant Morrison whispered as he left the house. "She's young, and you know how seventeen-year-old girls can be. She's a good kid."

"Thank you, Sergeant. I can assure you this will *never* happen again!" Sylvia shut the door brusquely behind him.

It's going to be a very long night. Stephanie resigned herself to her mother's ranting. She knew she clearly deserved it.

As Stephanie cried herself to sleep that night, she stared out her bedroom window at the moon whose light had betrayed her. *Traitor moon,* she thought, *you ruined my whole life. Without your light Sergeant Morrison would never have recognized me in Spencer's car. And so another fairytale comes to a tragic end.*

Steph woke up with swollen eyes. It was all she could do to get out of bed. Grateful for her before-dawn job, she dressed and tiptoed past her mother's room, hoping she wouldn't have another confrontation before work.

"Stephanie Frances, I want you home right after work today. Restriction starts now," Sylvia spoke emphatically.

"For how long?" Steph dared to ask. *I can't miss the gym. Not now. It's the only social life I've got. And what about church?*

"I'll let you know when it's over. Is that clear?"

"Yes, Ma'am."

"And if I even hear his name in this house, I'm walking straight over to that fire station and giving him a piece of my mind! What kind of grown man dates a seventeen-year-old girl? That's eleven years difference in age! *Eleven* years!" she yelled.

"It's not *his* fault, Mom. I told him I was twenty."

"You lied! You lied to him! You lied to me!"

"You never asked me how old he was, Mom. I didn't lie to you."

"I can't trust you anymore, Stephanie. You deceived me! You knew I'd never approve of you dating a grown man! I raised you better than this!"

"Mom, I have to get to work now. We can continue this later. You don't want me to lose my job, do you?"

"You're just like your father! Always leaving when things get tough. Go on, get out of here. I have half a mind to kick you out!"

"And just how would you survive without the money I'm bringing home, huh?" Stephanie clenched her fists and embraced the drama. *It doesn't matter now. I'll be stuck at home for the rest of my life,* she thought. "All you do is sit around here, feeling sorry for yourself all day, every day, waiting for Dad to come home. Well, I got news for you Mom, he's not! I've taken the whole burden of this family on my shoulders this last year, and yes, I'm *only* seventeen! It's time for you to quit playing the poor pitiful me song and pick yourself up. Get some help if you need it, Mom, and come back to us." She paused with her hand on the door. "And I am *nothing* like Dad! I honor my commitment to this family—more than you have in the past year. So get over yourself and be a mom to your two other kids. I can take care of myself! I'm leaving to go provide for all of us now. So, what are *you* gonna do?"

"This talk is not over, Stephanie Frances!" she screamed as the screen door slammed shut.

By the time she got to the bakery, Stephanie was ready to punch someone. Lyra was kneading dough with Molly. *Perfect,* she thought, *I can punch out some dough.*

"Morning, Steph," Molly said, her smile dimming. "Hey, what's wrong?"

"Nothing," she replied.

"How'd the big date go last night?" Lyra posed the question, clearly recognizing that things must not have gone well.

"I don't want to talk about it." She clipped her nails, washed, dried, and floured her hands and began smacking bread dough around with the ferocity of a prize fighter.

"Hey, what'd that dough ever do to you?" Molly asked.

"Dumb, stupid dough!" She smacked it harder onto the kneading table.

"Okay, what's up?" Molly insisted.

"I'm not ready to talk about it," Steph mumbled into the distressed dough.

"Well, I'll let you two girls 'not' talk about it while I go put out the pies and get the coffee going. And don't take it out on the dough. The bread will turn out like hockey pucks." Molly stepped out of the work room.

"Now, spill it, Steph," Lyra prodded anxiously.

"I just can't talk about it in front of Molly. She'd think I'm terrible like my mom does."

"Tell me what happened. It's obvious you've been crying. Did he try to take advantage of you? Cause if he did..." She picked up the dependable industrial sized rolling pin and slapped her palm.

"No, nothing like that. He was a gentleman." Stephanie told her the whole story, complete with her mother's and the police officer's reactions. "But the worst part was the look on Spencer's face when I was put into the backseat of the police car! He looked so mad. Why did I lie to him, Lyra, why?"

"Police car?! I tried to tell you this wouldn't end well. Lying is the worst thing you can do in any relationship, but I'm so sorry you got hurt," Lyra put a sympathetic floury hand on her friend's shoulder.

"You wouldn't understand, Lyra!" Stephanie pulled away.

Lyra flinched and looked down at the rising dough. "No, I guess I wouldn't," she said under her breath.

LEAVING LYRA

Steph grabbed Lyra's wrist. "I'm sorry. I didn't mean it like that, Lyra. Really, I didn't. I'm just so upset. There's going to be more yelling when I get home, and I'm not looking forward to it. I didn't mean to take it out on you. Forgive me?" She plastered on an attempted smile.

"Yeah." She paused. "So what are you going to do now?"

"Live on restriction forever. Never see Spencer again. I'm sure he hates me now! I can never look him in the eyes. Why did I lie to him, Lyra? Why?"

"Because you need love like everybody else. Maybe even more so because your dad ran off and left you all. You want to matter to someone. Spencer gave you attention. You were craving love, and it was important enough for you to lie in order to feel loved. But love will never work when it's based on a lie. At least he knows now, before this went any farther. It would only be harder to tell him the truth the longer you kept it from him."

"I've lost him forever. I really thought he was 'the one.'"

"The one to what? The one to help you with all of your problems? The one to never leave you? To give you unconditional love? You and I both know there's only one Person Who can do all that. Jesus."

"I know it in my head, but I don't feel it in my heart."

331

"My mom used to say the distance between the head and the heart is the longest eighteen inches in the human body," Lyra recalled.

"I wish I had a mom like yours. All my mom ever does is yell or sleep." Stephanie looked out the flour-dusted window.

"I wish I had a mom like mine too." Lyra patted Stephanie's shoulder and got back to work, grateful for the short time she had known her mother.

Spencer hadn't slept a wink that night.

How could I have been so stupid? Only seventeen? Why would she lie to me? I can never trust her again. Obviously. I've gotta forget about her, but there's just something about that girl. No, Spence, forget about her! She humiliated me in front of Sergeant Morrison. Now he thinks I'm a perv. What if there's something wrong with me?

Spencer battled himself, flipping over and over on his mattress all night. *I've gotta talk this over with someone I trust who'll be absolutely straight with me. McIntyre. I've gotta talk to him. He won't pull any punches. I should call my sister too. She knows me better than anybody. God, why did Stephanie have to be seventeen?* He tossed his extra pillow across the room.

CHAPTER 24
Shirley's Hot Buns

"I don't know why, but I keep getting tons of phone calls lately with people trying to sell me the strangest things. I must've wound up on some crazy call list. It's getting to where I don't even want to answer my landline anymore. Are you getting them too, Molly?" Phil asked.

"Nope," Molly replied. "I hardly ever get phone solicitors anymore." She took another bite of the excellent crock pot chicken dish Phil had prepared for dinner. The potatoes, pearl onions, and carrots were done to perfection. "Did you fill out some form to enter yourself in a contest or something? That's sometimes how you get on those call lists. They sell your info to other companies, you know."

"I know. That's why I don't enter contests. The one I got this morning was really different. They wanted to sell me on hiring clowns for corporate events. I told them there were enough clowns in corporations already."

Molly gave a shiver. "I hate clowns. They're so creepy."

"The calls get weirder every day." Phil shook his head nd narrowed his eyes.

"Well, why don't you get even when the next one disturbs your peace?"

"How?" Phil asked innocently as he propped his chin on his fist and gazed at her across the table.

"You could pretend you know them and attempt to carry on a conversation. Eventually they'll just give up and won't call back." She sat upright. "So what's for dessert, hmmm?" Molly raised a single eyebrow wistfully.

Sure enough, the next morning after returning home from Molly's bakery for his usual breakfast, the phone rang. Phil hesitated in answering, but eventually, with new resolve, he picked up the hand piece. "Hello," Phil said in his friendliest voice.

"May I speak with Phil McGuire?"

"This is Phil."

"Well, Mr. Phil, I'm Ted from the Save the Lemmings Foundation..."

Phil didn't give him the chance to say another word. He piped up, "Ted, you old bean, how the heck have you been, man? Long time no hear from. How's the wife? How did the lobotomy turn out for your brother? How's about I meet you at the old watering hole tonight around seven? Sure been good talking to you there, Ted. See ya tonight." With that, Phil hung up, thoroughly satisfied and oozing with well-earned vengeance.

Molly had Phil over for dinner that night at her place—raviolis and special bolognese sauce with her always popular Garden of Eatin' green salad with everything in it but anchovies. The variety of fruits, nuts, and veggies incorporated into the salad was always a hit anywhere she took it. As they munched, Molly asked Phil about his day, a game they often played with each other, always trying to ask the other person about their day first. This question could only be officially asked after twelve noon each day, according to the rules. Seems they had both forgotten the game today, until now.

"Oh man, you got me. Okay, I'll go first. Well, this morning I got another solicitor's call." Phil related the conversation from the morning as Molly smiled with glee at his newfound skill of annoying telemarketers.

"Bravo, Phil! I wish I had been there to hear it."

"Now we have to come up with more ideas. This was way too much fun. I can't wait for my next unsuspecting victim to call." Molly and Phil brainstormed a few more devious plans for the future telemarketer's calls.

The following morning Phil had already prewritten his monologue and was ready for the next assault. When the phone rang at nine o' clock he answered, putting his phone on speaker mode so he could record it and share his moment of triumph with Molly later. "Hello?" he spoke in the strangest accent he could muster.

"Hello, I'm calling on behalf of The Texans Against Tailgaters Association. We are raising funds for our yearly media blitz to remind drivers to drive more friendly and always leave a Texas-sized amount of space between themselves and the cars in front of them. How much can we count on you to donate this year, Mr. McGuire?"

"Magway get hit by bus," was his broken English reply in an accent hitherto unknown to linguistical science.

"I'm sorry, what was that?" the caller drawled politely.

"Magway get hit by bus! He in hospital. Make big mess. You doctor?" Phil kept the charade going.

The lady on the other end of the line stifled a snicker. "I'm sorry, I must have the wrong number." She hung up, openly laughing by this time.

Almost instantly the phone rang again. "Hello," Phil answered quickly in his most recent accent.

"Hello, I'm calling on behalf of Texans Against..."

Phil cut her off mid sentence. "Magway get hit by bus."

The caller could no longer contain herself and started laughing hysterically. She must have had her phone on speaker at the call center because Phil could now hear other people in the background laughing as well.

"It not funny! Magway get hit by bus! You hit him? I find you! I trace call. I get on bike and find you now. I avenge Magway!"

As the weeks passed Molly was continually entertained by Phil's prowess confounding the phone solicitors. One Friday morning he had taped a particularly irritating caller asking for donations to a vacation fund for the local assemblyman. Phil had had enough. He decided to pull out all the stops. In his finest British accent, he became an automated voice. "You have reached Arsenals R Us. We're your paramilitary go-to guys for all your armament needs at competitive prices.

"To order your own personalized nuclear warhead, press one. For tanks and heavy artillery parts and servicing, press two. To order our latest publication, 'Waterboarding for Surfers,' press three. For our exclusive dating service, press four. Press five or remain on the line and a representative will be with you shortly. Due to unusually high call volume, our current wait ime is approximately twenty-five minutes. Your call will be

337

answered in the order it was received. Your call is important to us and will be monitored for security purposes. Please stay on the line."

Phil could hear a button being pushed on the caller's phone and, having no idea which number had been selected, he thought quickly and chose a number at random. "Hello," he said in his most coy and convincing attempt at a female voice, "This is Shirley. I am five foot four and a vivacious companion. I like candlelight dinners, extravagant desserts, and long walks into oncoming traffic. I am approximately thirty years old and don't go anywhere without my stiletto heels. I always look so hot. Please leave your number after the beep and I'll call you back. Beep..."

"What do I do now?" the distraught caller whispered, presumably to his supervisor, as Phil hung up, smug in his craftiness.

That evening at dinner, Phil served up the minestrone soup he had made that afternoon. He and Molly were sitting down to enjoy their meal together, and Molly asked him about his day.

"Drat! You get me every time! Oh, all right, I'll go first. Not to brag or anything, but I pulled off one of the best stunts in the history of telemarketer retaliation. Let me play the recording of this masterpiece."

Molly listened intently and laughed with abandon at his opus until the very end when the caller had asked his boss what they should do. "You know, Phil, this is hysterical, but you may have crossed a line here that could get you in big trouble."

"Nonsense!" Phil crowed. "I won! Pure and simple! Take that, telemarketers! Bam!"

"I don't know, Phil, you might want to be careful. You may have gone too far this time."

After dinner they retired to the couch to watch "Father of the Bride" and share a cavernous bowl of Cherry Garcia. Just settling in, they heard a fevered pounding at Phil's front door.

"What the..." Phil rose, hoping it wasn't the return of Ronnie, the nightmarish vision of the past.

"Homeland Security!" came the commanding voice in charge. Phil cracked open the door and had to dodge as it was kicked open. "Get down on your knees!! Down...on...your...knees! Hands behind your head!"

Phil and Molly complied instantly. Molly's eyes were as round as sunny side up eggs.

"I'm afraid there's been some mixup, officer," exclaimed Phil. "It all started with these telemarketers..."

"Shut up and stay down! Johnson, McCalhainey, search the place." Sneering, he turned to Molly.

"And you must be Shirley!" He pointed accusingly.

"Her name is Molly. I'm Shirley," Phil protested.

"Shut up! Search them, Frazinetti," he thundered.

"Wait! I can explain!" Phil was visibly shaking.

"And you will, to the head of Homeland Security. Get on with it, Frazinetti."

"Do you have any explosive devices on the premises?" Frazinetti demanded, his eyes bulging with fury as he lifted Phil up by the shoulders. "Keep those hands on top of your head."

"No, no, of course not. This was all a joke. Really!" Phil pleaded.

"Well, none of us are laughing." Frazinetti frisked him down and cuffed him.

Molly began to cry.

"This was all just an innocent prank on a telemarketer. I didn't mean to..." Phil attempted again.

"Shut up. Get back down on your knees," Frazinetti growled.

"Well, looky what I found here, Commander. Found this detonation device under the pillow on the couch," McCalhainey held up a suspicious-looking black box with buttons and a joystick.

"That's for my remote control helicopter," Phil pleaded.

"So you admit to blowing up the helicopter," the Commander roared.

"What helicopter? I'm talking about a toy here!" Phil's voice broke.

"So it's all just fun and games to you then, huh?" the Commander said. "Johnson, put him in the car. Get him out of my sight."

Phil was forced to a standing position when a dark figure appeared in the doorway.

"Not so fast! Back down on your knees, McGuire," the shadowy figure ordered.

Phil complied.

The man clearly in charge stepped inside. "Bow! Bow to the new King of Prank!" a familiar voice boomed.

"Mitch! You Neptunian scum trawler! How did you pull this off? Was that you making all those telemarketing calls all this time?"

"No, I had my employees do it for me so you wouldn't recognize the voice or phone numbers," Mitch said, shining his nails on his pocket as he swaggered forward. "Sorry to put you through this, Molly. War is not without its collateral damage, I'm afraid."

"That's it!" Molly exclaimed. "This has got to stop, you two!" She rose, rubbing her sore knees.

"Yes," Mitch patronized, "with me as the all-time victor."

"I concede," Phil humbled himself momentarily. "But wait til the next round, he muttered."

"No more rounds!" Molly shrieked.

"The game's not over until we've used up all our lives," Phil asserted.

"Game over! I'm going home. You've crossed the line here!" Molly huffed. "So much for a romantic evening", she grumbled to herself as she drove home.

CHAPTER 25
Frosted or Pretty in Pink and Digging for Clams

"Let me make myself perfectly clear, gentlemen," Molly cleared her throat. "There will be no pranks, practical jokes, gags, funny business, or tricks of any kind at the wedding tomorrow. This is one day that I'm insisting that you call a truce. Our wedding is a sacred occasion and I am *not* going to let it be spoiled with your nonstop tomfoolery! Do I make myself absolutely clear?"

Phil and Mitch looked down at their shoes, crestfallen. "She's taking all the fun out of it," Mitch whispered.

"I think she means business," Phil said under his breath.

I heard you both." Molly raised an eyebrow. "I need your word on this, both of you."

"Okay," they said in sad unison. Phil kicked at the gravel path with his shoe.

"Now on with the rehearsal," Molly told Pastor Joe.

Joe was a bit unhappy at the thought of no pranks. Phil and Mitch were legendary after all. Joe had thought of a joke himself for the ceremony, but now laid it aside as he didn't want his supply of coconut cream pie to be suddenly cut off.

The rehearsal went off without a hitch. "See? That wasn't so hard, now was it, guys?" Molly asked.

The guys mumbled something unintelligible.

Molly rewarded Phil with a big kiss as the group headed off to Beni Hana for the rehearsal dinner.

By late afternoon the next day, the grounds at the Old Monterey Inn were enchanting. Light pink gerbera daisies floated serenely in the three-tiered fountain near the white satin pathway. There was a backdrop of four white doors accordioned together where the ceremony would be taking place. Molly had painted the panels light pink, then white, and antiqued them a bit with sanding so that some of the pink would peek through here and there. A multi-faceted chandelier hung on a filigreed bracket above the doors. Its prisms cast their rainbowed glory like confetti all around. The battery-operated tea lights were each set in their own mini lanterns hanging on filament wires from the many surrounding oak tree branches. A remote control was the solution when the time came to light them all just before the guests arrived. White chairs were set in rows with pink moire taffeta sashes wrapped around the backs of each. The hedges were manicured to perfection, and the nearby maze of azalea bushes would invite after-wedding strolls.

The guys' room was in total chaos two hours before the wedding. Photographer Marianne, one of Phil and Mitch's former classmates, was trying her best to keep them in line and on schedule.

"Look, guys. The wedding starts in just two hours, and we need to get all of your pre-wedding shots done soon. I'll be back in twenty minutes and I expect you all to be dressed and ready to rock. The girls have already finished their shoot. We've got to get you all done before guests start to arrive," Marianne lectured.

A boutonniere went sailing by her face as the men burst out in laughter.

"Very funny, guys," she said, rolling her eyes. "But I mean business! Get dressed! Now!" Marianne stomped off.

"Okay, dudes, let's get ready." Phil smirked. A shoe went flying across the room and smacked Phil in the rear end as he unzipped the bag his tux was in. "What the...?" Phil exclaimed.

"It's just a shoe," Mitch said flatly.

"No, not that, you bilge rat! What have you done to my tux?" Phil pulled a pretty-in-pink-colored tuxedo shirt and neon green bow tie from the garment bag. "Where's the white shirt and black tie? Molly's going to kill me!"

Mitch couldn't help but double over laughing. "Yes, she is! You gonna die, yo!"

"That isn't funny, Mitch! Where are my real shirt and tie? Marianne is going to be back here in a few minutes, and we've got to be ready!"

"I have no idea where they are, Phil. I'm innocent," Mitch snickered.

"Check out the rest of our bags," Phil's brother Matt said. "Maybe Mitch hid them in one of our bags."

The rest of them unzipped their bags. Shock rang out across the room as each found the same putrid color combo of shirts and ties.

"What are we gonna do?" Phil shouted. "Mitch, this isn't funny. Where are our real clothes?"

"How would I know? I just picked them up. I'm not responsible for what's *in* the bags," Mitch claimed, his face red with laughter.

Marianne knocked on the door. "Fifteen minutes, you guys."

Phil opened the door. "We've got the wrong tuxes! Mitch is playing games again. What are we supposed to do?"

"I suggest you all get dressed in your wrong tuxes and get yourselves out to the garden. We have to get started shooting right away."

346

Phil held up the fluorescent green bow tie and putrid pink shirt. "You gonna die, yo," Marianne said as she walked away, hand to forehead.

"Mitch, you've gone way too far this time," Phil said through gritted teeth.

"Don't blame this on me." Mitch said. "I just picked them up; *you* ordered them."

"Yeah, right," Phil shot back.

"Okay, everyone, just get dressed," Matt said. "I'm sure whoever is responsible will come clean before the wedding."

"So it was you, Matt, my own brother!" Phil accused.

"No way, Phil! Do you think I want Molly mad at me? You heard what she said yesterday about pranks. Apparently one of you wasn't listening."

"Let's just make the best of it and get dressed," Dorian said. "Guests will be getting here soon."

As the men were in various states of dress, Mitch called out, "What? Phil, you slime wad. What have you done?"

"Mitch, you've never looked so good, dude!" Phil belly laughed. "Now *that* is funny! Serves you right! This must be the latest in Paris, or German fashion, my friend."

They gawked at Mitch holding up electric green lederhosen. The upper portion connecting the suspenders almost obscured the Pepto-pink shirt. "I can't wear this! Phil, what have you done to my pants? These don't even come to my knees!"

You unconscionable bloggerbutt. I can't let Cindy see me like this! We've only just started dating. What am I supposed to do now? This'll be the end!"

"Hope you have time to shave those legs of yours," Phil busted up laughing until he thought of Molly.

Phil pulled his tuxedo pants out of the garment bag and slid them on. "Wait, what?! These slacks are at least six inches too short!"

"Ours too," Matt and Dorian screeched.

There was a knock at the door. "Five minute warning," Marianne called.

Phil opened the door.

"Oh my... What have you gone and done to each other? And what have you done to Molly? We're taking these pictures in five, ready or not. Whoever is responsible better come clean and fast." She walked off, shaking her head.

The tension had built to seismic proportions as the men scrambled to get ready.

"I can't believe you would do this to me on my wedding day, Mitch!" Phil huffed.

"Yeah, well look at what you've done to humiliate me! I feel like a German toreador here." Mitch retorted. "Do you think Cindy is going to take a second look at me dressed like this? You've already won *your* woman."

"Yeah, she'll take a second look all right! But what are you worried about? Molly could call the wedding off when she gets a load of what *you've* done here," spat Phil.

"At least the tux jackets are normal. You'll look back at all this someday and laugh," Dorian finally spoke up cheerily.

"Shut up, Dorian!" Phil and Mitch sounded in unison.

The final knock came at the door as Phil was tying his last shoe. "Ready or not, here I come," Marianne said, pushing open the door. She stood there staring in utter disgust. "You guys look like a bad anime. Which one of you is responsible for this mess?"

Phil and Mitch pointed at each other.

"Well, come on then, the whole lot of you. Guess I'm gonna have to shoot knees up and convert them all to black and white. When I find out who did this..."

They winced as she shot them a withering glare over her shoulder and marched them out to the garden area.

After shooting the guys' pre-wedding images, which Marianne and her assistant Glenda had to admit were the funniest they'd ever shot, they escorted Phil and his groomsmen back to their room. "If you still want Molly to walk down that aisle to you, I suggest that you get serious and fix this. You've had your fun." She pointed at Mitch's lederhosen and the hideous shirt, bow tie, and clamdigger combos. Marianne rolled her eyes, took a deep breath, and slammed the door behind her.

"Okay, Mitch, this was a pretty brilliant prank, but where are the real clothes?" Phil was at the end of his patience.

"And where are my pants, Phil. Hmmm?" Mitch countered.

The two men stood face to face, arms crossed in a standoff.

"While you two are being stubborn, didn't you have a letter and a gift you wanted delivered to Molly before the wedding?" Dorian asked.

"Oh yeah," Phil remembered. "Mitch was supposed to deliver it, but he's not exactly dressed for the occasion." He cast a deadly glance at Mitch. "Dorian, would you take this over to the girls' room for me?" He handed the black velvet box and envelope to Dorian.

"She's gonna see my shirt, tie, and these high-waters. What am I supposed to do?" Dorian replied.

"Put it outside the door, knock, and run for your life before they see you," Mitch suggested.

"Well, just don't blame me if they see this get-up I'm wearing and go home," Dorian said, heading out the door.

"Okay, you two. Enough is enough," Matt said, his sense of humor worn thin. "Let's put the pranking aside for a while and get ready. Dorian's right. Molly may just turn and run when she gets a look at you. Is that what you want?"

"Make him give me my pants!" Mitch insisted.

Leaving Lyra

"Like I know what happened to your pants!" Phil yelled. "Give me my clothes, Mitch! I mean it!"

Dorian returned, winded. "Whew! No one saw me. I just knocked and ran. Are you two still playing games? Man, are you stubborn!"

Phil went over to the bed, sat down, and pouted in silence for a few minutes until there was yet another knock at the door. Dorian answered it. "Lyra! Wow, do you look amazing!"

There stood Lyra in her ballet pink, full-length dress. Her expression did not match her outfit, however. "It's not funny, guys! Molly is not amused. Wait, what are you wearing? And Mitch, have you been digging for clams? You better get real, Phil, if you want this wedding to take place. And that letter you sent was not the least bit amusing."

"What are you talking about, Lyra? I sent her the sweetest, most romantic letter I've ever written," Phil stood up for himself.

"Oh yeah, like her face was the texture of petrified mesquite, and her hair reminds you of a used Brillo pad. Real classy, Phil. She's charmed. And that corn kernel bracelet you strung is so divine." Lyra held up a string of corn kernels. "What were you thinking?"

"What? Mitchell!" Phil roared.

Lyra stomped out.

Phil tried desperately to call Molly's cell phone, but she wouldn't pick up. He texted her repeatedly with no response.

Just minutes before the ceremony was to begin, the wedding coordinator tapped on the door. "Ready, gentlemen? It's time to go," she lilted. "Oh my," she said, trying to overlook the fashion travesty, but not able to get past Mitch's lederhosen pants. "Unusual style trousers. Is this a fashion statement?"

"No! Phil here is pulling a fast one on me, I'm afraid, but the show must go on. It's *his* wedding, and if he wants me to look like this..."

Phil was too angry to reply. How could his best friend pull all these stunts on the day of the wedding? He knew that Mitch must have given himself the stupidest pants to throw suspicion off of himself.

Dorian reminded Mitch to get the box with Molly's wedding band before they headed out. Mitch slipped it in his jacket pocket, and they went off to face the gathered crowd. Even facing the gallows would have been far more preferable.

Leaving Lyra

The violin, cello, and harp played airy pastoral music as the guests waited anxiously. There Phil stood with Pastor Joe at his side, awaiting Molly's entrance. Joe's eyebrows were raised at Phil's arresting attire. He whispered to Phil, "You gonna die, yo."

Stephanie and Matt were first down the aisle. Stephanie was wearing that "It Factor" look she always possessed. That girl could wear a flour sack and still make the best dressed list in <u>People</u> magazine. But even she couldn't make Matt look good.

Next in line were Lyra and Dorian. Lyra looked truly lovely. What an amazing pair they made. Phil wondered if someday they would be walking down the aisle together at their own wedding. Seeing them together this way just felt right.

Denise and Mitch were the last couple out of the chute. Even though Phil was madder at Mitch than he'd ever been in his entire life, he had to admit that Mitch really did pull off that German toreador look. Chuckles and snickers were escaping from even the most composed guests, but Mitch played his part and acted like the situation was quite mundane.

Man, am I ever gonna get even with Mitch when this is over, Phil promised himself. *I'll spend the rest of my life plotting revenge! I pity the poor woman who marries him.*

There was a short pause in the music. The melody of "Jesu, Joy of Man's Desire" began as the guests stood to their feet. A few seconds went by with a conspicuous absence of the bride. Had she taken one look at him and changed her mind?

After what felt like a half an hour, she stepped onto the runner, radiant and glowing. There was a soft swish of gown flowing over the satin runner. She was smiling beyond reason, staring at him and only him. Phil marveled that she didn't even seem to notice the bizarre clothes he was wearing, or that his best man was wearing glorified Bermuda shorts with a bib. Her gown fit like a second skin.

She held out her hand to him as she approached, handing off her pink gerbera daisy bouquet to Denise on her left.

Phil couldn't take his eyes off her. In spite of everything, he had never been happier.

The ceremony continued. Joe told a few anecdotes about Molly and Phil and how they'd each come to his office separately to talk about the other. He had known they would be together right from the start.

Phil delivered his vows earnestly without a hitch.

Molly started in with her vows. "I, Molly Marie Tauber, take you, Phillip...What's your middle name?" she whispered, "to be my awfully wedded...oh, I mean lawfully wedded husband, to have and to hold, from this day forward, for better or for worse." She paused and looked Phil up and down then shook her head. "For richer, for poorer, in sickness and in health, to love and to cherish you, in spite of your pranks, until death do we part."

Vows were followed by the exchange of rings. Phil's was a bit hard to get on his finger but finally succumbed and slid on.

Mitch handed Phil the box with Molly's diamond channel-set wedding band. Opening the box, Phil was stunned to find a gold band with fourteen tiny plastic carrots sprouting off of it.

Molly blinked very slowly at the fourteen carrot ring and sighed loudly, allowing Phil to slide it on her finger.

Phil shrugged, knowing that revenge on Mitch would one day taste so saccharinely sweet.

Joe rolled his eyes at Phil's attempt at another horrendous prank, then announced that their first act as a married couple would be communion. Phil helped Molly onto the antique kneeler. He took his place beside her. As he knelt down, he heard the crowd begin to snicker again, followed by a few guffaws. Unbeknownst to him, on the bottom of his shoes were written, "Help" and "Me!" He had no idea what they were laughing at now and he didn't really care. He and Molly were married, and that's all that mattered.

After communion they returned to their position before the guests. Mitch whispered to Phil, "Hey, buddy, look at the bottoms of your shoes."

Phil raised each foot and he and Molly laughed out loud at the message. He found it amazing that Molly had laughed and wasn't furious at all the shenanigans. He knew he would have a high price to pay later though.

Joe hurriedly pronounced them husband and wife before another prank could be played. "You may kiss your bride," he told Phil.

Phil took Molly in his arms. At this point even a broom closet would do, but he would have to settle for just a kiss now. It was epic!

Molly melted like buttercream frosting on a cake straight out of the oven.

"Now go get a room," Joe whispered.

On their way back down the aisle Molly sarcastically congratulated Phil on his numerous pranks.

"But Molly, I didn't do any of this...really."

"Sure, Phil. We will definitely talk about this later," she threatened sweetly. "For now, let's just enjoy the rest of our day, and no more tricks, mister," she fingered him on the chest with each word.

"You've got to believe me, Muffin, I had nothing to do with all this."

"Uh huh, right," Molly retorted.

"I'm gonna get even with Mitch if it's the last thing I do," Phil vowed, casting a death ray over his shoulder at him.

Lyra and Dorian were seated for dinner with Denise and Clyde, Mitch and Cindy, and Steph and Matt. They couldn't help but overhear Clyde's jumbled sentences. It seemed the more nervous he got the more his letters rearranged themselves.

"Molly and Phil look like a mappily harried couple...I mean..."

"It's okay, Clyde," Denise patted his hand. "I get you."

Clyde turned his hand over and held hers. "Thanks, I get so tired of having to explain myself all the time. I've talked like this since I was a teenager. It gets old pretty fast." He thought to himself, *This started about the time I met Denise. When I fell off that ladder, watching her walk by. Marry me,* he mused, *now there's a phrase I can't mess up.*

"I always thought your turn of phrase was charming." She smiled.

"Huh? So am I. I mean, I wish I were. I always thought it was charming when you flicked your hair back."

"Uh, flicked my hair?"

"Yeah, you know..." He swept his head sideways with what could loosely be called flair.

Denise flicked his blond hair with her manicured thumb and forefinger "And that, my dear, is flicking. This...is tossing." She threw her huge mantle of fiery auburn curls over her shoulder with a toss of her head.

"That's tut I'm walking about!" he announced a little too loudly.

"I'm lad you gike it," she laughed.

"Your hair is lositively povely," he continued.

"Yours flicks well," she returned the compliment.

357

Lyra and Dorian, having managed to hold back their laughter thus far, both burst out in hysterics.

Mitch spewed black coffee from his nose, seriously staining his lederhosen.

Cindy voiced his deepest fear. "That's it; you've ruined your lederhosen. I just can't be seen with you." She tried to stand up, but sat back down laughing.

Mitch gave her his best whimpering puppy dog face. She patted him on the head. "Well, okay, but you slobber one more drop, and I'm outta here."

Not a moment too soon, their food arrived.

The dinner of Cornish game hen stuffed with wild rice, grilled asparagus drizzled with truffle olive oil and blueberry balsamic vinegar, ten-grain rolls that the girls had baked up, daisy-shaped butter pats, and Molly's famous Garden of Eatin' salad left everyone on the verge of a food coma.

"And now ladies and gentlemen, the best man, Mitchell Steinbeck, would like to toast the bride and groom," the DJ announced.

Lyra and Dorian elbowed each other at the mention of the word "toast," as Mitch took the microphone.

"When Phil asked me to be his best man, my first thought was, 'How can I outprank the master?' This would be the perfect opportunity to *really* get even. Believe me, I had some great ideas, kidnapping the groom, having him arrested—oh, but wait! I already tried that one. Indelible felt pen goatee drawn on the night before the wedding while he was asleep, clown suits, tiny cars, tricycles, tattooing him with the Megakill Hover Flame of Doom...you get the idea. But fearing for my life, I decided that on such a sacred and solemn occasion, pranking my best friend would be the wrong thing to do. However, Phil did not seem to take this solemn event as seriously as I thought he would, therefore, I bow to the King of Prank. You win, Phil. Game over." He raised his glass. "Here's to the bride and groom. May she forgive him his legendary practical jokes." Everyone raised their glass.

As Phil clinked Mitch's glass, Phil said, "We both know you're responsible for all this nonsense, Mitch. Someday you'll pay."

The DJ continued, "Now we'll hear from the Maid of Honor, Denise Kaughman."

Denise stood up and took the microphone. "Molly is my oldest and dearest friend, my confidant. I remember back in high school we'd talk about boys and crushes and dreams and shoes. Well, Molly would do most of the talking about shoes." People laughed knowingly. "The years and the miles between us haven't changed that. You've always been there for me like a sister and a best friend. Back in high school we both decided to wait until the right man came along to get married and never settle for less. In spite of everything that happened today, it looks like it paid off for Molly. I couldn't be happier for the both of you. Here's to you, Mr. and Mrs. McGuire. May you have many happy, healthy years together, and God forgive you, Phil, for pranking Molly's wedding day." She turned to hug her best friend.

Phil's parents, Harry and Charleen, stood up to welcome Molly into the family. Harry spoke, "When Phil brought Molly home to meet us, I was impressed with her pies. By the end of the visit, her pies paled in comparison to her sweetness, and I soon realized that she would make a wonderful addition to our family. We have three marvelous sons, but Charleen and I always wanted daughters too. Now we have a new one to celebrate. Welcome to the family, Molly. We couldn't be more delighted, unless of course you could get Phil to quit pulling these ridiculous stunts. Good luck, my dear. As you can see, you're going to need it."

It was Dorian and Lyra's turn to toast the happy couple. "Since bread is your bread and butter, we thought we would appropriately toast the bride with this half-baked ditty, "Midnight Snack Going Anywhere," sung to the tune of Journey's, "Don't Stop Believing," Dorian said. They harmonized together:

Just a slice of toast,
Lookin' like it's seen a ghost,

LEAVING LYRA

She turned the setting knob to more than fair.

Just a piece of bread

But to a boy that's not been fed

He took her raisin toast with much fanfare.

Burnt toast makes a smoky room

As the bread goes to its doom.

With a loaf they can share a bite

Til it's gone, it's gone, it's gone, it's gone.

Hunger fading,

Up and down the toaster bar.

Their shadows nibbling in the night.

Crumby people

Livin' just to find some toastin'

Searching for the next bite.

No stop, I'm heavin,'

My stomach's really reeling.

Too much toast now, oh wahhhh!

Oh stop, I'm heavin,'

My stomach's really reeling.

Too much toast now, oh wahhhh!

    The song ended with the crowd's exuberant laughter. Dorian spoke up. "Seriously, guys, we'd like to toast Phil and Molly for giving us all such a great example of what love looks like. May you have many amazing years of life together and a lifetime of pranks to keep you forever young."

The DJ chose that opportune moment to open the dance floor for Molly and Phil's first dance together to the very song Phil had chosen as a backdrop to his proposal, "When You Say You Love Me," sung by Josh Groban. Molly laid her head on Phil's shoulder and closed her eyes.

"This is the most wonderful day of my life," Phil whispered into her neck.

"Me too. Fluorescent clothing, lederhosen, clamdiggers, corn bracelets, insulting love letter, fourteen-carrot ring—every girl's dream." She snuggled in closer.

"Believe me, Muffin, I had nothing to do with all that..."

She looked up into his earnest eyes and laid her finger on his lips, silencing him. "Shhh, we'll talk about it later." She returned her head to his shoulder and they finished their dance with a graceful dip.

The DJ invited all the guests to the dance floor. Inspired, Clyde looked at Denise and said, "Donna wance?"

"Founds like sun." She grabbed his hand and led him off to join the other dancers.

"I didn't spew through the entire meal, so wanna dance?" Mitchell asked Cindy eagerly.

"Sure."

As they stepped onto the dance floor, Mitch gave a nod to the DJ. The music suddenly and tragically turned into an accordion-driven polka, everyone's favorite, "Roll Out the Barrel." Mitch breathed new life into his best polka moves, and Cindy did her best to keep up, trying against all hope to remain inconspicuous.

Phil turned to Molly, "If you can't beat 'em, join 'em." They bounced their way over to Mitch.

"So there it is," Phil accused. "This just proves you are responsible for these ridiculous costumes we're wearing. It's no coincidence they're playing a polka when you're dressed for it." Phil's voice rebounded with each vigorous dance step.

"Nope."Mitch said in his defense. "Just making the best out of a bad situation. I tipped the DJ to dig up a polka song. He said it was the first time anyone's ever requested one. How odd."

As they polkaed off, Phil looked over his shoulder. "I'll get you for this. You're guilty. The lederhosen never lie."

Dorian and Lyra sat uncomfortably at their table, watching Bette Anne and Timothy cutting a pretty mean polka. "You wanna, like, dance or something?" he asked, watching her tap her foot to that hot polka beat.

"I thought you'd never ask." She stood up and gestured. "Come on, it's funner than it looks!" She grabbed his shoulder and opposite hand and off they went. As they rocked, bounced and twirled onto the floor, she coached him just like she had done at the quinceanera, until he got the hang of it again. Before they realized it, Mitch and the other dancers were frozen in their

363

tracks at the awe-inspiring sight of *True* Polka. As the accordion ground to a screeching halt, Lyra and Dorian became aware that they were the only ones still dancing. Everyone clapped for the newly-crowned polka royalty.

The DJ brought them all back with a nice slow dance which Dorian enjoyed, understandably, much more than the previous one.

"Whatcha thinking, Dorian?" Her eyes shone in the twinkling tea light.

"I...like...I...uh.."

"Are you always this eloquent or do you just save it for special occasions? Like polka festivities?" Her bangs had grown a bit too long and were catching on her eyelashes.

Dorian ignored their past experience and gently brushed her hair from her eyes.

She froze momentarily then collected herself and smiled nervously. "Thanks, Dorian." Though she tried to hide it, her shaky voice and trembling hands came across as anything but casual.

At least she didn't run this time, he congratulated himself.

"I guess I'm due for a haircut," she said, tugging on a strand and letting it slide through her fingers.

"It looks nice long," he offered.

Regaining control, she said, "So does yours." She changed the subject. Lyra nodded at Phil and Molly lost in their starlit world. "Are they cute or what?"

"I've never seen Uncle Phil so happy. Or dressed so fluorescently."

"And Molly's over the moon." Lyra smiled. "That just proves that true love is colorblind."

The DJ announced on his microphone that it was time to cut the cake. Phil remembered the last wedding cake that he and Molly had shared at his ex-almost girlfriend Ronnie's wedding. What a fiasco! Today was a whole new day, and seeing that so many pranks had already been played by his best man, he would now be the utmost gentleman and feed Molly delicately, even if she filled his sinus cavities with cake.

Marianne led them to the daisy-accented confection, handed them the knife, and stood back—way back—to capture the moment. There was no telling what would happen with these two. She took aim and asked them to proceed.

Suddenly Phil shrieked as a large frog came hopping around the second layer of the cake, frosting between his webbed toes.

What hesh frell is this?" Clyde whispered to Denise.

There was a large portion missing from the back side of the cake which the frog appeared to have thoroughly enjoyed. Phil continued to scream like a girl as Molly reached out to rescue the frog from the cake.

Phil backed away as she came forward wielding the squirming amphibian. "Put that down, Molly!" Phil demanded. "You know how I feel about frogs."

"Yes, I do, Phil," she threatened, wiggling it near his face.

The guests were in an uproar.

Molly dipped the froggy in a bowl of water and wiped its legs and feet with a pink napkin before letting him go in the far side of the garden. She returned to the cake and the recovering groom.

"You see, *I* was the one who planned the tux mishaps of fluorescent green and pink, the clamdigger pants, the lederhosen for *poor* Mitch, the fake letter and corn bracelet gag—and believe me, it's no easy task to string corn kernels. The substitute wedding ring was my creation, as was the writing on the bottom of your shoes, and yes, even the frog frolicking on the cake. The real cake is indoors, safe and sound. Now tell me, who is the Queen of Prank, huh?" She laughed maniacally.

When he'd regained his composure, Phil knelt and proclaimed with all the humility he could muster, "Long live the Queen!"

Fred, the DJ, called all the single women over to Molly for the "bouquet" toss. Molly held a lovely evening bag in the shape of an elegant flower. She unzipped the bag to show off the various gift cards within, such as Designer Shoe Warehouse, Godiva Chocolates, Macy's, Twinkle Toes Pedicure Salon, Swiss Sisters Coffee, and Cheesecake Factory, to name a few.

"Now that's something worth fighting for," a woman shouted, as the single ladies started jockeying for position.

Molly threw a smile Phil's way, as if to say, *See? I knew this idea was better than duct tape.* She wondered if he would truly throw a roll of duct tape at the guys. Molly turned her back to the ladies in waiting. She shifted her weight from foot to foot and shouted, "One, two, three..." On three, she tossed a cloud of mini marshmallows over her head.

"No fair," yelled Denise.

"Come on," Steph and Lyra shouted together.

"Okay, here it comes. One...two...three..." Whoosh. The silk purse did cartwheels in the air. It was headed straight for Lyra. She put up her hands to catch it, but was bumped out of the way by Stephanie, whose quick reflexes nabbed it before it reached the ground.

"Oh, yeah," Stephanie shouted, bobbling her head back and forth. She spun around in a victory dance, holding the purse high above her head. Unfortunately for Steph, it was unzipped and began raining down various gift cards from on high. Suddenly, bedlam broke out, like kids under a busted piñata. Lyra grabbed as many as she could and handed them back to Stephanie who quickly zipped them back into her new evening bag. "Thanks, Lyra. You're the best. These really should've been yours. Let's split 'em."

Lyra beamed.

Next, Phil stepped up to the plate with a large plastic storage box.

"What the heck is he up to?" Mitch said to Dorian and Matt.

"Who knows?" Dorian replied. "This is my Uncle Phil we're talking about."

All the single guys gathered around, curious.

Phil bent over the box, his back to the restless mob, and began flinging things backwards over his shoulder: rubber chickens, a clown horn, a box of ziplock bags. The guys started by dodging the items before they realized that these things were totally harmless.

"Hope he doesn't have a ball-peen hammer in there," Matt yelled, as Mitch returned Phil's serve, striking him square in the butt with a rubber chicken.

Undaunted, Phil continued hurling items. Next came a chub of salami, barely missing Clyde's head. "Man, that's geally rood aged salami. Gimme that." He snatched it off the floor and breathed in the garlicky, grease-infested aroma.

"Oh, *there* it is!" Phil exclaimed. He spun around, armed to the elbows with cans of neon silly string, "vaporizing" the guys, like the web-slinger he had always dreamed he could be. As the men unraveled themselves from Phil's surprise attack, he was at it again. Small paper airplanes continued the assault, each made from different denominations of cash, ranging from ones to fifties. It was rapid fire with an occasional round of super balls, pink erasers, and Groucho Marx nose glasses. Fake gold coins a la Mario came last.

"What's with the plastic coins?" Dorian shouted.

"It's a contest, guys! Who can get the most coins? There's a major prize in store!" Phil roared.

The coins flew with abandon. Grown men were on the floor, grubbing for plastic coins, shoving, pushing, scuffling, sweating!

"Time's up," Phil announced. "Count 'em up, boys!"

"I've got fifteen!"

"Twenty!"

"Twenty-nine!"

"Can anybody beat twenty-nine?" Phil called.

"Thirty-seven!" Mitch proclaimed slowly in a baritone voice. "Beat that, koopas!"

"Looks like Mitch is the big winner! Mitch, come forth and receive your prize. Kneel," Phil decreed.

Mitch obliged.

"My friend, I'm sorry to have doubted you. Come, here is your just reward." Phil reached into the plastic storage container and placed a raccoon hat on Mitch's waiting head. "Now fly, be free!"

The Super Mario fans cheered. The rest looked confused.

"But wait, there's one more surprise left in my treasure chest. The One True Ring must be claimed, and with it, all honor and responsibility. Are. You. Ready?"

More sweating, grunting, and shoving. They were ready.

Phil turned his back and loosed one last item into the fray. Dorian caught it.

"What? This is a roll of duct tape! Some prize!"

"Yes, and with it the power and responsibility to unite all kingdoms and fix just about anything," Phil replied.

"But it's just duct tape."

"That's what you think, young padawan. With this great responsibility also comes great reward." Phil handed Dorian a fine leather wallet filled with gift cards to Floppy's Pizza Cave, Farfy's Ice Cream & Other Stuff, Swiss Sisters Coffee, movie tickets, Molly's Sunshine Bakery, Clyde's Fine Dining, Henk's Hardware Emporium, Oozy's Shooting Range & Pawn Shop, Herbie's Haberdashery, Flunky's Video Game Shack, Mr. Pancake Head, Pachinko Palace, The *New* Jerky Store at the mall, and the Craving Carnivore Steak Barn.

Phil flashed his smile of superiority at his bride.

Journal Entry:

Today I got a good picture of what real love looks like. It allows each person to be themselves, not just accepting, but enjoying the other's uniqueness. It's playful, even childlike sometimes, forgiving, and creative. It doesn't demand perfection. It's ultimately honest when the day is done and the party's over. The looks that passed between Molly and Phil were priceless. That love can exist in neon clothing is proof that it's real. I see so much of these traits in Dorian. Could that be love?

I looked up love in my Bible concordance. Here's some of what I came up with. I'm gonna mark this for future reference:

1 Corinthians 13:1-13

If I could speak all the languages of earth and of angels, but didn't love others, I would only be a noisy gong or a clanging cymbal. If I had the gift of prophecy, and if I understood all of God's secret plans and possessed all knowledge, and if I had such faith that I could move mountains, but I didn't love others, I would be nothing. If I gave everything I have to the poor and even sacrificed my body, I could boast about it, but if I didn't love others, I would have gained nothing.

Love is patient and kind. Love is not jealous or boastful or proud or rude. It does not demand its own way. It is not irritable, and it keeps no record of being wronged. It does not rejoice about injustice but rejoices whenever the truth wins out. Love never gives up, never loses faith, is always hopeful, and endures through every circumstance.

Prophecy and speaking in unknown languages and special knowledge will become useless. But love will last forever! Now our knowledge is partial and incomplete, and even the gift of prophecy reveals only part of the whole picture! But when the time of perfection comes, these partial things will become useless.

When I was a child, I spoke and thought and reasoned as a child. But when I grew up, I put away childish things. Now we see things imperfectly, like puzzling reflections in a mirror, but then we will see everything with perfect clarity. All that I know now is partial and incomplete, but then I will know everything completely, just as God now knows me completely.

Three things will last forever—faith, hope, and love—and the greatest of these is love.

CHAPTER 26
Beatles in My Toast

Lyra had been up half the night working on a new toast song for Dorian. Toast Wars was going full force, and it was her turn to come up with one. She had chosen a song they would both know—a classic by the Beatles—"Michelle." It was a bit shorter than her usual jams, but she knew it would hit the mark for Dorian.

French toast is verbose,
Give me subtle wheat toast with some jam,
Slathered in jam.
Burnt toast, like French Roast,
These are dark excuses for light tan,
Toast that's light tan.

Don't burn it! Don't burn it! Don't burn it!
You know I like it light.
You'll wreck my appetite.
And if you do, I'm warning you
's you that I'll bite.

Keep it light.

Lyra finished off the last notes of her "toasting" song for Dorian when he came by the bakery after class.

"Bravo!" He clapped heartily for Lyra's opus. "That's going to be hard to top. I like the Beatles theme we've got going on. I'll have you know I'm already working on my next one."

"Can't wait to hear it. Bring it on."

Lyra was getting ready for bed when there was a knock at the door. She opened it slightly and peeked outside. Dorian's guitar strumming greeted Lyra as he serenaded her with his version of the Beatles' song, "Help."

Help! I need some toasting!
Help! Not just any toasting.
Help! You know I need some toast.
Help!

My toast was buttered, only buttered every day.
I never thought that toast could be
Much better than this way.

Leaving Lyra

But now I've had your toast and I'm not so self-assured.

Now I find my toast is dry,

Your jam's the best I'm sure.

Help me if you can, I've popped it down,

And I do appreciate it turning brown.

Help me hear that popping-up sound.

Jam and cream cheese, help me!

And now my taste has changed in oh so many ways.

My knife with butter just won't help me beat this craze.

I think about your toast, the one that I adore.

Now I know I need it more than I ever have before.

Help me if you can, I've popped it down,

And I do appreciate it turning brown,

Help me hear that popping-up sound,

Jam and cream cheese, help me,

Help me, help me, help me, ooooo"

Lyra's laughter doubled her over.

Dorian gloated, thoroughly proud of himself. "So there,"
he said with a flourish, "Now it's your turn. Good night."

"Wait, wait!" Lyra opened the door wide. "Want to come
in for a night cap? I have raisin bread and pumpernickel."

"Well, maybe just a slice or two," Dorian smirked.

Lyra would not be outdone. Dorian's take on "Help!" was quite the masterpiece. She started mentally working on which song to "toast" next as she and Molly rolled out pie crusts early the next morning. Lyra started humming various tunes to herself before deciding on the Beatles' song, "Yesterday." Throughout the day she jotted down lines here and there with a floury pencil.

Stephanie finally asked her why she had been humming the same song all day. "You must have that song stuck in your brain. Now you've got it stuck in mine," Stephanie grumbled, "and I don't even know that song."

"It's for Toast Wars," Lyra defended herself, "and it's my turn."

"You guys still doing that? I thought it was just a short-term thing," Stephanie said.

"Nah, it's turned into a real all-out battle. I'm meeting him for dinner at his new place, Molly's old house, so I gotta be ready. It was so nice of Molly and Phil to let Dorian rent Molly's house at such a low cost."

Lyra went on humming until it was time to close up shop. "See ya tomorrow, Steph," Lyra said as she left, heading home to get her guitar and feed Catzo on her way to Dorian's new home.

A few minutes later, Stephanie locked up and headed homeward, miserably humming the unknown song Lyra had left her with.

Dorian had prepared a virtual feast for his dinner guest—chicken pot pie, unfrozen and soon to be served piping hot from the oven. He hurried to the front door as the doorbell rang.

Lyra was standing on the porch, guitar case in hand, grinning like a Cheshire cat.

"You sure are happy tonight, Dorian observed. "What's up?"

"Oh, it's just the usual I-wrote-a-masterpiece kind of day," she bragged.

"Really? Well, come on in and let me hear it then. I expected it to take you a few days to come up with something to top my song from last night. Let's hear what you've got," he taunted.

"Okay. Continuing in our Beatles' tradition, I give you, 'Yesterday.'"

Marmalade. That's what I'm having on my toast today.

No more honey, that was yesterday.

Now I believe in marmalade.

Buttered toast—that's the kind I usually have the most.
'Specially with a cup of good dark roast,
Oh, I believe in buttered toast.

Why I have to toast, I don't know, I couldn't say.
Some say something's wrong,
How I long for toast each day ay ay ay,

Toast today, it's what's on the menu every day,
To change things would just be wrong I say,
Oh, I believe in toast each day.
Yum, mmm, mmm, mmm, toast each day.

"Oh man! Just how do you expect me to top that one, huh?" Dorian whined. "And I really do love marmalade. To tell you the truth, I've got another toasted song for you I finished today."

"What?" Lyra was disgusted. "I worked all day to get the satisfaction of being the victor for less than an hour? Well...go ahead, sing it to me. Let's get this over with."

"Ah, ah, ah! Not so fast. Dinner first, then the song."

"Well, at least I get the satisfaction of a short victory. So, what's for dinner?"

"Chicken pot pie a la Marie Callender."

"Smells amazing, but you shouldn't have gone to all that trouble on my account. What? Looks like you even turned on a real oven instead of the microwave."

"Don't laugh," Dorian said. "My mom showed me how to turn on an oven years ago."

"Microwave is out of commission, huh?" Lyra quizzed.

"Who told you?" Dorian folded his arms and raised an eyebrow.

The bunny-shaped kitchen timer hopped up and down on the counter, startling Catalina and sending her running for cover.

"See, that's a sure sign that Catalina's never heard that sound before...in her life! I'll bet this is the first time you've ever turned on an oven or used a kitchen timer."

"Yeah, well, Miss Kitchen Diva, like you have the energy at the end of the day to cook something."

"For your information, I cook all day long and I often put dinner in my crock pot in the morning so I don't have to worry about cooking when I get home. Then I can have leftovers for a few days."

"Crock pot, huh? Never thought of that. How does it work?"

"I'll have you over for dinner next and show you," Lyra promised. "Now can we eat?"

The two scarfed down their pot pies, burning their lips and tongues in their haste. As they finished up, Dorian demonstrated his spectacular talent for cleaning up, relegating pie pans to the garbage and tossing the unrinsed forks into the dishwasher.

"All right, I must admit the clean up is much faster than with the crock pot," Lyra conceded.

"See? What did I tell you? I really do know how to cook!"

"But the question remains, can you toast?" Lyra revealed her eagerness to hear the promised chart-topping Toast Wars song.

"I can toast with the best of them!" he boasted.

"That remains to be seen."

They headed into the living room, and Dorian picked up his guitar from its rack. They sat, facing each other on the couch.

"Here goes," Dorian said, looking suddenly nervous. "I hope you like it. I'm going to use another Beatles' song, 'And I Love Her.'"

Lyra heard him gulp before he began. *Why so nervous?* she wondered.

He began with a few lines of beautiful finger picking.

Quite impressive for Toast Wars, she thought as he began to sing.

I give her all my toast, that's all I do.
And if you saw my bread, you'd toast it too.
And I love toast.

She gives me raisin toast and poppy seed.
The bread my lover brings, she toasts for me.
And I love toast.

Our love of toast will never die
As long as I've got a toaster near me.

Light is the bread I toast, dark is the rye.
I know our love of toast will never die.
And I love her.

Dorian ended with another round of complex finger picking.

Lyra's eyes grew wide at the last line he sang.

"How did you like it?" Dorian asked.

"Fantastic, but I think you misspoke the last line."

"No. I didn't," Dorian replied.

ournal Entry:

What's that supposed to mean, "And I love HER?" This
toast we're talking about here. Or is it? I wish Dorian would

come out and say it if he has feelings for me, instead of just making a kind of slip up in a silly toast song. There's no way I'm going to let him know how I feel until he says it first.

CHAPTER 27
(A)Salt and Batter(y)

Expecting Dorian to take her to music practice at church, Lyra looked up, startled, as the door was flung open and crashed into the wall.

"So, have you missed me, Lyra?" Her father stood in the doorway, exuding cognac from each pore.

Lyra blinked in disbelief before she found her voice. "You're not welcome here. Now get out!" Her shaky voice lacked the necessary authority to repel a flea.

"You thought I didn't see you at the wedding," he slurred. "Well, you were wrong. You could've at least said hello. I saw you running away. You wound me, Lyra. You really do." Steadying himself, he took a step in her direction. "You should know better than that. Now come here and show your father some love. It's been a long time since we've played our little game."

Lyra froze, becoming for that moment, a terrified twelve-year-old girl whose idea of survival consisted of little more than quiet endurance.

"No!" She broke the spell as she backed away. "Get out of here! The McCrearys will hear me and they'll call the police, and my friend will be here any minute," she yelled at the top of her lungs.

"As if you had any friends," he mocked. "And as for your McCrearys, they are at this very moment, dining at a fancy restaurant they could never afford, courtesy of me and the special 'sweepstakes' neither of them could remember signing up for. Tonight they dine, so that you and I can have some time alone. You miss me, don't you?"

Lyra slid away from him along the wall, hoping to slip through the open door before he caught her.

Catzo's hair stood on end and she began to yowl at the intruder.

"Shut that three legged thing up, or I swear I'll kill it."

As he prepared to kick the cat, Lyra lunged at him and knocked him down. She grabbed Catzo and ran, but her father grabbed her ankle and dragged her back in before slamming and locking the door.

"Now where were we?" He scratched the stubble on his chin in a calculating gesture.

Lyra was drowning in a flood of horrible memories, feeling as helpless and hopeless to change her life's direction, now as she had then.

As Lyra reeled from the first blow, Catzo squeezed through a partially-opened window and made a beeline to the

McCreary's door, meowing frantically. When that failed, she dashed to the gate, left open by Lyra's father, and began calling to passersby, running back toward Lyra's cottage and looking over her shoulder, expecting to be followed.

No one acknowledged her until Dorian drove up. She risked running into the street, crying desperately.

Dorian knew immediately that something was wrong. Catzo would never be allowed out unsupervised, especially with the gate open. He followed the kitten to Lyra's house. It was there that he heard it. A fight—bodies thrown into things, curses, and pleas.

"You ungrateful, fat, stupid, dirty girl!" Dorian heard a man shout as he approached the door.

"It was you that made me dirty. But I'm not any more! And I'm not fat anymore either." Lyra spat each word, punctuated with powerful blows to his chest.

"You never did love me, did you? You just used me, just like the rest of them, you filthy, ugly girl."

"Lyra!" Dorian shouted. Pounding the door and finding it locked, he slammed his shoulder through the old wooden boards, and came upon a horrifying scene. Lyra was pressed against the wall with a tall, well-dressed man's fingers clutched around her throat.

Starved of oxygen and hope, Lyra was beginning to lose consciousness.

Her father released her and turned to confront Dorian.

With wood splinters poking out of his hair, skin, and clothes, Dorian attacked, staggering the drunk away from Lyra and knocking him out with a single ferocious punch. He hurried to Lyra's side and lifted her head. She recoiled.

"Lyra, it's me. Are you...okay?" His solemn eyes studied her with an intensity that left her with nothing to do but burst into tears.

Keeping a sharp eye on her attacker who had yet to rouse himself from the fist-induced slumber, Dorian held Lyra and stroked her hair.

"Who is that..." He pointed at her assailant as if the drunk was a stain on the carpet.

"My father," she said, sitting up. "Hey, your hand—it's all bloody. There's something sticking out of your knuckle. Is that a tooth? His tooth?"

"A trophy," he said. "If I'd known he was your father, I would've knocked out his other front tooth while I was at it."

Lyra's tears gave way to tentative laughter. "It's still not too late," she said as Catzo jumped, purring into her lap.

As promised, Dorian's justice was swift indeed, and now Judge Friedrich Rhinehardt was about to experience justice from the other side of the bench.

Dorian immediately called 911.

Journal Entry:

How could You do this to me, God? My father's a horrible man! How could You make such an awful person? How could You let him live and let Mom die instead? Where's the justice in all this? It was a pleasure to see Sergeant Morrison handcuff my father and take him away in the squad car. Was it wrong for me to be happy about that? You know how hard I've tried to forgive my father, and then this happens. What was I supposed to do? Just stand there and let him choke me to death? If Dorian hadn't come by I'd probably be dead right now. He took my father down with one punch and knocked his tooth out. I couldn't believe Dorian would do that for me. He took pictures with his cell phone of the choke marks on my neck and the bruises all over me. I can't bear to see them.

When my father regained consciousness, Dorian promised him that if there was ever a next time, he would lose a lot more than a tooth. I've never seen my father afraid before. It felt so good.

I don't want to forgive him! I don't and I can't. You're asking too much of me. If I forgive him again and let my guard down, he might kill me.

Am I supposed to just let him go free like nothing happened? And won't he just go on hurting people unless someone stops him? When Sergeant Morrison returned, he encouraged me to testify against my father for that very reason. If I do, how can I do it without dredging up all the hate, shame,

---

hurt, and hopelessness all over again? Could I even stand looking at him in the courtroom? Will I ever heal? How can I when he won't leave me alone? Help me God!

Lyra picked up her Bible and looked up the word, "enemy" in the index.

Psalm 18:47-49
He is the God who pays back those who harm me; He subdues the nations under me and rescues me from my enemies. You hold me safe beyond the reach of my enemies; You save me from violent opponents. For this, O Lord, I will praise You among the nations. I will sing praises to Your name.

Okay God, so You sent Dorian just in time. Why didn't You just prevent the whole thing from happening? You ask me to forgive my father, then you make it almost impossible. What's with that?

Is it wrong to want revenge? Nothing would make me happier than to see him spend the rest of his life rotting in jail, but somehow the word "redemption" keeps running through my head. What exactly does that mean? I looked it up, and it means atonement, restitution, or reclamation. Is that for my father or for me? Maybe I should press charges. Restitution—doesn't he need to make restitution for what he's done? Reclamation—do I get to reclaim my life, or does it mean my father's life? I'm so confused. I need to think about this for a while. I'm gonna look up "revenge," in the dictionary. Maybe that will help.

Revenge: It says, "To exact punishment for a wrong, especially in a resentful or vindictive spirit. Retaliating in kind or degree to avenge oneself or another."

I don't want to be a revengeful person. I just want him to stop.

She looked up a reference for revenge in her Bible.

Romans 12:17-21
Never pay back evil with more evil. Do things in such a way that everyone can see you are honorable. Do all that you can to live at peace with everyone. Dear friends, never take revenge. Leave that to the righteous anger of God. For the Scriptures say, "I will take revenge; I will pay them back," says the LORD. Instead, "If your enemies are hungry, feed them. If they are thirsty, give them something to drink. In doing this you will heap burning coals of shame on their heads. Don't let evil conquer you, but conquer evil by doing good."

This is NOT what I want to hear, Lord! My father knows no shame! How could I forgive him? Wouldn't that only make things worse? Wouldn't it be like saying what he did was okay? He was going to kill me to silence me. I know it. Maybe I should press charges like the policeman said, tell the truth, and let God be the judge, and not try to take revenge on him myself. I need to speak up for Estrella and who knows who else's life he may have ruined. Maybe it's justice I want and not revenge. I should let God do the avenging. And maybe forgiveness is something I need to do for my own healing!

Would You free me, Jesus, from my father's abuse? Show me what You want me to do so he can be stopped from doing any more harm.

After Lyra had considered putting herself through the trauma of a trial, she concluded a few days later that she didn't have the courage to dredge up her past. She knew that since her father was a judge, she would not receive a fair trial. Despite Sergeant Morrison's and Dorian's promises to stand by her in the courtroom, she abandoned her hope of putting her father behind bars.

Sergeant Morrison stood at the ostentatious front door and knocked with tenacity as the sun was touching the horizon. There was no response, so he pounded louder.

The door flew open wide. The presence of the small-town cop who had escorted Judge Friedrich Rhinehardt to jail outraged the judge. "What do you want?" Rhinehardt glowered from the doorway. "Haven't you done enough damage to my reputation?" He flicked his cigar ashes on the policeman's shined shoes.

"As a matter of fact, I haven't. I fully intend to see you in prison along with all the criminals you put there. Do you know what they do to child molesters in prison? And we now know there are others besides Lyra you've assaulted. You see, I've been doing a little investigating on my own. I intend for you to get *everything* you deserve in this life, Judge. Whether your daughter presses charges or not, I fully intend to bring you to justice with the testimonies of your other rape victims. And there are many."

"How much? How much cash to lose the testimonies of these women and forget all this ever happened?" Judge Rhinehardt extinguished his cigar in the decorative urn by the front door.

"Are you attempting to bribe an officer of the law? I'm not the only one who knows about all this. There's quite a big investigation going on. And all those poor sexually-harassed and assaulted women you've worked with all these years just can't stop talking."

"I have power over every one of those women! They'll never testify in court! I'll have your badge!" the Judge roared. "I know people!" he repeated his well-rehearsed threat.

"And I'll have your gavel. Oh, did I fail to mention I've been recording our entire conversation? See you in court." Sergeant Grant Morrison turned and walked casually back to his squad car. "Oh, and if you violate Lyra's Restraining Order by even one inch, I will take it personally. Very personally. Have a nice day, Your *Honor.*"

The next morning, Sergeant Morrison found Lyra working in the garden. "I don't mean to disturb you, Lyra, but I've got something I need to talk to you about."

Lyra stood, wiping her dirty hands on her jeans. "I still haven't made up my mind yet, Sergeant Morrison. I don't know if I have the strength to put myself through that."

"I know how difficult it was for you to tell me about your past. I'm not here to pressure you. I just wanted to let you know that I've been doing some investigating on my own. It seems that you are not the only victim of your father's abuse. There are numerous women who have worked with your father over the years that are prepared to present a united front against his sexual abuse, threats, and violence, not to mention a few underaged girls who have come forward. Whether you participate in this trial is up to you, but rest assured your father will be brought to justice. I had a little talk with him yesterday and made it clear that I would take any violation of the Restraining Order *very* personally."

CHAPTER 28
A Wall of Rising Dough and Other Charms and Protections

As the Andy McGee concert let out, Dorian noticed that time and again, fellow concertgoers would collide with Lyra, yet give him plenty of space. "Do you have some secret ninja skills you haven't told me about? People keep bumping into you as if they can't see you."

"I call it hiding in plain sight. It's interesting how people respond. Keeps you from getting picked on—as long as you don't mind being trampled."

"I don't get it," he said, perplexed.

"It's like you turn off any way for people to read you. Before long, you're shrunken, lose all confidence, and become invisible. If only it made me invulnerable." She murmured.

"Is that...like what you did before you lost so much weight?"

Wow, he noticed. I guess Stephanie was right, it was worth it. "Yeah, something like that."

Dorian turned her chin to face him. "You know your weight is just a number on a scale. It's not who you are. It never has been, especially to me. The question is how do you see yourself?"

She stared into his eyes.

As the crowd dispersed, they stayed there with her gulping down tears and finding no refreshment in them. Fortunately, she remained invisible to all those disinterested eyes. There was no need to hide anymore, and she knew it. She was safe with Dorian. Maybe it was time to change how she viewed herself once and for all.

Journal Entry:

No more hiding, Lord! I've tried to be invisible ever since Mom died. My Father made me want to hide to protect myself. But I'm not insignificant. In Your hands my brokenness can heal. It feels wonderful to be used by You! I give You the songs You've been giving to me. Use them for Your glory. Thank You for the latest song You inspired me with from the fourth chapter of Malachi.

All you weary and broken-hearted,
Battered by waves of doubt and fear that war in your minds,
There is One Who cares for you,

And He will come with healing on His wings
And He will fly throughout the land.
He'll set us free like calves from the stall,
And we'll go running joyfully.
Free, and we'll be free, we'll be free, and we'll be free.

All you weary and broken-hearted,
Shattered by a world, a world that's coming down on you.
Behold the King Who shed His crown for you.

And He will come with healing on His wings,
And He will fly throughout the land.
He'll set us free like calves from the stall,
And we'll go running joyfully.
Free, and we'll be free, we'll be free, and we'll be free.

Stephanie, do you think I still use my weight to keep people away?"

"Maybe not on purpose, no, but maybe you still do." She continued scrubbing the dough off her fingers without looking up, as if this conversation were not of critical importance. "You're pretty good at it too. I figured you knew what you were doing." Stephanie turned, her hands dripping. "But you've lost so much weight. And this is an issue because...?"

"Dorian pointed it out to me. He says that's what I'm still doing."

"Well, are you?" Smiling, Stephanie dried her chapped hands on a red checkered towel.

"Hey, I'm spilling my guts here, and you're just smiling like nothing's going on. What's up with that?"

"He *noticed*." Stephanie was positively smug.

Lyra grabbed the towel. "What do you mean?"

"Like I said, he no-ticed." She drew out the final word, effectively making her point.

It took a moment to recover her runaway train of thought. "Okay, so he noticed I've lost a lot of weight," Lyra conceded.

"What else did he say?"

"He wanted to know how I felt about it—my weight, that is. He said my weight means nothing to him."

"And how *do* you feel about it?"

"I still feel fat and ugly, even though I've lost all those pounds."

"And what are you going to do about it?"

"Eat a whole loaf of toast? Heck, I don't know. What am I supposed to do?"

"That's all in your head. Keep coming to the gym with me."

"Yeah, you're right, Lyra admitted.

"Besides, what do you have to lose?"

Lyra smiled in spite of herself. "Fifteen more pounds would be nice."

Journal Entry:

It's true. I'm still hiding behind my fat, even though I've lost over fifty pounds. It's still my wall of protection from the world. Stephanie and Dorian are right. It started with protecting myself from my father and then it grew to keep anyone who might hurt me away. I hate that I'm keeping Dorian at a distance. I need to get to a place where I allow him in, even if it means I have to risk getting hurt. Sometimes I feel like a lost cause. You've gotta do this, Lord. It's impossible, but You seem to enjoy a good challenge. Here are my loaves and fish. Do Your thing, God.

Isaiah 64:8
And yet, O Lord, You are our Father. We are the clay, and You are the potter. We all are formed by Your hand.

This pot can't make itself. I can't change me, but You can.

"Bette Anne! What a nice surprise!" Lyra looked through the peephole and opened the sturdy new steel-core front door to Bette Anne's cheerful face and her perpetually air-licking Yorkie.

"I came to see my girl," Bette Anne drawled.

"Hannah's in River Oaks?" Lyra asked, surprised.

"No, Sugar, I came to see you." Bette Anne administered a welcoming hug. "It's been awhile since we've seen each other, and I was wonderatin' how ya doin', girl. Why look at you, I do believe you lost even more weight! Good for you!"

Lyra ushered Bette Anne and her four-legged tag-along inside and onto the couch, then sat beside them. "Fifty-two pounds so far. Thanks for noticing."

"Nice place ya got here," Bette Anne admired the clematis vine that dangled its starry purple flowers teasingly in front of the window.

"I love it here," Lyra said. "And best of all, I get to help out in the garden. I've learned a lot since I moved in."

"How ya coming along in your healification?" Bette Anne asked.

"Oh, that." Lyra cast her gaze down to her cat who was on her haunches, trying to get a sniff of the dog through the designer carrier bag. "I seem to have hit a wall, Bette Anne. It's so hard to believe that I can ever be free from unforgiveness and sense of dirtiness, especially after my father came back and attacked me again. I'm sure Dorian has filled you in on how he came at just the right time and saved my life. How can I ever be free of all this? I pray about it all the time, and nothing's happening."

"Well, how 'bout that? Freedom's just what I dropped by to talk about."

"Dropped by? You live in Southern California." *What could be that urgent,* Lyra wondered.

"Do ya ever feel like there's a war going on inside ya?" Bette Anne asked.

"Yeah, I guess I'm fighting old feelings about myself and my father. I try to replace them with good things, but it only lasts until those same old voices come back, telling me I'm worthless and will never have enough faith to move past all this. I'll never be able to forgive him, no matter how hard I try. To be honest, I'm pretty miserable and depressed by the whole thing."

"Well, Sugar, the bad thing is that by yourself you will never have that kind of faith or will power. The good news is that in giving you His Holy Spirit, God has made those changes possible. If ya try and do it on your ownliness ya won't get far. Jesus is the vine and we are the branches. No branch by itself can produce fruit, like love, joy, peace, patience, kindness, goodness, faithfulness, gentleness, or self-control, no matter how hard that branch tries. The power has to come from the vine. You can say to yourself, 'I will be forgiving,' or 'I will produce a grape, I *will* produce a grape,' but it ain't gonna happen unless that branch is attached to the vine. Jesus is the

vine, and He sends His Holy Spirit's power into the branches.
No amount of your own tryin' can produce that fruit. That's the
Holy Spirit's job. Only He can make that fruit grow on your
branch. Only He has the power to produce that fruit in your life.
We don't. Pray for His Spirit to change, guide, and comfort ya.
You'll be amazed at what He's able to accomplish. You can talk
with the Holy Spirit anytime ya want. He's living inside ya.
Can't get any closer than that. He's even provided you with
spiritual armor to protect ya from those old voices both day and
night."

"How does that work? What do I have to do? I've been
trying so hard."

"Let go of trying to fight this battle by yourself, Lyra.
God's given ya everything you need. He protects your mind like
a helmet. Ya know you belong to Him. No one and nothin' can
ever take you away from Him. And your faith in God protects
the rest of ya like a shield you can hide behind. As a defensive
weapon, He gives you His words from the Bible, to use like a
sword, so you can defend yourself against the enemy's lies and
know what the truth is. You can trust Him, Sugar, even with
your deepest desires. Sometimes it's so hard to dare to dream—
ya give up or feel guilty for even wanting it." She gave Lyra a
knowing smile. "Don't be afraid to dream, Sugar. Sometimes
dreams can come true. He'll help you to want what is right and
give ya courage to withstand your doubts about yourself and
about Him."

"I do doubt sometimes, Bette Anne. Where was He when my father..."

"He was right there, hurtin' with ya."

"Why didn't He do anything to stop it?" A preliminary tear escaped.

"This world is broken. When people choose their own will over God's will, bad things have happenated ever since. In order for there to be real love, the opposite has to exist too. Otherwise, we'd all be robots programmed to love and be good. And love means nothing without a free will behind it. Light shines best in the dark, and this world is a darkful place. But ya can fight the darkness with the Word of God and take back what's been stolen from ya. The words in your Bible, they give ya the power to do that as you apply 'em to your life, and it gives ya the right way to deal with shame. You are not condemned for what your father did to ya, and ya never will be. Our good Lord Jesus took care of it for ya. And for me. He will protect your heart and keep it pure as you learn daily to trust in Him."

Lyra was biting her lip, trying not to flood her face as Bette Anne wrapped her arms around her and pulled her close. "What the Good Lord did for me, He'll do for anyone who asks Him, you included. It may take time, but He *will* do it."

Sandra Lee gave a mighty leap out of her carrier and licked Lyra's cheeks while Catzo looked on skeptically, her calr demeanor betrayed by the slightest twitch of her tail. She was ready for action should the tiny terrier prove belligerent.

"Any questions?"

"Why did you come all this way?"

"Because I love ya, Sugar." She fished around in her oversized leather bag and pulled out what appeared to be a picture frame lovingly wrapped in sky blue tissue paper. "And to give ya this." She handed Lyra the gift. "I made it for ya."

Lyra opened it slowly, gratefully. "Oh, Bette Anne! It's beautiful!" Lyra hugged the large embroidered sampler containing the words of Ephesians 6:13-17. The embroidered words were framed by clouds of daisies.

"Therefore, put on every piece of God's armor so you will be able to resist the enemy in the time of evil. Then, after the battle you will still be standing firm. Stand your ground, putting on the belt of truth and the body armor of God's righteousness. For shoes, put on the peace that comes from the Good News so that you will be fully prepared. In addition to all of these, hold up the shield of faith to stop the fiery arrows of the devil. Put on salvation as your helmet, and take the sword of the Spirit, which is the word of God."

"Dorian said ya like daisies, so I decided to add those after I finished the letterin'."

"This had to have taken you forever to embroider. You did this for me?" Lyra was full-on crying by this time. Sandra Lee was hard-pressed to keep up with the tears.

"Yes, for you. You needed these words, so I thought I'd permanentalize them for ya. Now ya can look at them whenever ya need remindin'." Bette Anne looked at her diamond wristwatch.

"Well, Sugar, I've got my boy to go see." She stowed the still-licking doglet in her carrier, gave the stunned Lyra a hug, and hurried out the door, pausing to wave. "By the way, see ya and Dorian at supper. Meet ya at his house at seven. I love ya, Sugar."

"I love you too, Mom." The last word slipped out, unnoticed at first until it settled deeply into her heart.

Journal Entry:

I feel like God gave me a new mom today. I accidentally called Bette Anne, "Mom," as she was leaving. I am still shocked that she would fly up here to give me encouragement. The embroidery she gave me is beyond beautiful, and the words will be life-changing if I put them to use. I owe myself that much and Bette Anne even more. I'm hanging her gift above my bed.

And she's right, I don't have the power to change by myself. I can't produce forgiveness or peace no matter how hard I try. And man, have I been trying. God, I admit I'm powerless to change myself. Holy Spirit, please produce this fruit in me. Let it be You Who does this work—the True Vine. I'm just a fruitless branch without You.

"I think ya oughta take a good, hard look at this girl, Dorian," Bette Anne said. She's got a heart the size of Texas, and a smile like a Tennessee sunrise. I know you've been hurtinating, but the past is the past. It's time to move forward. You say you're friends. That's the best way for any relationship to start."

"I don't know, Mom..."

"So how do ya really feel about Lyra?"

"I...I..." Dorian was saved by a knock on the door. He ran to answer it, leaving the question hanging in the air.

Clyde's restaurant was bustling, as usual. Lyra hadn't had such a sumptuous meal in many a year. Sea scallops in butter, wine, and cheese sauce, rice pilaf, and a delicate strawberry and baby greens salad filled her plate but not her stomach. She ate only half and saved the rest for the next day. "Thank you so much for dinner, Bette Anne," Lyra said.

"My pleasure, Sugar. It's good for family to gather round the table together."

"Yeah, Mom, thanks," Dorian said.

"So how do ya like your new home, Dorian? That was awful nice of Molly and Phil to rent you Molly's old house at such a great price, now that they're married and living in his. Got plenty of room for the future."

"Yeah, I feel guilty I'm not paying all that much rent yet..."

"So son, what are your plans for the future? How ya gonna make a decent livin'? How's the schoolin' goin'?"

"Music is all I know how to do, Mom."

"And ya do it well, son. Are ya thinking of going back into it? Ain't nothin' like that voice of yours."

"It's Lyra who's got the musical talent. She's writing the most amazing songs, like the one she wrote for you, and you've heard her voice. It's…it's beautiful."

"Thanks, but Dorian, we're talking about you here," Lyra said, dodging the compliment.

"Well, what I was ruminatin' on is that you and Lyra ought to get serious about working together as a musical duo. I think you two could make beautiful music together!"

"That's not a way to make a living, Mom. I already tried that."

"But it's a way to make a life," Bette Anne smiled

Lyra and Dorian left the courthouse hand in hand. "I'm so proud of you, Lyra," Dorian said.

"I couldn't have done it without you, Dorian. You have no idea how much your support means to me."

"I want you to know I'll always be there for you," Dorian reassured her.

"That means so much to me. You don't even know. Testifying against my father was the hardest thing I've ever done. I just couldn't let all those other women that he abused face this on their own. I'm not wanting revenge anymore; no more secrets; I just want the truth to be told, and let God be the judge. My father thought he was above the law, but now the judge is being judged, and I've never felt so free."

"Guilty!" The judge's gavel came down like a meat tenderizing mallet on an especially tough cut of beef. The sound would echo in former Judge Reinhardt's memory for the rest of his life. Chances were that he would never live long enough in prison so see the end of his sentence.

CHAPTER 29
The Bun's in the Oven

Sitting across the table from Lyra at Molly's bakery, Dorian absentmindedly answered his cell phone as he finished his maple bar. "Hello."

Lyra saw his face blanch.

"Brittney? I thought you wouldn't be caught dead talking to me. Is there some problem with the divorce?...She what?!"

Hoping he'd reveal the purpose of the call if she lingered, Lyra watched his face turn from dismal to overjoyed as he listened to his ex-wife. His expression chilled her.

"I can't believe it," he said as he ended the call. "My name has been cleared! Seems that the girl who accused me also accused my replacement on the worship team and—get this— even accused the senior pastor, using the exact same story, word for word. Fortunately, they both had credible alibis. I knew she was delusional about me, but now I'm guessing it's about men in general. But you know, I think somehow she believed what she said. He took a deep breath, letting it out slowly. "You know what this means?"

"What?" Lyra asked timidly.

"I get my old life back."

"That's...uh, wonderful news, Dorian." Lyra mustered a smile. "I guess I'd better get back to work now." With a failing heart, Lyra hugged him and trudged to the back room. She managed to hold off the tears until she reached the rack of cooling muffins.

"Lyra, what's wrong?" Molly asked.

"I, uh…got burned. I think I'd better go home."

"Let me have a look at it," Molly insisted. "I have plenty of experience with burns, believe me." Molly pointed to a red streak on her forearm. "Occupational hazard." She studied Lyra. "This isn't about a skin kind of burn though, is it?"

Lyra shook her head.

"Do I need to go punch him?" Molly offered.

"No, you need to congratulate him."

As he headed south on the freeway, all Dorian could think of was his return to his wife and the life he had loved. He would, however, return home a changed man, one less likely to judge on outward appearances. He had Lyra to thank for that. Sweet Lyra. He shook off a stab of regret as he thought of her. *Of course we could still be friends...Who am I kidding? Like that would really happen now that I'm going back to my wife.* He wished he'd had more time to know her better, but it was just as well he hadn't. It would only make leaving River Oaks—and her—that much harder. This wasn't as he'd planned it. He would return to his custom home and his lovely wife, recording new songs, and enjoying the acclaim of leading worship in one of the largest churches on the West Coast. It was all within reach—a few hours on the road—and it would all be his again. He tuned his radio to his favorite Christian station and drowned out Catalina's caterwauling from her crate.

Then it happened. One of his own songs began to play, the first time since his banishment. He'd sung without real joy or sorrow though the words were right. Had he really lived his life with so little passion? Had he just been going through the motions? Where was the honesty—another of Lyra's gifts to him—honesty toward himself, toward God, toward his audience? He smiled as he remembered how she had shown him how one worshiped God—the God Who had truly saved her from ruin.

The little storefront church and its plain-spoken pastor had stripped away his illusions of holiness and wholeness. Church of the Broken. He'd had no idea how lost he was when he first entered that church. Lost and broken. And not realizing it. He shuddered.

This whole mess was clearly God's will. He would retur home a better man. He would bring changes to his church and t his home. Trouble was, it didn't feel much like home anymore. Home was where his friends were, and his best friend, Lyra. He turned off the radio. He'd never had a friend like her before, someone so wise and yet accepting and fun. The miles rolled by as he remembered, smiling.

It seemed the closer he got to home, the more compelling those memories became. *But my beautiful wife is waiting for me, and in God's eyes we are still married. Right?* He stepped on the gas pedal. *This little clunker sure doesn't respond the way my Beamer did. I never had to think about money when I bought that sports car. Now it's more car than I need or want. Who am I kidding? I don't belong in one anymore.*

He tried to coax his mind back to Brittney, to her flawless face and figure, but that was all surface stuff, he reminded himself. None of that mattered anymore. He hunted for recollections of her inner beauty and found her coming up short. But that would change once she saw the changes in him. It would have to.

The memory of Lyra's farewell bit into his mind, laid hold of it and shook it. He hadn't taken time to consider how sad those beautiful eyes had been. Her good-bye had been brief with heartfelt wishes for God's best. She'd bestowed a quick hug that left him wanting more. Before he could say another word, she retreated into the back room of the bakery, turning just once to wave. He hadn't even begun to thank her for all she had done for im, for all she meant to him. What *did* she mean to him, anyway? A voice in the darkness, singing the light of God to him, hours of shared laughter, courage, acceptance in the face of painful rejection. Toast. Lots of toast…

That old rejection still burned. How could Brittney and his old church suddenly welcome him back as if nothing had happened? As if his wounds didn't matter?

He turned the radio back on, and there it was, one of the classic Christian songs he and Lyra had sung at Gabi's quinceañera. He remembered the long walks by the lake, the touch so tender yet so electrifying that she ran away from it and left him standing in the rain.

And as Lyra grew farther and farther away, the windmills loomed before him with blades that seemed to cut past and present asunder. Dorian pulled his car over and watched the blades spinning. He'd reached the point of no return. He sat there watching as cars whizzed by. Running his fingers through his hair, he came to his decision. He would go home. To Lyra.

As he headed back to his life in River Oaks, anticipating the look on Lyra's face, Dorian's cell phone was blowing up. His ex-wife Brittney left message after message. He ignored them a he drove home. Home, where he belonged now. Pangs of guilt rose in his stomach. False guilt? Brittney had divorced him, after all. She had kicked him out of their house, their life, and refused to believe in his innocence when his integrity was called into question. He pulled over to fill his gas tank when his father called. He decided to pick up.

"Where are you, Dorian? You should've been here hours ago. Brittney's in tears. You aren't answering her phone calls."

"I'm not coming."

"You're what?" came the angry response. "Look, son, Brittney has planned this big welcome home party for you for tomorrow, so get your rear end home right now."

"Sorry, Dad, it's not home anymore. Gotta go." Dorian could hear his dad yelling as he dropped the call.

Eventually Brittney's calls wore him down, and he pulled over and called her back. He owed her an explanation.

"Can't we at least talk about this?" she pleaded. "I want you back home, where you belong. Don't all our years together mean anything to you?"

"Didn't seem to mean much to you when you divorced me. You bought into the lies about me and kicked me out. We've known each other our whole lives. How could you think I would take advantage of that girl?"

"Come on, Baby. You've been proven innocent now. I'm orry I didn't believe you. I'll make it up to you. I was wrong to oubt you. I'll never do it again."

"How do you think I felt with my own wife not believing me? You told me to get out and never come back. You vorced me. I shouldn't have had to prove my innocence to you. You knew me better than that. Was the scandal bad for your image? Why do you think I'd want to come back now?"

"Because I love you, Dorian."

The phrase stopped him right in his tracks. Did he still love her? He didn't really know. He loved her the way things were before, but now?

"Please, Dorian, you know God hates divorce. Just come home and at least discuss this with me in person. Please forgive me, Baby. You know, God wants us to forgive. That's what the Gospel's all about."

Against his better judgment, Dorian agreed to talk to Brittney in person. He owed her that much; at least that's what she told him, and he was too battered to fight. Reluctantly, he turned the car away from River Oaks.

Hours later he found himself on the front doorstep of their luxurious house. His key didn't fit the lock anymore, so he had to knock, all the while wondering whether or not he had made the right choice of coming back.

Brittney quickly answered the door and threw her arms around his neck. "Baby, I'm so glad you're home!" Her low-cut top and tight little skirt sent a shock wave to his long-deprived senses. And she knew it.

LEAVING LYRA

The scent of the flickering candles in the entryway stirred up intense memories of times they had put candlelight to good use, but he remained impassive. "Whether or not I'm home remains to be seen," he stated flatly.

"Well, come in, Baby, come in," Brittney coaxed.

"Wow, I don't recognize the place," he observed. "The furniture is all new, and my piano is gone."

"Yes, well, my folks helped me change things up a bit after you left. I was so depressed..."

"You mean, after you kicked me out?"

"Now, Dorian, I told you I'm sorry. You know that. I would do anything to go back and do things differently now that I know the truth."

"Why didn't you believe me, Brittney?"

"That girl was just so convincing. She made us all believe her story."

"If it had been you who was accused of something so awful, I would have stood by you."

"I'll never doubt you again. Please, come back home to stay. I love you." She moved in closer.

"I don't know how I feel anymore. You just tossed me aside when I needed you most, Brittney. Do you know how that feels? You *chose* not to believe me."

"I'm so sorry, Baby! I was so wrong. Please forgive me." She wiped her eyes dramatically. "What can I do to get you back? I'll make it up to you, I swear." She pulled him to herself and kissed him. "I've missed you so much. I've been so lost without you." She caressed his face and felt his resolve melting under her fingertips. "Come on, Baby, haven't you missed me too?" she spoke into his neck, sending a delicious shiver down his spine. She kissed him again and again until his resolve was spent.

She pulled the wedding ring he had left behind out of her cleavage and slipped the warm ring easily on his ring finger. "Come on, Baby," she whispered in his ear as she led him to the bedroom.

Dorian excused himself and went into the bathroom to regain some semblance of self-control.

"I'll be waiting," Brittney purred from the bed.

He couldn't just let this happen. Dorian fidgeted with his wedding band. He started praying and as he did, the ring fell off his finger and into the trash basket. *Oh man*," he thought to himself, *is this a sign or what?* He fished around to the bottom of the basket where the heavy gold ring had settled. *What's this?* he wondered as he pulled up a positive home pregnancy test under a mound of tissues. He stormed back into the bedroom and tossed the test onto the bed where Brittney was waiting in her filmy lingerie.

"So you're pregnant! That's what this is all about, huh? We both know this can't be my child, don't we, Brittney? We haven't been together since you kicked me out months ago. You're just trying to make this pregnancy look respectable, like it's my child. Whose is it anyway? The guy who took my place in the music ministry? You were trying to use me here tonight to protect your reputation. You don't really love me! I don't even know who you are anymore!"

"Wait, Dorian, I can explain. I love you!"

"Is this your pregnancy test?"

"Yes, but I can explain. You were gone, and I got so lonely. I thought we were over."

"We are!" Dorian tossed his ring next to the pregnancy test on the bed and stormed out the door, slamming it behind him for the last time.

CHAPTER 30
The Crumbs Will Lead You Home

Lyra was putting the last of four dozen glazed doughnuts into a box for Irene Perkins who was having her annual garage sale. It was a Perkins' tradition to have her renowned garage sale on the same Saturday every year and give free doughnuts to her first forty-eight customers. People anticipated it, coming from miles around. They found the best gently-used items on sale in her roomy garage, driveway and front lawn. This year it was even spilling out onto the sidewalk. Irene Perkins was the queen of organization, packing in an amazing array of items. If you couldn't find at least a few things you wanted at this annual event, then there was something wrong with you—perhaps you were missing the bargain gene.

Lyra was planning to head over during her lunch break. Maybe she could find something to cheer her up. Dorian's leaving town—leaving her—and going back to his ex-wife and his former high-profile life had brought an end to her dreams and left her feeling completely hollow. Even her kitten's antics could not bring a smile.

LEAVING LYRA

Why did he ever have to come to town in the first place?
Lyra agonized. *I was surviving just fine without him. But that's
just it. I've spent my whole life just surviving. It was only in the
past few months I've really felt alive. I thought I meant
something to him. After all we've been through together, and
after my father's trial he said he'd always be there for me. He
said it to my face, and I believed him. I thought I could depend
on him, but I guess they were just words.*

His sense of humor and dark eyes had charmed her, and
it seemed as if he might have been thinking of her as more than
a friend. Dorian's departure swept that hope away.

They had so much fun playing music together, taking
nighttime walks around the lake, staying up late, laughing and
talking about anything and everything, and then there was Toast
Wars. He was, in short, the best friend she'd ever had, and now
he was gone.

Dorian was approaching the landmark windmills once
more. They seemed to serve as a turning point for him. Up
ahead he saw emergency lights flashing and a broken-down
powder blue T-Bird alongside the road. A woman was pacing
next to it. "You'd think I'd learned my lesson, trying to help
people," he muttered as he pulled over. "Need a hand?" he asked
the tall, attractive woman in designer jeans and teal silk blouse.

419

"I could sure use your cell phone, if you don't mind. I can't seem to get a signal."

"Dead zone," he said, handing her his phone to prove his point.

"Just what I was afraid of." She handed it back with a rare frown. "Now what am I supposed to do?" She looked up. "Hey, you're Dorian McGuire. I used to see you on TV." She stuck out her hand. "I'm Grace Alexander. My gramma and I used to watch you when I'd come to visit her. It was really nice."

Nice? Someone's gramma? Not exactly flattering. There goes my relevance to my generation.

Dorian thanked her graciously, nonetheless. An awkward silence ensued. Dorian knew he couldn't leave her there, but he didn't feel comfortable taking on a female passenger. "It's a long walk to the nearest gas station," he observed noncommittally.

"Yeah, I'm not exactly dressed for a hike." She displayed her stylish strappy sandals which looked pleasantly out of place on the broken glass and gravel roadside.

I...uh...guess I could give you a ride," he said, trying to drum up some enthusiasm.

Gracie's life in the business world made her a shrewd judge of character. He was charmingly nerdy enough with his sideways grin, and altogether harmless. She had no qualms about accepting his offer.

LEAVING LYRA

"Here, let me get my stuff off of the seat." He fumbled
with coffee cups, protein bars, fast food wrappers, and CD
cases. "Sorry, I've been, like, living on the road lately."

"No worries," Gracie said, pulling her long, sleek
brunette hair back and fixing it with a clip. "So what brings you
out this way?"

"I'm going home," he said with conviction.

"Oh, I thought you lived in Southern California. Isn't
that where your church is?"

"I'm...uh...retired now and living in a little town called
River Oaks."

"Shut up! That's where I'm going too!" She laughed, a
lovely melodic sound. "What are the odds of that?" She tossed
her luggage in the back, narrowly missing Catalina's carrier,
setting the poor animal to yowling again. "Oops, sorry!" Gracie
seated herself.

Dorian started the car, dreading a drive with a stranger
when he had so much on his mind. Still, duty called. He needn't
have feared; she was pleasant company. Grace was leaving
behind her city job and her city boyfriend to take over her now
deceased grandmother's country home and embrace a simpler
life. He took a deep breath, dispelling the dread, and offered to
drive her to the nearest town. She accepted gratefully. Once
here, she hired a tow truck to bring her car to the local repair
enter. Dorian waited, drinking tired coffee that had, like him,
een sitting for way too long.

421

The mechanic was grim. "You have a busted head gasket, little lady. Won't have the parts in for a few days, I'm afraid."

"Well, what am I supposed to do? I can't just stay here for a few days. I've got to get home."

"I can take you to River Oaks, I'm going there anyway," Dorian volunteered, anxious to be back on the road.

All she wanted was to set foot in her grammy's beloved home and greet the sweet, bereft sheltie dog who had been left in the care of a neighbor. She couldn't wait to sleep in her own little room Grammy had set aside for her many years ago. "I'll take you up on your offer," she said. "Thank you so much."

It was actually nice having someone to talk to on the long drive back to his new life. Before he knew it, they were involved in what proved to be a revealing conversation.

"I have my sheltie dog and my old pony. Anything special you're going home to?" she asked.

He paused to consider it and couldn't hold back. "Yeah, there's this girl—Lyra. She's my best friend. She's the most...real person I've ever met. She's funny, smart, talented, giving, and spiritually off the charts..."

Gracie couldn't help but notice he made no mention of her looks. Refreshing. She was coming from a world that was all about appearances and was looking forward to a life that wasn't

"Dorian! What are you doing here?" Lyra led her bleary-eyed friend holding a cat carrier into her little house as Catzo cavorted at his feet. She let Catalina out to visit with Catzo. The two cats rubbed against each other in greeting.

Trying to avoid the cats, he staggered.

Lyra took his hand. "Dorian, are you alright? You look exhausted." She didn't want to use the word, "terrible" in reference to his pasty skin and dark, ill-focused eyes, sunken in deep purple wells. He looked beat up, but emotionally, he was pulverized. "What happened, Dorian?"

She sat him on the couch and took her place next to him.

"I came home," he said.

"And then what happened? Why are you back in River Oaks?"

"I came home. Here to River Oaks. With you." He'd said too much but was too tired to care.

Lyra's heart was hammering. Home? To her? Of course, he was tired. People can say some stupid things when they're tired. She summoned her practicality front and center. "Can I get you something? Some coffee, maybe? Toast?"

He smiled. "I've been on the road too many hours. I guess I'm just tired. Could you just sit with me awhile?"

"Sure thing." If only she *felt* sure. She sat perilously close and stifled a shimmer of delight when he leaned his head on her shoulder. She could explain it all away later. For now, she'd go with it. She put her arm around his shoulder. "You just stay here as long as you like."

He fell asleep to her calming nearness.

Lyra was anything but calm. Her heart had never flip-flopped as it was doing now. The hope she felt defied logic, but perhaps that's just what hope does.

He slumped against her, and eventually her arm fell asleep. She eased him down on the couch and watched him longingly, lovingly. Could this really be happening? She scooped up Catzo, who was stalking Dorian's hand. Such beautiful hands, she noted as if for the first time—artist's hands. She had fled his touch that rainy night. His touch had stirred a fearsome emotion—love. There it was again. Love. She loved Dorian McGuire, and it seemed like he just might love her, too.

While Catalina drowsed, Lyra busied Catzo with a catnip mouse until the little tabby joined Catalina. Lyra quietly took her guitar out of its case. Softly, so as not to awaken him, she began to play a song of homecoming, a song that would become the soundtrack for his dreams.

Hours later he awoke to the sound of her voice. She was singing. He was home.

The Taylor Sisters

Molly and Lyra's Recipes

Phil's Favorite Fritters

Ingredients:
1 qt vegetable oil (for deep-fryer)
1 ½ C unbleached all purpose flour
2 Tbs white sugar
1 Tbs cinnamon
2 tsp baking powder
2 tsp pumpkin pie spice
½ tsp salt
⅔ C milk
2 eggs, beaten
1Tbs vegetable oil
3 C cored and chopped apples
1 C sugar mixed with 1Tbs cinnamon (for sprinkling on fritters when hot out of fryer)

Stir together in a large mixing bowl: flour, sugar, cinnamon, baking powder, pumpkin pie spice, and salt. When mixed, add milk, eggs and oil. Blend well. Add chopped apples and mix.

Heat vegetable oil in deep-fryer to 375 degrees F.

Drop batter by large spoonfuls into hot oil and fry until golden brown on both sides. Fry a small number at a time; don't overcrowd the fryer. Cooking time is approx. 5 minutes or more, depending on the size of the fritters. Be cautious with the hot oil and remove fritters with a large slotted spoon. Drain them on paper towels and toss them with the cinnamon/sugar mixture while they are still warm and serve with your favorite cup of joe.

Lyra's Fun-Filled Eclairs

Eclair Ingredients:
½ C butter
1 C boiling water
1 C all-purpose flour
¼ tsp salt
4 eggs

n a saucepan, melt butter in boiling water. Add the flour and alt all at one time. Stir it vigorously. Continue to cook and stir onstantly until the dough forms a ball that stays together. emove from the stove and let cool slightly. Add each egg, one a time, beating until dough is smooth between each additional egg. Shape the dough into rectangles on greased cookie sheet. Bake at 400 degrees F until puffy and golden, 30-35 minutes. Remove from sheet and split lengthwise. Let cool completely (no nibbling) before filling with vanilla pudding.

Vanilla Pudding Filling Ingredients:
½ C sugar
2 Tbs cornstarch
¼ tsp salt
1¾ C milk
2 beaten egg yolks
2 Tbs butter
2 tsp vanilla

In medium saucepan combine sugar, cornstarch, salt, and milk. Cook and stir continuously over medium heat until it thickens and gets bubbly. Cook and stir constantly, about 2 minutes more, making sure the mixture on the bottom does not burn. Remove from heat. In a bowl, stir about 1 cup of the hot mixture into the beaten egg yolks. When well blended, return this mixture to the rest of the saucepan mixture. Bring back to a boil. Boil two more minutes, stirring continuously. Remove from heat. Stir in butter and vanilla until all the butter is melted. Pour pudding into a bowl and chill in the refrigerator with plastic wrap touching the top of the pudding to prevent a skin forming. Whe completely chilled, spoon pudding into the cooled eclairs. Lick the spatula thoroughly. Sprinkle tops with powdered sugar. Save one for your own personal Dorian.

Allison Hamaker's Sarafina Slinger Old Fashioned Tea Cakes

(Contest Winner)

Ingredients:

3 C sugar

1 C melted shortening

1 tsp vanilla

3 eggs

1 C buttermilk

1 tsp baking soda

1 tsp baking powder

⅛ tsp salt

5 C flour

Cream sugar, shortening, vanilla, and eggs. In a separate medium bowl, put the baking soda into the buttermilk (watch it volcano). Add this mixture to the creamed mixture above. Mix baking powder, salt, and flour. Add to above mixture. Add milk and flour alternately a little at a time until mixed. Place the dough on a floured board and work in enough flour to roll out and cut with cookie cutters. Bake at 350 degrees F for 10 minutes. Remove from cookie sheets and cool.

Optional Lemon Icing Ingredients:

½ C butter

2 Tbs real lemon juice

1 tsp vanilla extract

3 C powdered sugar

Combine all ingredients and beat with mixer on high until fluffy and light. Add more powdered sugar if needed. Ice tea cakes only after they are completely cool.

Marie Ortman's Ultimate Carrot Cake

(Contest Winner)

Ingredients:

2 C flour

2 tsp baking soda

1tsp salt

2 C sugar

1 tsp cinnamon

1½ C cooking oil

4 eggs

2 C raw carrots (grated)

1 small can of crushed pineapple

Mix dry ingredients together. Add in wet ingredients and beat well. Bake in three 9 inch greased and floured layer pans, for 30 minutes at 350 degrees F. Remove from pans and cool on wire racks.

Icing Ingredients:

1 8 oz pkg cream cheese (softened at room temp)

1 cube butter or margarine

½-1 box powdered sugar

1 4 oz pkg of coconut

1 C nuts of your choice (chopped)

With a mixer, blend all ingredients in order listed. Frost carrot cake layers when completely cool.

Jan Williamse's Almond Butter Gluten Free Bars

Contest Winner)

gredients:

¼ C coconut oil

⅓ C honey and maple syrup blend (half of each to make ⅓ C total)

¼ C almond butter

1 egg

½ tsp vanilla

Mix above ingredients. Separately in another bowl, combine:

1¼ C almond flour

½ tsp baking powder

⅛ tsp baking soda

½ tsp salt

When dry ingredients are mixed, combine with wet ingredients. Add chocolate chips and/or dried cranberries. Bake at 350 degrees F for 15-20 minutes.

Aunt Alice Taylor Voigt's Buttermilk Brownies

Ingredients:

1 cube butter or margarine

¼ C cocoa

1 C water

½ C vegetable oil

1 tsp baking soda

½ C buttermilk

2 beaten eggs

1 tsp vanilla

2 C sugar

2 C flour

½ tsp salt

Heat oven to 375 degrees F. In a small saucepan, bring margarine or butter, cocoa, water, and oil to a boil while stirring. Remove from heat and set aside. In a small mixing bowl, dissolve baking soda in buttermilk, then add eggs and vanilla. In a large mixing bowl combine sugar, flour, and salt. Add cocoa mixture to flour mixture, then stir in the buttermilk mixture. Pour into greased and floured jelly-roll pan or large cookie sheet with sides. Bake for 20 minutes. Frost immediately.

Frosting Ingredients:

I cube butter or margarine

⅓ C buttermilk

 C cocoa

box (1 lb) powdered sugar

C chopped nuts (optional)

tsp vanilla

Heat margarine or butter, buttermilk, and cocoa to boiling while stirring. Remove from heat. Stir in powdered sugar and mix well. Add nuts and vanilla. Leave in pan until the brownies are served. These are cakey, not fudgy brownies.

Molly's "Let Me At Mmm... Lemon Blueberry Scones

Ingredients:
2 C flour
⅓ C sugar
1 tsp baking powder
¼ tsp baking soda
½ tsp salt
3 Tbs very cold butter (brrr…)
½ to 1 C fresh blueberries
½ C sour cream
1 large egg
zest from one lemon

Preheat oven to 400 degrees F. In medium bowl mix flour, sugar, baking powder, baking soda, and salt. Use large holes on a grater to grate butter into mixture. Use your hands to work butter into mixture until it looks like coarse meal, gently stir in blueberries and coat them with dry ingredients. In another bowl, combine egg and sour cream until smooth. Add lemon zest and stir.

Stir sour cream mixture into flour mixture with a fork, until large clumps of dough appear. Use your fingers to press the dough against the bowl into a ball. It may seem sticky in spots and dry in others, but as you press gently, the dough will form together. Do not overwork the dough. Use a lightly floured board to turn the dough onto. Form dough into about an 8 inch circle that is ¾ to 1 inch thick. Sprinkle with about a tsp of sugar or less. Use a knife to cut the circle into 8 triangles (pie shaped pieces). Place triangles onto cookie sheet lined with parchment paper. Bake 15-18 minutes, until golden. Cool for at least five minutes before serving.

Auntie Annie's Easy Igloo Macaroons

Ingredients:
1 package of shredded coconut (14 oz)
⅓ C flour
⅛ tsp salt
1 tsp vanilla
1 can (14 oz) sweetened condensed milk
1 package semi-sweet chocolate chips or butterscotch chips

Combine coconut, flour, and salt in bowl. Stir in sweetened condensed milk and vanilla until all ingredients are thoroughly moistened. Drop by Tbs about 1 inch apart on ungreased cookie sheets. Bake at 250 degrees F for 30-35 minutes or until golden brown. Immediately after coming out of the oven, place chocolate chips or butterscotch chips on top of each cookie. Let the chips melt a moment and then use the back of a spoon to smear the melted chips on top of each cookie.

Molly's "Gotta Go" Bran Muffins

Ingredients:

3 C baker's bran

2 C buttermilk (or 1½ C milk mixed with ¾ C orange juice)

Mix these ingredients together in one large bowl. Let the liquid absorb about 3 minutes.

In another medium bowl combine:

2 C flour

4 tsp baking powder

1 tsp baking soda

¼ tsp salt

⅔ C brown sugar

Back into the first bran mixture bowl, add:

2 eggs

½ C canola oil

½ C golden raisins

1 small can of crushed pineapple

2-3 tsp cinnamon

Optional items to add:

2 grated carrots, or 2 mashed bananas, or 1 large finely chopped apple, or 1 orange peel, zested

Next, add the dry ingredients from the flour mixture bowl to the large bran mixture bowl all at once, stirring just until moistened. Fill muffin papers in muffin tins ⅔ full, giving them room to rise. Bake at 400 degrees F for 20 minutes. Makes approx. 2 dozen.

Momma Alli's Bread

ngredients:

packages yeast

C warm water (80-90 degrees F)

½ C hot water

Tbs salt

¼ C brown sugar

3 Tbs butter

3 Tbs molasses

1½ C milk

1 C wheat germ

3 C whole wheat flour

4 C white flour (or more if needed)

Small amount of salad oil

Dissolve yeast in warm water. Add salt, brown sugar, butter, and molasses to hot water until butter melts. Add milk, and stir. Add to yeast. Stir in wheat germ. Add flour. Knead until smooth and elastic. Coat with salad oil. Let rise until it doubles in size. Punch down. Let rise again. Form into 3 loaves. Let rise about ½ hour. Bake 30-40 minutes at 350 degrees F. This bread will bring them home for the holidays.

Mr. Greg's Good Tasting Molasses Cookies

Ingredients:

¾ C butter (softened at room temperature)

1 C sugar

¼ C molasses

1 egg

2 C flour

2 tsp baking soda

½ tsp ground cloves

½ tsp ground ginger

1 tsp cinnamon

½ tsp salt

In a large bowl, combine softened butter with sugar, molasses and egg. Beat well. In another bowl, sift together flour, baking soda, cloves, ginger, cinnamon, and salt. Add these dry ingredients to the butter mixture bowl. Mix well. Chill in refrigerator. Form 1 inch balls. Roll balls in granulated sugar. Place on greased cookie sheets. Bake at 375 degrees F for 8-10 minutes. Watch them disappear.

Molly's Banana Bread

ngredients:

½ C vegetable oil

C sugar

eggs

C flour

Tbs milk

1 tsp baking soda

2 mashed ripe bananas

Mix all ingredients together thoroughly. Pour into greased bread pan. Bake at 350 degrees F for 1 hour. It's the perfect use for those "dead-beat" bananas.

Gramma's Apple Crisp

Ingredients:

4-5 apples cored and sliced into bottom of pie pan

¾ C flour

⅔-¾ C sugar or brown sugar

1 tsp cinnamon

¼ C softened butter

Mix flour, sugar, cinnamon, and softened butter in a bowl by hand. When thoroughly mixed, pour them over the sliced apples in the pie pan. Bake at 350 degrees F for 30-40 minutes. Makes one apple crisp.

Maggie's "Flour Power" Granola Cookies

Ingredients:
½ C softened butter
½ C sugar
½ C brown sugar
1 egg
1 tsp vanilla
1 C flour (feel the flour power?)
½ tsp baking soda
¼ tsp baking powder
¼ tsp salt
2 C granola
½ C shredded coconut

Mix softened butter, sugar, brown sugar, egg, and vanilla until well blended. In a separate bowl, mix together remaining ingredients. Stir second bowl's ingredients into first bowl's mixture until well blended. Bake at 350 degrees F for 10-15 minutes. Makes 3 dozen cookies.

Made in the USA
Middletown, DE
27 September 2022

11368987R00267